# Heart of Ice

**Heart of a Highlander, Volume 6**

Rebecca Ruger

Published by Rebecca Ruger, 2022.

This is a work of fiction. Names, character, places, and incidents are either a product of the author's imagination or are used fictitiously, and any resemblance to actual persons, living or dead, events, or locales is entirely coincidental.
Some creative license may have been taken
with exact dates and locations to better serve the plot and pacing of the novel.

# Chapter One

HIS JAW WAS SET GRIMLY, which was the only noticeable hint of displeasure about his proud visage. Otherwise, he appeared to ride leisurely into Carbery, a small village on the south west shore of the Dornoch Firth, his large hands loose upon the reins. He did not turn his head around the old burgh, but his eyes took in everything as he and his retinue walked their steeds down the main road.

The village, which was of considerable extent if measured by size and not inhabitants, was of irregular form, that it was not compact and orderly, but strewn about along the road, winding over hill and into glen. They passed first a woolen mill, built near where a river took its course, and then saw no other building for an eighth of a mile until they came upon a row of houses, six or seven on each side of the road.

On the north side of the road, a woman with a bucket on one hip and a bairn on the other stood in the doorway of a decrepit croft, her expression as worn as the thatch on the roof. The child in her arms wore hope yet, his pink-cheeked face tinted with curiosity as he pointed wordlessly but with some excitement at the soldiers marching through.

To his left, two old men sat on stools before another croft with a lidded barrel used as a table between them. They were perched up against the wattle-and-daub; if they removed themselves from the wall of the croft, they'd be sitting in the road. The younger of the two cast one eye, the only one he possessed, at the passing riders while the other man, mayhap as old as seventy, sat with one leg crossed over his other knee and crinkled both eyes with some conjecture at them.

Beyond the main road, and visible as the elevation was higher, freshly tilled acres of brown dirt stretched as far as the eye could see and imbued the air with an earthen, not unpleasant fragrance. Up ahead sat the old parish church, as unassuming as was all of Carbery. Though white-washed and tidy in appearance, it claimed neither tower nor spire. And though the windows were tall and wide, they were not fitted with glass as some modern kirks were. Like the joyless cottages in its periphery, the kirk walls were constructed of wattle and daub and not the more stable—and surely enduring—ashlar blocks. However, it boasted no corbels or lintels or arches to say that it served so nobly St. Columba, for whom it was dedicated. Outside the church lay a huge standing stone, a relic of the Picts, said to be a grave marker, carved with images of a tree of life and purportedly, the biblical David killing the lion, among other etchings.

They passed the church, no words spoken now between Nicholas MacRory and his men for the last quarter hour, and then kneed their destriers into a light gallop when Carbery was left behind, and over the next mile until they reached Kincardine itself, and the manse of John de Graham, who had summoned Nicholas on some urgent, but unnamed business.

Only when they rode inside the waist-high wall—more aesthetic than functional—of the de Graham house did Baldred, the captain of the MacRory army, once more bring his concerns to his chief.

Baldred was not more than a handful of years older than Nicholas, powerfully built even as he was shorter by three or four inches than the great height of Nicholas. He possessed what Nicholas' sire had called an *old soul*, and though he owned a keen mind for warfare as well, he entertained more caution than most and often felt the need to vocalize any misgivings to his chief. Having dismounted in the vacant yard, he held the bridle of his steed and moved toward his chief, where Nicholas put his feet on the ground as well.

"I see this woeful holding and I understand even less why we've ridden straightaway to answer so cryptic a summons," groused Baldred, casting his gaze all around, his brown eyes showing a distinct lack of enthusiasm.

"Aye, the manse might well be unimpressive," Nicholas allowed, "the wall alone nearly amusing for whatever its intent had been, but ye ken that de Graham's army is twice the size of ours. Like as no', with such numbers, he needn't worry about the height of his wall." Nicholas raised one dark brow. "And consider, if ye will, what those numbers would mean to Scotland if we persuaded him to fight for freedom, and no' with the mongrel English."

"'Tis said his greater holdings are there, in Longshanks' realm, so I'm no' sure how ye expect to turn around his loyalty."

Nicholas leveled Baldred with a speaking glance, reminding him of what William Wallace had said to them not so long ago. "No man chooses the shackles of tyranny over freedom. But many a man will sometimes choose peace and ease over war with the tyrant."

Baldred harrumphed his dislike of this. "I dinna trust a man such as that. Ye fight for right, for what's just, and no' for convenience or ease. Or, God's bluid, dinna fight at all."

Nicholas grinned and smacked Baldred on the shoulder as he walked past. "No' all men are created so brave and true, my friend."

The de Graham house might not have been impressive by the standards of Nicholas and Baldred, but it was not as miserable as Baldred made it out. It was a two-story stone dwelling, resembling more an English manor than any great Scots' castle or keep, with peaked, timber roofs and showcasing leaded glass windows in wide frames on the ground floor, unlike the slim, arrow-slit apertures to which they were accustomed.

The door to the hall opened and a woman stepped into the yard. Having determined that no great expense was laid out for the home or the grounds or the village of de Graham, Nicholas determined that all income must then be spent not only on the sizable army, but also to clothe the women within so finely.

Dressed in a sapphire léine of wool, whose short-sleeves were fur-lined, and under which was shown long-sleeves of brocaded linen, the woman did not remain near the door to accept them or question their coming but strode forward and beckoned with crooking fingers a lad from the stables, which were situated adjacent to the house.

"Fergus, come see to our guests' horses." Before the steeds were collected, and while the rest of his men dismounted, the woman said, "I am Eleanor de Graham, and I thank you for responding so quickly to my missive."

Nicholas exchanged a subtly quizzical look with Baldred before questioning the woman.

"You sent the missive, ma'am? 'Twas signed by your husband, John de Graham."

Without the barest hint of apology, she queried, "Would ye have responded to a request from only his wife?"

Nae, he would not have. He'd have answered the note, though, would have addressed his response to her husband, seeking clarification. He felt all at once irked and then as if he'd just wasted many hours in the saddle, when those hours might have been better spent at his own home.

Because she'd displayed no contrition at all, Nicholas sized her up, this bold woman. Eleanor de Graham clung to the remains of a beautiful person, not without success, being middle-aged with hair that might have once been shiny and soft, and skin that had not yet been damaged profusely by years. Her smooth skin nearly compensated for her thick, coarse hair and while her eyes were likely smaller, more sunken than they had been in her youth, they were not unattractive, being bright blue, and standing in sharp contrast to that pale complexion and her black-as-night hair.

"Ye have me at a loss, ma'am," he confessed, "as I can no' imagine why ye should have sought me out. We have no' crossed paths, and nor I with your husband."

"We have not," she said, folding her hands together serenely in front of her. "But I have indeed encountered your reputation, sir, which is sung as loudly as our hero, William Wallace."

Nicholas smirked, wholly confused now. "Mistress de Graham, ye call the man your hero even as I stand here, and I ken full well your own husband's army has and might again take up arms against him, and all our plans for independence."

All civility was lost then, replaced by no wee amount of annoyance, shown in her pursed lips and the whitening of her knuckles. "My husband has committed his army as such, against my counsel and to the detriment of our own union. But enough spoken out of doors, come inside. Please."

With one more perplexed glance at his captain and then behind him to Dungal, Henry, and Malise, he inclined his head to indicate they should follow the woman inside. With his hand on the hilt of his sword, and knowing his men would have likewise primed themselves, Nicholas walked in the wake of Eleanor de Graham.

The hall of the de Graham home might be only a third as large as the hall at Braewood Keep and was not met directly inside the door but through a fair-sized corridor which bent around one corner first, the darkness of which enlivened Nicholas to move his fingers to curl around the hilt of his weapon and not only rest upon the butt.

Happily, no evil plot or brigand revealed itself and the MacRory men gained the de Graham hall unmolested.

There, the Mistress de Graham swept regally across the small room to where a man—her husband one might assume by his dominant position at the raised table and in so ornate a chair—lifted his face and cast a heavy scowl upon his guests.

And mayhap wedded trials were a book laid open here that she announced freely before she'd fully reached his side, "Pray give me no grief for what I have set into motion, sir."

Aye, the man's response—a rather long-suffering roll of his head—advised that indeed this woman was not above provoking her husband to fits of pique. To his credit though, he did not bark at his wife, though the coming strained expression about his mouth suggested that he might actually be holding back an irked response.

"I have summoned Nicholas of Lorne, the MacRory, to give aid in that one endeavor where we have failed," Eleanor said airily, and seemed to pay no mind to the blood surfacing just under the cheeks of John de Graham, nor the way his eyes bulged with so much latent fury.

And while Nicholas and his soldiers stood in front of the de Grahams and their cloth-covered table, John de Graham turned to his wife as she approached on his left and asked bitterly, "And what, dear wife, would be the aid this man might give?"

At this, the woman straightened her back and cocked a thin brow. "He might bring our daughter home, husband, as we have been unable to do."

Neither Nicholas nor any man of his so much as blinked in the next few moments as the de Grahams indulged in a profound battle of wills with only their eyes. Nicholas could not say who might have been the victor as both husband and wife turned to face their audience at the same time.

Remembering himself, he tipped his head politely at de Graham and had to believe that this man would have realized as he did, that there was no threat to them attached to that cryptic missive, and no harm foreseeable in their coming here.

Appearing only mildly annoyed now, none of which Nicholas supposed was directed at him, John de Graham returned a nod in greeting and informed Nicholas, "I am afraid my anxious wife has called you on a fool's errand." He turned to convey his lingering annoyance onto his wife and said crossly, enunciating words that surely had been spoken previously, "And to a matter that might only work itself out in time, if she would but allow it that."

Because he had travelled for many hours, Nicholas expected that he was owed some greater explanation. "Where is your daughter, sir?"

He never had met a man, not in all his life, who might speak quicker than any woman. As it was, John de Graham had barely parted his lips before his lady wife had begun to answer. "Stolen. Taken by Longshanks himself, kept under house arrest in England," she cried out, her anxiety now wholly exposing itself. "A year now. She's been gone a year, ripped from my arms in the very yard in which I greeted you. And for all I know being abused or tortured or suffering any—"

"And I've begged ye, have I no'?" Her husband interjected. "To leave off with all that conjecture? She is no mistreated. You've had three letters that said as much. Why do ye—"

"Three letters," Eleanor repeated shrilly. "In twelve months. I'd have to be daft to believe anything else, but that she is being maltreated." With her fisted hand clutched to her chest, she faced Nicholas. "If you knew of Alice, and of our sweet and enduring bond, you, too, would ken that something was amiss. Three letters in twelve months when I should have baskets filled by now."

"If I may," Nicholas inquired of John de Graham, "why did the English king take custody of yer daughter?" He could not, despite the already fraught environment, keep the censure from his tone when he further wondered, "Ye already provide him arms and men—coin, no doubt as well—so why would he punish ye by taking yer daughter from ye?"

"It was no' because of any one thing—"

"Silence, wife," commanded de Graham. "I'll respond with truth and no' with your wailing sentiments." He addressed Nicholas then, his tone calm now, "Edward recognizes that my wife's allegiance lay boldly and proudly in contrast to his own agenda and thus—"

Ignoring her husband's admonition to be silent, Eleanor stated proudly, "I am the daughter of Alan Durward and the great-granddaughter of Gille Christ, Mormaer of Mar, and descended from Máel Coluim, mormaer of Atholl—"

"—he did not trust my pledge of fealty on its own merit," John de Graham finished with an aggrieved snarl to his wife.

Nicholas was able to dismiss the drama attached to both de Grahams and whittle it down to fact: this house was divided. He narrowed his gaze at John de Graham, meaning to assess the man behind the barely-tolerant bluster.

Before he might have ascertained anything, John asserted, "Aye, I've sided with the English. It was no' a difficult choice to make. I've lost already one child, gone with those poor souls at Dunbar while I rode away unscathed. I've lands and a barony inside England itself, which help to feed and maintain all these good people of Carbery. And mayhap it escaped yer attention, lad, as ye were sauntering down from your safe Highland keep, I am, at any given time, naught but a few hours away from any garrison of Edward's or any part of his vast moving army. It is no' about what is most rewarding for me, but what is safest for me and mine."

"Except that yer daughter is no' safe, apparently," Nicholas was compelled to point out.

"Aye, and she is," John returned, his brows moving up into his forehead, "so long as I preserve my good behavior."

So, de Graham had fought at Dunbar, Nicholas thought. He knew and often relived his own horror from the chaos of that meeting with the English. Losing his brother there had almost been the easy part.

Concentrating on the matter at hand, Nicholas asked, "And if yer daughter were freed from her English prison, where would ye rest yer loyalties then?"

"Bring my child home," Eleanor answered first, and solemnly, "and we will commit all of the de Graham army and resources to the Scottish cause."

Ignoring her, despite her powerful role in this union, Nicholas kept his gaze locked with John de Graham, waiting while the man wrestled with the possibility of other English reprisals. It was his answer and his promise that was required to make Nicholas break his vow to never again set foot into England, if he should decide to take up Eleanor de Graham's plea to bring her daughter home.

He might. It might be worth it, to revisit the place where he had once spent a year as a guest of the English, simply to have the weight and might of de Graham's army on the proper side of freedom.

It was a long moment before de Graham finally nodded. And the remainder of the bluster dribbled out of the man, diminishing him as he sat so that he was noticeably smaller in his grand chair.

"Aye, bring my daughter, Alice, home, and I will pledge all the de Graham army to our independence."

"YE CANNA BE SERIOUS," Baldred griped when they were barely outside the short wall of the de Graham home two hours later.

While he was inwardly as displeased as his captain, Nicholas was indeed serious, intent on rescuing the fair Alice de Graham from the clutches of the evil-doer, Edward Longshanks. And not for one minute did he suppose his reasons for doing so could in any way be construed as selfish. It had nothing to do, he told himself, with seeking revenge against anyone or the English system in general for his own stint as an English prisoner. Nae, he was not so self-serving as that.

He had to give some credit to Eleanor de Graham for the breadth and depth of the scheme she'd concocted behind her husband's back. She hadn't only called him down from Lismore Abbey with naught but hope and a very basic plea to bring her daughter home. Once Nicholas had agreed to consider the idea, she'd laid out more of her deliberating. No sooner had Nicholas wondered himself why de Graham wouldn't have sent some of his own army to reclaim his daughter than Eleanor had said, "If any de Graham soldier were discovered attempting to recover Alice, 'twould mean a price put immediately on my husband's head, gold marks to whomever might wish them. Patronage," she pressed on, "is the first art of government, as well ye ken. England's king is known to be miserly, but on occasion he can—if he realizes some benefit to himself or his own kin or heirs—be persuaded to exercise benevolence. I believe he will no' persecute my husband if he canna prove who might have stolen Alice away from him."

'Twas a weak belief, and one that was not his concern.

Now, to Baldred, Nicholas said, "Aye, I will go to England. And when I return the maiden to the bosom of her family, I will ride away with an army six hundred strong and bring them directly to Wallace's position, in addition to our own proud numbers."

"Ye need an *if* and no' only a *when*," advised the ever-practical Baldred.

Dungal, a half a length behind them, chimed in, "Ye mean to march into England and only suppose no one will notice yer own army, or have heard of the Brute of Braewood Keep, and think ye can—"

"No' an army," Nicholas corrected him. "No' so great a number that I can no' move undetected."

This piqued their interest.

Malise wised up. "Ye will use stealth, then?"

"Aye." And while they mulled over this, Nicholas conceded, "And will I no' need it, whatever plot I decide upon?"

Baldred quipped, with little humor, "Aye, and when we return, God willing, we'll beg ol' Marta to peer inside that skull of yers and see what became of the wee critter who once dwelled there, moving the gears steady-like, but who now is gone."

Once they were out of view of the de Graham, Nicholas reined in and turned to face his men.

"I will charge no man with any crime or deficit if he chooses no' to attend me." In the whole of his army, he might expect some opposition, some wish to be excluded from so haphazard and confounding a plot, but these men, some of his officers, he fully expected to rise to the challenge.

And so they did.

"Ye ken I'll no' leave ye to yer own demise," Baldred said pointedly, one corner of his mouth lifted. "Aye, and will ye no' do me a favor then, and carve it in my tombstone? *Here lies a guid man, who perished on the whims of a daft one*."

Malise smirked at this. He was but a year younger than Nicholas, olive-complected and owning deep-set brown eyes, though his shaggy mane often concealed so much of his face. "Been a day," he said, "since last we did anything worthwhile with our swords. Might rather use mine on English soil."

Nicholas looked to Dungal, seeking his response. He was called *the old man* for good reason, approaching half a century, by Nicholas' reckoning, barrel-chested with legs so lean it was sometimes a wonder he did not tip over in a strong wind. His blue eyes were often narrowed, as now, and were only made bluer by the shock of white hair, long and thick upon his head, and the gray-white beard that covered his chin and jaw and the top of his chest.

"Ye've had less dim-witted ideas, lad," he conceded gruffly. "But aye, yer no' the Brute of Braewood for no guid reason. Would no' be the worst way to go, scribbled down as legend, snatching back a fair damsel in distress."

# Chapter Two

Alice de Graham held her small dagger to the throat of Baron Lisle, Hugh de Lisle, and advised through gritted teeth, "If you so much as lay one more finger on my person, sir, you'll have less fingers to lay anywhere else."

The silver blade was bright against the sudden pallor of his façade, which was already made sallow by the peacock color of his costume. His tunic was of emerald green and his surcoat of red and gold striped silk. His hose were a softer shade of gold, made of fine linen, and his pointed shoes were of good leather, and embroidered in red and gold threads.

The lad, not more than Alice's own nineteen years, recovered himself and pasted on a simpering smile, one meant to appease her but that which only heightened her exasperation. Carefully, he removed the hand that he'd a moment ago placed with too much familiarity upon her waist. But he did not rein in his appreciative gaze, letting it rake down over her. She was fully clothed, but he made her feel as if she were not. Her stomach curled in reaction.

Alice might not have thought anything of such a simple touch, which might only be construed as a courtesy, making sure that she did not stumble as they passed each other in the narrow corridor; the touch seemed harmless enough. But she'd been a guest of the de Lisle house for more than a year now and be-tween this fawning boy and his more irksome uncle and then any guard whose occupation it was to advance her safekeeping, she'd learned fairly quickly that there was no such thing as an innocent touch. Handsy, all of them, and if not for the engraved silver dag-ger her mother had given her many years ago, she'd have been a victim of more than only an unjust imprisonment.

God's blood, she hated England and everything and every-one in it.

"Gone three months, I've been," said the baron, "and I was quite sure you'd have missed my company."

She did, but only because it was actually less loathsome than his uncle's. Edward de Lisle was a predator, intent on conquer-ing, while this dullard only sported with her.

"Gone three months and nothing has changed, Hugh," she told him, managing to keep the tremor from her voice—*never show fear*, her mother had cautioned her. "I still do not wish for you to make free with yer hands." Alice did not let up on the knife, keeping the flat of the blade pressed against the bulge at his throat, the tip barely scraping the underside of his chin.

"You Scots are a fearsome lot," he said, grinning as if she held not any weapon at all. "But oh, how tempted am I to brave the thorn to have the rose." He inched closer yet, so that the tip of her knife now indented his chin.

Joanna had warned her about just this, that there were men who would prove excitable, stirred by the fierceness she only pre-tended at. Mayhap such a man might be willing to chance injury or worse to know if the wildness was imbued deeply, in every-thing she did, and not only roused by her defensive instinct.

"Made reckless, those kinds," had been Joanna's exact words. "Aye, and dinna they think they must be the one to tame ye. Ye only whet their appetites, lass, and be careful with that. So put them off, aye, but ye need to be a heathen about it, speak of bloodletting, lest they imagine yer only playing coy."

"I've told you," Alice said to Hugh now, letting the words come out as a low and dangerous snarl, "I can slit your throat whilst you sleep and be back inside my own bed and nestled with my dreams before the blood stops pooling." With her back against the door to what was supposed to be her private chamber, Alice pushed one hand behind her and lifted the handle.

"Pray tell, what would you do," asked Hugh lazily, as if now amused by her threatening his life, "without your trusty little blade in your possession?"

"I'd use my claws," she promised him and pushed open the door, slipping inside.

Once behind the door, Alice faced Hugh de Lisle while she closed it, keeping her scowl intact until the door was shut on his leering face.

Exhaling a rush of breath, Alice leaned her back against the door. And now her hand, white-knuckled around her dagger, shook so vehemently that it startled her.

Joanna, her maid, rushed her. "Aye, and he caught ye, did he? I told ye, lass, no' to wander about without me."

Aye, she had. And normally, Alice knew better than to go anywhere inside this house without Joanna. But then, one would not imagine a nighttime foray to the garderobe at the end of the hall would provoke so much cause for concern.

"Did ye tell him yer father would split his gullet?" Joanna persisted.

Sighing, as they'd had this conversation—so many times—Alice reminded her of her most recent answer to this same query. "They are not put off by that anymore, Joanna. It's been a year. They know he is not coming to see us freed."

"See *ye* freed," said Joanna, with some pertness. "I'm no' a prisoner, no' exactly. I'm here at yer mam's behest and I'm no' saying I would no' have come of my own volition, to keep ye safe and all, but I am free to come and go as I please. But I could no' look yer mam straight in the eye, all the rest of my life, if I'd no' done this, come here to this dark bit of God's earth with these evil curs."

"And if we ever see mam again or any blessed part of Kincardine," Alice said, weary now, "you will no doubt be richly rewarded." No sooner had she uttered these words than she regretted them. Leaning her head back against the door, she closed her eyes and prepared her rote answer for what came next.

"Ye say richly, as ye have," Joanna began, "and do ye speak of coin? Or mayhap I'll only be fobbed off with some fine léines and a pair of cast-off shoes? Yer mam is just and fair, to be sure, but it is no hen's secret that she can be tight with the coin."

"I will make sure that you have whatever it is that you wish," Alice said mechanically and remembered to include, "within reason." Opening her eyes, she saw Joanna lift her brows and open her mouth to question even this, that Alice was compelled to add one more codicil. "And my mother shall be the judge of reason, in this instance."

Joanna harrumphed, though managed to make it sound fairly pleasant. "So the léines and shoes it is. Though maybe she'll throw in the odd worn mantle. Never did have one of those." And apparently, having that settled in her mind, she returned to her previous argument. "I warned ye no' to leave the chamber. I said the toady lad'd be sniffing around, ken there'd be trouble with that."

Aye, and she might well have used the provisioned chamber pot, but on occasion—this night being one of them—Alice only desired a release from this dreary chamber. And from Joanna herself. A dear woman, by St. Andrew's favor, who was a good decade older than Alice, but who knew not what to do with companionable silences and so thought to alleviate them with her chatter. All the live long day.

As usual, as happened often when she knew such uncharitable thoughts of her companion, she was suffused with guilt. Joanna was right: she herself was no prisoner but had taken on the task set to her by Alice's mother. Embraced it, she had, being both daily attendant and then a teeth-baring hound rising often to Alice's protection.

Edward de Lisle liked to insist that even Alice was not truly a prisoner, that she had freedom within the de Lisle house and was even allowed out upon the grounds. The grounds, as it were, were naught but a walled-in space of green, no bigger than this chamber, which housed only one tree, and afforded little in the way of freedom or even any view in which to dream upon, the wall being taller than Alice. The house itself was situated within the market shire of Hallam, chosen either for the gratuitous groveling of its owner toward the English king or mayhap for its proximity to the barracks at the edge of town, where hundreds of English soldiers were garrisoned. Outside the town itself, there was nothing but the uncrossable rivers Don and Sheaf on the east side and naught but forests and fields as far as the eye could see on the western horizon—nowhere to run.

There was no freedom, however, not if one could not step outside any of the stone that constituted part of the de Lisle house. Alice had not seen the front of the de Lisle house since she had stepped through the door more than a year ago.

She climbed into the narrow bed beside Joanna and thought as she did every night, that tomorrow might be the day she was retrieved and returned to her home.

THEY WAITED UNTIL MARKET day to step foot inside the small town, imagining that their presence might escape notice among the crowds expected. Even then, they split up, Nicholas and Dungal strolling down the main street well before the other three followed.

As with the market towns in Scotland, this one linked the burgh to the surrounding countryside, which brought in so many more people than Hallam knew otherwise. The street was lined with booths and stalls, bakers, tanners, chandlers, and fishermen among those hawking their wares. A peg-legged ale-taster checked the quality of the brewer's ale, for there were in many burghs regulations set and meant to be followed, same as in Scotland.

Nicholas was assaulted by sights and sounds and smells, and his Scottish eyes and ears and nose found them obnoxious, lacking any single bit of charm or redeemable quality. The venders employed shrill voices to be heard, screaming overtop each other; the stalls must be engaged in some desperate duel to be noticed, one's arrangement of draped linens more garish than the next; his nose was offended by raw hides and meat, and day-old fish and unclean bodies.

None of this mattered, of course, save that it was unpleasant. And since crossing the border two days ago, Nicholas found that his mood had only soured, his return to England—despite the noble objective and the benefit to Scotland—lost somewhere in the return of memories of his own imprisonment several years ago.

They'd left their horses and anything that would identify them as Scots, most notably their plaids and any other bit of MacRory tartan, just at the outskirts of town. They spoke to no one, avoiding even the aggressive tactics of some venders with sneering silence, or in Dungal's case, a well-used growl that widened the eyes of that fishwife.

A week ago, in the midst of the Mistress de Graham's conjecture on where her daughter might be found—based solely on hints inside said child's few letters—her husband had surprised all by revealing the exact location here in Hallamshire.

Shock did not quite convey the depth of Eleanor de Graham's reaction, which Nicholas had believed to be tainted with no wee amount of scorn as well.

"All this time you've ken?" Was all the stricken woman had asked of John de Graham at that moment.

*And did nothing to bring her home*, was not uttered but assumed by the bloodless, gape-jawed look she'd turned upon her husband.

"Aye, I ken," returned John de Graham, with some heat, in defense of her unsaid charge, "Aye, I might have made some effort to recover her but ye ken that's a wee bit difficult to do when my entire goddamn army is outside my reach at the moment!" His voice had only increased, ending on a roar. And then, after a moment of twisting his lips, he did admit, "But I made some inquiries, needed to ken where and under whose roof she was held."

At this moment, Nicholas could not say that the wife was yet speaking to the husband.

As it was, though, he'd been given a precise destination, that of the home of the baron de Lisle—"naught but a child, is what is told," de Graham had stated—inside the burgh, upon High Street, adjacent to a traveler's inn. The man might well have said the house sat atop a brothel for the reaction of his wife, who gasped and covered her mouth while her eyes widened in horror.

Again and still, none of his concern, but for the actual location that he might retrieve the lass and gain an army for Scotland's freedom.

The house. Nicholas exchanged a glance with the likewise baffled Dungal when they came upon it.

This was it? This non-descript pile of stone, as narrow as any alley here within Hallamshire? Aye, it was three stories and stretched quite a distance to the rear plots, but 'twas certainly no prison. He'd expected a fortressed dwelling in the middle of the burgh, with a curtain wall and towers and battlements. Not this...this unexceptional residence with nary a guard in sight. He could discern no defense at all, and the various roof lines afforded plenty of footholds that he was sure he could climb the side of the house without difficulty, mayhap without breaking a sweat.

The next look he shared with Dungal was fairly arrogant. His entire mood improved. This would be child's play, wresting a lass from these clutches, such as they were.

Spying Baldred across the road, he inclined his head to indicate the target dwelling and thus, the MacRory men spent the day ambling about, watching the comings and goings of the de Lisle house.

The rear of the house, unseen from the road, and like almost every other building around it, was wholly undecorated, being naught but a straight stone and timber wall from the ground to the third story roof. There were only two windows, one on the first floor and one on the third. There was a forestair, a narrow staircase built outside the house, attached to the side of it, which went directly to that third floor. Likely its original design had been intended for tenants' use and not only prisoners, and in all probability the door up there was now barricaded well to prevent escape.

Nicholas catalogued all this information while he planned his invasion of the house. However, he would make no move until his exact target had been located, until he knew for certain that Alice de Graham was kept within.

People came and went from the front door with more frequency than he would have expected of a house this size. A kitchen serf exited with an empty basket slung over her arm and disappeared into the milling and shopping market crowd. A post boy delivered a letter, handing it through the barely cracked door. He accepted a coin in exchange and while still upon the stoop, clanked the coin between his teeth to test its authenticity before dashing away, his leather bag flapping against his hip as he ran. Just after midday, a loudly dressed man approached the door and rapped precisely three times, looking left and right as he waited for the door to open. The door opened once more, the greeter unseen, and the visitor said only a few words and then scurried away, looking about himself often as he, too, merged into the crowd.

When no one came or went at the front door for more than an hour, Nicholas wandered around to the rear plot once more. The wall enveloping the tiny de Lisle courtyard was as tall as Nicholas himself. He scaled that bit easily, and only long enough to poke his head over and discover the yard empty save for a weary birch tree and one narrow bench made of stone. Before he dropped back down to his feet, he took note of the worn path in the gravel and leaves, from the lone door at the back of the house to where some feet might plant themselves in front of that bench.

The alleyway which brought him here moved uphill as it lengthened and Nicholas followed that path, to the rear of the next yard and then further, almost to the side of the building on the next street over, until the elevation afforded him a clear view of the de Lisle yard. And he set himself up to wait, only pretending to walk through the alley if any person happened by.

He was rewarded after only a short time, when the rear door opened, and two women stepped out into the compact courtyard. The first woman moved purposefully, head down and focused only on gaining the seat of the bench, doing so immediately. The first thing the second young woman did as she stepped outside was lift her face to the sun.

This Nicholas understood, recalling well the very first time he saw the sun and the sky and the grass on that day he was released from his English imprisonment. How sweet had been the scent of the grass, how overwrought his joy at the sight of something so simple and unpretentious as a clear blue sky.

He knew in an instant this was Alice de Graham. She had the same height and midnight hair as her mother. He was far enough away that no particulars availed themselves to him, naught but a long and lean figure in a blue wool léine, the skin of her arched neck pale perfection. Her long black hair was wound with pale ribbons and her waist was trimmed in a beaded belt. She pivoted, ignoring the chattering of the woman with her, so that her face was in direct sunlight and Nicholas was shown her profile, which appeared to be carved with both delicacy and strength.

A full minute passed in which she did not move, only let the sun warm her and adore her.

Nicholas squinted, unable to resist the urge to move closer, telling himself he needed to hear as well as see to determine these ladies were indeed Scots, that this must be Alice de Graham. He strode purposefully but slowly, down the alley from the house that backed up to the de Lisle property, keeping himself near to the wall and close to the fringe of ivy.

"Dinna tip your face as such," the other woman was saying when Nicholas was close enough to hear.

Aye, their thickly accented English was easily discernable now.

"Yer freckles'll come full force," said the other woman, who must be the servant, Joanna, who would likewise require rescuing, per Eleanor's instruction. "And yer mam'll take that out on me."

The lass whom Nicholas was sure must be Alice sighed visibly, her chest lifting and falling.

"A moment will do no harm," she assured her companion. Her voice was mild, almost resigned, the sound of it as soft as silk.

"Aye, and dinna ye say that last week?" challenged Joanna, "And weren't it a good thing we were no' called home then and yer mam saw that damage?"

Alice's shoulders dropped and she lowered her face from the sun. Apparently, it was not worth putting up with that one's fussing about it.

But the badgering did not end, even as Alice sat next to her on the bench. It was only transferred to something else.

"Ye spent all the morn on a letter—only ye and our sweet Lord ken what all those scratches were—and then ye tuck it away, dinna finish, dinna send it off. Why do ye bother?"

"I was trying to pen a note...and struggling to project a cheeriness I do not feel—"

"Struggling to project?" Joanna cut her off. "Ye say what ye say. What needs to be said. *The baron de Lisle is a pig. His uncle is a bounder. Bring us home. Love, Alice.* There."

"I do not wish for mother to worry—"

A huge, unattractive snort was interjected here. "And ye think keeping secrets from her will chase all that away?"

"I do."

"Aye, and the truth of it is that you're sore," Joanna said next. "Sore and believing they've forgotten all about ye—and by extension, me, more's the pity. Naught but half a dozen sad letters—in all the year—from yer own dear mam, who says she loves ye, but how can ye be sure?"

*Jesu*, but was the woman Joanna actually in the employ of the English? To be filling the poor lass's head with such absurd doubt. His brow furrowing, Nicholas continued to move closer. Since she sat, Alice was in profile still, and he wanted to see more, and clearly.

But he moved without giving attention to the ground and his foot kicked an abandoned and empty bucket that sat near the wall.

It was not terribly loud, but it did draw Alice de Graham's attention. She lifted her face and stared directly at him, half of her obscured by Joanna's head. For the space of a heartbeat, she looked directly into his eyes. Her pink lips parted, and she blinked before Nicholas recovered himself and looked away, pretending he was only using the alley as a path between two roads, walking out of sight toward the front of the de Lisle house.

And somehow he felt duped, as if he'd been tricked by her parents, as if they'd purposefully left out what seemed to him, inexplicably, to be of great import, the fact that their daughter was the most magnificent creature Nicholas had ever laid eyes on.

"St. Andrew save us," he mumbled reflexively, as his stepmother often had when something irksome troubled her.

He walked all the way around the block to return to the alley at the higher elevation of the house whose courtyard abutted with the de Lisle yard, keeping that discreet distance. Baldred and Dungal joined him after a while.

"*Jesu*, is that the de Graham lass?" Dungal asked, not bothering to hide his severe displeasure, which was explained by his next statement. "Ye ken one who dinna look like that would be a hell of a lot easier to spirit out of England."

"If that be Alice de Graham, I fear getting her out of England will be the least of our troubles," Baldred groused, sounding about as put out as Dungal. "Aye, and praise the Lord we dinna bring more of the army to trip themselves up over her."

Nicholas rolled his eyes at them, well accustomed to their similar fatalistic speculating.

Half an hour later, when the two women had abandoned the courtyard and returned to the house, Nicholas waited a few minutes and then picked up and tossed a small stone at that third story window. It sailed through the opening. Within seconds the woman, Joanna showed her face in the window, looking straight up, as if the stone had come from the sky. Alice appeared in the right side of the mullioned window seconds later, leaning against the hands she pressed to the sash. She displayed a bit more cleverness and looked out and not up. Her gaze passed over the top of the wall where that overgrown ivy concealed Nicholas but did not stop. After a moment, both women disappeared from the window.

And now he knew, indeed, she was kept in that chamber.

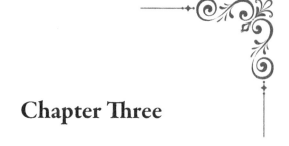

# Chapter Three

D ungal insisted that they should use that forestair and burst through the door, which might well open directly into Alice's prison chamber. Dungal would do almost anything not to have to scale the outside of the house.

"We dinna need to rouse the entire household," Nicholas clipped at him in the dark of night. "Aye, then ye wait down here."

They'd left their steeds once more just outside of town. It was easier to remain unheard or unseen when on foot. And because the town saw so few horses, bringing theirs in at this hour would only raise any still wakeful brows.

"Baldred and Malise, with me," he instructed. The lad, Henry, had stayed with the horses. He reminded them, looking pointedly at Baldred, "I dinna expect that either of the lasses will be able to climb out and down the wall. We'll be forced to lower them by ropes, but then I also dinna expect that to go so smoothly or quietly, so then we're off on a race, getting out before we are discovered."

"Aye, and let's get it done before we're found now, loitering in places we should no' be," said Baldred, looking around the de Lisle courtyard and even over the wall into that alley.

Nodding and then establishing Malise's readiness, which came with a tight nod, Nicholas led the way, jumping up to grab hold of the low hanging roof of what might be the kitchens. Hoisting himself up onto the roof, he stepped carefully over the tiles, keeping near the house itself where the roof would be sturdier until he was directly below that third-story window. He was able to stretch his leg out onto the transom at the top of the ground floor window and pull himself to stand on that, curling his fingers into the mortar joints of the wall. From there it was just a climb upward, against the stone, which might have been easier done if he'd doffed his boots so that he could find greater purchase with his toes, but which was not impossible. He needed only three moves to gain enough height to reach his hand over the sill of that third story window and then only arm strength was required to pull himself up.

Once perched inside the casement, Nicholas pushed aside the oil cloth curtain and peered inside, scanning the room for any impediment. There was no noise, either inside or out, save for Baldred's slight panting directly below him. As soon as his captain's hand slapped onto the window sill, Nicholas hopped down inside the chamber and kept his gaze on the curved form under the bedcovers.

No sooner did he decide that it appeared to be only a lone figure inside that narrow bed than a knife was thrust at him from his right, where a body had been pressed against the wall.

He did not take the time to placate the lass, whichever one it might be, but lifted his left hand to circle the trembling wrist. With a grip of steel, in control of the hand that held the dagger, he yanked the body toward him, swinging his right hand around her head to cover her mouth before she might have screamed.

"Ye dinna want to do that," he whispered at the side of her head, pressed against his face.

This brave lass, the one who'd just confronted a thief come in the night, was Alice. He knew this instinctively, and not only because of her height, several inches taller than the other one, Joanna. He held her hand and her weapon, which she'd not dropped, tight against his left thigh. Her back and left hip pressed against his right side, and while she was rigid with fear, she was soft against him and smelled faintly, enticingly, of roses.

"I've come to bring ye home, lass," he said when Baldred finally landed two feet inside the chamber. "Get that one from the bed," Nicholas instructed him.

A wee bit of chaos ensued then.

Baldred move toward the bed just as Malise appeared in the open window. Having given the lass this good news, Nicholas was surprised when she responded not with a softening of her rigidity, but by lifting her foot to stomp down on his. It was not so painful, the stomp of her slipper clad feet, but was shocking enough that he momentarily loosened his hold across her mouth. With her free hand, she scratched at his, uncovering her mouth just enough for the beginning of a good screech, which Nicholas thwarted, though not quickly enough, by clamping his hand tighter over her mouth, able to withstand the scratching and clawing of her hand to be freed.

Joanna, inside the bed, was roused by this and let out a shriek of her own before Baldred could throttle that attempt in a similar fashion, with his hand over her mouth. Her position on the bed gave Joanna some leverage as it was difficult for Baldred to keep her silent while trying to drag her off the thin mattress. She fought and kicked and rolled away, falling to the floor at the far side of the bed.

"Sweet St. Andrew," the woman, Joanna, whimpered acerbically, upon all fours, scrambling to her feet, "here comes the end."

Alice began to exert more force in her own struggle to be free, so that Nicholas was compelled to squeeze her wrist until she dropped the dagger. When she did, with her own whimper behind his hand, Nicholas pulled her more tightly against him, her back to his front, his left arm secure around her middle, imprisoning her arm as well.

"Shh," he commanded her as Baldred leapt over the bed at Joanna, and Malise grumbled something unintelligible before closing in on that lass from around the foot of the bed.

"Run, Alice," wailed Joanna, while falling to the floor in a heap and covering her head with her hands. "Save yerself."

"God's bluid, woman," Baldred hissed at her, "that's what we're aiming to do."

When Joanna was well in hand, pulled to her feet and held between Baldred and Malise—though looking yet like she was just now to be led to the doomster's block to have her head lopped off; her shoulders sagged and possibly her knees buckled, so low did she stand between the two men—Nicholas lessened the force of the hand covering Alice's mouth.

"Dinna scream when I release ye." He waited for her acquiescence, which came after only a moment and with a shaky nod. "We've been sent by your father, John de Graham, have come to bring ye home, lass," he conveyed as he lowered his hand.

Alice twirled in his arms and faced him. For one fleeting moment, he stared gape-jawed, so entranced by this moonlit lass, standing in the light of the window, staring at him with wide eyes and so much hope. 'Twas not enough light to study her fully or know if her eyes were blue or green or black, to know if only nighttime shadows made the fringe of lashes surrounding her remarkable eyes appear so thick and long.

"My father?" She questioned, her voice airy, her chest rising and falling.

*Jesu*, but her lips were amazing, generously curved and parted with the gasp of her question.

He patently ignored the very clear imprint of his hand on the left side of her cheek, four smudges of color—gray in this light—where his fingers had clutched at her with too much force.

"Aye," he said before too many seconds had passed. "To bring ye home."

The wide eyes were no more. She narrowed her gaze at him and challenged, "He would not have. To do so would jeopardize his own position. I am to stay here until—"

"Nae, ye are bound for home," Nicholas informed her. "And we move now."

She hesitated, blinking with bafflement and removed her gaze from him. The hysteria had left her, replaced by confusion. Her lips moved, as if she might question this more, before she clamped them tight, seeming to accept this. In the next second, she said, "Very well. Let us depart."

Turning those wide eyes onto him again, she nodded, and bent to retrieve her dagger.

Nicholas' chest expanded with some relief that he would not have to drag the lass, kicking and screaming, from this house. The relief was short-lived, however. Straightening with the blade once more in her possession, she slashed at him, cutting his forearm when he belatedly lifted his hand in defense.

"Bluidy hell."

"Lies," she accused at the same time. "Liar."

What the—"Why would I bluidy lie about that?"

"I cannot say," she charged while the two of them squared off. "My da would not keep company with the likes of you. And he'd come himself, or"—she paused, relaxing her fighting stance—"did he send a note with you? A letter to introduce you?"

"A letter to introduce—?" Nicholas scoffed. "This is no' the court of kings, lass. We've no' waved banners to announce our presence—"

"My mother warned me that some attempt might be made—"

He tried to reason with her, using the truth, but was unable to keep the harshness from his voice. "We canna travel with papers and notes, giving away all the plot and all the parties involved." When she remained stalwart in her disbelief, Nicholas growled low his impatience and once more, easily disarmed her. He was sorry to use such force and for how brutal he might seem, but they'd been too long, and it was possible that even their disrupted screeching had wakened others in the house. Clasping her flailing arm once more, he plucked the dagger from her hand and secured that in his belt, next to his own dirk, and shocked her by fisting his hand into the bodice of her shift and pulling her up against him. She slapped her hands against the fabric, pressing her nightrail against herself since Nicholas' tug had pulled it away from her body. His breath was hot on her as he charged, "Yer own mother, Eleanor de Graham, summoned me to her, begged we rescue her daughter—went behind yer sire's back to do so. But yer da had been spying on yer welfare, had discovered ye were kept here, and bade me fetch ye home. He promised me his army for Scotland's cause in return. Ye're coming with us."

In the face of his controlled fury, she boldly shook her head, her fingers laid over his at her neck, trying to dislodge them. "Nae. If I leave here, my da will be charged with treason, hunted down or worse. At the very least, he would be ruined, stripped of all his English holdings. He would not have—"

"Dammit, but he did. Will I need to bind ye and gag ye to get ye out of here?"

"Aye, you will," she growled at him, her tone as fierce as his. "I'll not betray my father willingly. I see your game—you've just revealed it. You mean to take his daughter to fatten your own army, but 'twill be his life on the line for your actions."

In truth, he hadn't really considered that this part—getting the lass to accompany him away from the de Lisle house—was going to be the hard part. His fury only rising for this unexpected inconvenience, Nicholas gnashed his teeth and said to her, "Aye then. Bound and gagged it is." He tightened the fist in the linen neck of her shift and brought her face even closer. "And that's the only pass ye get for drawing blood, Alice de Graham. Dinna ever raise a blade to me, never again."

"I will. I will see you dead," she seethed at him, seemingly without fear, "before I play any part in my own father's demise."

OH, BUT HER LEGS WERE jelly.

This man was too...much. Too strong, too big, too menacing. She knew this man. Not by name and not before today, but she had spied him just this afternoon standing outside the wall of the de Lisle courtyard, was sure this was the same man.

In all her life, she'd not ever been this scared.

But it made no sense. Why would her father—now, after a whole year!—decide to thumb his nose at Longshanks' edict that she was to be held in captivity to assure her father's fealty?

Alice felt, deep inside, that this was a ruse, perpetrated by these evil men. She believed as she'd said, that they meant to turn her father's allegiance, by force, to the Scots' side. And while she was sure that her father, if given a choice without unjust persuasion, would have chosen to fight on the side of right, for freedom, she knew for certain he did not want to engage Edward I as a personal enemy. 'Twould be a death warrant, for there were many who might be willing to prove their own loyalty to Longshanks by slaying one who was not.

But she was trapped, she knew. There was no way she and Joanna, who had given in quickly, could take on these three men, barbarians by the looks of them. That was how she knew this man did not keep company with her own father. John de Graham was a baron, who mingled with nobles and like-minded men, not men of this ilk, wearing no plaid and having his large, muscled arms bare and showing such a gruesome scowl that he appeared more beast than man.

"Tell me why now?" She asked of the man, who had yet to identify himself. Not that his name alone would erase any of her concerns or suspicion. "If you are privy to this—me being here—then mayhap you can tell me why my father would wait nigh on a year to come for me?"

"Ye can take that up with him when I deliver ye to him."

"Will you? Deliver me to him? Or is it your intent only to spirit me away to another prison for your own selfish reasons?"

Still holding her by the neck of her shift, he seethed at her, "I've stated my business, said that yer own sire and yer mam bid me come to free ye. I've said I'll take ye to them. I will defend my position no' more. I am no' a liar."

In the dimness of the bedchamber, with naught but the dying embers of the tamped fire and the bare light of a silvery moon, Alice studied him. He was remarkable for his height and breadth, being taller than any man she knew and as broad shouldered as none she'd ever met. Extraordinary as well for how his eyes searched and probed her face so thoroughly, and for how they glittered with fury. They were close enough that he should be able to see all her face at once, but he made a point to investigate each part of her face individually, darting his eyes over her own and up to her brow, then down across her nose. More than once, he settled the heat of his glittering cat eyes on her mouth. At one point, his own lips curled with disfavor while he studied hers.

She was left breathless and weak-kneed and thankfully, that was when Joanna recalled her own voice, which had been unaccountably, amazingly, silent for a long minute by now.

"And git yer slimy hands off me, will ye now?" She struggled in the grasp of the other two men.

"Wrap 'em up and drag 'em out," snarled the one holding Alice.

Her eyes widened, aghast that she was truly to be taken away from the baron's house. Again, she struggled with him, twisting to be free, clawing at the hand that held her.

His next words rendered her motionless, her dread now reaching new and ridiculous heights.

"Dinna fight me, lass. If ye give me but one more bit of grief, it will be yer friend's neck that will be slit."

Alice gulped down her fright. And while he seemed to wait for her to digest this and give him some indication that she would do as commanded, she nodded pitifully at him. Though she didn't mind one bit hissing at him what she thought of his character and his plot. "You are evil. And when my father is killed because of this, it will be blood on your hands. And then I will make it my life's mission to—"

"Hush," he growled without an ounce of contrition. "Ye'll do no such thing, as well ye ken. And ye'll see soon enough, when ye've been taken into yer mam's arms in a few days, that I did no' lie." Unblinking, he narrowed his gaze again at her. "No' another word or yer friend will feel the blade."

"Aye," said the man holding Joanna, tugging on her arm, "and the same goes for ye. Get out of line and that one will get it."

Joanna, ever adept at stirring one's ire by her habit of pointing out common sense arguments, dared to suggest, "I dinna imagine ye'll harm Alice. If what ye say is true, she's only good to ye if she's kept alive."

"And that's enough out of ye," said the man, more irritable now. "Move on, then. Let's go." He shoved her forward, around the bed so that all of them stood near the window.

The hand at the neckline of Alice's gown loosened and then fell away. "Will ye leave of yer own volition?" The beast asked her. "Or will I spill the blood of yer friend and toss ye over my shoulder?"

Pertly, annoyed with her own helplessness, Alice wondered, "Will you simply exit the same way you entered? And expect that I or Joanna might climb down the side of a house, like goats on a hill or cats on a roof?" Still suspicious of him, she hoped he would say that they would exit through the house, and that she might be presented with some opportunity to rouse the household or the guards. The door to this chamber was locked each night, timed to the lighting of the evening lamps and to her knowledge, after the first few weeks of her captivity, no longer did soldiers keep watch just outside the door.

Another thought occurred to her. "And will ye expect that we go out into the night and journey—as ye say, across a hundred miles to my father and mother—wearing naught but our shifts?"

For one split second, his face displayed the truth, that he hadn't thought about this minor detail. But his surprise over this was quickly hidden behind yet another furious scowl. "By all means, Lady Alice, please do take a moment to garb yerself more appropriately for yer own kidnapping."

He was being snide of course, but Alice understood that was only to conceal his own lack of forethought. But she was released as was Joanna after a moment, and the pair quickly collected a gown each from the only cupboard in the chamber, both facing the cupboard in the dark corner as they pulled their léines over their heads. How utterly mortifying.

"Like as no', I should pack what little we'd come with," Joanna said, bending to pluck one of the valise's from the bottom of the cupboard. "Yer mam will split my head if I leave the finer—"

One of the men who'd restrained Joanna hissed at them, "Ye'll pack nothing, ye daft wench. Throw on yer cloak and yer sturdy shoes and off we go."

And so they did, collecting and donning their cloaks, while Joanna critiqued Alice's choice of léine.

"Ye should wear the gray wool, lass," she said. "This one is too light, will show all the dirt and filth yer likely to pick up along—"

"Lord save us, woman," said the man, bearing down on them in the corner. He yanked at Joanna's arm. "Move, now."

Spurred into swift action, Alice left off changing her shoes and woodenly returned to the beast waiting on her near the window. His dark eyes were steady and menacing upon her, his sneer still in evidence, effectively fading her own. Dread overtook her when he reached to his side and pulled a length of rope from his belt. Clamping her lips, meaning to show not even an ounce of her current fright by way of her quivering lips, Alice lifted her hands to him, assuming he meant to bind them.

The beast stepped forward, forcing her to fold her arms up against her chest. He stood too close again, his boots scraping the hem of her léine. Alice gulped and held her breath while he reached around her to circle the rope around her waist several times. She turned her face away from him and closed her eyes when his thick hair brushed her chin as he bent to the task.

When the rope was secure around her middle, he took her arm and turned her toward the open window.

"I'll lower ye down," he said to her. "Dungal waits below and ye'll no' make a blessed sound as he will no' hesitate to twist your neck to save mine." His dark brows rose, awaiting her acquiescence.

With his face in the window, directly under the moonlight, Alice saw that his cheeks were stubbled, the short hairs silver upon his skin. A scar, unseen until now, was drawn from the corner of his mouth across his angular cheek until it disappeared into his hairline. 'Twas old and not grotesque, but surely he suffered much because of it, then and now.

Having no other options available to her, she nodded, and listened to his next instructions.

"Ye hang on, face the wall," he said, "use yer feet as needed for leverage."

He lifted her hand and pressed the rope into her palm, his warm and strong fingers closing hers around the hemp. Alice stared, a bit wide-eyed at the fingers covering hers, so much darker and larger than her own.

"I'll no' drop ye," he said, his voice quiet now.

She hadn't thought he would. He appeared supremely capable of so many things.

"Unless ye shout yer distress and raise my ire again."

Alice shook her head and stared at his chest now. She might be dreaming, so foggy was she. The reality of the situation crashed into her that she felt she could look at it now, the whole of it, what was happening. Someone had come for her, but it was not her father nor any de Graham man. A beast had come, bound to take her away from what had been a miserable existence for more than a year. But to leave might well put her father in danger. Her heart sped again, her eyes pooled with tears.

She met his piercing eyes. "Tell me true," she begged. "I would rather die here than bring danger to my sire."

"Aye, I ken ye would," said the beast. "Climb up," he ordered, tapping the sash of the window. And when she hesitated, needing more assurance from this man, he sighed and said to her, "Yer mam frets for ye, having received only three missives in all the year. Like as no', they destroyed many more than what they allowed to be delivered or sent."

Alice considered him, wondering if she would know anymore if a person lied to her or not, having so little interaction with persons other than Joanna and the few inside this awful household. He had more reason to speak untruths than to assuage her worries. He returned her stare unblinking, almost as if he dared her to call him a liar again.

Mayhap it didn't matter. What was true moments ago remained so: she had little choice. Swallowing any remaining anxiety, she put a hand on each side of the window frame and pulled herself up, not unaware of the brute's hands so familiarly upon her waist to give assistance.

Halfway between the third story and the ground, she thought she should scream an alarm, when no one was near to silence her. But Joanna was still at risk, still within the chamber with those ruffians, and Alice was forced to choke down any cry for help.

When she was on her feet, the man she'd been told was Dungal untied the rope, and it was pulled back up for Joanna.

Joanna, on her descent, must have taken her own earlier words to heart, believing that Alice truly was not in danger, was only a pawn more useful alive than dead.

And so she did scream her head off as she dangled about the side of the de Lisle house.

# Chapter Four

"**B**luidy hell," cursed Nicholas as the daft woman let loose a wail he might have only ever heard from a wild boar, or any other undesirable and threatened animal. His charity abandoned him as the noise pierced his ears and Nicholas felt no remorse for releasing the rope completely when answering shouts and calls were heard only seconds later from somewhere inside this house. A thud from below cut off Joanna's screeching and was followed almost immediately by footsteps pounding up the stairs.

Having only seconds did not allow for escape by way of the window for all of them. Descending the side of the house would take several minutes, which would make them easy targets. But he and Baldred could hold off a few here and afford Malise enough time to make his way down.

"Go on," he clipped to the lad, inclining his head toward the window as he drew his sword and then faced the pounding at the door. "Ye and Dungal get them away," he advised, referring to the two women, and having no fear that he and Baldred wouldn't be following in a few minutes.

Metal scraped against metal as a key was employed in the door, which was thrust open only seconds later. Despite the fact that he knew what was happening, Nicholas displayed as much shock as the man who entered. Boy actually, naught but a pup. This was the only response of her captors? To send half a man in his nightclothes and with the key as the only possible defense?

Baldred had the same thought and even went so far as to sheath his sword, since no other footsteps were forthcoming. "I'll wait ye down below," he said and climbed out the window, following Malise down the stone wall.

The young pup squawked, "Who are you? And what have you done with—?"

"Hold," Nicholas barked, aiming his sword at the pale lad, though still a good distance separated them. With the lad gone still, Nicholas peered out the window to assess the situation below in the courtyard. Three men, these ones armed, had burst into the courtyard. Another was outside the wall, having come from the front of the house. Malise and Dungal had two well in hand. The third inside the wall was trying to drag Alice away from the heap on the ground that was Joanna, who was again wailing with some volume. Baldred was almost to the first floor, would join that fray soon.

All was well.

He turned again and gave his regard to the youth in his nightclothes. "Ye ken it's no' worth death, aye?"

Without answering the question, the young man asked instead, "You've come for Alice?"

A fine time then to plant a seed of doubt over de Graham's involvement. "Is that the beauty's name? I only spied her in the courtyard earlier and decided she might serve me well." A not unreasonable possibility, given Alice's loveliness.

Nicholas was surprised by the snort of laughter that erupted from the man. "And good fortune with that. I certainly found none. Sweet-cheeked and silver-tongued, she'll slit your throat if you but lay a hand on her."

Good for her, Nicholas thought. Furthering his pretense of not knowing who she was, Nicholas lifted a brow at the man and challenged, "No' so great a fight to save your own kin—your lady wife, mayhap?"

The man gasped. "Lord in heaven, no," the man said. "She's a filthy Sc—she is nothing to me."

And now Nicholas smirked, letting the lad see all his justifiable scorn.

"Aye, then, this filthy Scot will take that other one," he said blandly and sheathed his sword before pivoting to climb through the window. He expected no challenge, no fight or additional protest from the young baron. And there was none.

By the time he reached the ground, less than a minute later, Baldred and Dungal and Malise had the situation well in hand. Four men lay incapacitated on the ground and Alice and Joanna were huddled together on their knees, Alice's arms around her friend, whose head was buried and whose wails continued.

Wanting to be away, and quickly, Nicholas took up Alice's arm as he strode by, pulling her to her feet with little care for tenderness. "Let us depart," he said as he wrenched her away from the unquiet woman.

Before he might have instructed Baldred to collect Joanna, that one gave life to another squealing cry, one that roused several nearby hounds so that the night was then filled with answering barks and howls.

"*Jesus Christus*," fumed Baldred as he hauled Joanna to her feet.

Nicholas rolled his eyes and continued moving, toward the gate at the very back of the small yard, from which they'd found entry earlier. At his side, held close by his hand on her arm, Alice was silent and skipping to keep up with him.

Only a quick dash, made in the shadows through the sleepy town, was required then, though they did increase their speed when calls were heard behind them. He thought the baron might have exited the front door and was screaming for assistance in a high-pitched squeal. Moments later, answering cries were heard, not from the burgh itself but further away from where Nicholas and his party were, likely from the garrison at the opposite end of town.

When they reached Henry, minding the steeds outside of town, Nicholas was tempted to toss Alice on her stomach over the destrier and make her ride in that ignoble position for hours, for all the grief he'd been given so far. But they might yet be pursued, and swiftness was required and that would be more easily achieved by having her upright on the steed. Thus, he only took a moment to don his plaid, not wasting time on pleating it as neatly as he'd have liked.

While Henry held the bridle for him, Nicholas put his hands around Alice's narrow waist and lifted her up into the saddle so that she faced him, seated sideways, and he quickly gained the saddle behind her. Reaching both arms around her, he retrieved the reins from where they'd been loosely wrapped around the pommel and pivoted the horse to gauge everyone else's readiness. Baldred had not simply lifted the woman, Joanna, into the saddle but was allowing her to mount by herself, which then had the woman struggling to lift her foot so high into the stirrup while

Baldred attempted to hold it steady for her, his eyes bugged wide with significant frustration.

"Lord love a sinner, man," groused Dungal while his steed pranced a bit in response to his rider's agitation. "Get 'er up there."

"Or drag her by her hair while ye ride," Malise offered as a suggestion, impatience tinting his tone as well.

"Up ye go," Baldred said, placing his hand upon the woman's rump and giving a good shove when she finally managed to set her foot into the stirrup. Being boosted so ignobly had the woman howling with indignation, even as she slung her leg up and over the horse and the skirt of her gown rode up to almost her knee.

"Och, the tragedy of it," she wailed and then slumped dramatically, her posture pairing perfectly with the whinge in her voice.

Nicholas rolled his eyes and led his party away from Hallamshire.

SHE WAS A DECENT HORSEWOMAN but had never cared to ride sidesaddle. Alice was certain that if not for the strong arm around her waist, she might topple right off the side of the horse at any moment, given the speed and what she considered recklessness of their getaway. She had no choice, it seemed, but to cling to the arm around her, but managed to do so stoically, sitting stiffly to keep herself from touching too much of this man. He might yet prove to be the liar she assumed, naught but a desperate brigand about in the night, attending his own self-seeking agenda.

She said not a word. But then, neither did any of these five men, not even to shush the constant nervous chatter of Joanna, who had indeed regained her voice. If not for Alice's own niggling doubt and fear about the true intentions of these men, she might have known a bit of amusement, might have inquired of the beast with whom she rode if Joanna's unending and mostly nonsensical prattling had been expected, or was appreciated.

Alice's delight was rattled a bit when she happened to hear some of what her maid was saying to the man with whom she rode.

"Oh, and she wailed and wept and kicked and clawed at her mam when she was taken," Joanna was saying, her voice not exactly hushed, even as it should have been expected that stealth and silence were hoped for. "Left drag marks on that poor woman's arms, no doubt. And I was sent to soothe her and so I did, best I could, told her all would be well. We've all a part to play, I said to her."

Most everything over the next few minutes that emerged from Joanna's mouth depicted Alice as the subject. Joanna made her sound weak and whiny and then brash and bold, and Alice found herself clamping her lips lest she do what she'd only dreamed of in the last year, told the woman to *clap her trap*, one of her father's favorite commands.

"I dinna ken what might have become of her if no' for me," Joanna said at one point. "Tears and gloom she does well, but dinna get me wrong, she'd cut out de Lisle's heart—either he or that uncle of his—for all the manhandling they got up to. 'Twas only this eve she put the baron under her wee knife, told him he'd lose his fingers if he touched her again. No doubt it was my own admonition to her, to no' be cowed by any of them, that saved her from ruin."

"Aye and weren't she so fortunate to have ye by her side, every blessed waking moment?" her riding companion intoned carelessly, a sigh detected in his voice.

Joanna missed the nuance of irritation in the man's words and willingly agreed. "She was and dinna I remind her."

"Aye, I wager ye did," said the old man, riding abreast of the pair. "Every blessed waking moment, I am sure."

Out of the corner of her eye, Alice was allowed a view of her captor, the beast with the dark and probing gaze. A slight tilt of her head put his chin at eye level, and she thought either it was clamped as was her own, annoyed with Joanna's inability to be silent, or his jawline was simply that square and that stonelike. He did not look down at her but he did tighten his arm around her waist and Alice sighed, letting her shoulders fall a bit.

She was good and stolen from the de Lisle house by this brigand of the solid jaw, whom she might have believed was untroubled by Joanna's continued yapping, until he revealed some of his own annoyance at the lack of silence by wondering near Alice's ear, "She dinna ever quiet?"

Surprised by the question, given with much less exasperation than even Alice herself knew, she answered promptly, "Not so often." She thought it wise to advise him of this now, ahead of their return to Scotland, that he might prepare himself for the onslaught of words to be spewed over the next several days or however long it would be before she saw her mother again. Feeling particularly lighthearted at the thought of seeing home and her mam again—or of this man's possible regret over Joanna's nimble tongue, if his intentions were not as he said—she added jauntily, for his ears alone, "Shock sometimes has the effect of taking away her words and thoughts. That might well see you the boon of several minutes unencumbered by noise."

"Jesus, Mary, and Joseph and the arse they rode in on," grumbled the one named Dungal, the oldest man in this party, "will ye quiet already? We'll no' ever see our sweet Alba again if ye plan to announce to all the world every step we take."

Being spoken to so harshly might be accounted as shock-inducing that Joanna did quiet, though her mouth formed a large O at being chastised so gruffly. The beautiful silence was short-lived.

"No' any other unsavory soul about at this hour to hear our passing," Joanna guessed. "Will ye truly see us all the way home?"

"The lass, aye," said the man riding with Joanna, his tone suggesting his own pique, "but ye may well be abandoned 'fore we reach the borderlands if ye dinna close yer mouth."

Joanna was undeterred. In fact, she snorted a laugh, one of her most well-loved expressions. "Fat chance ye have then of convincing her da or mam that the lass was unmolested on the journey, if ye do away with me, the only one who might give evidence to the contrary." A pause, and then, "Unless, aye, yer no' who ye claim to be and molesting is all ye have in mind."

And on it went. Alice tried to distract her saddle-mate with conversation of her own that he might ignore Joanna's.

"Ye have not told me your name," she accused, with less severity than should have accompanied her complaint. The man had, after all, pilfered her from a relatively safe place and was now holding her hostage, riding about at midnight through an inhospitable country; she had a right to know his name.

"Nicholas MacRory," he said, "summoned, as said, by yer—"

"Saints be warned," hissed Joanna, having heard the man's name—which meant nothing to Alice until Joanna followed up with, "and now we're in the hands of the Brute of Braewood. Och, but our days are numbered, Alice. There go all our sweet ambitions for life, all our good fortunes, and aye, all our hopes for any future no' labeled as this man's victim."

There was more, of course, but Alice had gotten stuck on *good fortunes*? Good fortunes? When and where had those been?

And who was—aside from a man named Nicholas MacRory—the Brute of Braewood?

"I'll no' say it again," said the man sharing the saddle with Joanna, "no' another word. I'm no' above twisting a hood o'er yer head after filling that yawning trap with my fist."

"Joanna, please," Alice begged. "Shush."

"Aye, I'll shush," promised Joanna, but she did not. "And that'll be after and no' before ye tell me just how it is the MacRory came to ken the mighty de Graham and be tasked with coming for Alice de Graham. I canna see a reason that her dear mam would have—"

The horse upon which she rode stopped suddenly, the man yanking hard enough on the reins to interrupt Joanna's current tirade. The four other men, including Nicholas MacRory, reined in and watched the man dismount and pull Joanna—not gently—from the horse as well. Not one of the men asked what he was about. Alice stared, frowning in confusion.

Joanna, of course, wanted answers.

"And ye'll be telling me now why ye handle me as if I'm no' so much but a—"

And that was all she said before she was struck dumb as the man turned from his saddle bags with a length of rope, which he swiftly used to bind Joanna's hands. When that was done and just as Alice cried out her dismay, the man did not fill Joanna's mouth with his hand but did push a scrap of fabric inside. Joanna's eyes were wide and horrified in the pale moonlight. She lifted her bound hands to remove the scrap of fabric, but the man slapped them down.

"Leave it," he ordered and began to affix another rope around her head, holding the muzzle in place.

The beast advised an anxious Alice in his deceptively quiet voice, "Dinna speak, lest the same fate befall ye, lass."

And all Joanna's following words—and there were plenty—were muffled by the kerchief in her mouth and the rope that held it, and then more so by the hood that was draped over her head.

"Aye, and we'll keep that in place," vowed the man who'd bound her, "until ye learn to bite yer tongue."

Aside from Alice's gape-jawed horror and Joanna's angry and inaudible murmuring, no other person showed any reaction to this turn of events.

"Please, you mustn't—" Alice began.

"Aye, we must," said Nicholas MacRory, kneeing his steed to turn him about. "She'd been warned. As ye have as well."

And then, as if they'd not just bound and gagged the poor woman, Joanna was unceremoniously tossed back up into the saddle and they moved again at a slow canter, further north toward Scotland.

It was several minutes before Joanna's surly and unintelligible mumbling was reduced to soft keening and then quieted all together.

And while she wouldn't have said that these men had been particularly careful or considerate with Joanna, they truly had done her no harm. For quite a while the only noise made or heard was that of the horses' hooves parading over the soggy grass of England.

A maze of tangled emotions rose within her, not least of all a great dismay for Joanna's present degrading condition. But then Alice entertained hope, that she might actually be returned to her own home, to her parents. Had her mother truly gone behind her father's back and commissioned this man to fetch her home? If he'd said that her father had put the task to him, she'd have struggled less to believe him, would have known for certain that Nicholas MacRory had been lying. Her father was a gruff man who had so often ignored Alice—she, naught but a mere daughter. She did not recall that he had expressed any great distress when she'd been taken away from their home, not at all as her dear mother had, wailing and weeping as Alice had: regarding that, Joanna had not exaggerated. Her father, however, was not unkind and had never raised a hand to her, but aye, he was not, as Joanna termed it, warm and fuzzy.

Still, she knew a great delight that she had been removed from her prison at the de Lisle house, and an even greater excitement to be reunited with her mother.

Thus, Alice felt some of the tension leave her. After a while, she sagged against the man who held her and soon, she was asleep in the arms of the brute.

# Chapter Five

He would have preferred not to chance that the woman, Joanna, would actually keep her mouth closed and her thoughts to herself, but when the sun began to rise over the rolling and misty hills in the east, Baldred claimed that surely she'd learned her lesson and might be permitted to be both hoodless and unbound. She was, for some time, actually quiet. The woman did not sleep though, Nicholas presumed, since she had not wilted against Baldred as Alice de Graham had against Nicholas for the last several hours.

Wilted indeed, and comfortably so, much to Nicholas' vexation. Mayhap the circumstance was more intriguing than vexing, he allowed after a very short amount of time. He judged it no coincidence that she only settled so easily *after* Joanna's noise and grousing had been silenced, forcing him to wonder if they'd known each other longer or better, if she might have thanked Baldred for the boon he'd given her, a moment's peace.

As it was, Alice's back was curved along his right arm, her head tucked into his shoulder. Her pale-skinned cheek was pressed into his chest, her black-as-pitch hair curtained around her face. Her arms were folded at the elbow, her hands clasped together at her chest. Admittedly, it was impossible for Nicholas to find any fault with this circumstance, having the soft and warm Alice de Graham cradled in his arms. Try as he might, he could not stop himself from stealing glances at her, though he did resist the urge to move away the mantle of hair to better see her face. When he realized how many minutes he rode blindly, staring instead at the sleeping beauty in his arms, he knew a wee bit of fury to be so distracted by her. This would not do. Grinding his jaw, he staunchly moved his gaze up and away from Alice and set it on the vista in the distance.

And that's when he saw it, in the early morning light, the billowing plume of black smoke just beginning to rise over the forest that lay beyond the meadow over which they rode now.

"Baldred," he said, only loud enough to be heard by that man but not with enough volume to rouse the slumbering Alice.

Baldred only briefly turned his attention to Nicholas before he put his gaze where Nicholas had, beyond the meadow and the upcoming trees.

"That should be Bewlie," Baldred commented, narrowing his gaze at the ominous smoke rising.

Aye, they had crossed the River Tweed not so long ago, had glimpsed the pale stone facade of the Coldingham Priory from a great distance, swathed in early morning light as the sun rose over the rocky promontory of St. Abbs' head. Since then, they'd angled northwest, walking alongside the Ale Water, a tributary of the River Teviot in the borderlands.

"That's no' the morning mist," said Dungal, maneuvering closer to Baldred and Nicholas.

Nicholas studied the tree line intently, the forest that separated this small party from the little village of Bewlie. Just as he determined that there might be an orange glow filtered through those trees—possibly the origin of that wafting smoke—a hair-raising scream, muted only by distance, sounded across the land.

"The English are up and about early this day," decided Baldred, his expression grim.

At once, and without direction from Nicholas, all five men spurred their steeds from their ambling walk into a hard gallop along the even ground of the riverside.

Instinctively, he'd tightened his arm around Alice's form when the horse had shot forward but Nicholas could not say if this tightening or the jolt into speed might have roused her. She stiffened and lifted her head, letting out a breathy, little gasp as she woke.

He appreciated that she did not rile him with useless questions but said sleepily, having likely spied the growing plumes of smoke ahead, "Something is amiss."

"Some trouble, aye," was all he allowed, not enlightening her about the scream they'd heard only moments before.

One of her hands, which had been held close to her chest, was now attached to him, her slim fingers curled into the plaid he'd flung over his shoulder, which draped diagonally across him. He could not say or know if this was evidence of fear or if the swift ride bade her hang on tightly. The gallop across the meadow was effortless but they were forced to slow down inside the forest of trees, winding their way around and about pine and birch trees and the thick underbrush therein. As they moved closer to the telling smoke, the orange glow noted only minutes ago brightened. The crackling and roaring of flames soon assailed them, the noise an eerie and riotous backdrop to the numerous cries heard now as they drew closer.

"Need to unload this baggage," Dungal suggested and pointed to a thicket of tightly grouped birch trees surrounded by a tangle of tall undergrowth.

Nicholas and Baldred shifted their direction to that area and reined in.

Baldred said blandly, "Get off," to the surprisingly silent Joanna and all but pushed her from the saddle. The rope that had held the gag in place earlier was still coiled loosely around her neck. When her feet hit the ground, she turned and gave Baldred a scowl that possibly contained a promise of retribution.

With greater care than the hasty Baldred, Nicholas took Alice's hand and lowered her to the ground. She was stunned and confused and clung to his arm even after her feet had touched the ground. Her blue eyes, wide with panic, found his.

"You cannot leave us here," she protested.

"I canna fight with ye in the saddle with me," he told her, pulling his hand free. "Stay low, stay quiet," he clipped. He spared a glance at Joanna and knew a moment's disquiet over the chances of that. Considering the danger far enough away, he met Alice's bright and searching gaze. "Wait here, lass. We'll no' be long."

"Please," she begged, casting her glance beyond him, to where the smoke rose in grotesque clouds over the verdant green tree tops. "But if you do not...return," she said, a wobble to her voice, the hesitation likely an effort to avoid putting into words the worst possible scenario.

Of course, he should not have been bothered by the look of despair she gave him, should not be affected by Alice de Graham at all, whom he'd only just met. She had defied him, had taken a knife to him, had slept in his arms, that was all. She should have no effect on him.

"I'll return, lass," he vowed, sure of this. If the rampaging party was small enough, the MacRorys would make quick work of them. If there were too many infidels about, Nicholas and his men would not engage, would make haste to vacate the area. "Alice," he said, using her given name with purpose, "dinna fret. I'll no' leave ye." Nicholas expected that the look he gave her showed he knew no fear, and so should advise that neither should she.

Seeming to pull herself together, she pressed her lips together and nodded, separating herself from Nicholas and his steed. He moved away from her but felt the heat of her troubled gaze on his back as he joined the others.

They did not charge headlong into the fray but slowed at the edge of the woods to survey the goings-on.

The village—Nicholas did not believe it was Bewlie after all—was only a cluster of a dozen or so crofts, three of which were presently on fire. Mounted and walking Englishman—identified by a red cross emblazoned on the chest of at least one marauding man and by the shiny helm of another, from which chain mail was draped, covering the entirety of his neck—roamed about the area, seemingly pleased just now to cause more panic than injury. Though two bloodied bodies were noted, prone and unmoving on the high street, otherwise people only ran about, screaming their fright, dodging this way and that to evade the raiders.

"Eleven," said Dungal, guessing at the number of mounted and menacing men seen.

"Twelve," corrected Baldred, as another man showed himself between two crofts, intimidating a middle-aged woman, poking and prodding her with the tip of his blade. The man had a shock of red hair atop his head and covering most of his face, and the cackle he used while harassing the woman was chock full of evil glee.

The enemy was not clustered in one spot but spread out around the terrorized village. That would make it easier to attack. Rushing four men out against a group of closely-situated enemy was showing the deficit of their own numbers and put the MacRorys at a disadvantage. Being able to come at individuals rather than a group, when outnumbered, was preferred.

"Henry, this spot should serve ye well, aye?" Nicholas asked.

"Aye," said the lad as he slid from the saddle and collected his long bow and quiver. He leaned the quiver against the wide trunk of an old oak tree and stood just next to it. He planted his feet apart, standing sideways to the action fifty yards ahead of them, and gave Nicholas an at-ready nod.

Henry's apparent calm so often begged a second glance. To look at the lad—lanky and pale and not yet in need of a daily shave—one would not suppose that he might approach a harrowing scene with so much tranquility and fearlessness, or at least the façade of such. But he did, his long and lean face showing nary a furrow in his young brow, his hand firm and gentle upon the grip in the middle of the bowed yew. No tension was detected in the line of his shoulders or the turn of his closed mouth.

Baldred and Dungal alone had seen more fights and battles than Nicholas and Henry and Malise combined might ever know and generally ran with seething arrogance into any fray. Having escaped or cheated death so many times filled a man with a sense of invincibility, which the two older men used well. Henry was different, however, had only this past year taken to the road with the MacRory army, soon after his skill with the longbow had been made known to Nicholas. *An old soul*, Dungal called the young man—not without an often narrowed gaze upon the lad, as if Dungal distrusted that by itself, that a youth should be imbued with so much wisdom and patience and confidence, things that should only come with time and age.

"Take out that flame-headed mongrel first," Baldred directed Henry, "'fore he gets too much of what stirs him."

"Let's move," Nicholas said to the others and kicked his destrier into motion. This particular horse had served him now for more than a year, had seen his share of combat, and knew his master well. The animal snorted as he lunged forward, giving voice to his restlessness to get to it, having sensed Nicholas' bloodlust.

The first Englishman to fall was indeed the man with the red hair. Henry staggered him as he loomed above the fallen woman, as he worked at the ties holding his breeches in place. He glanced down in shock at the arrow protruding from the exact middle of his chest. The strike was forceful enough to lift him off his toes and he was seen teetering, for one, two, three long seconds on his heels as his jaw gaped, before he fell backward. Whatever sound he or his landing might have made was swallowed by the roar of the flames consuming the thatched roofs of the crofts and the louder, more urgent cries of the peasants as they tried to escape their tormentors.

Eleven now, Nicholas thought, only seconds before he engaged the first man he came upon. The man wore only a russet-colored gambeson, a padded defensive shirt, but no chain mail, suggesting he was not a knight, but perhaps only a footsoldier.

As at least six of these attackers were dressed similarly, Nicholas wondered if they were only disgruntled or disaffected men of Longshank's great cause, defected from their unit and about no other objective but to wreak havoc around the borderlands.

As it was, the gambeson offered little defense against Nicholas' meaty blade, which pierced the jacket and whatever lay beneath and then the thick flesh of the paunchy man. While Nicholas withdrew the blade from the man's middle and before this man, too, toppled backward, he stared at Nicholas with some frowning confusion, as if he might question where Nicholas had come from and why he had struck him.

Putting the man from his mind, Nicholas spurred on his destrier to the next target. This one was mounted and presented a greater challenge than the first. They fought in close combat, their horses' flanks touching at times and turning closely around each other. But the man recognized what Nicholas had done, come astride to his non-weaponed hand, so that the man was forced to wield his sword across his body. Before half a minute had gone by, the Englishman was laying on the ground with a neat slit on the left side of his chest.

The trajectory of the assault on the village shifted in a matter of minutes; the flight of Henry's arrows, the falling men, and the coming group of riders turned the Englishmen's violent intent from offensive to defensive. One sorry infidel actually blanched and wheeled his horse around to escape. Nicholas paid him no mind, knowing that Henry would make quick work of him, so long as he didn't get more than two hundred yards away.

The immediate horror and close pursuit of the English removed, the villagers began to run toward the very woods from which the MacRorys had come. Some Englishmen gave chase, seeking their own escape or possibly pursuing hostages. Henry had since changed positions, having remounted and given chase to the first cur to run so that he was unable to pick off the fleeing enemy.

One woman ran for her life, holding a howling bairn on her hip and dragging a young girl behind her by the hand. The little girl appeared to fly, her feet only occasionally touching the ground as her mother tugged her along. A leggy youth and an older man led the race into the trees. A waddling woman of indeterminate years, hoisting her skirts above her knees, brought up the rear. The closest Englishman was almost upon her, his sword raised, when Nicholas pulled a hatchet from the leather holster attached to his saddlebag. Pressing his heels repeatedly into the destrier's flanks, demanding greater speed from him, Nicholas raised the hatchet up over his head, ready to hurl it forward. He waited as long as he could, wanting to be closer so that he did not miss, and when he was within twenty feet of the charging adversary, hurled the well-honed weapon through the air before the man might have struck down the old woman. The man let loose a not unfamiliar battle-time howl and crumpled over the neck of his horse.

Nicholas pursued those other escaping Englishmen, two on foot and one more mounted, as they chased the horrified villagers into the woods. The next—but last—thing he expected to see through the trees was that flash of blue and black as Alice stepped out from her hiding spot, waving her arms wildly to draw the attention of the fleeing peasants. Joanna was not seen, presumably still wisely tucked deep into that undergrowth.

"This way," Alice called to that woman and her children, her strong voice giving no hint of any fear.

The man chasing that small family closed in enough that Alice began to run forward—to what purpose, Nicholas had no idea. He knew a baffling rage at her carelessness and bellowed her name in warning.

"Alice!" He called out. "Get back! Get down!"

She did not. She continued on and pushed the running-scared woman behind her just as the Englishman leapt off his charging horse. Nicholas's heart stopped in his chest as the man slammed into Alice and the pair went down, rolling on the ground. He was yet too far away to help Alice and watched in horror, even as he continued to race toward her as the man gained the upper hand—though not before Alice had swiped savagely several times with her small blade, cutting her foe's arm and cheek. The brigand heaved himself on top of her and caught her flailing arm with one hand as he lashed out with the other, striking Alice across her cheek with enough force to turn her face to the side. In the next second, he lunged to his feet, Alice's knife in one hand and a fistful of her hair in the other. Savagely, he hauled her upward onto her feet as well and might have, just then, sliced her throat with her own dagger, but that he saw Nicholas bearing down on him and heard the ferocious roar that burst from Nicholas' chest.

The man acted swiftly, spinning Alice around so that they both faced Nicholas, who reined in with great force and abruptness when the man put the dagger to Alice's neck.

"Hold," the man called out, breathless, panting, his mail-plated chest heaving.

Nicholas did and then did not. He stopped his horse only ten feet from the pair, from where they stood before a towering yew. But he did dismount, imagining a better chance of freeing Alice if he were on level ground with them.

He'd fought in enough battles, had been a prisoner of the ruthless English long enough to understand that to show any emotion only gave them leverage, put them in control. But then, if he'd wanted to remain aloof or appear unaffected, he shouldn't have looked at Alice's face.

She faced him squarely and though she'd stopped struggling with her captor at the sight of Nicholas, both her hands remained lifted over her head, her fingers locked on the thick hand fisted into her hair. Only her chest moved, surging up and down with her exertions and fright. Her chin was lifted, and stiff, giving a greater impression of defiance than fear.

Ah, but her eyes. In the clear light of day, Nicholas saw that they were an unusual light and bright blue, truly remarkable, but liquid just now with tears. She returned his gaze with an unfathomable expression, so that he could not say if she expected him to save her or if she thought he might sacrifice her to save others, himself included.

Well, that would not do, Nicholas thought. She should not fear—either him or any other while she was under his protection.

"Here," was called out from behind him and Nicholas recognized Henry's voice. "*Ullamh a nis*," he said. *Ready now.*

Perfect. Until this moment, Nicholas hadn't been exactly sure how he would go about freeing Alice.

"All is well, Alice," Nicholas told her, his voice level, reassuring. "No harm will come to ye."

She whimpered then, the first sound she'd made since she'd been hauled to her feet. The sorry noise was filled with disbelief.

She blinked once, slowly, pushing out a lone tear, her gaze asking him how he imagined anything at all was well.

The woods, erupted with so much uproar and noise only seconds ago, was eerily quiet now. The woman with the bairns had been drawn into the brush by Joanna. Fighting continued inside the village, but the sounds of Englishmen dying and horses whinnying and flames devouring homes was dulled at this distance. Nicholas sensed people around and behind him but knew it was those other villagers, including possibly the old woman, whom he'd passed trying to get to Alice.

"Back up, mate," snarled the man holding Alice, believing he was in control. He blinked repeatedly, his gaze frantic upon Nicholas. "Keep going," he said when Nicholas only took one step backward. "Swat the rump of that steed," he said next, inclining his head toward Nicholas' steed, which had stayed close to his master.

The man's abandoned horse was nowhere inside Nicholas' periphery. "Ye canna take my horse," Nicholas said. He might well have said, *the weather is fine* or, *this mutton is flavorful*, for how smooth and relaxed his voice was.

This widened the eyes of both Alice and her captor, the former likely with some grievance that Nicholas should protest the taking of his steed but not yet her, the latter showing surprise that his commands would not be followed.

"Move the horse here or she'll taste the blade," threatened the man, tightening his grip on Alice's hair, straightening himself to appear larger and angrier. "I'm riding out of here, and she's coming with me," he vowed. "And what might you say to that?" asked the ignorant man.

Nicholas showed him a smirk that contained no humor. "Henry," was all he said while holding Alice's watery blue-eyed gaze.

A split second later, the momentary and complete silence of the woods was punctured by the whoosh of a coming missile. Mayhap the man's blood was pounding in his ears during this dangerous confrontation, or perhaps his attention was focused so singularly upon Nicholas as to ignore all else. Whatever the case, he neither saw nor heard the arrow coming at him. Likewise, and thankfully, neither did Alice. She hadn't time to react, to scream, to struggle greatly which might have changed her position to one of danger, that she was as shocked as her captor when the dart landed twelve inches from her face, in the forehead of the man holding her.

Time was frozen, as was the furrowed brow of the man, for the space of a second until he dropped to the ground, taking Alice with him as his fingers were yet tangled in her hair.

Nicholas lunged forward and went to his knees beside Alice, his first objective to remove the knife from the man's hand. He wrested the dagger away from the fingers twisted around it and then uncurled those other fingers knotted into Alice's soft, black hair. When she was freed of the man's grasp, Nicholas lifted her onto her knees to face him and took her by the shoulders, shaking her hard.

"In the name of all that is holy, what were ye thinking?" He demanded of her, uncaring that as they knelt and faced each other, a corpse lay beside them. Alice wore a blank face, all the blood drained as surely as the man next to them. But she did not reject the strong hands on her arms, nor shout any justification for her wayward and dangerous actions. "Ye stay where I tell ye!"

Nicholas went on, his fury unrelieved. "If I say duck and hide, ye duck and hide. If I say run, ye run! Do you understand me? Dinna ever disobey again. 'Tis naught but a swift path to death."

*Damn her*, for raising such peculiar concern in him.

# Chapter Six

Honestly, she heard not one word of his tirade. He was yelling at her, she understood, but the why of it and the what of it escaped her. As did her interest in it. She stared at him, struggling to make sense of the thoughts churning about her head. She'd known plenty of fear and anxiety over the last year, but nothing had ever scared her more than what had just happened. She'd not ever heard a voice so coolly malevolent, as that of the man who'd just put a knife to her throat. For long seconds while the brigand held her, she couldn't imagine how she might live through it, how she wouldn't wind up dead.

But then, Nicholas. He'd been so calm, so serene, had shown not a whit of worry or fear; he'd only been angry at the man, she had decided— easily enough from the curl of his lip. Mayhap he'd known no worry because he knew that he—and thus she—would emerge unscathed. How remarkable, Alice thought. How wholly fantastic to be instilled with so much bloated and justified confidence as this man, the Brute of Braewood.

He was, she decided then, magnificent. Of course, she still wasn't entirely convinced that his own ambitions in regard to stealing her from the English were selfless and good, but that did not dissuade her from judging him a splendid person. Admittedly, his entire person—not only his self-assured and victorious actions just now—was impressive.

In the light of day, she got her first good look at him. He was not a beast at all, but a god. Never mind the grotesque scar, raised and white and puckered, which traced a path from his ear all the way to one corner of his mouth. Alice wouldn't have said it added to the allure of the man, but it most certainly did not detract. Could not detract, not from those pronounced and sculpted cheekbones or the perfect squareness of his jaw. He hadn't shaved, mayhap not in several days, that his sun-kissed skin was shadowed by brown whiskers, some as dark as mahogany, one patch as light as honey. His mouth was wide, his lips smooth and full and only a few shades darker than his skin. His hair was short, cropped close to his head, though not without a charming curl to the thick mahogany locks with gold highlights. He was rugged, with creases around his eyes and that scruffiness of several days unshaven, but then sublimely beautiful for how clear and compelling were his eyes and how, aside from that lone scar, he was unblemished in every other way.

His eyes. Alice was quite sure she'd never met eyes like his. They were sharp and assessing—she'd gathered that much even inside last night's darkness—staring through and into her as much as he stared at her, but they were also a most fascinating shade, a light chestnut color that appeared more golden than brown. With his strong hands still clamped onto her arms, she was close enough to discover that the pupils actually were gold and flecked with bits of brown and green. Remarkable.

He'd stopped speaking—hollering—at her, she realized after a moment. Other things became clear as well. Joanna and that terrified woman and her bairns had emerged from the thicket of underbrush. The MacRory men came, one by one, from the village, into the woods.

Transfixed by the magnetic gold of his eyes—indeed by all of him—Alice nodded mechanically, imagining that was a reasonable response to his reprimand, which by now had been done for almost half a minute. In reaction to this, or to her mesmerized and blatant gawking at him, Nicholas MacRory narrowed those golden eyes at her briefly before rising to his feet and helping Alice to stand as well. He tarried no more but turned away from her almost instantly to address his men again.

And Alice breathed again.

*My, my, my.*

"Let's see what can be done with those fires," Nicholas said and strode to where his horse stood; the animal had not moved since his rider vaulted from his back. Once atop the large destrier again, Nicholas wheeled around and faced Alice, running his gaze quickly over those around and near her. "Safer in the village," he said and tipped his head in that direction. "Let's go."

She gave him another nod and drew in a deep and settling breath before turning to where Joanna—inordinately quiet all this time—gaped at her with wide eyes.

She found her voice again. Joanna always found her voice. "Oh, and dinna I believe ye dead? Dinna I see the end coming? And I sobbed inside, pondering what I might say to yer poor, sweet mam. Aye, we were liberated from the dastardly baron but och, she met her death at the hands of an evildoer—alas, upon our own soil. Lord love a sinner, but aren't I pleased not to have to deliver that tale?"

The woman, the one with two clearly terrified children, blinked several times at Joanna but was given no time to consider that ponderous flood of words.

"Aye, and we'll get back with them," said Joanna, lifting her skirt and her feet over the protruding roots of a tree. "Safer, he says, and dinna I ken it, if we stay close to those ones." She began to march toward the village, her gaze on the mounted men ahead of her, but stopped when she sensed that no one followed. Turning, she cast a frown onto both Alice and the young mother, and then included an old woman off to her left, whom Alice only just now recalled as well. "Frozen and gawping seems a dangerous pastime, I should imagine," Joanna charged and pivoted to resume her march.

Alice let out a shaky laugh. There was some benefit—a beautiful familiarity that set so many things right—in Joanna's manner, returned to normal.

Glancing at the young woman and her two bairns, Alice now discovered their distinctive fright. They'd just been terrorized in and from their own home, might have witnessed more horror than Alice's brief and resolved encounter. She met the blue-eyed gaze of the young girl half-hidden behind her mother, clinging to her hand.

Smiling generously, Alice extended her hand to the wee lass. "Will you hold my hand and walk with me?"

The lass tipped her head back and met her mother's gaze, seeking permission, any sign that it was safe. At her mother's shaky nod, the girl, not more than four or five, moved out from behind her mother's skirt and toward Alice. She did not, however, put her hand in Alice's but lifted both her arms, wishing to be carried.

Awash in boatloads of sympathy, Alice obliged, lifting the tiny girl into her arms and holding her close. "You are safe now, love."

"Oh, but what providence," said the girl's mother as they walked now, following Joanna, "that ye should come along at just the right time."

Alice turned to make sure the older woman was walking with them. She was, slowly, still breathless from her earlier sprint, which mayhap she'd not done in years. The few men who'd run toward the woods had returned immediately when the MacRory men had given notice that the threat was gone.

"Fortunate indeed," Alice agreed, thankful as well. What might have become of them, of this darling little sprite in her arms if they'd not arrived when they had?

Even as the trees cleared as they drew closer, the haze of smoke shrouded so much of the scene.

Joanna stomped along, looking for any task she might undertake. That was one of her more endearing qualities, that she was not afeared of labor and was quick to offer assistance when needed. It was tied somehow, Alice had always believed, to her similar need to keep her jaw busy. For some reason, in some way, silence and stillness disturbed Joanna, Alice had learned. Joanna needed noise and motion to keep her calm. Joanna stopped near one flaming croft and claimed a broom standing near the door, which she dipped into a nearby rain barrel and then used to beat against the flames along the roof line. Little good it would do, Alice determined, but left her to the task.

"Is your own house unharmed?" Alice asked the young mother, walking beside her.

The woman nodded and lifted her face to indicate an un-scathed croft further ahead. Alice followed her gaze and found Nicholas MacRory in her line of vision. With rake in hand, he was scraping the burning thatch off another small cottage, stamping it out when it fell to the ground. He paused and called out to one of his men, "Collect those bodies next. We'll bury them when the fires are out."

Alice gasped and only then, swinging her gaze around, saw that several people had died, either defending their homes or themselves. Three bodies lay in different locations about the small village. Instinctively, she tucked the child's head against her shoulder and neck, so that she could not see that particular wreckage. The nearest body was that of a young man. He lay on his stomach, his back covered in blood. Stricken by this, Alice turned to the woman. "Is that...?"

Wearily, with watery green eyes, the woman shook her head. "My man left this morn, went with three others, took the grain to the harbor."

Small blessings then, Alice thought. "We can dig the earth for...them," Alice suggested, even as she didn't know how to go about that, or where a shovel might be found, or where the graves might be dug.

"Aye," said the woman, shifting the toddler boy on her hip. "The barn at the end of the lane will have shovels."

Alice followed her then, walking past a couple huddled to-gether on the ground, weeping into each other's shoulders, and then past a teenaged lass crying over another lifeless body while an older woman tried to pry her away. A screech from behind them made Alice turn. Her fright hadn't a chance to develop as she saw that the cry had come from Joanna, who had only tripped and landed on her backside. The MacRory man who'd gagged her and covered her head jogged over to the fallen woman and pulled her to her feet. He took the broom from her and continued about the work that Joanna had started.

Five minutes later, Alice and the woman joined two men at the edge of the village, one of them the proficient MacRory archer. As those men were each digging a single grave, Alice and the woman worked together on the third while the young children sat on the brown grass and silently watched, their regard languid.

NICHOLAS WIPED THE sweat from his brow and glanced around the village. Every now and again, he needed to give conscious thought to unclenching his teeth. He was never keen to engage in battle—thought any man who said as much should be looked upon with misgivings—but freedom and rising above gluttonous tyranny required such things. Outside of war or his own work of the last few years, he abhorred violence, and senseless violence such as this most of all. The borderlands were a territory subjected to frequent skirmishes but this now, with only a dozen offenders, seemed naught but vile men searching to assuage their own depravities, horrifying and slaying innocent people for no other reason but that they could.

He didn't mind that his party would now be delayed. Certainly, he wouldn't leave this modest village, now depleted by three persons, to their own protection and burying of their dead. They might as well stay on for the night here, more of a *just in case* decision than with any idea that other English troops might arrive as well and cause more harm.

He worked nonstop, keeping himself moving and industrious, so that there was no need for his brain to torture him with images of Alice de Graham being held under the knife of that now dead brigand. Disregarding what a foul turn of events that would have proven—to have rescued her from the English, have returned her to the good, green earth of Scotland, only to have her murdered by a derelict Englishman and how he might have explained that to her already mourning mother— Nicholas allowed his attention to be turned from the ashes he was shoveling into a black kettle to where Alice worked. She stood at what looked to be the end of the lane but was instead only where it turned sharply and dipped low and out of sight. She used the long sleeve of her kirtle to wipe her own brow and though a good fifty or more feet separated them, he could see her perfect lips moving as she spoke.

She smiled soon after, and then scrunched up her face at the child sitting close to her. Playfully, likely with some attempt to distract the wee lass from being tortured by the events of the day, she leaned forward against the earthen hole in which she stood, deep enough now that her thighs hit the side of the hole, and pulled out a bright green leaf from behind the child's ear. She pretended a great surprise at this, her mouth open in a long *O* and her eyes large. The little girl's response was delayed by her astonishment until her eyes widened as well and she straightened, pulling herself onto her knees. Laying a hand on Alice's shoulder, she checked behind Alice's ears, first one and then the other, no doubt looking for more leaves. Alice shrugged her slim shoulders, feigning innocence, and unbeknownst to the lass, plucked a white tipped thistle from the grass beside the child and then made a show of 'discovering' that behind her tiny ear as well. Her sleight of hand was impressive. Only Nicholas' rapt interest had allowed him to notice what she was about.

Mayhap he grinned inside, but he did not let it surface. It had been years since he'd known either the ability or the want to show any cheerful sentiments. On any given day anger, disinterest, and annoyance were among the most often used expressions. Those emotions were known and comfortable and revealed no weakness. They kept him safe, and in so many regards.

Having finished with the burnt thatch from the last of the damaged crofts, Nicholas then helped two men from the village carry the bodies of the dead toward the curve in the road, where the opened earth waited for them. Many had gathered around those freshly dug holes, though not the young lass who skipped and stumbled alongside Nicholas, as he carried the forever-young man, to whom she'd apparently given her heart.

"Please dinna leave me," she was saying to the dead man, almost unintelligible for the choking fragility of her voice.

Nicholas paused, turning to the girl. "Gather what ye want to go with him," he told her, recalling how his father had tucked a note and his signet ring inside the shroud his stepmother had been buried in.

The brown-eyed lass ceased her weeping and stared at Nicholas, captivated by this suggestion. He nodded at her, encouraging, "Go on," he said. "And ye think on what words ye want to give to send him off. We will no' start without ye."

At the graveside, the women of the village made themselves busy with lengths of linen, sewing each body into the donated or scavenged cloth. It was quiet, the undertaking. Nicholas kept a respectful distance, his hands on his hips while he considered the vista down into the glen beyond that curve in the lane. The land was painted in lush green and earthen brown, rolling lazily up from the valley to the mountain range miles away. The sun shone brightly and the wind was gentle, but that was all that was perfect about this day.

Shortly after, the dead were buried. Solemnly, Nicholas and his men stood near and at attention, until his regard was stolen by Alice once more. She stood across from him, across the expanse of those three holes in the ground. She held now or again that wee tow-headed lass, the one she'd entertained earlier, and stood near that child's listless mother, who yet held her tiny lad in her arms.

Alice should be wretched now, as were all the others. She'd had her own fright, as well as these harried, tortured people. Aye, she was weary and there was evidence that she'd cried at some point today, given in the clean line down the center of her cheek, the one that dragged away the dust and grime to reveal her porcelain skin. Her hair was mussed, and her hands were dirty, but her eyes were clear now, and whenever the child looked directly at her, Alice managed an exaggerated smile for her benefit.

His attention shifted and settled briefly on Joanna. To her credit and Nicholas' surprise, she made no sound at all during the burying, only stood patiently with her hands folded in front of her while she bowed her head.

When a few words had been spoken over each lost soul, when prayers had been murmured and one hymn had been sung with no small amount of tuneless desolation, Nicholas and the MacRory men watched as the mourners ambled away from the gravesite.

"We ought to stay the night," Nicholas suggested, glancing overhead once again to gauge the hour.

"Aye," agree Baldred. "We'd no' get so much further this day as it is. And I dinna like to leave them to their own devices, should any English come looking for the dozen villains lost."

Nodding, Nicholas ordered that they take turns with the watch, same as they would on any given night of travel. "South and east, I should think." If any English were to come, it would likely be from only those directions.

Dungal offered no resistance but did add, "But on the morrow, we make straightaway for de Graham's place. If we depart as the sun rises, we should no' need but a day and a half."

Out of the corner of his eye, he'd watched Alice and Joanna and that mother and her bairns walk through the village and into a sparse thicket of trees on the north side. He already knew that a small loch was just beyond those trees but thought it not wise that they visit the place without protection. To distance himself from what he'd felt earlier, which for one errant moment had assumed that Alice meant something to him and had put that fear into him when she'd had her own knife to her neck, he sent Malise to keep an eye on them.

They supped with the denizens of this tiny settlement—not Bewlie, but an unnamed hamlet of Lilliesleaf inside the civil parish of Roxburghshire, they'd been told—who had not retreated into their homes for the evening meal, but chose instead the comradery of a communal meal, where they mourned together. Baldred and Dungal had hunted with two men from the village in the early afternoon, dismissing those men's fear over what would be poaching on the parish lands.

"I'll be the one shooting," declared Dungal, "that'll be on me. And I dare any man to say ye've no right to eat when nothing has been done to protect ye on that same land." And so they'd gone and had returned in under two hours with a red deer that would likely feed these people for an entire week. And they scrounged up a half dozen hares, which were given to the village women and cooked in the early evening.

The sun was yet on its slow, descending path when they supped, though the village was cast in shadows by the sky-touching mountains to the west. Dungal, who could easily speak to any person on any subject, ensconced himself with the peasants and maintained a steady conversation even as these people were still listless and solemn for the horror they'd known today. Malise and Henry were gone on watch duty and would sup later, when Nicholas and Baldred relieved them.

Alice and Joanna kept company with that woman and her children as they had all day and neither complained or asked any questions about when they might depart or why they were hanging around when trouble was done, and the dust had settled.

After dinner, Alice walked away from all the small groups of people and disappeared into the trees once more. Attuned more so to her than any other person's movements in the growing gloom and shadows of late evening, to his own chagrin, Nicholas made note of her departure. Frowning when she did not return after a few short minutes, Nicholas got to his feet and followed.

# Chapter Seven

Having witnessed Joanna pick and poke at some bit of food lodged between her teeth, having been amused by how little restraint Joanna had employed to remove the trespasser, which had scrunched up her face and opened her mouth disturbingly wide, Alice had opted instead to return to the loch to attend a similar predicament. She didn't mind that the water gave witness to her own efforts to extricate a bit of rabbit meat from between her own teeth, and then swished a bit of water around her mouth when it was done.

The loch was pretty now, the water reflecting flawlessly the sky above of orange and purple painted clouds. At the far side, a hundred feet away, a red deer and her fawn drank of the crisp water, their ears twitching in harmony. All things considered, including events of the last few days, Alice had known little distress in her young life. She marveled now that all the rest of the world carried on so exquisitely when only hours ago more evidence was presented of how mean and cruel it could too often be.

Rising from where she'd knelt at the water's edge, Alice startled when she sensed a presence near her. Instinctively, she swiveled and though it had done her little good on the last two occasions of use, she withdrew her small dagger from the quilted sheath at her waist.

"Ye've been gone too long."

The sound of Nicholas MacRory's voice, recognized only seconds before he showed himself, gave her instant relief.

The woods here around the small loch allowed even less light from the setting sun. Thus he was, for the first few seconds, only a dark figure emerging from the trees. Unmistakable all the same, for the size and shape of him, oddly known to her already after so short an acquaintance.

"You should not sneak up on a person as such," she said, sheathing her mostly useless blade. With relief came a sudden and overwhelming exhaustion, which she had managed to avoid all day long. As her shoulders relaxed, so then did her entire body wilt and slump with fatigue. With little thought, she lowered herself to the ground, facing the silver black water of the loch, and sighed out her weariness.

"'Twas less sneaking than ensuring," he rationalized with no sign of remorse.

His boots appeared in her periphery, close to her on her right side, and only feet from the drape of the skirt of her léine. In the next moment, he surprised her by sitting as well, apparently none too eager to return her to the company of the group in the village.

"The quiet is welcome after so chaotic a day," she said after a moment.

"Aye."

Alice did not feel any particular need to fill the silence hovering about them with the noise of words. Truthfully, she was too exhausted to know any discomfort for the lack of conversation, only knew some peace that she could enjoy this respite without any alert fear or caution now that he was here.

It was several long minutes later when he introduced conversation. "Ye did well with those bairns," he remarked. "Made the day more bearable, I imagine."

She smiled at this, with recollection of how charmed she'd been by the little girl. "The child is Marion," she told him. "Not to be confused with Martin, her father, she'd advised me. She has known five summers and is not so great an admirer to her younger brother—was much happier, she'll tell you, when it was only she and her mam and da. She's quite precocious, even asked of Joanna what her mouth looks like when it's closed."

As she had her face turned, she witnessed the slight and then gone quirk of the corner of his lip. Mayhap she'd only imagined it. Mayhap it was only a twitch in that scar.

"Ye seem unaffected by...all of this. Everything, in fact," he said.

Everything? Ah, yes. "I have little choice but to believe what you say, that you aim to return me to my family and my home. This here today...I consider it fortuitous that we happened upon the grisly scene. What might have become of them—of all of them, of precious little Marion—if we'd not happened by?"

The quirk returned and stayed for a while. He angled his handsome face at her. "Did yer Joanna no' give ye that answer? And in fine detail?"

Alice smiled fully, appreciating his quip even as she was quite surprised by it. "She did. Or, she began as much. I shushed her 'fore Marion's eyes or that of her mam grew too big." After another space of silence, she did wonder, "We will stay the night?"

"Aye, and head north at dawn's light."

"And," she asked further, "barring stumbling upon any other burgh or village under attack, should see me in my mother's arm...?"

"Soon," he answered. "Within a day and a night and half of the next."

"Sweet joy," she mused. "Was my father well when you saw him?" He had not been unwell when she'd been taken, but he was a man given to high anxieties. So many times in her life, she'd witnessed the dangerous reddening of his face when his anger or frustration got the better of him. At those times, her mother would caution him that he would only affect his own demise if he didn't take better care with his reactions. Alice had to suppose that having your daughter stripped from your very arms and secreted away to parts unknown might well cause mayhem on his humors.

"He appeared a man aggrieved by—or mayhap resigned to—your mother's covert schemes, but otherwise well."

With these words, Alice realized even more deliverance from worry. Nicholas MacRory had just described her parents as they always were, her mother ever pushing the boundaries of her father's long-suffering patience, ever hatching one idea after the next that he knew he could not stop from becoming his new reality. It put her at ease, this intimate knowledge shared, allowing Alice to believe unreservedly that indeed this man spoke the truth. Certainly, he'd met with her parents if he'd gleaned so accurately their dynamic.

"Ye dinna ask after yer mother's health," he said then.

And for good reason. "My mother is the strongest person I know. She must be fine. If what you say is true, the fact that you are here, sent by her, says that she is well, as fierce as ever."

"Aye, and so she is."

When she'd sat down only minutes ago, Alice had laid her hands in her lap. But now she crossed them over her chest and hugged herself briefly, imagining her mother's sure arms around her. Soon, she told herself.

"But it's late now," He said, rising gracefully to his feet. "We'll get on back now, tuck ourselves in for the night."

He reached down a hand to her.

Alice glanced up at him, towering over her and with little hesitation, set her hand in his, which was swiftly engulfed as he closed his large fingers around hers. One smooth tug, and she was pulled to her feet.

This put her very close to him. Nervously, Alice swiped her free hand over her bottom, brushing away any grass or dirt, her eyes on his chest, unaccountably nervous at this proximity. They'd been closer already, in her prison cell at the de Lisle house, upon that horse, when he'd been hammering her with a scolding earlier.

But now, in the dark and quiet of the evening....

He did not release her hand, did not move in fact, but stood unnervingly still and focused upon her.

Alice braced herself and lifted her gaze to him but made no move to retrieve her hand.

His gaze was diligent, moving over her eyes and cheeks and mouth, the golden brown of his gaze darkened by the lengthening shadows and something else, some emotion she could not name. She only knew that she felt as if he had this probing examination to complete to make some final assessment of her, that he wanted to know her secrets, of which she had few.

Save of course for how he unnerved her and how he fascinated her.

And then his gaze shifted no more. While her hand still sat within his grasp, his amber eyes settled on her lips and did not move. Alice's heartbeat tripled in time, and she was fairly certain he must feel her racing pulse in her hand. He clamped his lips and a muscle ticked in his cheek.

She hadn't realized she'd been holding her breath, not until she opened her mouth to speak and her breath was released so that the words came out breathy, wispy. "You want to kiss me," she surprised herself by announcing her speculation.

"Aye, I'm thinking on it," he surprised her by admitting so freely, surprised her more that so titillating a response should come so severely, from under a hood of dark eyes.

She had no notion where that idea might have come from, that he was debating just this. She'd not ever gotten anywhere near this close to being kissed. But then, she'd not ever seen such a steadfast look of longing in a person. Longing? Perhaps not. Mayhap, like she, it was more a zealous curiosity. Whatever the case, she was beyond titillated at the very idea that a man such as this, brave and beautiful, should want to kiss her. Something else occurred to her in those few seconds while he continued to stare at her but made no move to actually kiss her. He was older, seasoned, had in all probability lived so much more than she had as of yet. Certainly, he had kissed or had been kissed before. How fascinating that he knew what it was about and was just now toying with the idea of doing it to her. With her? She wasn't sure, had no idea what a kiss was between a man and women. Oh, but she wanted to know it with this man.

"Are you still thinking on it?" She knew exactly what she was really asking. Was he going to kiss her or not? *Will it only be a thought, or will you satisfy my eager fascination and act upon it?* Her heart thudded rapidly inside her chest. *Please.* Alice curled her fingers into a fist at her side and boldly advised, "I believe you should."

He nodded, one dip of his head, given slowly, his regard still probing as if he were still trying to discover something about her, seeking it in the depths of her eyes. But he did not move immediately, and Alice wondered if he were now trying to talk himself out of it. Before he might have managed that, she stepped forward, closing the distance between them to less than one foot.

Her cautious step forward enlivened him, and he displaced the remaining space that separated them.

She sensed a restraint in him, as he slowly moved their joined hands out to the left, his golden gaze locked on hers.

His free arm and hand snaked slowly around her waist, drawing her near. "Close your eyes," he said, his breath warm against her face, just as his lids fell like drapes over his amber eyes.

That was the extent of his control though, for in the next second he crashed his lips upon hers with a force that was as exciting as it was unsettling. As persuasive as it was, his lips were smooth and warm, and she did not feel as if she were in danger. She melted against him almost instantly, thrilled by this thing they were doing, that she was being kissed by this man. She felt his kiss everywhere, in the singing blood of her veins, in the drumming heartbeat sounding in her ears, in the heat of him pressed against her. He glided his mouth over hers and then used his tongue to trace the seam of her lips, to coax her to open for him. This he did softly, a feather of a caress across her lips. Alice gasped, opening for him. His tongue was warm and sweet inside her mouth. Alice met his searching tongue with her own and a primitive growl erupted from his chest. She felt powerful, that she could invigorate this man to nearly lose control, and then weakened by the sheer force of it, by her body's response to it.

Clinging to the padded leather of his breastplate, she arched her chest forward. Nicholas crushed her against him, and the kiss grew wild and hungry, yet still maintained a dreamy intimacy. Alice felt heat swirl throughout her entire body, down to her toes, beguiled by the devilry of his kiss. Having always imagined herself a placid and sensible person, she was shocked to know such ridiculous greed and hunger right now. She wanted to know and feel everything all at once, wanted to explore this fully.

For one brief and glorious moment, she was lost, happily so.

And then he stopped. Just like that, growling low again as he pushed her away.

"Cease," he commanded in a hoarse whisper, as if she'd been the one waging that beautiful war on him.

Breathless and suffused with a heretofore unknown desire, Alice stared at him. Her chest heaved. She touched her fingers to her swollen, heated lips and watched him seethe at her now.

"Let's go," he clipped, his expression returned to that grim one that she was familiar with.

They walked side-by-side back through the trees and up over the knoll, Nicholas' hand on her elbow. Too immersed in her own response to his kiss, to the kiss itself in fact, Alice gave little thought to his quick about-face.

Nothing had changed, she thought distractedly. She was still Alice, still had hope that she was indeed being returned to her mother, was still dark-haired and blue-eyed, she guessed. And yet she was different, would never be the same again.

All because of a kiss from this man.

Alice had all she could do to keep from grinning like a fool as they walked back to camp. Nicholas gave her one last sideways, unfathomable glance accompanied by a barely courteous tip of his head before he moved left to join his men. Alice walked over to where Joanna had made their beds.

The woman pounced on her immediately, her eyes wide.

"Saints be merciful, what have ye done?"

Alice's frown was instant. Was it *that* noticeable? The flush returned to her cheeks. Ignoring this, and Joanna's open-mouthed suspicion, Alice sat on the ground next to her and pretended a complete innocence that she certainly could no longer claim.

"I have not done anything," she told Joanna, as calmly as her still racing heart would allow.

"Aye, and my mam is a red deer," sneered Joanna, "gone to the forest now, should be returned by morn." Then, ignoring Alice's rolled eyes at that outlandish fabrication, Joanna pestered her, "Ye go off with none but yerself and return with the brute at yer side, and neither one of ye is wearing a convincing expression so I imagine he revealed his true self and ye, ye daft girl, ye let him."

Closing her eyes, Alice buried her head in the arms she crossed over her raised knees, in some fruitless attempt to not hear her. She wanted instead to relive the entire episode, not be badgered by Joanna and her favorite pastime of twenty queries.

Alas, she was to have no peace.

"Och, and it's all my fault," whined Joanna. "I should have made better use of our time at the de Lisle prison, should have picked up right where your dear mam left off, instructing ye on the proper ways of a good lass, what ye give and what ye hold dear. Aye, and now I've this to explain to yer mam—och, and yer da! Sure, and will he no' have the brute's liver for dinner? I see wreckage in that one's future, that's what's coming. Did ye fight at all? Pretend to fight at least? Or did he assail ye with those cat eyes of his, lure ye in with a glib tongue. Tell me now, and make it true, ye got one good lick in, aye?"

Annoyed beyond reason, Alice lifted her face and snarled at her friend, "Will you please, for just a precious few moments, allow me to enjoy the memory of his kiss? Pray do not force reality so soon that I must accept that it was ill-advised, not one of my better decisions?"

Perhaps the fact that Alice had never, not once, spoken to Joanna so harshly, was what had stricken the woman with silence. Once more her mouth was open wide, this time with either or both shock and indignation.

Alice didn't care. She closed her eyes again and laid her head on her arms.

Amazingly, almost five minutes passed before Joanna said another word. When she did speak, her voice was softer.

"But...was it nice? He looks as if he kens his way around a woman's heart and body," Joanna said. And then, most amusing, and possibly true: "Those eyes alone might well see kirtles and léines and all sensible inhibitions dropped to the ground as swiftly as the unwitting squirrel when met with a good, slung shot."

A small gasp of a laugh burst from Alice. Picking up her head, she turned a wondrous smile upon Joanna.

"Was it nice though?" Joanna pressed, her brows lifted into the middle of her forehead, her expression nearly pleading that she not be disappointed.

"It was better than nice." Alice breathed. It was brilliant.

HE'D HAD BETTER IDEAS, he thought much later. Later, as in long after the spell she'd cast upon him should have released its grip, but when it still had not.

He was almost thrilled when it came time for him to relieve Malise of his watch and assume the duties himself. But he was no less agitated as he prowled the perimeter of the village on the west side, the memory of her kiss the only danger he encountered through the night.

When the sun began to rise over the mountains in the east, Nicholas returned to the village, eager to get on the road now, more keen than ever to return her to her family, his current impatience having little to do with the army he would earn for his trouble.

He and his men had some discussions with the local men, the latter advising of their plans to enact better defenses so they were not caught so off guard if the unimaginable should happen again.

Alice hugged the wee lass, Marion, teary-eyed Nicholas thought, though he made some effort to not let his gaze stray too often to her. Joanna had a broom in hand, stirring up the dirt around some dried blood in the lane, in some attempt to erase it, right up until the moment Baldred collected her to mount up.

When her goodbyes were done, Alice approached Nicholas, where he stood cinching the saddle straps tight under the destrier's belly. Her eyes only darted on and off him, as if she might fear looking too long upon his dour visage, and thus read what he was thinking. Her cheeks were flushed so becomingly that he already dreaded a day in the saddle with her, in that forced proximity that would no doubt favor him only with more desire to kiss her, the very thing he'd assured himself he should not do. Ever again.

There was not any part of him, not one ounce, that wanted this mission—and the benefit Scotland would know from it—upended by his ungovernable, untimely, and wholly inconvenient attraction to her.

He muttered a curse, wondering what had become of his famous willpower, his ability to segregate emotions and desires from duty and honor.

If he'd gleaned any sign of hope or courage in her initial flitting gazes, neither of those were evident after his foul curse. Holding the bridle, he beckoned her forward and without a word, lifted her in the saddle, joining her there, his movements abrupt and impersonal as he pulled her against him as was needed for an easy ride.

Dungal led them away, down the turning lane and off into the quiet glades and old growth of the landscape. Baldred and Joanna followed ahead of Nicholas and Alice, Henry and Malise bringing up the rear.

Nicholas knew very little of Joanna, other than that he'd not like to ever be stranded with only her and her constant jawing, not anywhere or anytime. But he did find some appreciation for her abilities when she started right away, no sooner had they pushed out.

"Sure and are they no' still vulnerable, sitting grouse, waiting on the next hunter to come?" Joanna began, in reference to the people they left behind. "But 'tis no' our responsibility, is it now, to keep their feathers intact anymore? Och, and with all those bairns throughout," she bemoaned. "Canna say they'll see many more years, perched so precariously as they be. Like as no' they'll be naught—"

"Aw," interjected Baldred, his tone sharp, "and dinna start already. Give a man at least an hour to digest the bread and ale, will ye?"

"Ye'll no' be speaking to me in such a—"

"Aye, I will, and I'll continue to do so until ye *stop* speaking."

"Never have I known such unkindness," Joanna said with a bit of a gasp, as if no one in all her life had ever called her out for her constant prattle. "Never has a—"

"Aye, they have," Baldred contended. "If no' to ye, then about ye. Now save me from running this girl off the next cliff we find, will ye no'? Just give me one hour of quiet, that's all I beg."

Naturally, she did not, but continued to argue with him about what she called his *crustiness*. Baldred, to his detriment, gave it right back, which only encouraged more contention and not the silence he so desperately wished.

Alice turned her face on her shoulder and looked up at Nicholas. He did not return her gaze but clenched his jaw and stared straight ahead. He didn't need to see her eyes to know that they were the bluest he'd ever known, and that a man could get lost in their depths, or to be reminded that so much of her power—unknown to her—was contained right there, in how she looked at a person, how many emotions were so easily accessible in her bonny eyes.

"A fine day for a ride," she commented. "Wouldn't it be tiresome if we had to contend with rain or strong winds or bitter cold?"

Nicholas gave a curt, "Aye."

"I imagine you are accustomed to the saddle, and long hours in it."

He nodded.

"I don't know that I've ever spent more than an hour upon a horse for any occasion, not before I met you."

"Hm."

Her voice smaller, she carried on. "What will you do after you've delivered me home?"

"Return to my home." But only until de Graham had gathered up his own army that Nicholas would then bring to the forest where William Wallace presently collected an army.

"Oh."

He read her well, knew exactly what she was about, gauging his mood and trying to determine what their relationship was now, if it had changed at all. She was friendly, but cautious, likely seeking clarification for his change of manner since he'd kissed her so greedily and fervently last night and now was so remote.

He must put a stop to it. It needed that he return them to their previous roles. Ah, but that was no good, captive and savior. No, he would need to invent a new circumstance for them. Hired sword, he should be, since for so long he had been just that. And she, the means to an end.

After a length of grim and stiff silence, she employed a clipped tone of her own, suggesting, "If...if you are, um, regretting having kissed me, then mayhap we should just pretend it never happened."

Nicholas leapt at the idea. "Aye, let us do that."

As if that were possible.

# Chapter Eight

She should have been growing more and more excited with all the miles and hours put behind them, bringing her closer to home. Instead, she felt rather morose, uncharacteristically so—the cause of which she put solely on Nicholas MacRory. She was sure she'd been correct to have expected some kindness from him today, believing she wasn't out of line to suppose that a kiss shared should have made him more amenable in the aftermath. Wasn't that how it worked?

Keeping up her stiff posture in the wake of his coolness was as fatiguing as what trauma they'd known yesterday. Alice gave up on it after an hour and when her spine began to ache. What did she care if the angry man was bothered by her slumping against him?

She thought about making some complaint to see her removed from his horse and his company but could imagine no such charge that might succeed in that endeavor. She considered asking if he might prefer that she rode with Joanna, and thus bore the brunt of her babbling, but did not know if either she or Joanna could manage a beast so large as these war horses.

By late morning, exhaustion took its toll and she slept for a while only to be woken with a start by a piercing shriek from Joanna. The arm around her middle tightened.

"'Tis fine," soothed Nicholas. "Snake crossed their path. Apparently, she would ken that snakes have legs and might pose some danger to her while seated atop the horse."

Before she might have thought better of it, Alice mumbled, "Aye, but some snakes do have legs." Immediately, she felt childish and churlish to have said as much. "I apologize. That was...impolite." She'd almost said it had been unwarranted, but part of her believed that it was not.

And because he made no response to either her remark or her apology, Alice assumed that as before he did not want to engage in any conversation with her, which she decided suited her just fine—though she was at least honest enough with herself to admit that this was not her first choice.

For quite a while, when Joanna had either run out of energy or ideas, she, too, was quiet. As ever, the silence did not last long. She spied a capercaillie with its black plumage, bright blue chest, and its distinctive red-ringed eye, and began to regal Baldred with the recipe for her favorite stew.

"Ye canna slow cook it, lest ye want that it will taste like liver," Joanna was saying. "And dinna bother with the older birds, too gamey. Get yerself a nice young one with the mild flavor. And ye can be sure the larger the ring around his eye, the tastier he'll be."

When behind her it sounded as if Nicholas were breathing—seething actually—through his nose, Alice hoped Joanna spouted every recipe and method she could think of for ways to make use of the grouse.

It was late afternoon before they stopped, for which Alice was pleased. She had pressing needs, and she and Joanna made haste into a thicket of trees.

And then they were on the move again. Alice did not hear it from Nicholas, but from Baldred, who kindly advised Joanna that once they cleared the harshest of the borderlands, they would stay the night in Melrose, a medium sized burgh in the shadow of the Cistercians' Melrose Abbey, he said, where they would be afforded a private room and their own bed, if either of the travelling inns had any vacancies.

"And any room that's let will be after ye feed us and no' before, I am sure," Joanna stated.

"Aye and here's me praying that ye dinna chew with yer mouth open," quipped Baldred.

To Alice's surprise, Joanna actually laughed at this even as Baldred was clearly hoping that feeding her would therefore silence her.

Up and down the south peak of the Eildons they went, eschewing climbing and descending the other peaks for their greater height. Alice leaned back into Nicholas' chest as he walked the horse down the bare trail, fearful the steepness would see her pitched over the head of the horse.

The party of six walked their horses down the high street of Melrose, where the dry dirt of the lane was painted gray by the lengthening shadows. The town itself was situated at the base of the north side of the Eildon Hills, and boasted, as far as Alice could see when they were still elevated above it, a few dozen buildings, squat and tall, decrepit and not, with very few frontages not facing the high street.

They reined in before the first of the two inns, with Nicholas dismounting and searching for a lad from the livery, which surely every town had, to relieve them of their horses. When none was found, the MacRory named Henry volunteered to escort the animals to the yards. Without further delay, Joanna and Alice were plucked from the saddles and the group moved into the three story building, which Alice thought must be as wide and long as it was tall, a very large inn.

The streets of Melrose had not been bustling with people, so many of which might have been accounted for inside the tavern. There were but a few empty tables available, and Dungal led the way to the farthest one. The oversized square room was pungent with leather and grease and soot. Alice thought her eyes might water and sting if she spent too much time inside. She followed behind Joanna, with Nicholas walking directly behind her, and one by one, they settled into a booth that sat against the furthest wall, taking up the entire corner with a bench along each wall and the table accommodating each side.

As it turned out, Joanna and Alice sat in the v of the corner, perpendicular to one another, with Nicholas to Alice's immediate right and Malise next to him. Baldred and Dungal sat at Joanna's left, respectively.

Once seated and while she surveyed the establishment, which seemed, despite the sour odors, to be very tidy, Alice decided it was a fine circumstance. And had it not been, she would not have complained since her stomach had been calling for food for hours by now. Laying one hand over the other directly before her on the table, the wood worn smooth and black from the settling grease and subsequent scrubbings, Alice noticed for the first time how much attention their party was receiving.

Likewise, Joanna took note of all the eyes upon this corner as well.

"What? Have we painted our foreheads bright green or such, that they stare so?"

Dungal smirked at this. "Might as well have."

"They dinna take kindly to strangers," explained Baldred, "and then less so to Highlanders."

Malise, whom Alice wasn't sure she'd ever heard speak, said, "And sure when ye come with yer blades attached and sitting with the chief, so says the brooch at his plaid, they begin to wonder if we've an entire army just beyond the door and if we might be thinking to lay siege to their bonny little burgh."

Dungal added, "And then they'll be wondering about ye lasses, what yer doing with such rabble as us?"

"Good Lord, but that's a lot of anxiety you've created," Alice commented, "simply by walking into the place."

"None of it unwarranted, I should think," Joanna added her own opinion. "Each one of ye looks meaner than the last. Ye ken, a smile, even a wee one, might remove some of their concern."

"Highlanders dinna smile," claimed Baldred, straight-faced.

Henry finally joined them, sliding into the booth at the end of Alice's side, which forced both Nicholas and Malise to move toward the center, closer to Alice. She bristled, wishing Henry had taken a seat on the far side and had not moved Nicholas into contact with Alice. As it was, their arms were pushed against each other as Alice had her hands on the table and Nicholas had only that arm, his left, raised and resting on the table also. She hadn't noticed that she was cold until she felt the heat of his flesh through the layers of their sleeves, all that separated them. Under the table, his large thigh was wedged against hers, though she had her legs situated demurely, knees touching each other as her mother had instructed *ad nauseam* while she was growing up. His leg as well seemed to cast off its own heat.

On Henry's heels came the innkeep. Alice had only ever once visited an inn, around the occasion of her mother's sister's wedding, when they'd traveled down to someplace near the Solway Firth. She had shared a trestle table and benches with her family when they'd stopped midday to break up the long journey. Surely, Joanna had been there as well. The innkeep at that time looked not unlike this one that approached them now, potbellied and possibly aged beyond his years for his daily labors. His hair was wiry and thick, sticking straight out on the left side of his head, while the right side was combed neatly. Alice pictured him scratching the left side of his head when aggrieved, which his current expression suggested might be often.

He set down pewter tankards by the handful and began to fill those with ale from a tall pitcher.

"Wine for the ladies," Nicholas advised before the man had filled all the tankards. "if ye have it."

The innkeep scowled at Nicholas, indifferent to his stature and apparent position as laird, and less charitable in his gaze for the perceived slight. "Finest tavern ye'll find for a hundred miles. Aye, we have it."

"And whatever's cooking," Baldred said, "assuming it's hot and flavorful, enough to feed a hungry group of weary travelers."

"But nothing with onions in it," Henry added, lifting his finger at the man, while he gave an exaggerated shiver to express his dislike of the cooking staple.

The innkeep huffed and planted his hand on his hip, staring down Henry with little patience. "There is no pottage worth serving if it dinna meet with an onion. Ye'll manage. Pick 'em out one by one as ye cross 'em, same as every other daft soul who dinna ken good food when it's laid under their nose."

"Och and he'll be fine," promised Baldred, "have no fears there, sir."

Alice grinned at this. Though young, she'd been witness first-hand to what the lad was capable of with bow and arrow. How silly that Henry should fear an onion.

NICHOLAS WISHED THAT she wouldn't smile. Not ever again while she was in his company. She was bonny enough simply sitting and watching and shouldn't be allowed to exacerbate the fascination he'd spent all day trying to reject.

And damn Henry for not taking a seat on the other side of the corner booth, and thus compelling him to shift his own position until he made contact with her—unavoidable if they were all to fit in the booth—and have it thrust at him how soft and small she was.

He kept his gaze straight ahead, his eyes wandering around the interior of the noisy tavern. Their position, at this far corner booth, afforded him a complete and unobstructed view of the entire taproom and its occupants. And aye, they'd drawn much notice, some of which still lingered, but Nicholas had not taken note of any that should cause them trouble. If he were wrong, it wouldn't be the first time some boastful tipper, drunk on sour ale, thought to increase his local status by picking a fight with the warriors come to town.

No one was surprised that Joanna provided much of the discussion. And hell, maybe he and the MacRorys were already accustomed to her and her inability to sit quietly so that she was able to engage them, and conversation was actually pleasant and entertaining while they waited their meals.

Still, he couldn't be sure how the topic of malt was introduced, or by whom. It might have come about when Joanna finished off the wine set before her and requested ale as her next
round. Naturally, she had an opinion to share on the subject of
malt. And a story to tell.

"They dinna crush the malt so well in this one, aye?" She put
out, rolling her tongue along her teeth and lips to give evidence
of her disfavor. "And the oats are no' fresh, I dare say. Aye, we had
one like that, did we no' Alice? Matefrid of Barnwall come to
the village, starts her brewing when ol' Stephen Miller turned his
toes—death by dismemberment and that's what befalls ye when
ye challenge a young lad with an old blade. But aye, that Matefrid
she liked to use the unfresh oats, and we'd be none the wiser but
that William Brid did take two bushels of her oats—in a wrong-
ful manner, mind ye, but his heart was right—so then we all saw
what she was about, letting the mold and whatnot consume the
oats that were bound for the cask. Fined sixpence, William was,
for the *unjust detainment of her oats,* but aye, we all pitched in
and henceforth, the ale did improve."

Nicholas wondered if he had ever, all told throughout his
life, put out so many words as Joanna had in the last few seconds.
But she wasn't done.

"She had a lad, that Matefrid—another Stephen, no' the
limb-lost one—and weren't he a sight? Teeth like the black
grouse and a face like the backside of a beaver, with the tail serving as his nose, am I right, Alice?"

Nicholas was not the only one whose brows lifted at the
clever way Joanna had just expressed that the poor lad possibly
had no teeth, since the black grouse most certainly did not. Al-

ice, he noted, took no part in any of it, not even nodding when prompted by Joanna.

"He was sweet on Alice, were he no', despite all the laws of nature that said he should no' be."

"Joanna," Alice chastised then. "They aren't interested in Stephen."

"Och, but we are now, lass," said Dungal. "And what ho? Laws of nature?"

Joanna ignored Alice and seized on Dungal's interest. "Aye, ye ken an unfortunate, such as he was, canna be going against the laws of nature that say all the bonny ones should be and keep with all the bonny ones. And those who are no' should keep with those who are no'."

Dungal shouted out a chuckle at that absurdity, while Alice chided her friend softly, "Beauty is no' simply superficial, Joanna."

"But the lack thereof most certainly is," Joanna countered after she'd snorted out her disagreement. "And ye're goin' to say to me that ye found him pleasing to the eye?"

"Stephen was—*is*—sweet, is very kind, with a pure heart. And I enjoyed his company, being that he is generally so quiet and thoughtful."

Joanna missed the gentle dig. The collective grins of his men said they did not.

The trenchers of hearty stew arrived, and all was peaceful for a time.

Until a shadow fell over the table, this one not belonging to the innkeep. Lifting his gaze, Nicholas failed to recognize the man approaching until he was within only a few feet of the table and had removed the hood of his cloak.

"I dinna ken I want to partake at such an establishment that admits the likes of this curious round-table," said the man.

Grinning, Nicholas stood—as much as he was able trapped inside the booth—and extended his arm across the table to Graham McKenna.

"I might have had my own reservations," Nicholas said as they clasped forearms in congenial spirit, "had I noticed ye first. Bluidy hell, but what brings ye out of yer cave, McKenna?"

"No' nearly so enticing an objective as has pulled ye from yours, lad," he returned.

The use of *lad* was not quite a disparaging epithet from this man, as he likely had ten years on Nicholas. The way he looked at Alice when he'd said *so enticing an objective*, on the other hand, reduced Nicholas' smile by half.

"I'd invite ye to sit, but we've no' the space," he said as he sat back down.

"Nonetheless, I would be obliged to decline," said McKenna, his gaze still rapt upon Alice.

For her part, the lass only smiled politely at the towering figure of the man, her eating knife unmoving in her hand. Possibly, she only gave attention as a courtesy, did not continue to eat and chew and gawp as Joanna did.

When McKenna finally removed his regard from Alice, Nicholas then ignored his own hot stew in favor of lending his complete attention to the man, whom he'd not seen in years, not since the debacle that was Falkirk, from which they'd barely escaped with their lives.

"We're only moving through," said McKenna, his thumbs tucked into the belt at his waist. "Meant for Melrose, where they're expecting some trouble."

Nicholas nodded, understanding that *some trouble* meant the English had their eye on Melrose as well. "Aye, and I will see what orders await after I stop near Carbery. Expect to leave there with more than five hundred."

McKenna raised his brow at this. "More bodies, more possibilities," he said in appreciation of those stated numbers.

And then he returned his appreciative gaze to Alice, and Nicholas found himself irked by the man's lack of subtlety.

"Melrose will still be there when I get there, lass," he said directly to Alice then, "if I ken ye were no' meant for Carbery."

Alice, possibly unaware of what exactly the man was implying, answered simply, "We are all bound for Carbery, sir."

Dungal asked McKenna a question, about the size of his moving body of men, and McKenna still did not take his gaze from Alice. Later, Nicholas would wonder why he cared, why it bothered him at all who looked or leered at Alice, so long as they remained respectful and kept their hands to themselves. But he did care. His lip curled and his blood simmered a wee bit so that he felt he had no choice but to lift his arm up and lay it over the back of the wooden booth, along the rail. He made it out to be casual, since he next perused the platter of cheese and sweet breads in the center of the table, frowning over his deliberation before he chose the hard cheese and plopped that chunk in his mouth.

And he sat back and left his arm there, ostensibly around Alice, and he met McKenna's knowing smirk.

He returned the smirk with a keen eye and a deceptively lazy grin.

*Aye, she is with me.*

"SURE AND THAT WAS NO' the finest pottage ever to pass my tongue," said Joanna as she climbed into bed beside Alice that night in a narrow but tidy room let in the same establishment as they'd dined. "But the company and easy cheer were welcome, aye, lass?"

To which Alice responded that aye, they'd passed a pleasant evening.

And that was all, for rare was the night that Joanna did not fall hard asleep within seconds of attaining her bed. Tonight was no exception, leaving Alice on her back and staring at the ceiling, keeping her own company while she reviewed the entire day.

Her thoughts fought to be heard since Joanna sleeping was no quieter than Joanna wakeful. Alice expected at any moment for her to raise the rafters with her snoring.

But the thoughts found purchase inside her head, beyond Joanna's snuffling, those ones that wanted to be the center of attention clawing their way to the fore. The kiss, of course, and how could it be ignored for long, having been her first? She recalled with startling clarity the thrill she'd known being held against his strong body.

So that was a kiss...'twas no wonder such things were frowned upon between a man and woman who were not joined properly in matrimony, for Alice could see how easily a pious servant of the Lord might well be led astray by such sensual delight. Happily—eagerly?—led astray in the arms of Nicholas MacRory, she might suppose. Certainly all rational thought and any bent toward virtue had abandoned her at the first touch of his lips.

But no matter how many times she revisited the splendor of those few short minutes, it could not be maintained, thwarted and diverted every time by Nicholas' behavior of today. By how harshly he'd said, *Aye, let us do that*, when she'd desperately suggested that they forget he'd ever kissed her in the first place.

What an impossible man.

So then it didn't help that she'd been scrunched into the booth so close to him, and then even more when Henry had joined them. She'd spent so many minutes sitting stiffly, so afraid to provoke him into further unkindness. But he had not been—unkind, that is. Not to her, or to anyone. She'd noted his attention to Joanna's rambling tales and had even thought she'd spied a grin in her periphery at some parts. He displayed no dislike of the fare, which had been quite hearty. And he'd been pleased to find an acquaintance among the occupants of the tavern, though Alice had sensed a swift and inexplicable cooling of that initial warm welcome.

But he'd said not one word to her, had not looked her way at all, had shown her no exceptional courtesy beyond requesting wine rather than ale for her and Joanna.

So that was how it was to be, she guessed, thankful now that so few hours separated her from her mother and home when she might be relieved of his company.

She yawned large and felt her eyes begin to shutter and wondered what the morrow would bring. Would he preserve his remoteness? She wasn't quite sure how another kiss might come about if he did.

# Chapter Nine

Nicholas had never encountered an inn whose taproom by the light of day was not less scenic for the fewer number of guests but then so much more ungodly, for what the light shone upon. This one was better than most, he supposed; the hand he laid upon the worn wood of the table did not stick to last night's spilled ale.

He was the first to rise this morn and show himself in the taproom and idly broke his fast with cheese and bread and ale, waiting on the others to join him. Dungal and Baldred came next, the former's hair standing on end and decorated with bits of straw from a night spent in the alehouse's stables. They might have taken rooms themselves but that the last one to let had been given to Alice and Joanna. Unbeknownst to either of the ladies, Nicholas had spent the night just outside their door, with his long legs stretched out on the hard floorboards and using his plaid as a pillow. He hadn't specifically expected any trouble and then was pleased to encounter none.

"Quiet this morn," Dungal noted groggily, casting a weathered gaze around the room, filled with naught but a dozen souls.

"Aye," said Baldred, "but I ken she'll show herself anon and dispel all this fine peace."

All three chuckled at this, his obvious reference to Joanna.

"We should be able to make the Fintry hills today," Nicholas predicted. "Should be safe to camp there tonight."

Baldred nodded. "And to Carbery on the morrow." He lifted his refilled flask as a salute to his liking of this. "And then, if God be guid, greater peace."

"What peace do ye suppose ye'll ken with the army we'll be taking away from de Graham?" Dungal asked, reminding them of their mission.

"I'll send word down to Comyn and Fraser from de Graham's place," Nicholas said. "Advise of our change of circumstance. If there is no pressing need, I ken it makes most sense to take the army home first and begin training."

"Ye ken de Graham's army is no' trained?" Baldred wondered with a frown.

"I ken nothing about his army," Nicholas replied. "But I ken I dinna want to find out inside a battle met that they are no' prepared to our liking." Nicholas had always taken great pride in the fact that his MacRory army was well-honed and well-disciplined, their fighting instincts sharpened regularly, that never had he cause to doubt their capabilities or their willingness to engage wholeheartedly whenever needed.

Both men nodded their agreement.

They were joined next by Malise and Henry, the latter requesting of the serving wench who approached the table a hearty bowl of porridge in addition to the bread and cheese already laid out.

Within minutes of their arrival, Alice and Joanna appeared.

"Lips already flapping," Dungal commented, though with little animosity, about Joanna, who was indeed talking with her hands and mouth as they entered the taproom.

Of its own accord, Nicholas' gaze went to Alice. She should be travel-worn, bedraggled even, for having been plucked from the de Lisle house in the dead of night, not allowed to gather so much as a comb for her hair or a change of clothes. Indeed, the hem of her léine was discolored with dust and dirt, though it seemed some effort had been made to address this, since Nicholas thought yesterday had seen it even filthier. Her long midnight tresses were gathered into a braid but mayhap that had been done last night before she'd slept since her hair was not tight and sleek around her face but loosened and full, framing her features softly. She was, overall, as disheveled as any of them but damn if she still weren't so vibrant. Her bluer-than-the-sky eyes found him almost immediately and Nicholas did not strain himself to remove his gaze from her, and then was not sorry that he hadn't since the answering blush that stained her cheeks at his silent but steady perusal was possibly as beguiling as was the rest of her.

Alice bid good morning when she and Joanna reached the table, her smile easy as she addressed his men. Nicholas smirked, since her greeting did not seem to include him, her gaze otherwise occupied now. Almost instantly, he chastised himself for his churlishness. Truly, there was no need for all the great weight he'd given his misstep that was their kiss.

He was a seasoned warrior, a paid mercenary, a killer of men. His hands were awash in blood and his heart and mind were, accordingly, blackened by the misadventure of his former deeds. He simply wasn't worthy of that rapturous and wonder-filled expression she'd worn after he'd kissed her.

Unless he meant to do her harm, which he did not, he would be wise to keep his distance. As he'd deliberated overnight when sleep refused to come, there wasn't any cause for concern. He wasn't some untried youth, engulfed in the bliss of first love or any of that rubbish. He was a full-blooded man, a heartless one, who merely appreciated a fine lass and a sweet kiss. He could effortlessly turn his mind from the appeal of Alice de Graham and concentrate instead—again—on the task at hand. They had only one more day until he would be relieved of her too-tempting company. He could certainly manage to engage without being made smitten.

Or any more smitten.

Presently, they occupied one of the trestle tables and not that crowded corner booth, so there was plenty of room even after the two women had joined them, both merging onto the bench beside Dungal and Baldred.

"Much prettier by morning light," Joanna noted of the tavern as she sat and helped herself to a chunk of hard cheese, plopping that in her mouth and possibly only savoring and not chewing as it sat thickly in her cheek and she continued to speak. "I'm no' sure where ye made yer beds last night, but I canna say I'm sorry to have taken that last chamber and bed. Is that no' so, Alice? Slept like bairns, we did."

Baldred rubbed a spot on his neck, massaging a crick it seemed, which had not been evident earlier. "Och, and dinna fuss about me, lass. This ol' neck'll come right by midday."

Whether or not she believed his aching condition were real, Joanna was unfazed. She snorted out a hearty laugh. "Sure and better ye than I, lest ye wish all the day to hear me grousing over it."

This widened Baldred's eyes, at what he'd escaped. "*Jesu* and praise the Lord and our good innkeep for sparing that chamber for ye."

"Some of you made your beds in the stables, did you not?" Alice asked, reaching up to pluck a piece of straw from above Dungal's ear as she sat directly beside him.

"Aye, and that's my thinking bit, lass, and give it back," Dungal intoned with a feigned snarl, taking the strand from her. He placed one end of the straw between his lips. "But dinna deride the hay as a bed. Soft and warm and we dinna lose sleep for any jawing. The horses dinna say too much, ye ken."

Alice cast a glance at Dungal and appeared to fight to contain her grin, likely understanding that he referred to Joanna. "'Twas nearly silent, sir, for we are known to sleep fast."

And next, Alice darted a look across the table at Nicholas. In all probability, this was in reaction to what she surely felt, the heat of his probing regard, as he'd yet to figure out how not to stare at her.

No blush came now, and neither did her sunny gaze stay too long on his, but she knew that he watched her still. She pretended an interest in what Joanna was presently saying to her, but she blinked too often, and her chest began to lift and fall noticeably as if her breathing had accelerated. Her hands, which had been folded in front of her on the scarred table, tripping over each other, now disappeared beneath the table. Aye, she knew he couldn't keep his eyes off her.

He really didn't need to charge himself with so daunting a mission as that, to keep his gaze off her. They had only one more day until he would likely never see her again.

Within an hour, they were on the move again, riding as they had previously, Baldred burdened with Joanna while Nicholas had taken Alice up with him. Of Baldred's circumstance, Nicholas might have said there was less negativity attached to having Joanna ride with him.

Baldred had quite cheerily—and irreverently—said to her when the horses were brought forth, "I canna keep pushing ye up by yer arse, lass, no matter how much ye might wish that I do. C'mon now, get that foot up there." And Baldred had then taken hold of the foot Joanna had been trying to lift, fitting it into the stirrup himself. "And there ye go."

Yet, he'd still had to use his hand on Joanna's bottom to hoist her upward, which had the entire party grinning, Joanna not least of all. Her tone had been just as jovial when she'd gained the saddle and had charged, "Ye say ye will no' but then ye do, ye daft man, so I canna be the only one wondering who might be wishing for what."

Of Nicholas' own circumstance, with Alice within his arms and thighs upon his huge destrier, he only shrugged internally, having no desire to make the lass wretched for his poor disposition of yesterday.

"Was it truly quiet abovestairs in that chamber last night?" He asked, by way of opening conversation.

He'd startled her. She rather stiffened as she turned her face, her head bent to avoid meeting his gaze, so that she might only be staring at his thigh or the sword that hung from his belt.

She nodded first. And many seconds passed before she said, "'Tis true."

But nothing else then, as she returned her gaze over the steed's head. Nicholas was not one to look too deeply into a woman's prerogative to remain aloof, certainly not in this case, when the cause of her coolness was well-imagined.

He pretended the cause of it might be something else. "Ye still cling to yer original belief?" He asked. "That we were no' summoned by yer mam, that we dinna mean to deliver ye to yer parents?"

"If I did," she replied, "or if I believed that more than what you claim is truth, I would not be sitting here on this horse with you."

"Would ye no'?"

"Nae. I would have compelled Joanna to make an escape with me overnight. Or mayhap we'd have slipped away when we ran into that carnage in the village, while you were otherwise occupied."

"And ye ken ye'd have gotten verra far? Away from me?"

"I've just survived an entire year in the house of an English baron, sir. I doubt there is little I could not do if I put my mind to it."

Aye, he might have suspected that about her, had learned already that she was intrepid and certainly did not want for courage.

He challenged her no more. This was fine, as they were right now: she wary, possibly wondering at his reasons for starting a conversation with her when yesterday he'd gone so far out of his way to avoid the same; and he, returned to that immensely comfortable role, one he knew and practiced well, that of hired sword, one that did not allow for distraction such as all those soft and weak and useless emotions that came with kissing a lass as bedeviling as Alice de Graham.

The day and their travel were uneventful then, until with the sunset came the rain.

"I dinna guess ye planned this so well," Joanna said to no one in particular. "No inn in sight and now with the rain. And last night, no rain but that fine bed."

"I ken ye imply that we're mighty," Dungal intoned, "but even we canna control the rains."

They had yet an hour to go before they would reach the Fintry hills. Nicholas instinctively tightened his arm around Alice when she lifted her hands from his forearm to arrange the hood of her cloak around her head.

Simply to be accommodating, he recommended, "Lean in, lass, against my chest. Will keep the brunt of it away from ye." What had started as a light rain had erupted into a full shower, spurned by a strong gale which shoved furiously against Nicholas' back. Through squinted eyes he saw that at times the rain was blown sideways, horizontal to the ground.

Alice did as he suggested, leaning her shoulder against him, huddling under the protection offered by his broad chest and shoulders. "Heavy rains never last long, my da always says," she said with a wee hope flavoring her tone.

Her father lied. Or his supposition was disproved when more than thirty minutes later they were still struggling against the same hard rain. And that was when they came upon the steep hills of Fintry.

"We cannot possibly climb that," Alice predicted, the hope detected in her voice different than what she'd presented earlier.

The incline was treacherous even when dry, which it most certainly was not at the moment. The bottom of the mountain side was naught but grass and the occasional growth of some wild brush. Above that, after more than a hundred yards were climbed, the landscape was peppered generously with trees, tall pines and downy birch. Presently, the grass directly in front of and above them was lined with wide trails of water, rivulets of rain traveling downward from the top of the mountain. Taken as a whole, the mountain was not so much tall as it was steep.

"We canna remain down here," Nicholas explained. "We're yet in the borderlands. Safer up there at the crest."

"'Tis no' known to be hospitable just here, at the base," Henry added to Nicholas' argument. "Reivers are no' ever far away in this area."

"I say aye, let us take our chances with reivers," Joanna called out over the rain as Baldred reined in next to Nicholas and Alice.

Nicholas glanced sideways at Baldred. "Will take us hours to get around it and then we'd have to cross the river on the west side, which might be more dangerous than this."

"I ken we should—" Joanna started.

"Ye ken nothing," Baldred barked at her. "So hush, will ye, while those who do ken get on with a decision?" To Nicholas, after a roll of his eyes, he said, "Aye, up and over might be the most practical and soundest course."

Swinging his leg over the back of his steed, Nicholas dismounted, finding that Dungal had as well, and was holding the bridle of his horse, which might be how they would have to climb, tugging the horses along. While the destriers were justly fit for their occupation, with powerful hindquarters, they only rarely had to contend with this manner of gradient.

Nicholas turned and lifted his arms to collect Alice from the saddle. "We have to climb on foot, lass, canna take the chance the horse will stumble and drop ye or throw ye."

She leaned forward and allowed herself to be pulled off the horse, affixing an expression that was possibly meant to convey she was not looking forward to her own march uphill but that she understood the reasoning. "I was afraid you might say that."

Malise and Henry, with no burden to consider, started up the hill. Dungal followed, more slowly than the lads, and was huffing and puffing after naught but ten steps.

Nicholas inclined his head toward Baldred and Joanna, who followed. Joanna was nearly comical, since she did not bother to attempt to keep herself upright but put her hands to the nearly vertical ground and climbed upward in that fashion, while Baldred grumbled to her after only a moment that she was going crooked up the hill.

Stretching out his hand to Alice, Nicholas invited, "Shall we?"

"I fear we must," she said with a grimace. "But you do not need to hold my hand. You have the horse to manage, and I need my hands to hold up my skirts. Or to prevent myself from falling on my face when I go down, which seems inevitable. I'll be right behind you."

"Nae, lass," he corrected her. "On my side."

Thus, they began their climb at the same time, side by side. The first fifty feet went well, Nicholas with a firm grip on the destrier's bridle while Alice took slow and cautious steps, keeping her gaze on the ground. Soon, they were only feet behind Joanna and Baldred, the former still hunched over the earth and clinging to it as she climbed.

Alice slipped several times, but caught herself, once casting a nervous glance at Nicholas, who had reached to steady her. But she had lagged a few paces behind him that he was not close enough to get to her and she righted herself before she might have fallen.

"I fear these slippers are not made for scaling the side of a wet mountain," she said. "They're only getting more slippery as they are soaked."

"Slow and easy, lass," he advised and returned his attention ahead of them, just in time to hear Joanna yelp, the sound echoing throughout the glen, and then watched as she lost both her footing and her grip and began to slide backwards with great speed.

"Son of a—" Nicholas cursed.

Joanna was too far left for him to stop, and Alice was still a few paces behind him that he could not prevent Joanna from crashing into her. But he tried, rushing left toward Alice as her feet were swiped out from under her. The collision stopped Joanna's forward—downward—progress but sent Alice tumbling and sailing downward.

He had only forethought enough to release the bridle, lest the horse crash down as well, before he dove across the slick grass, hoping to reach one of Alice's flailing arms as she slid away.

He missed one of her hands by inches and then needed to stop his own trajectory, not without difficulty, so that he could rise and jog down the hill after her.

"Och, and sweet Mother Mary," cried Joanna, who'd somehow managed to not slide any further, "there she goes."

Her voice continued to trail after them as Alice slid dangerously downhill and Nicholas gave chase.

"You should no' have left yer sturdy boots behind, lass!"

He was not surprised when he lost his own footing and went down, landing on his arse and now following in much the same manner as Alice.

With nothing to stop their downward spiral, they slid all the way to the bottom, gaining speed as they descended. Nicholas strove desperately to slow or stop his fall, afraid if he did not he would crash with great force into Alice when finally they stopped. But he could gain no purchase on the slippery ground and his swipes at the grass proved ineffective, as the grass he tried to cling to only tore off in his fist. If he put his foot down, he feared he would only forfeit what little control he had, mayhap might only roll end over end.

Alice's panicked scrambling had turned her around several times that toward the end, she slid down on her belly, her face and hands lifted up toward Nicholas. She barely missed crashing into one of the few growths of brush that sprung from the side of the hill and because her eyes were squeezed tightly closed, she did not see the hurdle that she might have used to stop her swift decline.

But Nicholas recognized the benefit of the tangle of weeds and stronger branches of the green plant and was able to latch onto that and stall his plummeting. When he had stopped completely again, he stood and jogged down the remainder of the hill to where Alice had come to a stop at the bottom, face down in the puddles and mud at the base of the hill.

His heart dropped to his feet when he saw that she was not moving, and he crashed onto his knees at her side while Joanna wailed loudly above them.

"Alice!" He shouted, gingerly turning her over onto her back.

Her eyes were open, possibly the only unmarred thing on her face. She was stunned, her mouth gaping and trembling, her hand flopped over her middle.

"Lass...?" Aw, *Jesu*. His throat closed up. "Alice?"

He thought for sure she was about to cry, and he wouldn't have held that against her. But then, while she stared with so much horror at him, she began to laugh. 'Twas at first only a bark of incredulity until it grew, and she became almost hysterical, shaking and giggling so thoroughly that her eyes watered, and she covered her mouth with a dirty hand.

Nicholas' breath escaped him with his relief, and he sank onto his ass, peeved by so absurd a situation.

From above, he heard Baldred scold Joanna. "Now how can she be dead and be laughing, will ye answer me that?"

"Ye ken we still have to climb, lass?" Nicholas asked Alice, his chest still heaving with his exertions, as was hers.

"I know," she said when she could control her misplaced mirth, "so some of this might be tears, at the very idea."

Glancing over his shoulder and up the steep hill, he saw that Malise had his steed well in hand. His attention returned to Alice, he stood and helped her to her feet and then felt wretched for only belatedly thinking to inquire formally if she were seriously hurt at all.

"Naught but my pride," she said, looking at her dirty hands, which she wiped off on her dirty cloak. She lifted her blue eyes to him. "Allow me to express my appreciation to you, for dropping right behind me so I was not forced to suffer this indignity by myself."

"It was no' as if I had a choice." He grinned at her. Or thought he did, but mayhap he'd not done it well, so that she appeared unsettled either by his response or by a grin that more surely resemble a grimace.

But then he did smile, almost fully, for what an unholy mess she was. There was not a clean or dry spot on her cloak or léine, it seemed. Her hair was a wild tangle of black, caked with mud and grass, and her face had not escaped unscathed, both cheeks being streaked with mud.

Nicholas lifted a hand and plucked several blades of grass from her hair near her temple before moving a long lock of black hair behind her ear. Of its own accord, his thumb traced a fresh scrape on her face, which followed exactly the arch of her high cheekbone. Her perfect skin was abraded, not in any ghastly fashion, though even in her present beyond-untidy state, the imperfection was out of place and quite unfortunate. He ran his thumb softly over the tender abrasion until he realized how he touched her and then clamped his jaw and pulled his hand away.

Alice had held herself perfectly still when he'd stroked his thumb over her cheek but now blinked rapidly to dispel the nearly intimate moment once he'd removed his hand.

"On the bright side," she said jauntily, her cheeks suddenly bright red under his scrutiny, "you no longer have a steed to guide, and I will happily take your hand this time."

And before he might have wondered about her skirts, Alice bent at her waist and collected the hems of her léine and her cloak, sodden as they were, and tied them into a knot so that none of the fabric fell past her shins.

Nicholas took Alice's hand then and didn't mind calling up to where the others waited. "Someone hang onto Joanna, lest she chase us down a second time."

They started up the hill again, her grip as sure and tight as was his. Her hand was soft and warm, her skin almost ridiculously smooth, and he did not dislike it at all, the way her hand felt wrapped in his.

# Chapter Ten

They managed the climb successfully. Every time Alice slipped, which happened more than once, Nicholas' hand kept her from falling onto her face. When they reached the rest of the party, waiting on them where the trees began, Alice thought the going improved, or mayhap only the smooth, rain soaked soles of her slippers found better leverage against the carpet of leaves and pine needles and over roots lifted out of the earth.

Malise did not return the bridle of Nicholas' horse to him, but trudged on ahead, seemingly with only half as much effort as Alice supposed she expended.

"I think I might be all right up here," she said to Nicholas, tugging to have her hand returned now, not wanting to be a burden, or any more of a burden than she'd involuntarily already proven.

"I'm no' letting ye go, lass," sounded intimately inspiring until he followed that up with, "I'd rather no' have to chase ye down or climb back up again, no' even one more time."

After they'd climbed possibly another fifty or more yards, they came to a lower, flat-topped peak, buffeted on one side by the wall of the mountain that rose even higher, and on the west side from where the wind came by a coppice of scrub, juniper and willow, and a low-growing rowan tree.

Not anyone was spared from suffering some effects of having made so perilous and taxing a climb. Joanna and Alice were the first to sink to their knees.

"Lord spare me if any one of them starts yapping that we've yet more to climb," Joanna said, wheezing a bit. "I dinna ken that I would no' do harm to the man who might dare suggest as much."

Alice might have smiled at this, she couldn't be sure. 'Twas not terribly cold but her face was rather numb, mayhap from the continued falling rain, and she felt as if she had no control over any of her body even as she was cognizant of muscles and bones aching. "I do not want to think about the descent tomorrow."

As this was to be their camp for the night since darkness had fallen some time ago, and because the rain was still bothersome, the group settled fairly quickly. Horses were hobbled and small bits of cheese and bread were shared. They huddled collectively and closely under the green canopy of one of the rowan trees, whose limbs were twisted, some touching the ground, which created a shelter of sorts.

The shelf of this lower peak was not especially wide or large, which also necessitated them gathering close for the night. Alice curled up on her side next to Joanna, using her arm as a pillow, expecting that she might start shivering soon since she was soaked to the bone, and it was so much cooler at this elevation. She was grimy and rather uncomfortable but had no fear that sleep would not come, her exhaustion being greater.

Nicholas and Henry took up positions on one side of Alice, and the other men sat or laid down close to Joanna.

And then, as if the last few hours had not been harrowing enough, the wolves started to howl when the rain calmed to naught but a gently falling mist.

Wolves, sounding entirely too close for any to rest easy.

Joanna bolted upright. "Och, and here they come, the night creatures."

Next to her, Baldred attempted to soothe her concern. "Wolves dinna want to encounter us no more than we them. They'll keep their distance."

"They might," Dungal said, and then effectively ruined what little assurance Baldred had meant to convey. "Or they might no'. Recall that incident that was told to us by that butcher at Haddington's market few years back?" He asked into the night. "Four wolves terrorized some godforsaken village for weeks, took three people off into the night, one at a time."

"They did no'!" Joanna challenged, aghast.

"Sure and they did," alleged Dungal. "Came for one man—a robust soldier, in fact— and weren't he surrounded by half a dozen more of the same. Bit down on his head and dragged him away. If there were any screaming none had heard it, but then they would no' have, for his face being clamped inside the jaws of the beast."

"Now why would ye conjure tales to frighten the—?" Baldred began.

"Ye were there," Dungal charged, "heard the same sorry story I did. Aye and the lad they'd made off with had been soused and mayhap, ye ken, he dinna ken what bit him. Recall what the butcher said next, from those who lived to tell the tale, that they never found any more of him but part of his foot and one lost eye, which rolled back into camp unaided the next morning."

Malise's chuckle sounded over Baldred's griping that Dungal should keep his tales to himself.

"Ye're a vast brute, Dungal, with yer ghost stories," accused Malise. "Dinna pay him no mind, lass."

"I will no," said Joanna, "but ken I'll be pushing him in front of me should the beasts come now to haul one of us away."

Alice added to the silliness. "I have no fear, Malise. I believe I am quite safe here, tucked in the middle. But fare thee well, those of you on the perimeter."

This roused sleepy chortling from several, Joanna included.

Alice turned her head over her shoulder to study Nicholas, who was sitting up, his back against the wet and hard trunk of the small tree. He was staring at her was all that she could fathom in the darkness, could discern only his glittering eyes upon her though not his expression.

"You will not sleep?"

"I will," was all he said.

After one more second, she returned her face to the pillow of her arm and closed her eyes. Exhaustion aside, she knew she would sleep well. She had no fear that any harm would come to her while Nicholas MacRory kept watch over her.

MALISE WOKE HALFWAY through the night and took over the watch and thus Nicholas was able to stretch out, claiming a bit of sleep for himself. He'd spent the previous few hours alternately staring at Alice while she slept and considering with no small amount of either shock or wonder that neither she nor Joanna had grumbled at all about their circumstance—not the distressing uphill climb nor the irritating rain and not even about their sleeping quarters or the cold of the night.

He thought that by now both had realized for certain that his claim had been true, that he meant only to return them to the de Graham house, that he hadn't any ulterior, possibly nefarious motive for having stolen them from the de Lisle house in England.

Truth be told, he could find little fault with Alice, not in any aspect. She was bonny and brave, and kissed a man with a passion that certainly he had not expected or had ever known from so well-heeled a lass. And while he didn't begrudge whatever she might have read into his less hostile mood of the day past, he would be pleased to be devoid of her company after tomorrow. A lass such as Alice raised hope inside a man, that he could be made whole again, that he wasn't entirely irredeemable, that all the blood on his hands might be washed away. A dangerous contemplation since he knew damn well the misdeeds of his past could not ever be erased. Chances were, he firmly believed, that he could not be saved, but more likely that she—or any good woman—would only be tainted and tarnished by what he was.

Still, Nicholas reconciled often that he would cheerfully commit all his sins again rather than live as his father had, so weakened and diminished by his love for Nicholas' stepmother that he'd withered and died when she was gone, naught but an ineffectual, enfeebled man by the time he'd passed. How Nicholas had hated him for that, as if all his worth had been tied up in his love for his wife. True, his stepmother had been worthy of admiration, for she was clever, and strong-willed and efficient, but Nicholas had always known and abhorred that his father only walked in her shadow, had not led or governed or accomplished anything of note that his wife hadn't first decreed and set into motion.

As he often did, Nicholas quelled any thoughts of his father, since he was so often made bitter by any memory of that weak-willed man.

By this time tomorrow, he would be marching with an army three hundred strong, away from Carbery and toward William Wallace or toward Braewood Keep where an abbreviated but exacting training would commence immediately.

As much as he didn't mind being on the road, he did lament the lack of communication with so many different persons, and thus his lack of knowledge about all current situations. Hopefully, John de Graham was kept well abreast of any new developments and might share what information had come to him, if any, in the last week or so.

His sleep was not so restless as it sometimes was and he woke, nearly dry now, just as the sun was rising. When he opened his eyes, he was greeted by the sight of Alice, who must have turned in her sleep and now faced him. She was asleep yet, her lashes fanned over her cheeks, with streaks of now-dried mud still marring her cheeks and chin. Her hands were curled loosely and tucked up under her chin, the backs of them also coated with dirt. Incredibly, she was still so damn pretty.

The quiet of the morn allowed for solemn reflection, but all that came to mind was the taste of Alice's kiss. He still maintained that had been an unwise move on his part, though he knew damn well all the reasons behind it, not least of which was his desire to taste and touch something innocent and good.

It was naught but an hour later when the small party marched down the far side of the Fintry hills, the going so much easier for its gentler decline. Still, they walked the horses down and did not gain the saddle until they'd reached the bottom, at which time Alice was once again mounted with Nicholas and Joanna with Baldred.

They did not pause to rest and water the horses at midday since they were within only a few miles of Carbery by then. Nicholas knew exactly when Alice began to recognize the landscape of home when she straightened in front of him and leaned forward, as if she might encourage the horse to a faster pace.

"I cannot believe we're almost there," she said, a great excitement in her tone.

"Ye canna believe I dinna lie?" He questioned. "Or is that only an expression of delight?"

"Both," she answered pertly, "but more of the latter than the former."

A gasp sounded beside them, where Baldred and Joanna rode. "Och, lass, but what if they're no' here? What if yer da's heart finally gave out for all the bristling and bridling he does? What if yer mam has succumbed—"

Many voices, including even Malise and Henry, expressed immediate annoyance with Joanna's frightful and untimely speculations. Their frustration was spat all at once.

"Aw, now, why do ye gotta be like that?" Baldred moaned.

"Many a fine blessing were likely ruined by yer distressing theories," Henry said.

"Are ye daft?" Barked Dungal. "Putting such a fear in the lass?"

Riding lead, Malise shook his head. "Never did meet one such as ye. I can no' figure out yer head."

"It's fine, sirs," Alice allowed. "Joanna only worries. It's been so long."

"But we saw both yer mam and yer sire within the last fortnight," Dungal reminded her, his tone still aggrieved.

"There. See, Joanna? All will be well."

Apparently, nothing could dampen Alice's buoyant spirit on this day.

They rode through the same outspread and sleepy village and once they'd gone beyond the last croft, kneed their steeds into a swifter stride. When the de Graham house came into view, Alice lifted both her hands from where they'd sat on Nicholas' arm to cover her mouth. She glanced over her shoulder at him, her eyes sparkling while all around her fingers was evidence of her large smile, as her cheeks were lifted and her eyes crinkled. Nicholas was powerless to withhold a returned smile, as her joy had a life of its own, being rather infectious.

And just now, experiencing this quiet and teary-eyed delight from her, Nicholas finally appreciated this facet of his mission. Until now, it had all been about the benefit to him and the army he would gain by delivering the de Graham daughter safely home. But as her color heightened and her energy grew, he realized a sense of satisfaction because he'd been the person to make this happen.

"I'm going to leap from this horse and run, Nicholas," she told him when the squat stone wall and empty yard came into view, "straight into the house. Apologies given now for abandoning you in the yard."

Over this, he chuckled outright, something he could not recall doing in a very long time. Certainly, it had been ages since any laughter had erupted unaccompanied, for mostly such an outburst would be tainted by scorn or righteous fury or mayhap annoyance. This pure amusement now was different. Only Alice de Graham would forecast her intention and announce her contrition before the event that would necessitate it.

"No leaping, lass," he requested. "Take hold of my arm again and at least allow me to lower ye down."

She did, clasping one hand tightly in his while she gripped his forearm with the other. "Oh, but I wish I didn't look such a fright."

"Yer mam will no' be disturbed by a little mud and dirt," he said, believing that to be true.

They entered the small yard and Nicholas pulled back on the reins within ten feet of the door, and did as he'd said he would, moved his arm away from his body, and Alice slid down to the ground. With a squeak of excitement, she lifted her skirts and dashed toward the house.

The door there opened before she reached it but upon seeing that it was her mother who pulled it open, Alice did not slow her sprint but threw herself at a slack-jawed Eleanor de Graham.

They wept and spoke and laughed all at once.

"Mother, I'm home!"

"Oh, my darling!"

"I've missed you so much."

"Everyday, lass, pray and worry, 'twas all I could do." She pushed Alice away, at arms' length. "Aye but let me look at you. Oh, you poor dear. What a state you're in!" And she laughed and hugged Alice again.

By now, Joanna had arrived and dismounted with help from Baldred. She approached the clinging pair slowly, perhaps the first bit of trepidation Nicholas had ever noticed in the maid.

"Oh, and Joanna, too," cried Eleanor de Graham, though she made no move to include the woman in her and Alice's gathering.

Alice, though, was a generous person, a good friend indeed. She neither forgot nor ignored Joanna's presence as that one sidled closer to the hugging women. Alice separated herself to open her arm to Joanna and with a fresh cry of joy from all three now, Joanna was swept into what was now a three-person embrace.

Eleanor de Graham was suddenly and fully ten years younger. Possibly not even the longed-for second coming of the Lord could compete with the bliss she knew at this moment. It shone bright in her eyes, so like her daughter's, and in her weepy smile. And just when Nicholas was sure that the embracing was done for now, another happy cry burst from Eleanor and she pulled Alice close once more.

Nicholas glanced sideways, at Baldred and Dungal on his right. Both men wore grins that likewise said what Nicholas felt, a tremendous pride for what part they'd played in this reunion. Next, Nicholas imagined an answer to a question that was spoken only in his mind: Aye, he was sure that Alice de Graham knew very well how loved she was. He didn't suppose she was the type to only assume or take for granted the noble affection of her mother and similarly, he might assume that she understood that she was blessed.

Still clinging to her daughter, Eleanor de Graham raised her gaze to Nicholas and his men.

"Please, come!" She invited with a wave of her hand. "All of you. You must sup with us this night."

The woman turned and stepped fully inside, and Nicholas and the others dismounted, leaving their steeds with the same gangly lad who'd taken charge of them once before.

"Here's hoping there comes an offering of a soft bed along with any fare they might present to us," Dungal said as they entered the de Graham house.

"Aye," agreed Baldred. "I'd no' mind one night upon linen or furs."

Nicholas supposed that if an offer of such hospitality came their way, they might as well accept. Until he had possession of the de Graham army, he was in no hurry to go or be anywhere. And though he knew it existed inside him, he rejected any great ponderance of the idea that he wasn't ready to leave Alice just yet.

As he and his men lagged a bit behind the three women, by the time they stepped into the hall, Alice was already separating herself from her father's embrace. John de Graham appeared both stunned and relieved, but then he was not as effusive in his joy as had been his wife.

De Graham lifted his gaze over his daughter's head as Nicholas' party approached the high table. Alice's father did not smile nor show any enormous appreciation toward the men who'd rescued his child, but he did walk around Alice and step off the dais, striding toward them.

He stretched out his hand to Nicholas, his gaze steady. When Nicholas met the outstretched hand, John de Graham laid his other hand over their joined ones and said solemnly, "Ye have my gratitude, lad." He let his proud gaze convey the extent of such. In turn, he shook the hand of each of the MacRory men.

And while his appreciation appeared genuine, Nicholas sensed some other charged emotion beneath that.

Quietly, Nicholas asked, "Although now ye've other considerations to contend with, do ye no'?"

Standing before the five men, John de Graham nodded soberly. "Aye, and..." he began and then waved a dismissive hand, "ah, but none of that matters. My daughter is whole and well and returned, sirs. All is well."

But it wasn't, Nicholas understood. Now the greater part of de Graham's treason against Edward I would begin. He would recall his army from England's forces and commit them to the Scottish cause. The logistics alone of simply bringing his army to Carbery were dangerous, for they might be seen as deserters. Word would spread quickly throughout the ranks no doubt, and Longshanks would swiftly be made aware of de Graham's denunciation of his fealty.

As Nicholas contemplated the increasing pensiveness that pervaded de Graham's proud visage, Alice spoke up behind the group of men.

"Father, pray do not detain them," she begged, her mood yet light. "We must see to their comfort, for all that they have arranged ours over the last few days." She turned to her mother. "Might they be granted baths in the garderobe?"

"Canna say I'll squabble too robustly against that," Dungal murmured at Nicholas' side.

"Yes, yes, indeed," Eleanor approved. "And you as well, my darling. Off with you, abovestairs."

Taking Joanna's hand, Alice tugged her along as she crossed the hall to stand beside her father. She swept her gaze and showed her smile to all five men but then settled her vivid blue eyes on Nicholas.

"You will stay to sup, will you not?"

Nicholas was well aware that John de Graham was yet studying him though he could not say what the man might be looking for, or if he only was now assessing this interaction with his daughter. Casually, Nicholas laid his hand over his sword hilt and nodded at Alice.

"Very well," she answered, her lips curving. "I know it wasn't done strictly out of pity for either my parents or for me, but I thank you all the same for bringing us home."

"Aye," said Joanna, "and for no' letting us be kilt along the way, as there were plenty of times that seemed naught but inevitable."

Nicholas inclined his head once more, eyeing Alice with apparent indifference. "It was my pleasure, lass," he said, and which he knew to be the absolute truth.

John de Graham gave a curt but pleased nod for his daughter's stated gratitude and turned back toward his wife near the high table. This allowed Nicholas to chart Alice's departure from the hall with his eyes, the feigned nonchalance surging into that keen and hungry awareness that mostly accompanied any glance sent her way.

# Chapter Eleven

A fter his bath, Nicholas was summoned to the lord's solar. Appreciating being clean for the first time in more than a week, he was led to the second floor chamber by the same wench who'd attended his bath, expecting that details of the transfer of de Graham's army would now be defined. The solar was well-appointed, with thick wool carpets and an abundance of daylight provided by two large windows, and what he might suppose was furniture crafted beyond the border. The table behind which the baron de Graham sat was unremarkable but the chair under and around him was quite fine, oversized and padded with a tufted tapestry.

"My Lord," Nicholas greeted him with little reservation as the maid ducked back into the corridor, closing the door as she left.

De Graham waved his fingers at the only other chair in the chamber, which sat in front of his desk. The desk itself was well-used, cluttered to such a degree to suggest the baron's holdings or interests might be greater than what Nicholas had suspected. In addition to the ledgers and scrolls and loose documents, the tabletop was strewn with two inkpots and a flat wooden board offering a variety of quills; unlit candles set in pewter holders crowded one corner; and in the middle of the desk in front of

Nicholas sat two copper seal matrices and an oft-handled stick of red wax.

Returning his attention to the baron, Nicholas was given pause by a prickle of foreboding.

John de Graham's expression was so far different from what restrained joy he'd exhibited earlier at Alice's return. The fact that he could not or would not meet his eye directly now gave Nicholas pause as he wondered if some foul treachery was afoot. He didn't immediately suspect that de Graham had played him false, despite de Graham's cautious, cheek-biting regard, but was determined not to be surprised if the man faltered and stumbled through some surely derisory excuse for why the army might be delayed. Or possibly why he could not, in truth, commit to the numbers that Nicholas anticipated.

He was offered wine from a sandy-clay jug with a sagging base, which he refused. The baron's about-face in demeanor made Nicholas desire to have the words and the truth put out without delay.

"I have returned your daughter," Nicholas began when the man seemed unable to spew whatever it was that clearly disturbed him now. "In return, you have an army to put into my hands, as we agreed."

John de Graham sighed wearily and met Nicholas' eye with a resigned gaze. " I should no' have promised ye any such thing, and for that I am sorry, lad."

And now Nicholas wished that he had not taken the seat, would have rather that he'd remained standing, with his legs shoulder width apart and his hands set formidably upon his sword and hip, a display of power and all the aggression he presently felt. Barely controlling the sudden rage that coursed in his blood, Nicholas reminded him through gritted teeth, "But ye *did* promise me—and Scotland—yer army."

"Even if I wanted to—"

"*If ye wanted to*?" Nicholas snarled, his wrath detonated. "Ye bloody well said that ye did. I risked my neck and that of my men to return the lass to ye! Will ye prove so dishonorable—"

"'Tis no' so effortless as ye make it out to be!" De Graham snapped, slapping his thick hand against the table top.

"Dinna matter whether simple or otherwise, ye gave yer word, de Graham," Nicholas fumed.

"'Tis self-destruction! Only begging to be hanged!" He lifted both hands, palms thrust forward at Nicholas. "I'll no send ye off without compensation. I'm willing to pay ye—"

"Aye, and with yer army, de Graham, as agreed, unless ye wish to ken me as an enemy. Trust me, sir, ye dinna want that."

The older man's shoulders sagged, all his bluster shrinking. "At this verra moment," he said, "the de Graham units are entrenched with Edward himself. To remove them now would be an act of deliberate self-destruction."

Surging to his feet now with enough force to upend the chair upon which he'd sat, Nicholas spat, "I dinna care one whit what it means to ye. I dinna want yer coin. I expect yer army."

In a torrent of self-criticism for trusting the word of one he did not know well enough, and whose circumstances might have been estimated to be dire enough to propel the false promise of an army, Nicholas curled his lip and reproached himself for accepting this man's pledge when he'd proven he was no better than Nicholas' own father, ruled by a woman, weak and too ineffectual to stand strong with his own decisions or against his lady wife.

"As much as it pains me to recant my vow," said de Graham, "I cannot subject my wife and daughter to a life tethered to a man accused of treason—"

"But ye dinna mind having yer own name thrust about as that of a traitor to the cause, and worse, as a man without honor," Nicholas guessed.

"Better that I suffer rather than they."

Nicholas scoffed heatedly at this. "Think ye they will no' suffer for yer treachery?"

The baron did not exactly shrug in response to this, but did show a declining posture, the robust man diminished greatly behind the desk.

"Ye will truly do it?" Nicholas asked. "Renounce a pledge? And all for cowardice?"

John de Graham did not answer, but then he did not look any further than the scrolls on his desk.

And so it was clear. The baron would not be intimidated into compliance—now the man decided to show a strength of will that had previously and obviously been lacking!

Still deriding the trust he'd allocated to the man, Nicholas considered striking him down where he sat, so enraged was he over this betrayal. Steel hissed as he drew his sword.

"Ye've made an enemy, de Graham, and one I'll make ye sorry to ken."

But he did not raise his sword to John de Graham, who had not even bothered to stand at the threat of the weapon drawn. Only later would Nicholas acknowledge what—or more precisely, whom—had kept him from skewering the baron.

With a growl of pure rage, he pivoted and withdrew from the chamber.

Damn the man. And damn his daughter as well, that 'twas her face he saw when he considered briefly ending de Graham's life, as he had every right to do for the fraud he'd perpetrated.

Swift, angry strides carried him down the stairs and into the hall.

Eleanor de Graham, setting bouquets of flowers along the high table, gasped as she turned and noticed his stormy arrival, and the shiny blade swinging with his furious gait.

As soon as his men caught sight of his brandished sword, they drew their own.

Ignoring the baroness who let out a sharp cry, Nicholas cursed to his men, "He bluidy broke his oath."

Already a plan was forming for an immediate retribution against de Graham. While Eleanor de Graham stuttered and spewed her own disbelief and then screamed her husband's name, Nicholas instructed Malise, "Ready the mounts, two minutes." Of Baldred and Dungal, he inquired, "How many soldiers about?"

"No' more than a dozen," Dungal answered.

"What are you planning?" Eleanor asked, rushing him, pulling on Nicholas' sleeve. "Please, just allow me a moment with my husband. I had no idea of his—please!" She cried when Nicholas growled at her and shook her off. "There must be some misunderstanding."

He paid her no mind, and she ran straight for the stairs, calling once again for her husband.

"Be ready to take them on," Nicholas advised, "and move away quickly. Now." With that, he turned and followed where the baroness had gone, up the stairs.

"What are ye—?" Baldred began.

"We're no' leaving empty-handed," Nicholas called back, his shout infused with all the rage that was summoned to the surface inside him.

Believing the family apartments to be housed on the third floor, Nicholas bypassed the second floor—ignoring the shrieks of Lady Eleanor as she violently upbraided her husband, still entombed in his solar—and marched purposefully down the passageway, throwing open doors until a pair of screeches greeted him as he found what he sought.

He was taken aback himself, having discovered Alice half-clothed, apparently just risen from her own bath, garbed only in a thin shift of cotton, which left little to his imagination, while a young girl applied a cloth to her wet hair, wringing all the water from the long black tresses. Alice's feet were bare beneath the hem of her chemise as were her arms, which she instinctively clutched over her chest.

She said nothing right away, only stared at him with wide, frantic eyes.

Recovering himself before she did, he clipped at her, "Get dressed."

"But—what is happening below? So much hollering and uproar in the last few—"

"I said get dressed," he growled. His wrath propelled him into the room and allowed him to leave at the door such benevolent considerations as propriety and correctness. He flung open the doors to the cupboard in the corner of the chamber and with little regard withdrew a dark léine and tossed that at the maid.

The stricken girl caught the gown and scrambled to arrange the open bottom in her hands to throw over Alice's head while Alice continued to stammer questions at him.

"Nicholas, whatever are you—why are you wielding your sword inside—?"

Keeping an attentive ear on any noise outside the chamber, Nicholas bore down on Alice and snarled from less than a foot away, "God dammit, Alice. Be gowned by her or by me but do so now."

BY FAR, THIS RAGE OF his was so much worse than the brief one she'd known from him when first he'd entered the de Lisle house and she'd accosted him with a knife at his throat. And vastly more terrifying. His eyes were darkened with fury while the scar across his cheek, which she'd so often overlooked, whitened against his bronze skin.

Having no clue what had transpired, or why he felt the need to brandish his sword or confront her in her chamber, Alice obeyed, allowing the petrified Hylnn—who only moments ago had been smiling and laughing with Alice, regaling her with tales of what had gone on in her absence—to drop the léine over her head.

"What is amiss?" She begged finally, her voice returned. "Is father all right? Mother?"

"They await ye below stairs," he answered, stepping over to the door to peer out into the hall.

"My God, are we being put to a siege?"

"Don yer boots," he commanded, standing in the doorway.

Hylnn, jumping to do his bidding quicker than Alice, fetched her footwear and thrust these at Alice.

"But my hose—"

"Put on the bluidy boots, Alice," he ground out.

She did so, but was not allowed time to tie the laces before Nicholas took her by the wrist and ushered her from the room.

"Hylnn," she cried. "We cannot leave—"

"She stays. She has nothing to do with this."

"With what? Nicholas, what are you—"

"Cease."

Alice yanked on her arm and dragged her feet inside the stairwell. "I will not cease. Tell me! What is happening?"

Nicholas, one step ahead of her, stopped and turned on her, his mien as fierce as she had ever seen it. "Yer sire revoked our spoken contract, refuses to recall his army. If ye dinna want his blood spilled for his treachery, ye'll do exactly as I say."

And he began moving again, while Alice's head spun with what few scraps of detail he'd given her. Only her utter confusion allowed her to be pulled along again without further protest. Upon the first floor, inside the hall, the tableau that presented itself to Alice was striking for how surreal it was. Just twenty feet from the stairs from where came Nicholas and Alice, her mother and father were shouting at each other, her father with sword in hand, swinging that wildly to punctuate his arguments. Near the middle of the hall stood Baldred and Duncan with their swords drawn against her parents, hollering for them to be quiet. At the open door to the yard, with his back to the room, Henry had assumed a fighting stance, feet set apart, his long blade aimed at the door, while more shouting was heard from outside. In front of the high table, upon her knees with her skirts billowed around her, Joanna added a high-pitched wail to the scene, her hands clasped together and lifted high in supplication.

Alice blinked several times until the truth was thrust upon her. They were not under attack, but from Nicholas MacRory himself.

Her mother realized her presence then, held firm in Nicholas' grasp, and her shouts became a wail that sang in time with Joanna's. "Merciful *Jesu*, have pity on me, my lord," she beseeched of Nicholas. "Do not punish me for my husband's sins." She crawled forward on her knees, begging, "Take me! Take me, not Alice. Not my Alice."

*Take her*? And the full weight of this tragedy was understood then—her father's perjury, her mother's panic, her own imminent kidnapping—and confusion was dashed away by panic. Alice began finally to struggle against Nicholas' grip, slowly at first, only trying to dislodge his hold, but soon enough she scratched and clawed at the hand that held her wrist and dug her nails into his flesh. It was a useless endeavor, his grip was not loosened at all, and she was pulled across the room amid all the shouting and weeping to where Baldred and Dungal were stationed.

"Let's go," Nicholas ordered, and the men backed up toward the door.

Alice added her own cry of protest. "Stop! What are you doing?"

A deafening roar filled the room, whipping Alice's head around, just in time to see her father charge at the MacRorys, his own sword now lifted high and shaking with his rage. The bellow of anguish that was torn from Alice's throat at the sight matched that of her mother. Dungal positioned himself to meet the assault, disarming her father after only a parry left and then right. While John de Graham's sword clattered noisily on the ground, he ducked his head and charged full force at Dungal.

Alice's sire might only be ten or so years older than Dungal but he was not a warrior, did not train regularly or perhaps at all, so the Dungal barely adjusted his stance and with lighting speed struck his meaty fist forward, his punch reaching de Graham's face square on before the baron could get his hands on Dungal. The blow staggered the baron, and sent him backward as if time had slowed, reeling and teetering until he could not maintain his balance and collapsed onto the floor of the hall.

"I warned ye no' to make an enemy of me," Nicholas said in a dangerous growl. "Ye send that army up to Braewood as ye pledged. The entire army. And I'll return yer daughter then."

Realizing she had precious few seconds to secure her freedom before she was once again stolen by the Brute of Braewood, Alice resumed her struggle, digging in her heels as Nicholas attempted to drag her outside. She lifted their joined hands, meaning to sink her teeth into his arm but was thrown off balance by a sudden jerking movement from Nicholas.

With embarrassing ease, Nicholas swung her around until she was held with her back to his chest. He clamped his forearm around her neck and his voice was an icy snarl at her ear. "If ye fight me, resist even one more second, I'll leave no person alive inside this house or yard."

She went miserably liquid against him, all the fight robbed from her with his threat, which his tone promised was not only idle. "You are despicable," she murmured wretchedly.

"Must be something in the air of this house that made me so," he snapped at her as he propelled her forward.

Limp with her own defeat—she would not struggle only to see people die because of her—Alice was then easily led out into the yard, where Malise held those huge MacRory destriers at the ready.

What few de Graham soldiers were housed with the family were stationary in the yard, eyeing each other with confused gazes, some of them having not even drawn their swords. Possibly they did not understand the present chaos, what exactly was happening, or mayhap they did not move to intervene in light of the MacRory men's apparent competence with their swords, held aloft to keep those few men at a good distance. Malise, particularly, danced his steed around the gathered de Graham soldiers, showing a proficiency with his sword as he passed it from hand to hand.

As he had so many times already, Nicholas set his hands on Alice's waist and lifted her into the saddle.

At the same time, Joanna came scrambling from the keep, charging toward Baldred who had just gained his saddle.

"Shameless cur of the north," she railed. "Highland swine! Is kidnapping all ye ken, you conceited lout?"

She clutched at his leg and his boot, but Alice could not say that she was trying to unseat him or otherwise, and she feared that Baldred's twisted and dark countenance might suggest he was about to kick her away. As it was, either Joanna's frantic clambering or Baldred himself moved the horse into a circular prancing, which saw Joanna's feet sometimes lifted off the ground as she grasped at Baldred's leg.

"Joanna!" Alice called out a warning.

At the same time, Joanna yelled at Baldred. "Well, lift me up, ye bluidy blackguard! I'll no' be leaving her—no' ever—and certainly no' in any of yer despicable hands!"

Nicholas had pivoted the destrier upon which they were seated, minimizing Alice's view of that shocking circumstance and its outcome, and now they faced the open door of the house, where Alice's mother, powerless and anguished, was slumped. Alice's heart caught in her throat at the sight of her mother, who shook with her dismay and hugged her arms around herself. She did not meet Alice's gaze though; Eleanor de Graham's tortured gaze sat wretchedly upon Nicholas.

"These are the workings of yer husband, my lady," he said in a hard voice which offered little charity for the woman's agony. "'Twas no' only unnecessary but spineless, his behavior. Yer daughter will be no more ill-treated than she was in the custody of the English, but she will be imprisoned until the terms of our original covenant are met."

"But she has nothing to do with this!" Eleanor de Graham cried, her cheeks stained with tears. "She is innocent."

"As is every man who dies by the blade of the English while men such as yer husband only prolong the war with their dishonor and deceitfulness, and in full truth, such cowardice as what he has shown."

"I beg of you—" Eleanor implored, stepping away from the door, out into the yard.

Nicholas ignored her, and whatever pleas she might have uttered next, yanking on the reins to turn the destrier around again. With a fierce, "Hyah!" he kneed the animal's flanks and the horse bolted into a run, toward the low stone fence, and then through and away from home.

Alice slapped at the tight arm around her and turned her face, trying to see beyond Nicholas' broad shoulders and thick arms, to have one last glimpse of her mother, one more time.

Hearing Joanna's voice so close though they'd cleared the yard swung Alice's gaze around, to find her friend had indeed gotten her way and was securely seated behind Baldred, both arms wrapped around the warrior's waist.

"Never ye fear, Mistress!" Joanna brayed over her shoulder as she was driven away on the back of Baldred's steed. "I'll keep her in good stead, same as before!"

Numb now with her lingering confusion and shock, Alice dropped her chin to her chest and wept for her mother's misery. She herself was not frightened as he might have supposed or preferred. She was irked beyond measure, and justly so.

# Chapter Twelve

M iles and miles later, in which time Joanna had been the only speaking person, Nicholas' temper had yet to settle, had yet to come down from the heightened emotions so often entangled with rage and so daring and spontaneous an escape. Joanna's scolding of the MacRorys was only a muted din now, as Nicholas had moved his steed well ahead of his party.

Alice had yet to say one word to him, nor he to her. She had not, though, set her hand upon his forearm as she normally did as they rode. Instead, she'd chosen to twist herself in her sidesaddle seat so that from the waist up she might be seen as riding astride. He imagined that she kept her hands on the pommel since they did not touch him at any point, and because certainly she clung to something as he kept the pace brisk. Unsurprisingly, she sat stiffly, not allowing herself to lean against him for comfort or in ease as she previously had. Her weeping had stopped some time ago, or at least her shoulders had stopped shaking and her face was no more bowed to her chest in grief or dismay.

And for all that they ignored each other so completely, he was as aware of her as ever, mayhap more so for the sweet scent of primrose that clung with so much dedication to her, and beckoned greater consciousness from him. Her hair had dried by now, but too often was lifted away from her slim shoulders and back to stroke his chin and neck.

Nicholas pushed a few ebony strands away from his jaw once more and blew out a slow, even breath over the top of her head.

So much of his life was spent in a state of rage, of varying degrees predicated by whatever the spark was—a battle or any part of the war itself, or his life inside that English prison, or inside his head with memories. He lived with anger and darkness for so long, 'twas those things that were not related to anger—joy, gratitude, hope, among others—that usually had him out of sorts. Today, it was the damnable shame for having seriously misjudged de Graham, for not having considered even the prospect of that man's deceit that saw Nicholas' brain brutalized. Thus, when the raucous indignity of his own ineptitude waned and he was left with only his good friend, anger, which for years he'd been able to pass off only as coolness, he finally slowed his horse to a trot and addressed Alice and their new circumstance.

"It will be as before," he said evenly. "Ye'll no' be harmed in any way—"

"Oh, will I not be? Haven't I already been served a grave harm? Stripped once more from my mother's arms and for what? Because you didn't get your way?"

He'd heard this voice from her before, this uptight tone, on the very night he'd stolen her from the de Lisle house. He did not retaliate with the obvious, that he might have slain her father for what deceit he'd practiced. That it had been his right to do so.

"As I said, same as it was when first we met. Dinna try to escape or cause grief, or it will be Joanna who pays for your sins."

"My sins?" she sneered. "Shall we first discuss yours?"

"Aye," he snapped, "by all means, and that right after we examine those of your own sire."

"And the actions of one nullify or...or condone the narcissistic and ruinous reactions of another?"

Nicholas scoffed vocally. "Aye, lass. That is how it is, how it happens."

"You won't harm a hair on Joanna's head," she charged. "I know that now. You are naught but a blustering coward, a peeved child who did not get his way. This now, is only you stomping your feet."

This enraged him, that she should imagine him weak, that she thought she knew him, his mind. She'd not be challenging him with such a zealously imperious manner, would be quaking in fear at her fate if she knew even one tenth of what he was truly capable of. He'd been respectful of her before, believing she would bring him an army. Part of that consideration had also been borne of his beguilement, he knew, but allowed *that* had only been feasible because of his optimism, having believed he was about to secure a sizable army for Scotland. Alice was naught but a prisoner now, a pawn, and one he wasn't sure was worth anything at all based on her own father's choices.

"Aye, ye are right," he acknowledged. "I have never raised my hand against a woman and would no' begin now. And yet the dungeon at Braewood is a terrifying place. I wonder how long Joanna would last in that dark and dank crypt before the scratching vermin or grating madness claimed her."

"You are evil. I have not wronged you in any manner—"

"But yer sire has, which makes ye my enemy."

"Are you of that ilk then? One of those half-wits? Who believe the transgressions of a man are passed on to his offspring?"

"So ye agree your sire did commit treachery?"

"But neither my mother nor I did, and that is who you punish now—you must see that. Shall I hold you accountable for all the sins of your father?"

He stiffened and hissed, "I am nothing like my father."

"Are you not? Then where, pray tell, did you discover your dishonor?"

"Ye try my patience—"

"As you do mine, you miserable excuse for a man."

Of course he knew that about her, that she was fierce in her own right, that her present circumstance would more irk her than unravel her. She would not wither in fright before him but would likely hurl her haughty vilifications at him with irritating steadiness. Nicholas almost chuckled now, in hindsight, when it occurred to him to know some thankfulness that her charge against him, that he would harm no person, had not struck her earlier, when he'd threatened the same only to see her removed without hassle from her home. But he did not take her to task on this.

She detested him now, and that was enough. All was well.

Dungal called for a halt when his horse, inexplicably, began to favor his right front leg.

Nicholas was not concerned for their position, being out in the middle of a vast field of green and gold that rose only as high as the destriers' hocks, with nary a tree in sight by which to take cover if needed. They had ridden through the tranquil valley of one of the Angus glens, safe in the Highlands now, and had only the River Dee and the Shevock water to cross and all told, another three to four leagues of meadows and smaller hills to navigate on the east side of the Grampians to reach Braewood.

Nicholas dismounted and without inquiring if she had any need or desire to do so, pulled Alice from the saddle as well. He smirked with little humor when she slapped at the hands he'd put upon her.

"Do not touch me, you corrupt heathen," she snarled before stalking away from him.

Leading his horse by the bridle, Nicholas paused near Dungal to see what might be amiss.

"Bruised sole," Dungal muttered, flicking out bits of dirt and grass and one tiny stone as he held the affected foot between his thighs. "And that'll be all the riding she'll stand," he predicted next.

While mulling over this sorry appraisal, which would see them delayed quite a bit if Dungal were forced to lead the steed home and not ride her, Nicholas took note of Alice's whereabouts. She hadn't gone far, was face to face with Joanna about forty feet away, standing knee deep in the tall meadow grass. She stood in profile to him while the setting sun painted her generously in a golden light. Her hands were at her waist, fidgeting around one another while Joanna was saying something to her that involved wagging her finger at Alice. In response, she nodded several times, glumly it seemed, her head bowed a bit. When Joanna stopped speaking, Alice straightened and drew in a large breath before she swept her gaze over the calming vista and absently ran her fingers over the tops of the seeding grass. The soft shimmering light of near-dusk softened every bonny inch of her to gilded perfection, sparkling in the black of her hair and rendering her gown in shades of yellow. Her cheeks, which might have picked up their sun-colored radiance over the last few days in his company, were decorated with a gleaming glow that gave her an otherworldly appearance. Angelic, he might have said, if his brain worked in such a way, to think and assume such contemptibly tender drivel.

And then more human she was, as she gasped at something Joanna had said and covered her cheeks with her hands.

Baldred joined Nicholas and Dungal after a moment while Malise and Henry opted to remain mounted, waiting.

"That right there," Dungal said, drawing Nicholas' attention, "is why ye took her?"

Nicholas' scowl deepened. "That right *what*?" He questioned, finding Dungal's narrow gaze focused on him.

"That there," Baldred answered instead, "the manner in which ye stare at her. That explain why ye felt the need to terrorize the lass yet more?"

Nicholas was less aghast than instantly stung by resentment. "Ye had some other initiative in mind?" He requested hotly of Baldred. "Some other plan to see the wrong righted?"

Dungal gently lowered his destrier's hoof. "Yer talking about what? Mayhap five hundred warriors? That what ye might have gained from de Graham?"

"Not for me alone," Nicholas reminded them through gritted teeth, "but for Scotland."

"Aye and all considerations met and known, what have ye with only five hundred more? When the English come at us by the tens of thousands? And that pitted against the harm ye've done to her, who dinna deserve either the negligence of her own father or this bluidy attempt to set that right."

"Bluidy hell," Nicholas growled. "I dinna need to hear yer buggered bleating about it—"

"Nae, likely ye dinna want it or expect it. But need it? Aye, ye do."

"Ye bluidy stood there, by my side," he was compelled to remind his old friend, "holding yer own sword to pervert the injustice—" Dungal's shrug halted the rest of Nicholas' tirade, widening his eyes until they bulged with enmity.

"Aye," acknowledged the seasoned warrior, "but that, ye ken, is how like my mam used to say to my da: dinna argue in front of the bairns and allow them to see the dissent."

Nicholas had no words, as stunned and stymied as he'd ever been. It was rare that his men took issue with any of his decisions, but then he'd not ever before kidnapped a woman to pursue revenge against her father.

"Aye and I wonder if that were for certain the beinn upon which ye meant to perish," Baldred ventured.

Likely his countenance showed plainly his growing astonishment and the raw fury that came on its heels at their opposition to his decision. Not the hill he wanted to die on? Nae, it was no. But when did these two turn their backs on those who would misrepresent themselves, who had without compunction reneged on a promise?

He might have asked either Dungal or Baldred what they thought he should have done, what they supposed his reaction should have been, but gnashed his teeth instead and turned away, not truly interested in their opinion at this moment, certainly not when the deed was done.

The other thing, their suggestion that his taking of Alice had anything to do with...whatever they assumed they'd read into his staring at her, provoked Nicholas to a more abhorrent fury.

"AS IF I'D ABANDONED ye now, when yer feet had barely known the precious earth of home," Joanna said. "I dinna fool myself I make it any easier, lass. I truly dinna. But I ken yer face when ye understood what was happening and I said to myself, *Aye, Joanna, she's no' wishing to be kissing him now. Ye better get on with her, make sure she dinna murder the beast while he sleeps.*"

This, in response to Alice's rather gusty query, which wondered what her friend had been thinking to have hurled herself at Baldred, to have insisted on accompanying Alice once more into captivity.

Alice was yet astounded, still unable to fathom entirely what had happened, and so swiftly that it seemed it was only moments ago she was sunk in her bath, lazing gloriously in that heated, scented water.

"What yer da did was wrong, Alice, ye ken that," Joanna pronounced softly now.

"I do know that, Joanna, but it not does excuse what these louts have done now."

"Nae, it does no', though I ken *louts* is a wee harsh. Sure and were they no' as shocked as yer dear mam, who like as no' even hours later, is still giving yer da grief for what he perpetrated." She shook a finger at Alice though her censure was directed at John de Graham. "But dinna be blaming yerself for what gruesome fate has befallen us now. We'll survive this one, same as we did the last one."

Alice nodded. After a moment, she wondered, "Good grief, Joanna. Is this to be my—our—lives? One horrendous tragedy after another?" She sighed and turned her face toward the falling sun, idly brushing her hand over the top of the high grass.

Joanna, who was especially calm for all that *had* befallen them, tipped her head at Alice. "Ye ken 'twas no' so horrendous, that last occasion with these MacRorys."

"Sweet Mary, Joanna. They've kidnapped us—well, me. And you...oh, my...you wanted to come. And not only because of me?" The question was put out without any basis, only with all the confusion Alice felt for Joanna's remarkable sacrifice.

Alice couldn't ever recall a time when Joanna had blushed. Or stammered. Certainly, she had never before committed to both of these at the same time. A dawning of understanding—only that something was afoot in the maid's mind, but not what that might be—made Alice slap her palms over her cheeks.

Not quite a sacrifice perhaps.

"What..." She could not fathom even a single query to pose to Joanna. "You want to be with...them and not specifically me." Each word came slowly, while complete clarity remained elusive. Until she worked out in her head that scene of Joanna pursuing Baldred, not any other, not upbraiding Nicholas. Baldred, with whom she'd previously spent so much time. "You didn't want Baldred to leave without you," she guessed, piecing all of it together now. "You were afraid you would never see him again."

Joanna's brightening blush answered while the maid pursed her lips, trying with little success not to smile as she stared only at her left foot, which she'd lifted and scraped back and forth about the dry grass. She was pretty now, more so than Alice had ever noticed before, her cheeks pinkened, her hair streaked with golden highlights, a dimple showing on either side of her mouth.

Alice's heart instantly turned to mush, and she moved her hands from her cheeks to cover her mouth completely, lest anyone see so much awe converting the one person in this party who should be, or at least feel, most ill-used right now.

*Saints alive*, but it was almost comical—her life ruined presently and Joanna possibly the happiest, most hopeful Alice had ever seen or known her.

She could not help but tease her friend, "By all means, Joanna, do not allow my untidy kidnapping to stand in your way. So pleased I was able to abet your cause." She'd not snickered or sneered those words, was truly humored by how ridiculous was Joanna's timing and her actions.

Joanna lifted a sudden frown to Alice. "But they dinna need to ken anything but that I'm here for ye."

"All right, Joanna." *You sly fox*, she thought, her own vexing predicament momentarily forgotten.

A few minutes later, Baldred walked his steed over to them.

"Slow going from here on out," he advised, "As Dungal's lady took a stone, mayhap two, and now we'll mind her pace."

Alice considered Baldred now, with greater notice than any she'd afforded him previously. Seen in a new light he was—apparently the object of Joanna's affection, she was just finding out—though before now he'd only been the MacRory captain, an outwardly even-keeled fellow with a sometimes short fuse for Joanna's verboseness but who at this moment was sending what he might have thought were surreptitious peeks toward Joanna—which provided the remainder of insight for Alice—and who was suddenly simply a man evidently smitten with a woman.

Alice nodded at his statement, belatedly, as her mind was elsewhere, while Joanna struggled to not look directly at Baldred and more, pretended she did not know he stole so many sweet glances at her.

*Good grief.*

"And now, lass," he said next, wearing a nearly-pained expression, "we dinna want ye to imagine we think poorly of ye, though it might be a wee difficult to ken otherwise, what with a kidnapping—this time for real—and that one," he said, hooking his thumb over his shoulder toward Nicholas, "behaving as if ye personally done him an injustice and ye should no be concerned that any harm'll come to ye, 'cause ye ken us by now, and ken that is no' our style—we dinna normally take out our pique against the, ah, weaker, ah...and well, just so ye ken, yer safe now, same as ye were, and God willing, we'll have ye back in yer mam's embrace...er, soon."

By the time he'd concluded that rambling, mumbled speech, given with so much foot-shuffling, Alice's jaw hung quite low. She caught herself, however, only a split second before Baldred lifted his gaze to her and gave a succinct nod, which thus concluded his—she wasn't sure it was categorically an apology. Alice managed a nod herself, also not entirely sure that she was required to express any appreciation for his kindly-meant words when the fact remained that he had willingly participated in her abduction.

Possibly she was more confused than ever and in the next second, she shook her head, hoping to clear the hazy, disbelieving fog, and turned away, imagining they might be about to move again.

Whatever it was that brewed and bloomed between Joanna and Baldred in no way diminished her resentment toward her own predicament, but between her newfound knowledge of it and Baldred's simplistic though meandering act of contrition, she felt abruptly less spiteful toward the entire scheme, despite how vexing it was.

But if she thought there might be some relenting, some lessening of the rage that had enveloped Nicholas after their brief and unexpected respite, Alice learned but quick that she was mistaken. The average person, such as Baldred, might know or entertain some form of remorse for what they'd thrust upon another, for what they'd done to one innocent of any crime. Nicholas MacRory, she recalled, was not an average person.

Standing beside his monstrous destrier, he waited her arrival, watching her with what she believed might be purposefully narrowed eyes, meant to intimidate her further. In this Alice knew immaculate clarity; Nicholas would much prefer that she was terrified, that she shivered and shriveled in fear before him.

*Oh, bother that*, she thought, so blessedly weary of being shoved around and controlled by callous brutes who thought only of themselves and their own ambitions.

Thus, she was loathe to accept any aid from him and brushed his hand aside with annoyance when he moved as if he might assist her in mounting. She didn't care that it took her several tries to lift her foot into the high stirrup, and she surely didn't concern herself with whatever he might make of the fact that she'd thrown one leg over the far side of the horse, desiring to ride astride so that she could ignore him completely.

Gritting her teeth, she stared over the horse's head, lengthening her back to sit proud and straight, as Nicholas mounted behind her. She ignored the arm he slid around her and held herself rigidly as he kneed the horse into a slow walk.

"We'll be forced to slow our pace now, in consideration of Dungal's steed," he said, his tone yet infused with so much misplaced aggression.

Alice did not deign to acknowledge this at all.

"Might no' reach Braewood on this night, as I'd hoped," he said next, annoyed by this likelihood.

She said nothing.

After five or so minutes had passed, his tone had soured further. "Ye'd rather that we no' speak at all, I gather."

He was miffed at her? At her! Because she did not want to engage with him?

"Aye, let us do that," she said bitterly, hoping to remind him of the icy words he'd spoken to her after he'd kissed her and then attempted to dismiss her. Recalling her own words at that time, which had instigated his harsh response, she added, "Mayhap you are regretting having kidnapped me and would like to pretend it never happened."

# Chapter Thirteen

The going was indeed slow, though there was little to be done about it. Dungal did not grumble or bemoan his circumstance, having to walk the remaining miles while he allowed his steed an empty back. Still, Nicholas was not eager to spend the night out in the fields when Braewood was within reach. So they marched on most favorably even as darkness fell in a heavy blanket as this landscape was well-known to them and most of it was over level, congenial ground.

He waited for exhaustion to claim Alice, for the stick to be removed from her back, so that she collapsed against him in slumber. His mood was yet sour enough that he would have collected even that as a victory. But Alice maintained her rigid posture, a feat of either great desperation to disprove her weakness or of sheer obstinacy, borne of an intent to thwart any of his suppositions about her.

He might have told her she needn't have bothered trying to prove anything to him. He was familiar with her fortitude, and he wasn't feeling particularly triumphant at the moment, or at any time since they left the de Graham house. There was no victory in this meager conquest, which was naught but his own desperation to have that army promised him. That was as far as his thoughts took him in that direction, despite the recriminations of Dungal and Baldred earlier. He did not in this instance consider anything beyond the basic facts: Nicholas had taken something from de Graham, same as the baron had stolen something from Nicholas, an eye for an eye. As soon as the baron's original promise was met, Alice would be returned once more to her family. Presently, it was fairly easy to disregard whatever trauma Alice might know for her unwitting part in this play, since he knew better than anyone that she would be wholly unscathed when she was once more delivered to her mother. One person's short-lived distress was of little significance when freedom was at stake.

He thought it might be nearing midnight when they finally gained the ground of the MacRorys. Malise rode ahead to announce their presence at the gate. Nicholas was sorry the moonless night offered so ungenerous a view of Braewood, the tall, curtain wall being naught but a black shadow around the keep itself. Inside the gate, only half a dozen torches were lighted, making bright circles against the stone where they hung, lighting little as the bailey was empty at this time of day.

"Is this..." Alice began and then cleared her throat. "Are we stopping here for the night?"

With all the pride usually attached to any announcement regarding his home, Nicholas informed her, "This is Braewood."

Her response was not as expected. Not at all.

She barked out an unkind, unladylike snort of laughter. And 'twas not only one brief, disrespectful chuckle, but it went on, with Alice tipping back her head to sound out her scornful judgement. Her soft hair brushed against his chin while Nicholas stiffened at her unexpected reaction.

"This is Braewood? But we might have reached this in only a few hours if not for Dungal's lame horse."

He was sure that she delighted in prickling his ire and was determined to ignore her, but she continued.

"This is where you intend to keep me? Naught but a few hours away from my father, who no doubt does gather his army now and with the intent to storm your house."

Through his clenched teeth, Nicholas reminded her, "Yer sire has proven he has no' the bo—" he caught himself and decided against the vulgarity of *bollocks*, "the courage to engage in such a fight, one he would ken he would lose." Almost immediately, he questioned why he thought he needed to spare Alice any profanity, so weak a concept, when he'd just kidnapped her at sword point, almost literally out of the arms of her parents.

"So what is to be my fate, then? Held prisoner all my life since you've just said you don't believe my father will come for me."

"Surely, I'm no' telling ye anything ye dinna already ken. Yer sire allowed ye to be taken—twice now and each time from his own hearth—and was it he who rode to yer rescue down to England? Nay, 'twas no'. He'll no' be coming to save ye now. But yer mam will, I'd wager. She'll round up the army herself if she has to, is my thinking. I would no' be surprised if they're here within a fortnight. I put greater faith in her strength of will and her care for ye than I do in yer sire."

Right away, he was weakened again by the sour taste of regret, for having raised a suspicion in her that her sire did not love her enough to either have kept with the terms of their agreement or to mount a campaign now to see her rescued.

Angrily, he thrust aside such frailty and brought his leg over the back of the saddle, smoothly dismounting. He did not offer to assist her, which was not a bow to her preference but only his dark mood partly hoping she was compelled to ask for his aid. And then he was not surprised when she managed to alight herself, albeit with about as much grace as she had mounted earlier this evening, swinging her leg over the back as he had done, but then only sliding down the side of the horse while she clung to the saddle until her feet touched the ground.

Godfrey, roused from his bed inside the stables, came lumbering from that building, wiping sleep from his eyes with the back of his knuckle. Nicholas laid the reins in his hands and took Alice by her arm to steer her into the keep. Dungal went directly into the stables with his mare, possibly to attend the bruised sole or to give instructions to the stablemaster, Fionn, about the care he wished for the horse. Malise and Henry would go off to the barracks and likely find their beds straight away. Baldred, with his hand similarly upon Joanna's arm, followed Nicholas and Alice into the keep.

At this moment, Nicholas was quite pleased for the late hour, hoping he encountered neither of his sisters, not in the mood to withstand the numerous and anxious queries that would inevitably come. He'd given only brief consideration to what might be done with the two women once they arrived, having disregarded the tombs below the keep as their prison as a last resort, to be used only if needed to coerce good behavior. The family apartments upon the second floor were all occupied, by himself and his sisters, while the fourth chamber upon that floor offered no bed but only a lady's solar. Thus, he planned to house them upon the next floor—separately, so that escape was less likely since he knew that Alice would not attempt to flee without taking Joanna with her; he had some baffling inkling that Joanna would not make an effort to escape at all. Upon the third floor there were several empty chambers awaiting the occasional guests Braewood saw, in addition to the smaller sleeping quarters of the house servants, those who did not work directly in the kitchen and keep rooms on the ground floor.

He marched Alice up the wide timber stairs from the great hall and proceeded to the end of the second-story hall to find the smaller, twisting staircase at the end of the passageway, where they climbed again, with the light of only a single tallow candle ensconced in the wall. Upon the top floor, he quietly opened the door to what should have been an empty chamber but was immediately startled by a figure jerking up from sleep upon a low and narrow cot.

A gasp came from within, and Nicholas mumbled a curt apology before pulling the door closed, wondering who that small person was, but not enough to intrude further upon their privacy. In addition to the sporadic visitors Braewood entertained, they did sometimes open their doors to weary travelers, and it was not unheard of that the keep might be full. He hoped that was not the case and pushed open the next door, this time not startling anyone though clearly the bed was inhabited, this time by a larger shape with a noisy and uneven snore.

"Full house, ye have," Joanna whispered in the darkened hallway.

"Bluidy..." he murmured now, contemplating little hope as he approached the next and last possible chamber where they might be accommodated.

Thankfully, this chamber was indeed vacant, the thin and rather short cot tidy and available to fill.

However, there was no way both women would rest comfortably inside that too-small bed. Cursing again under his breath, Nicholas pulled Alice away from the door and waved his hand so that Baldred and Joanna might enter.

"Joanna will be housed here," he clipped, his mood only worsening.

He'd been prepared to have to spend the night, possibly several, just outside the door to whichever chamber he installed Alice, taking what rest he could upon the hard timber. He had not expected that he would have no place to house her. "Go on," he encouraged sharply when Baldred and Joanna seemed to hesitate.

"But what—" Joanna began, sending a fraught glance to Alice.

"She will be kept elsewhere," was all he said. To Baldred, he advised, "Ye can manage this from here?"

"Aye," Baldred nodded, with so much less upset than expected.

Pivoting to retrace his steps, Nicholas caught sight of Alice's smug expression. She was quite pleased to see him confounded by this unexpected twist. He declined gentleness then, yanking on her wrist to urge her to follow. Her self-righteous mien alone should have seen him walk her straight down to the crypts, but even he wasn't that kind of monster.

They returned to the floor below and Nicholas threw open the arched door to his laird's chamber, propelling Alice inside. She spent a few seconds looking about, possibly encouraged by the large four-poster bed and thick coverlets in the center of the room but whirled swiftly when she heard Nicholas close the door behind him.

She swallowed noticeably and lifted one hand to clutch nervously at the neckline of her gown.

"What...?" She began to shake her head, slowly at first. "Oh, no. This is your—no, I will not."

"Apparently, there is no other available chamber," he said, not without a hint of remorse for this circumstance, the most unsustainable but which would have to suffice for tonight.

And everything that was soft and graceful about her evaporated, replaced by this frantic lass, shaking her head wildly, showing wide and desperate eyes. She lunged forward, compelled by panic to touch him, grabbing at his arm.

"You can't do this to me," she cried, her voice tremulous. "Nicholas, put me in the dungeon or the stocks or the stables, tie me to a tree. You cannot expect me to share a—my God, lock me in here and find your own bed elsewhere."

"I am no' about to give up my own bed for ye." He could not, and only be seen as gratifying the whims of a prisoner. It would diminish his own worth and authority inside Braewood if he showed such weakness.

More pitifully, she begged, "Please don't do this to me. I-I will be ruined. This is not a lark, this is my life."

"And no one outside of Braewood will ken where ye were kept," he said, avoiding her desperate gaze as he removed her claw on his forearm. He stepped around her and went to the hearth, where he knelt and began tossing peat and kindling into the belly of the fireplace.

A swishing of hectic movement behind him brought him to his feet quickly and sent him charging after her as she made for the door, and reached it, but thankfully fumbled with the latch in the darkness that he was on her just as she unlocked the door and pulled it open. Without reacting too forcefully, he laid his much stronger hand on the door above her head and pushed it closed against her while she struggled valiantly to pull it open.

When it was clear she could not outmaneuver him or over-power his want to keep the door closed, she dropped her fore-head against the cold oak while her shoulders sagged.

"You are...beyond despicable," she murmured in a small, de-feated voice. "And heartless."

They stayed like that for quite a few seconds, she sagging against the door, one hand splayed on the wood below his, and he directly behind her, close enough to be reunited with her primrose scent and to know she trembled, though with rage or despair, he did not know.

"Alice," he said, as gently as he could with yet so many wild emotions roiling inside him.

"Don't," she snipped at him. "Do not even speak to me."

SHE WAITED, HOPING he would assume her forlorn posture signified acceptance, and that he would abandon his position at the door. He did not of course, and likely would not until she moved herself away.

Holding back the tears that wanted so badly to come, and after a full minute might have passed, Alice turned and stepped away from the door, out from under his arm. Of her own accord, she walked listlessly to the farthest corner of the room and sank down against the cold stone wall, drawing her knees up to her chest.

This changed everything.

Her entire life.

This kidnapping had turned seriously ruinous. Whether she was ever recovered or not, she was destroyed.

Funny, she thought, she'd known today first confusion and then a rampaging fury at Nicholas for his actions, but she truly hadn't known fear, had not for one moment thought he would hurt her. But this now, this was devastating, a situation from which she could not rise above. She was indeed harmed, and irreparably now.

How simplistic was his view, supposing no one outside this keep would know of her position, kept within the larid's bedchamber. The tale would have been told dozens of times, from ear to ear, and likely before she met even the first or second or third person who carried the damaging narrative.

The fact that her mother might not suspect she'd been plummeted into so dire and irrecoverable a circumstance offered little relief. Alice flung her arms over her knees and nervously nibbled at one of her fingernails while her gaze followed Nicholas MacRory—a beast indeed—around his bedchamber.

He'd lifted the lid of the trunk at the end of his bed and stood before it, the small fire and its glow at his back. He doffed his plaid and spent quite a few minutes folding the long fabric into a much smaller and very precise square, which was laid in the trunk. He scratched at his jaw, his face angled just enough that the scar upon his cheek, which Alice now sullenly decided was grotesque and well-placed on him, was highlighted to malevolence by the short, flickering flames. He lifted the hem of his tunic up from his waist and raised his huge arms fully to pull the shirt over his head.

Alice had only a glimpse of his broad and muscular chest before she sulked and ducked her head into her arms, not wanting to see any more.

He continued to undress, she guessed, by what little noise he made, and Alice retreated into her own thoughts, tapping one foot in a rapid repetition that did little to soothe her.

She'd been angry earlier at his unwillingness to consider any other avenue or recourse with her father, for having resorted to his beastly tactics, kidnapping her, but she wasn't sure she'd hated him even then, despite what she might have said to him.

She did hate him now, she was sure. Or at least, she was determined to hate him or pretend as much. And yet of greater concern, far more important than what emotion she attributed to Nicholas MacRory, was the idea that if she did not escape on this night, there was almost no point in escaping at all. The damage would be done.

Her thoughts froze when she sensed his presence very close to her. She stopped drumming her foot and waited until he went away.

"Alice."

Judiciously, she raised her face, just enough to peek out of one eye. She thought she would go mad with rage if he were standing naked before her, even as she felt certain that a man such as he most certainly slept in the nude. But her squinty gaze above the arms in which she'd hid her face showed his powerful thighs first and those were yet clad in his breeches that she felt it was safe to lift her head and eyes completely.

Immediately, she understood she'd been wrong. It was not safe. He wore only his breeches, but nothing else.

Thus, she was forced to lift her gaze up from his legs, over his lean hips and hard-as-stone abdomen, alive with a surfeit of detail in lines and ridges. Above that, she confronted his massive chest, sparsely blackened with short, dark hair, but glorious in its symmetry, each side of his chest being raised and sculpted with singular, fascinating attention.

He offered a hand to her, the slight motion moving shadows and contours all over his chest and arms, across valleys and latent muscles.

"Ye canna sleep here," he said.

"I—I can." She cleared her throat, forcing her gaze higher, into his unfathomable eyes, more shadowed than any other part of him. "I will. Do not presume to increase the damage by insisting otherwise." *Please, I beg you.*

"I dinna trust ye here," he said without emotion. "I need to sleep. And I need ye beside me. I sleep lightly and ye would no' be able to move upon the mattress without my waking."

Meaning she would not be able to escape, even if he were sleeping. Haughtily, she advised, "You might as well end it here and now. Claim your sword, you vile brigand. Finish it. There is no way I will sleep in the same bed with you."

"I'm no' going to argue with ye. I can simply lift ye up and drop you in the bed."

Having no other choice at the moment, she allowed a hint of pleading to enter her gaze and her voice. "Please. I know there will be talk. I know that I will be ruined. But allow me this, at least, the ability to hold my head up in any moment in the future, knowing the truth, that I stayed right here."

He seemed to reflect on her words, and she knew a tiny satisfaction when his hand fell away and he turned from her. For a

moment he stood with his back to her, no less formidable or cap-
tivating as his front, so chiseled and hard, carved by a raw sculp-
tor who appreciated form and sinew and sharp lines.

He planted his hands on his hips briefly and turned his gaze
around the room before he moved again on bare feet toward
that trunk that had since been closed. With relative ease, though
the piece appeared monstrous and weighty, Nicholas shoved it
across the room and positioned it against the door. Likely, Alice
would be unable to move that thing at all, not even a few inches,
to squeeze herself out of this chamber.

Without another glance at her, he left it there and strode
across the chamber once more, this time laying himself across his
big bed on his stomach. He folded his arms beneath his pillow
and turned his face away from Alice and very quickly was still
and silent.

Alice stared unblinking for several minutes, wishing all kinds
of horror on him. She hoped the roof mysteriously caved in on
his head or wished what looked to be a very soft mattress might
be riddled with bugs. She prayed he woke with a fever, brought
by whatever god righted wrongs, and that it raged for days, and
he was made insensible and bereft of memory.

She did not detest herself at all for such cruel imaginings. In
fact, she then spent the better part of the long night crouched in
the corner plotting alternately either her escape or his demise.

# Chapter Fourteen

Nicholas woke, no more refreshed than he'd been in weeks, despite his return to his most comfortable bed and home. Immediately upon waking, he turned to his side, even as he did not really expect to find Alice there. She had sustained her obstinacy all through the night. Propping himself up on his elbows, he found her yet in the same corner in the same position, though her legs had fallen to one side and her head lolled on her chest. At least she had slept, for however long or well.

She would believe he planned it or that he reveled in it, this untenable situation of sharing quarters, though he did not. 'Twas only one more irksome thing with which he must contend. Not that he subscribed precisely to her certainty that word was bound to escape the keep and travel anywhere outside the MacRory acreage.

With a ragged sigh, he dropped back onto the soft, feather mattress and stared at the timber of the ceiling, gray above his head while the sun shone in from the window upon only one square on the floor.

So often any return to Braewood conjured reflections of this place and his role within it. Even a shorter journey such as what sent him initially down to the de Graham home and then to London on that fool's errand summoned musings of puzzlement: was he pleased to be here, or was he more at peace when away?

The bewilderment was mired wholly within, born of how miserable he'd been here as a child, disregarded at the coming of the new and very young wife of his father, witnessing with derision how his strong and proud sire had been so easily cowed and made weak by that woman, giving into her every whim and wish. When finally Nicholas had realized his long-held desire to be away, to put his sword to the test at the advent of war, he'd proven his valor and steadfastness again and again until that melee at Falkirk where he and several of his ilk and under the same tartan had been taken as English prisoners. And what did he crave then, while held in an unforgiving English prison but just these walls of Braewood. Upon being granted his freedom in one of those rare exchanges of prisoners—meaning the Scots had finally seized some Englishmen of value—and returning to Braewood, Nicholas had learned of his stepmother's demise and had witnessed firsthand and again the power that woman had maintained over his father. The once great Laird of Braewood was naught but a shadow of his former self, weepy yet though half a year had passed since her death, and ineffectual in his governance. Nicholas had been equally incensed and embarrassed for how far his father had fallen from greatness, from the pride of strength. He'd vowed then to be diminished by nothing, by no one, to never be so despicable a person as his sobbing father had been. After putting things right inside Braewood, installing Ranald as steward and Iòsaph as bailiff, ousting those his father had relied upon but who had proven both greedy and incompetent, Nicholas had taken his leave again.

He'd sought, for some time once returned to war, to prove his own mettle, to demonstrate his own resistance to vulnerability and impotence. He'd fought recklessly and wildly, having little care for his own safety. At the time, the idea of helplessness had terrified him. For as strong as he thought himself, it remained that he had been taken prisoner, had not managed to escape, had known fear inside that prison; for as strong as he wanted to be, he might so easily fall into despair as had his father, if he but allowed it.

Becoming a soldier of fortune had seemed the most expedient way to stave off any uncertainty about his worth and his strength and his ability to withstand either adversity or such feeble, damaging concepts as compassion or tenderness.

It had started simply enough, as he'd met with the bishop of Moray and John Comyn, to give evidence of his time in captivity. They'd taken his statements and then, with seeming innocence, had inquired what next he might do, if he would still fight for Scotland. He'd advised at the time that he would fight more, and better, and be a worthier champion of Scottish freedom. They had been pleased with this answer and wondered next if he might better prefer a more clandestine role, working independently.

And so it had begun.

His first task, with men of his choosing, had been simple enough, to disrupt the supply lines moving from England to their armies garrisoned inside Scotland. Next, he and his men had been asked to meet and disband those hired mercenaries brought by ships from Ireland at Loch Ryan.

After a while it became apparent that not only the bishop and Comyn knew of his covert endeavors, as more requests came for his sword. When the war lagged, usually over winters, Nicholas found other work. He had once spent two months with the MacDuff laird about his holdings in Kincardine, making war on his neighbor and enemy, who thought to unlawfully extend his own sheriffdom in the same region.

They had only been twelve men, Dungal and Baldred included, and all that when Nicholas had been naught but the presumptive heir to a northern keep, naught but a nameless mercenary. If his stepmother had born a son, he'd likely still be about that unkind business, would never have returned to Braewood.

And Nicholas had suffered no reservations about what his role had been for those few years, his conscience devoid of any remorse at the time, as he knew he was only conditioning himself against weakness while ridding the world of those who deserved the taste of his blade. Rarely had he questioned the justification of any hired work, nor the reasons behind it, be they authentic or valid or not.

For more than a year, so few knew the identity of the person they hired to protect their own interests or make war in their stead upon their enemies. He and his elite unit had worn chausses and helms and kept upon their persons no item that would identify them as MacRorys. For so long, Nicholas had not donned his plaid at all or carried the tartan with him. But then he'd not asked any client for discretion and took no greater precautions to remain unknown that soon whispers of the Brute of Braewood Keep had reached his ears, and by all accounts, every corner of Scotland. The Guardians of Scotland and the nobles had looked the other way, so often contracting Nicholas for those illicit and secret operations themselves.

At about the same time, word had reached him that his father had passed, that his young step-sisters had been orphaned, that Braewood was without a warden and defender. The growing alarm and threat that came with any mention of the Brute of Braewood Keep suggested that he, himself, might only have become a target so that he'd retired his hired sword and had returned to Braewood.

And then the truest and most difficult battle had begun, to settle into his role as warden and landholder and sheriff, which required more of those tender attributes he'd fought for years to quell. Guilt had crashed hard and mean upon him then, for how zealously he'd committed himself to so many heinous deeds and sins. He was unworthy of this role, as leader, as chief, as protector of such innocents as his step-sisters, his days as a mercenary leaving him decidedly unfit to rule justly or answer any squabble or slight in any other manner but by the tip of his blade. In all probability, he would never believe he was the proper person to lead these people, not when his heart was so black, when killing was what he knew best, not crops and crofts and sheep and shearing. For all that he had worked so hard to remove any weakness in himself, he feared that he no longer recognized the man he was, certainly knew no pride for what he had become, what he had made himself.

At the same time, he resisted any hint of wonder at the whispers of truth that lived within him, that he wanted to know and experience something that was not base and mean and destructive. Easy to reject, those musings, since that was weakness in and of itself, to be curious about something so worthless—as what? Joy? Peace? Delight in another? Any or all of those things were fleeting. One should not search their lives and sacrifice so much to find them, how wasteful. The alternative, what he did well—the lack of feeling—was sustainable, a level sea upon which to sail, unshaken by any waves.

Deciding he'd deliberated long and uselessly enough, Nicholas made to rise. Just as he threw off the bed coverings and put his feet on the floor, the door to his chamber banged against the trunk he'd wedged there as someone attempted to enter without first knocking or announcing themselves.

Alice was stirred to wakefulness in the corner, puffy-eyed, her gaze darting instantly to his as he faced her.

"God's blood, but what is this?" Was grumbled from the other side of the door.

"'Tis a deterrent," he called over his shoulder at the door, "and one I beg ye heed."

"I will not." His sister, Ellen, was not to be dissuaded. "Nicholas MacRory, unbar this door."

"*Jesu*, Elle, but can ye no' regard so verra substantial a hint?"

Alice rose to her feet but did not vacate the corner.

"But what is happening, Nicholas?" His sister persisted. "'Tis said ye've abducted a woman, and that ye have her here, just here in yer chamber. With ye!"

Nicholas sighed and rubbed his hand over his sleepy eyes. "Go on, lass. I'll join ye anon. But ye'll get nothing from me if ye dinna heed me now." He did not look directly at Alice now, not wishing to find her certain contempt, for his sister's near panic that matched Alice's of last night, because she'd been kept inside the bedchamber with him, and because this information had indeed already begun to circulate.

"Bugger him," Ellen complained, seemingly to another.

In all probability she spoke to Violet, his youngest sister, who like as not would make no response, mayhap cared little about such goings-on but was dragged here by Ellen.

He eyed Alice again, her face hidden in the shadows of the corner, while she stood with her arms folded around herself.

It dawned on him that they'd been forced to miss the supper her mother had planned for them last night, that they hadn't eaten in almost an entire day. For this, a wee guilt gnawed at him until he thrust it aside, even while his own stomach currently protested the lack as well. Coming to his feet, he invigorated himself with a slow and lazy stretch, flexing his arms above his head. Next, he returned the trunk to its usual position at the foot of the bed and garbed himself in a fresh tunic.

"We'll get on below and break our fast," he said casually to Alice, having some hope that civility might soon be known between them. He left his plaid inside the trunk, having no need of it today as he had no plans to stray outside of Braewood.

And mayhap a lack of animosity was her intent as well, but that she chose to remain silent for fear that she could not actually put forth any statement that did not portray any discourtesy.

Nicholas strode to the door and pulled it open, sending her one more level glance, inviting, "Come," before he left the chamber.

She followed but with enough hesitation that Nicholas was forced to slow his step upon the stairs.

In the great hall, he paused, his teeth grinding with a new unpleasantry, the identity of those visitors who'd been found in the bedchambers last night. Of all the poor timing...

Ellen noted their arrival and strode quickly to meet Nicholas and Alice, giving none of her attention to her brother but all of it to Alice, who remained upon the last step as Nicholas had stalled just off the stairs.

"Welc—" Ellen began with more cheer than one might suppose a host would use to greet a prisoner, and which was interrupted by Nicholas.

"Ye might have said that Edgar and Marjorie had come to call," he hissed at Ellen, turning his back to the hall.

Ellen scowled at him. "Aye, I might have, if ye'd opened the door and allowed that misfortune to be made known." She swapped out her scowl with the return of her smile as she faced Alice. "I am Ellen, the laird's sister—half-sister, he would insist," she said. "I'm no' certain what he's done or why, but I wanted to welcome ye to Braewood."

"I am Alice de Graham, and I thank you for the kind welcome. And yet forgive me if I hope I shall not need it for long."

"Och, and like as no', you'd wish no' to need it at all." Ellen skirted around Nicholas and threaded her arm through Alice's. "But we'll make it sweet while ye are here, as best we can. Come and sit with my sister and me and you can tell us all about it."

Rather than raise more brows throughout the hall than were already lifted, Nicholas allowed Alice to be led away from him and knew he had no choice but to greet Braewood's guests.

He approached the trestle table where sat Edgar Ailred, the self-important and intrusive brother of Nicholas' stepmother, who styled himself as a descendant of Máel Coluim mac Alaxandair. Edgar was pleased to disremember that his presumed ancestor was naught but a bastard of Scotland's King Alexander I and had never amounted to anything more than a failed pretender to the Scottish throne. At his side sat his daughter Marjorie, who was akin to her father in disposition, supposing a two-centuries-removed ancestor gave her rights and status above many others, and likely grateful daily that she was not also similar to her sire in appearance, being vaguely attractive, not as portly or as unfortunate looking as was Edgar.

Edgar, seated at the high table as he might have been for days or more now in Nicholas' absence, charted Nicholas' progression across the hall with a shrewd gaze, his small brown eyes flicking back and forth between Nicholas' approach and beyond him, to where he'd left Alice in his sisters' company.

"What brings ye round, Ailred?" Nicholas asked, refusing to call the man *uncle* as he'd requested, and refusing further to extend any welcome, as the corpulent man was known to take advantage of Braewood's generosity. The very sight of him, in his English fashion of silks and fur and pointed shoes, with that tricornered felt hat tipped cockily upon his head—so ill-suited to any northern province—rankled Nicholas more than most trivial things did.

Edgar replied in garbled noises, spewed from a mouth filled with the morning's repast. Nicholas did not understand a word he said, but then also did not desire clarification.

Briefly, with little sincerity, Nicholas bade welcome to Marjorie, who had always struck him as either thick-witted or too easily cowed by his scowls, those that were ever shown to her being the by-product of her hand-wringing anxiety in his presence—a vicious cycle then, as her mood fed his and vice versa until he could barely stand the sight of her.

Nicholas rounded the table and took up the laird's chair, not drawing it close to the table, but keeping it set apart and angled so that he could keep one eye on Alice, as she'd been brought to and seated at one end of the high table herself, flanked by Ellen and Violet.

"Forsooth," said the man, now three chairs away from Nicholas, and with a dollop of porridge hanging from one corner of his mouth. "And with fortuitous timing, I gather, as I found your keep left unattended, and gladly plied my proficiency to both your steward and bailiff. Have set several matters to rights, I reckon, for which I am sure you will be pleased."

"I suffer no ill-confidence in either office," Nicholas returned, "for Ranald and Ìosaph ken my wants and wishes and can manage well in so short an absence."

"And what did take you away from Braewood at such a dangerous time?"

"Braewood business," Nicholas hedged. Before Edgar might have pursued this further—he would have, for certain—Nicholas inquired, "And what of this dangerous time?"

"Of grave concern, the fears to the north," Edgar said around the food in his mouth. "The MacWilliams and the MacHeths, those incurable enemies of the Scottish crown—such as it is at the moment—have broken into rebellion against all those loyalists that surround them."

"Have they now?" The MacWilliams and the MacHeths of the north were always warring with someone. "I would put my coin on the loyalist forces, if that be yer concern, Ailred."

Edgar thinned his lips and glanced aside at Nicholas. "That is not my concern, lad. My concern lies in which side of the battle Braewood and the MacRorys will lean."

Nicholas scoffed. "Braewood, nor any of us within her boundaries, will claim any position in a fight that will undoubtedly be short-lived, and which has little bearing on our own survival."

"That, dear boy, is not the position you should adopt at this perilous time."

"And yet, that is my position, which you may feel free to report to whoever sent ye." He wasn't sure why the man should make the journey—in dangerous times—simply to know on which side of the fence Nicholas sat.

"I am not dispatched or directed by any person, as well you know."

Nicholas shrugged, and casually laid his gaze once more upon Alice, catching the hint of a frown about her as her head moved from one side of her to the other, between Ellen and Violet. Facing Ellen now, and thus Nicholas' direction as well, he supposed she called out his sister about something, easily recognizing that tense and anxious look of hers, which said she disagreed with either an idea or behavior and was now challenging it.

"I came in accord," Edgar went on, supposing he had Nicholas' attention even as he stared over his head at Alice and not at him, "with a thought only for the survival of Braewood, and with the offer of my daughter as your mate, to align yourself more closely with the line of Alexander, with whom those MacHeths and MacWilliams claim kinship as well, and not with any descendant of the usurper, that next Alexander."

Nicholas drank long and slowly from a horn of ale, supposing he should not be surprised by anything that gushed from this man's mouth. *That next Alexander* happened to be Alexander II, not at all a usurper as Máel Coluim mac Alaxandair most decidedly was. He'd reigned adeptly if not always ideally for nearly four decades and had been the father to their well-beloved and widely-mourned king, Alexander III, whose death had opened the door for the war with England in which they were presently engaged.

His gaze stayed with Alice, who had made quite an about-face in his sisters' company and was now smiling—albeit barely—at something Ellen said. She turned and faced Violet, who pulled her chin out of her hand and said something to Alice that widened her eyes and caused her smile to expand, until she tamped it by first rolling in her lips to smother it and then covering her mouth with her fingers to hide her response altogether, though it was still seen in her crinkled, laughing eyes.

All that glory left her, though, when she noticed Nicholas' silent regard. For the space of a second, she smiled at him, or so he chose to believe, even as he knew she did not. It faltered soon enough, her smile, but she did not tear her gaze from him. He could not say how much time passed, seconds counted by single digits or by tens, while he probed and tried to decipher her blue-eyed gaze. He did not blink until movement before and beyond Alice gained his awareness, the rapt gazes of both his sisters turned to him.

Giving away nothing by his expression, Nicholas once more forced his attention to Edgar Ailred, and addressed now his outrageous proposal. Briefly, and without explanation, Nicholas said, "I see no need to wed, certainly not in this instance." Or for any other reason. Shaking off the spell unknowingly cast by an unwitting Alice, which he was not keen to have possess him, Nicholas met Edgar's shrewd gaze. "Sadly, it seems ye have journeyed for naught, Ailred. And ye, Marjorie," he added, recalling her presence slightly on his right. "There is no union to be found here, and again, no interest in what bedevils those warring factions of the north."

Averting his gaze from the abominable man, Nicholas looked out over the hall and noticed two more visitors seated among the people at the trestle tables. Both garbed in black from head to toe, looking like malevolence upon two legs, Nicholas recognized them as Ailred's hired thugs, the muscle that the simpering Ailred never traveled without.

"Well," Edgar replied, seemingly unperturbed by the curt dismissal, "there's bits about your discharge on both accounts that I'll take issue with."

He had a way about him, an inexplicable incapacity to know any shame, that his next shocking statements were uttered without a hint of diplomacy or hesitation.

"As kin to the Brute of Braewood Keep, I've made vows in your stead, giving assurances of your commitment to the cause held dear by the descendants of Máel Coluim mac Alaxandair. I've said that aye, you'll take up arms with them." He shrugged, using a long fingernail to pick at some bit of food between his teeth. "Or, at the very least, I promised you were good for a bit of coin to finance any attempts to right former wrongs."

And while Nicholas now favored him with a ferocious scowl as his blood began to boil, the simpleton who was kin to his stepmother dropped the second shoe.

"As it is, 'twas no' only a swift journey, begging respite and aid for the cause, but we've come to stay, Marjorie and me. As kin to the wife of the former laird of Braewood, we ken our place would hence be found here since we were cast out of our humble home. The loyalists thereabouts think me a traitor, and neither the MacHeths nor MacWilliams would come to our rescue—"

"Unless ye returned with pockets filled with MacRory coin to convince them of your fealty," Nicholas guessed, this gritted through his teeth, his fury only rising when the full picture unveiled itself to him.

He lifted his hand with the intent of pounding it upon the scarred wood of the table to advise Edgar of his wrath but stopped his fist before it fell. 'Twas a grievance and rebuttal that did not need full attention of even the few souls that remained inside the great hall.

Uncurling his fist, he slowly laid his fingers upon the wood without a sound.

# Chapter Fifteen

"We've met your woman, Joanna, already," said the lass who'd given her name as Ellen.

Another shock. The brute who'd kidnapped her could claim sisters? And they were human and not beasts themselves? Young and bonny and this one with so impish a grin? Impossible. Shouldn't any kin of the beast be made with fangs and claws, same as the beast himself?

'Twas only her sour mood supposing such fanciful things. Inwardly, she was forced to admit that until yesterday, Nicholas MacRory had given her little cause to assimilate him with any four-legged brute. On the heels of this, Alice was then compelled to acknowledge that it had been her father's actions that had unsheathed the claws.

"She is quite something," Ellen went on, as she led Alice toward the high table, following in Nicholas' wake, "marched straight into the kitchen and made herself useful. I saw her first bearing the baskets of bread to the hall. And there was me, staring at this comfortable stranger in my home with my chin sagging, and doesn't she introduce herself, says I must be related to the laird because we bear such a striking resemblance—I've never heard that before, I can assure ye," she said, and then leaned in to whisper, "so it was she who alerted me to your circumstance and how she'd come to yer aid—what a good woman—and that was how I learned of yer existence and dashed straight away to Nicky's chamber, but lo, he's as crusty and cagey as ever, so that most of my life is only wondering what he's about." She indicated a chair, third from last at this side of the table and Alice mechanically sat down, her head spinning for how quickly the lass spoke. "And so...why did he kidnap ye? What did ye do to him?"

"Me?" Alice gasped and thumped her hand to her chest. "I haven't done anything to him." She cast a sharp eye about Ellen, judging her swiftly: of an age similar to Alice's nineteen years, with russet hair styled sleekly, not a loose strand to be found in her tight chignon, with lines already formed upon her brow between her hazel eyes, and whose silver léine appeared both costly and immaculate.

"Well, he's volatile and no' impervious to a grand fury , but he's no' unjust," Ellen stated. "Forgive me for assuming ye might have earned it."

"Earned a kidnapping?" Alice repeated. "I'm not sure that is even possible."

"Maybe he only stole a bride."

Alice's head swiveled around to the other lass, who'd taken the seat on her left, who until now hadn't made a sound.

"And you are?" She inquired with a raised brow, borrowing a bit of her mother's infrequent haughtiness.

The girl shrugged. "I am only Violet." She set her elbow on the table and her chin in her hand. She appeared as untamed as Ellen did refined, her auburn hair either uncombed or uncooperative, her green eyes not so bright as they were deep, wearing a saffron belted gunna overlaid with an embroidered mantle that was swept around her shoulders and neck in a fashion that was either outdated or not yet known to this realm.

Alice sat back in her chair, to afford herself a view of each sister on either side of her at the same time. "Earned a kidnapping? Stole a bride? You are both quite mad," she decided, "to behave so indifferently toward something so disastrous as an abduction." She knew no remorse for how bitter she sounded, or for what blame she laid at the feet of these lasses, for they were entirely too detached from the calamity of Alice's circumstance and their brother's part in it.

Neither appeared properly chastened that Alice's shoulders sank. No help here, then.

"Oh, but you've come," Ellen said, "willing or not, at the most opportune time."

"An opportune kidnapping, "Alice murmured, "how fortunate for all of us."

Ellen tilted her head at Alice. "Sarcasm does not become you."

"Indifference does little for you," Alice retorted.

Unaffected, Ellen continued, "That's Uncle Edgar and our cousin, Marjorie. We've been putting up with their grotesque company for three days now. Nicky can take his turn."

Alice made no determination about the chatty man, whose voice she'd heard almost non-stop, but thought the lass, Marjorie, at quick glance, appeared harmless enough. She did think it strange that both Ellen and Violet had not invited their cousin to dine with them at this end of the table.

Violet offered no opinion and did not tax herself to look toward her uncle and cousin even as Alice briefly sent her glance that way.

"I am right suspicious," Ellen went on, "since the oaf requested, upon his arrival, that I give up my own bedchamber for him."

Alice thought that alone should not have warranted such reproach. She herself had, over the years, sacrificed her own quarters for guests and visitors inside the de Graham house. She began to wonder why she cared, save that Ellen spoke of these matters as if they were of concern to Alice, or mayhap she wanted them to be.

"But you haven't yet explained," Ellen said next, "why Nicky abducted you."

"Mayhap you should ask him," Alice replied. She didn't know them at all, wasn't sure what they should know about their brother, or what she was willing to divulge to them.

"He won't allow us anything but some vague non-answer, which will in no way feed my curiosity," Ellen revealed.

"Perhaps he—"

"Did you attempt to harm him?" Violet asked. "Or another? Someone weaker than you?"

"Weaker than me? Trust me, no one feels weaker at the moment than me." She did not specifically think she might gain an ally—or two—but she did decide at the moment, she should not be charged with protecting either Nicholas' true nature, or even that of her own father, from these two lasses. "The truth is, your brother initially rescued me, from my first imprisonment."

Ellen's eyes widened while Violet's brows furrowed.

"Sweet Mother Mary, but from what netherworld do ye hail?"

Ellen's genuine reaction, which was amusing as it supposed something to be wrong with Alice, shocked Alice into a wee silent chuckle, but it was eclipsed by Violet's response.

"Bluidy bollocks, ye are a nightmare then, and so imprisonment is all that can be conceived to contain ye?"

The absurdity of this speculation was worse than Ellen's and elicited an unruly burst of laughter from Alice. How fanciful these two were!

No sooner had she lost control and laughed than Alice covered her mouth, trying to rein it in. A prisoner should not be giggling, even in the company of these two. Their brief, startled interlude of quiet laughter was interrupted as Alice discovered Nicholas' gaze upon her, as spied beyond Violet.

As ever, his golden mahogany eyes were nearly unreadable. All her misplaced mirth evaporated, replaced by whatever it was she felt whenever he regarded her in such a piercing manner, as if he wished to ascertain every secret she had ever hidden. Mayhap only those that related directly to himself.

With a quick gulp to swallow her reaction to him, which for a moment forgot altogether to aim any of her justifiable—but sadly forgotten-in-the-moment—anger at him, Alice wrenched her gaze from his.

She'd only returned her attention to his sisters but for a moment before Ellen gasped quietly, her gaze set beyond Alice and Violet, but which effectively turned their attention toward the center of the table.

Nicholas' jaw was clamped and his fist was lifted as if he would slam it with great force upon the table. He did not, though. While the man, Edgar, paled a bit at his side, though still chewed upon whatever he'd last shoveled into his mouth, Nicholas opened his hand and flexed his long fingers, and laid them softly upon the table.

As if they were better or longer acquainted, Ellen clutched at Alice's arm just as her brother began to speak to the middle-aged, portly man, his tone malevolent for its low and dangerous quality.

"Always, ye presume too goddamned much, Ailred," Nicholas raged quietly and slowly at him, enunciating each word to highlight his fury, "to come unannounced, uninvited, and un-welcome, and then to own so heavy a sac that ye say to me ye've set things to right inside *my* keep, and within *my* affairs. And ye say ye'll barter yer daughter for a union from which only ye would benefit, but in lieu of that, would take coin or mayhap a promise of an army for a cause that has no direct bearing on me." He blinked slowly and his jaw moved left and right. "Ye make promises in my name—which, for the umpteenth time is no' yer name—and pledges that I will no' adhere to. I owe no allegiance to any but mine—and ye are no' one of them, Ailred. For years you have taken willingly which has thus far been given without complaint, but I find in this instance my goodwill is at an end. For the sake of Ellen and Violet and even yer own Marjorie, who might be either an unwitting pawn or wholly innocent of yer self-serving schemes, I will no' insist upon yer leavetaking, but ken this, Ailred: my affairs and that of Braewood are no' any of yer concern and the next time ye make promises in my name or attempt to interject yerself into MacRory matters, ye will with-out concession be cast out from Braewood."

Flustered, the man's head swiveled in many directions, want-ing to see who or how many had witnessed this merciless up-braiding. His bleary gaze landed briefly on Alice and his nieces, no doubt all uniformly wide-eyed with astonishment before he faced the laird again and stuttered, "But, lad, ye mistake—"

"I am no' *lad*," Nicholas interjected in the same lethal tone. "I am *laird,* and no' anything else to ye."

With that, Nicholas stood from the table and further shocked Alice by striding angrily in the direction of her end of the table, barking at her, "Get up. Let's go."

Before she thought to refuse him—later, she would realize she wouldn't have; his fury was as frightening as what he'd shown at that de Graham house yesterday—Alice had risen from her chair and made no complaint when he took her arm in his hand and paused only to instruct his sisters, "Say nothing to anyone of what is our business."

His step-sisters made gestures of compliance, Ellen's nod given with so much more consternation than Violet's shrugging assent.

Alice didn't dare question what he wanted with her, not in his present mood, and might have supposed immediately that he only meant to place her in some locked or guarded room while he removed himself from the hall. But unless she was to be kept somewhere outside the keep itself, she was clueless then as he led her out the door and into the yard.

So strident and quick was his gait that Alice had only a brief impression of a quiet yard though was sure she felt eyes on them from the outbuildings, possibly from within the stables or farrier's or smith's shed.

"I canna leave ye in there, unprotected," he said, by way of explanation after they'd cleared the gate.

His hand fell away from her arm, which Alice rubbed unconsciously as she followed resolutely in his footsteps along the dry dirt of the lane. She spared a glance backward, upon the tall curtain wall, manned by watchful soldiers, and over the iron clad, thick oak gate, which was more closed than open. Facing forward again, she swept her gaze over the unending vista of hills and fields and white-capped peaks of faraway mountains. A chill shivered her slender frame, an unaccountable frisson of iciness that came in spite of the warm, summer sun, for the remoteness of this keep, the land about so barren as to be thought forsaken.

She wasn't quite sure that he hadn't abandoned her within because he was worried about her safety, despite his mention of protection. She thought more probably he was concerned that she might have reached out to the man, Ailred, to aid her own cause. Possibly, the man was not an outright enemy, but he was certainly an untrusted adversary, which Nicholas might imagine thus made Ailred her friend.

After they'd marched on for dozens of yards, he with his long, angry strides, Alice dared to ask, "Are we going somewhere?" There was nothing around but the quiet, still landscape. No breeze stirred the grass or moved the air. The sky overhead was only one long stretch of blue, devoid of even the smallest cloud. Nothing moved but them, it seemed.

"I am walking off the steam that rages to a boil inside," he said.

Alice slowed her step and then stopped and held her hand up over her forehead to impede the sun.

When he noticed this, he turned a questioning scowl onto her. Though he did not move then, he was poised for action. There was about him, as ever, that coiled energy, that restless vitality, which made her understand that inaction or repose or stillness was not done well by this man, and then less so when his temper flared.

And yet, "I have no steam to exhaust or expel," she told him, pleased to confound him.

NICHOLAS STARED AT her with still-seething eyes. She was not cowed, of course. She knew his wrath was not directed at her.

He sighed inwardly and set his hands onto his hips. He'd only taken her away from the hall because he didn't know what to do with her. The circumstances that had warranted her hostage-taking had not necessarily allowed him much forethought. He'd not worked out yet what might be done with her all day. In lieu of keeping her under lock and key, he wasn't sure how much he trusted her to not flee the keep. But then he had no recourse against her, not really. She knew as well as he that he would never raise a hand to her. Whether he would or not against her father was uncertain. Dungal's benevolent violence of yesterday aside—he'd shown commendable restraint—Nicholas wasn't sure he could cause Alice pain by any attack on her sire.

Weakness. Vulnerability. Flawed, all of it, which he detested even more than the treachery of others.

"I need to ken that you'll no' try to flee," he said to her. "If ye give yer word, I'll accept it as truth." Despite who and what her father was. "Otherwise, or in the event of any such attempt, I would have no choice but to lock ye away until…"

"Until my father's army is brought here," she finished. "Yes, I recall."

She was stoic and not without a certain amount of anger herself.

"Ye may walk about," he clarified, "but no' anywhere outside the wall but with me or an approved escort."

"Of course," she said, her lips pursed a bit. "And will I be tethered to any one person or mayhap different ones throughout the day? Shall you loop a collar around my neck and chain me inside your bedchamber at night? Am I allowed to speak to only certain persons—"

"That's enough," he snapped at her, his temper still riled from that scene with Edgar. "I dinna mind reminding ye—as often as needed—'twas the actions and cowardice of yer own sire that predicated my response."

She threw up her arms. "But of course. It's all perfectly acceptable then. Pray do not allow me to distress you with my bellyaching about something so worthy and righteous as an abduction."

Ignoring this provocation and the want to rebut, he growled at her, "Can you say, in good faith, that ye will no' attempt to flee, or will I chain ye to the bluidy wall?"

Her gorgeous mouth spread into a thin-lipped line, and he knew she wrestled with lying to him, vowing she would not try to escape simply to have the freedom to do just that. It took her near to a full minute to give her assent, and it did not come easily. A plethora of expressions crossed her bonny face, but mostly she was angry at him for extracting a promise from her. If she'd not been forced to give a vow, most certainly she would have tried to flee.

"I give my word," she said finally.

Enough challenge was presented in her fierce gaze that he believed she almost dared him to spew the thought in his head, which hoped her word was more reliable than her sire's.

Somehow he knew that it was.

Next, her face softened, the anger receding as the matter was settled, replaced, it appeared, by a bewilderment.

"What happened to that man who rescued me from the de Lisle house?" She asked, with her hand yet lifted to hinder the sun's glare.

Nicholas snorted his contempt for what she hinted at. "He was reminded of the weakness of men, of the deceptive minds of his enemies."

"But then which is real? That man or this one?"

"They are the same," he insisted. *But for what I allow you to see*, he thought. Aye, he'd been too solicitous of her in the beginning, made soft by the initial distraction of her—which had not faded but which he had under control.

Or maybe not. And damn her, for being so bold and bonny, for having not the proper fear that a hostage should.

His steady gaze bore into her, sweeping over her face and settling with intent upon her rosy lips. In a few short strides, he closed the gap of space between them and slid his arm around her waist, jolting the breath from her as he drew her against him. Before she might have protested—if she would have—he claimed her mouth in a savage kiss, meant to remind her of his power and his authority, and of her own weakness. He moved his hand behind her head, forcing her to slant her face against him as his lips twisted across hers, demanding and not gently. Where their chests met, he felt the hammering of a quickened heartbeat, but could not say 'twas only his that raced. She pushed against his arms even as she went limp in his embrace and moved her mouth with great torment against his. The kiss advanced swiftly to a hungry and mutual desire and tongues were met and joined. She tasted of the morning mead and smelled yet of those damn primroses. He slid one hand down over her softly rounded bottom and the other into the loose midnight tresses and held her fast against him. His body's response could not be either unnoticed or mistaken, his shaft leaping to life against her. Nicholas groaned within and flexed his fingers into a hard grip on her ass, and plundered her sweet mouth with his tongue.

And the purpose of this display of might and control was forgotten, his entire consciousness aroused by the feel and taste of her. Until her arms crept upward over his shoulders and around his neck, and Nicholas growled his displeasure at being drawn in and lost to his own game, and he tugged roughly at her hands and thrust her away.

Realizing what she'd done, what she'd yielded to him and how effortlessly, the final shove came from her. Her hands inside his grip managed to push against him, and they were thrown apart. Panting, their mouths burning, they stared at each other until Alice whimpered, the sound reflecting her anger at him, and the shame reserved for herself and her response to his fiery kiss.

With a cry, she drew back her arm and struck a vicious, openhanded slap across his face and then gasped at her own assault and held her breath in stunned surprise. He might have thwarted the blow but did not, supposing this too would serve a purpose.

He forced his lips to curl in scorn. "Ye forget yer wish to ken some freedom within Braewood, it seems,"

All the violence drained from her face, and she gaped at him, seeming only to wait his reversal of that verdict.

"Fear no', Alice. My word is my oath, same as is yers."

She closed her tantalizing lips with a snap and lifted her head proudly, pivoting on her heel to march back toward the keep.

With his grim smirk intact, Nicholas followed her.

# Chapter Sixteen

Knowing Nicholas was directly behind her, Alice strode briskly back to the keep and straight into the hall. There she was met almost instantly by Joanna, who let out a cry and rushed her just inside the door as if it had been more than twelve hours since they'd seen each other.

Joanna squeezed Alice tightly in her embrace, holding the pitcher from which she'd been serving out and away from her body.

"And dinna I fear, all the blessed night," Joanna said, keeping her voice to a whisper, as much as she was capable of, "wondering what hell ye'd endured, what dark crevice ye might have been caged in."

She drew breath to say more as they parted, but Joanna caught herself, clamping her lips as Nicholas appeared, and did not pause as he passed, though did wither them with another unpleasant scowl. And then she did not expend any time or energy by asking about any particulars of the *hell endured*.

Joanna lowered her head and her voice yet more when Nicholas was several paces away. "And then I heard, it straight from those sisters—and I dinna ken either of them yet, one too chirpy and the other too silent, and the latter is no' to be trusted, ye ken—that he kept ye in his own bedchamber. And he stayed there with ye! So now, I've failed, first night about my mission, and I dinna ken what I'll say to yer dear, sweet mam, who like as no' is sickly with the grief and her with no idea how—"

"Joanna," Alice interrupted, laying her hand on the woman's forearm, "why are you serving here?" 'Twas naught but a distraction, to put her into a more practical frame of mind. Indeed, Joanna's anxiety and worry had never done anything to soothe Alice's. "You owe neither time nor labor to this house."

"That is true, I dinna," replied Joanna, the severity of her uneasy mien lightened by this neutral topic. She shrugged. "But ye ken I'll no' only sit and watch. Would be batty by day's end, with nothing to do to fill the hours." She lifted the pitcher, waving it vaguely in the direction of the high table and possibly the kitchens beyond. "I've said I'd teach them how to dress the pigeons in a finer manner than what they were getting about this morn. They're cooking the bacon now, because ye ken I'll no' eat any squab that's no' cooked in pork grease."

Unable to help herself, Alice grinned. All was right in the world so long as Joanna was instructing someone, somewhere about the best practice for some*thing*.

Over Joanna's shoulder, Alice spied a young girl, twitching nervously, stepping from foot to foot, skimming her gaze around the hall. "Might that lass be looking for you?" She asked of Joanna when the child's wide eyes landed and stayed on Joanna's back.

"Och, and sure she is," Joanna confirmed after a quick glance over her shoulder. "Bacon must be done. Ye come on with me, Alice, and we'll keep ourselves like mice, scurrying about but bothering none."

"You go on," Alice advised. "I desire only solace at this time."

With a nod of little concern, other than what she knew for the roasting of the pigeons, Joanna took herself off and Alice strode through the hall, head held high as she climbed the stairs to return to her prison chamber. What use had she of making friends or more enemies inside the hall? Either her time at Brae-wood was to be short-lived or if not, she would only grow to resent these people more for holding her hostage. Of course, there was nothing to occupy her mind inside the chamber so that Alice only leaned against the single window in the room and watched the goings on in the side yard, over which it looked. Pitiful little activity there to engage or hold her attention, since she was offered a view of only one side of the keep, where sat the bakehouse and the kitchen garden. Thus, she was forced to reflect upon her own most recent foolishness, her utter naïveté, which was made so very obvious by how quickly she'd succumbed to his kiss.

It had not been as their first kiss, was neither desired nor softly given or taken. He'd kissed her only to show that he could, to put his power on display. Still, it had been potently effective, much to her dismay. Oh, how she wished she were made of sterner stuff, so that she might have resisted. At all. A man taking such liberties was bold enough, and to such easy play she'd given in previously. But now, he was strictly and most definitely her enemy and Alice knew a great shame for her behavior, for all the strong will she knew she possessed but which hid itself so cleverly when his lips touched hers.

She leaned forward, planting her elbow upon the warm stone sill and her chin in her hand. Beyond the bailey and the curtain wall, looking east, the vista was stunning, a majestic view of summer's bright green grass and the rolling hills in the distance. Soon, she hoped, she would gaze out this window upon a sunny day and see her father marching an army toward Brae-wood. She would be released, freed, and would finally return to her home for good.

And at that time—even if it killed her, and it might—she vowed that the moment she left the MacRory keep, she would never waste another second of her life with any thought of Nicholas.

A quiet knock turned her head around to the open door.

Violet stood there, looking about as pleased as Alice was surprised.

"Violet?" She said when the girl said nothing.

"Nicky requests," she began, her displeased tone and the slight rolling of her eyes giving away her thoughts on the matter, "that ye no' keep yerself cloistered all the live long day."

"I have no desire to—"

"I dinna want company anymore than ye want to expose yerself to all the talk and the certain lurid gazes sure to follow ye, but both yer life and mine will only be sweeter if we simply do as he wishes."

"You do realize that such unhesitating compliance only feeds a greater expectation of the same?" Alice thought to clarify.

"Aye, as ye do," she said. "But simple is nice, is it no'?"

Alice harrumphed a quiet laugh. "Aye, it is. And what am I to do with you?"

"He dinna say," she said and shrugged.

"So his specific want is left to our understanding," Alice assumed, grinning at Violet.

Who caught on quickly. "It might be."

"Then let us do what we will, Violet. Or rather, do as you would, and I will follow quietly and unobtrusively."

Violet's pretty face, mostly bland or charged negatively until now, showed brows lifted in wonder and just the hint of a grin, not unlike her older brother for its charm. "Aye, and I like ye so much better already."

Violet then disappeared from the doorway. Alice debated only briefly not following the youngest MacRory. If she stayed and thereby thwarted Nicholas' plans to keep her occupied—which Alice was quite sure also meant to keep eyes on her so that she did not attempt to flee—he might himself come to the bedchamber and cause her more grief. Thus, she lifted her skirts and dashed after Violet.

She remained about half a dozen paces behind the lass until they had left the keep and the yard, in the same fashion as she had with Nicholas only an hour ago. Once past the open gate, Alice skipped ahead to catch up.

"I will not pepper you constantly with bothersome queries," she said, noting as they walked along that Violet was almost exactly as tall as she was herself, "but where are we going?"

"Away," Violet answered simply. "To the quiet."

Intrigued by this, Alice walked on with the girl, her step lighter.

For a while, Alice did wonder if Violet knew precisely where *the quiet* was, since she seemed to travel in a circuitous and nonsensical route, westerly at first, through a thicket of trees, but in such a manner that Alice was quite sure they walked past the same aged and fallen oak. The landmark tree was rather unmistakable as it had not broken in half, the top of it falling away from the bottom, but the entire tree had been upended so that the whole base of it and all those tangled roots and so much earth surrounding it lay on its side, standing taller and wider than Alice, while the trunk was yet intact.

Before the trees thinned and opened completely, Alice had already a glimpse of sparkling blue and surmised they were approaching a loch. And when this was confirmed and she stood before the majestic lake, glinting with the morning sun, she gasped in awe at the splendor. They'd come from that wooded area, at the same elevation as the water, but as far as the eye could see in any other direction the loch was encased by hills of wildflowers, more color than Alice had ever seen all in one place, so bright and beautiful.

She imagined if she had brought some unsuspecting person to this stunning and bountiful—and quiet—place, she'd have stared at them with so much expectation, awaiting their reaction. Violet did not, only sat close to the water in the short grass there and began to remove her soft-soled boots.

Supposing the girl meant to dip her toes into the cool water, Alice thought she might like to join her.

But then Violet began to remove more of her clothing, shucking the affectation of a mantle and the very old gunna and then her hose, all of which she dropped carelessly in a pile on the grass.

Only her shift remained as she walked into the loch.

"Oh," Alice let fall from her lips.

Violet turned when she was knee-deep in the lake, while the skirt of her shift floated around her legs until it soaked up enough water and sank against her. The curious tilt of her head contrasted with the skinny-eyed gaze that probed Alice.

"I would wager ye never partake," she said. "Dinna crave the tranquility that comes as the water pulls ye in, away from the world, or the weightlessness, the calm."

"Um, well, no," Alice replied, feeling as if she were being judged. She waved her hand to shoo away a bumblebee that buzzed too close. "But then I guess I never really thought about it."

"Nae, I dinna suppose ye would. But here, in the water, everything that drowns in me can fly."

Alice didn't know what to make of this girl, who was entirely too young for the old clothes and her old soul and certainly such weighty reflections as these. *Everything that drowns in me?*

Presenting her back to Alice, Violet walked out until the water lapped softly against her thighs and then only seemed to fall forward, her hands raised in front of her. She disappeared completely beneath the surface in one smooth motion, barely disturbing the water but for what rolled and plunged downward with her. A few seconds and a few feet away, she reappeared, but only to draw breath before vanishing again beneath the blue water.

Alice wasn't sure if she were intrigued or not by the prospect of submerging herself so fully in the water. But having removed her own boots—she had no hose to doff since Nicholas had not allowed her time yesterday to don that luxury—she waded into the loch. Violet spared her no more attention, possibly seeking the calm and quiet, now twenty yards away, drifting listlessly upon her back, her arms flung wide and skimming the water's surface slowly up and down, as if they were wings.

The water was not as cold as Alice had imagined it might be. She lifted the hems of her skirts and moved her feet carefully over smooth flat rocks and the sometimes squishy floor of the loch, her gaze flitting often to Violet until either envy or a greater curiosity—mayhap a bit of both—sent her back upon the grassy shore, where she bravely doffed her léine after thoroughly sweeping her gaze around the area to be sure that no one was about to discover her half-dressed.

Her next entrance was both cautious and not without a wee dread for what came after, when they emerged from the loch, their shifts dripping with water. Assuming Violet had a solution for what seemed not only a trifling consideration, Alice boldly waded further this time.

She didn't ever swim, wasn't sure she knew how or wouldn't drown herself if she strayed too far or too deep, so she remained close to shore, where the water rose only to the top of her stomach, but knew a wee inquisitiveness for how Violet had floated on her back. Alice tried the same. It took several attempts to keep her legs and body afloat, to manage the drifting with some success. At one point, she was dunked completely when she panicked and floundered, briefly unable to find the bottom. But soon enough, she figured it out. And then the quiet of which Violet had spoken came, as the water covered her ears. Alice closed her eyes, enjoying this tremendously. When she opened her eyes, she saw only the blue sky and in her periphery the green of leaves of the surrounding trees hovering over the water. All at once, she felt incredibly vulnerable and then so very detached from anything else. This almost—not quite, but *almost*—made her abduction worth it, for this benefit she'd learned and earned.

Violet had made the floating look easy but Alice realized it required a bit of steady effort and she wondered if she looked more like a drifting and flailing red deer, not meant to swim, as opposed to Violet's graceful, swan-like coasting. Somehow even this did not bother her overmuch, so entranced was she with the serenity of this activity.

She closed her eyes again and swayed her arms and legs.

Her thoughts drifted as well, invariably, maddeningly, to Nicholas MacRory. And his kiss. And his kidnapping of her, and how effortlessly he executed both of these, seemingly with so little forethought. And how distinct they were, each separate action, how one clearly contradicted the other.

Unless...well, unless his actions were as simply explained as were Joanna's, who'd forced herself upon the fleeing abductors, not wanting to be distanced from Baldred.

Alice's eyes popped open and, torn from the serenity of drifting aimlessly, her arms and legs stalled, and she quickly began to sink. And then thrown into disarray again, she flapped her arms and legs until her feet found the floor and she stood motionless and stunned in waist deep water, her back to the shore. She gave only a vague awareness to Violet, closer than she'd thought her to be and still peacefully adrift, and stared blindly across the sun-streaked water while her jumbled thoughts began to unravel themselves.

A sudden noise in the tranquil area startled Alice and turned both she and Violet toward the water's edge, where sat Nicholas upon his great destrier. The horse pawed the earth and Alice believed that had been the sound that disturbed her. But Nicholas sat very still, his hands laid loosely over the pommel, as if he had not only just arrived but had sat and watched them for a while. Watched her, mayhap, as his blistering amber gaze chewed her up right now.

He was striking just there in that position atop a magnificent stallion, large and impressive, his tawny hair tousled and streaked by the morning sun, an apparition, it seemed, a feral hunting beast come looking for prey.

The scorching gaze he leveled upon her was not anything she hadn't ever seen before. Despite a sudden quickness of breath, she wasn't unduly concerned, had little fear for what looked to be a great exasperation. She wasn't sure his sister's presence would save her from any scolding if he deemed her indecent swimming worthy of reprimand, but she thought Violet's presence would certainly spare her another kiss that rendered her witless and wanting.

"I said to ye, no' an hour ago, that ye were no' to step outside the wall." His voice was low and angry, but not nearly as terrible as what he'd used on that man, Ailred, earlier. "I am left to assume that ye only beg to be tethered, as ye suggested yerself."

Her most recent musings about him resurfaced and, disregarding the menace of his words and the subject matter, and before her brain could stop her, Alice said to him, almost lightly, "I begin to think your kidnapping of me had more to do with want than need."

His furrowed brow softened only marginally though his lip curled in contempt.

"In much the same manner," she explained, "as Joanna not wanting to be left behind. You...you didn't want to leave me." It was all speculation, born only seconds ago, but Alice wanted to know if she might be right.

He scoffed at this, not with sound but only a darkening glower and the glint of steel that entered his hard gaze. "You are mistaking me for a much weaker man."

Of course, a man like him would see it as such. "I think you are mistaking weakness," she said softly.

No resolution then, to her supposition, as she could not read his expression aside from the very obvious and always simmering anger.

Though he stared her down, Alice did not wince or falter—not until he let his gaze roam with purposeful leisure over all of her that was visible above the water line at her hips. She swallowed convulsively and knew great difficulty not lowering her own gaze to see what was available to his, somehow managing to refrain from wrapping her arms around herself to conceal her near nudity. It infuriated her that with only this leering and tight-lipped perusal, he could make her feel so powerless, as is she were naught but the wary and defenseless prey, and he the mighty hunter. Damn him, for all that he seemed only to want to shame her now.

Alice stuttered in both rage and embarrassment, "Y-you were rather unclear about the direction given either to me or your sister. I imagined that since Violet was sent at your behest and charged with my keeping, that she was an *approved escort*."

"She is no', and I dinna want ye so far from the keep." He said all this while his golden-brown eyes remained transfixed by her breasts, where surely, and to her great mortification, her nipples were hard and poking through the soft, wet cotton.

How awful he was, she thought, to use this sort of intimidation. Still, she was not so much fearful as she was vexed.

And then the full weight of what she knew about this man twirled about her brain and she knew she'd been foolish, to have been blinded by her fascination with him, most of which was tied to his kiss.

Flushed of cheek, Alice tilted her head, wanting him to feel the weight of her scorn, lest she suffer hers alone, and brazenly said to him, "Just now, with your disparaging ogling, meant to shame me no doubt, you remind me of any man inside the de Lisle house, whom I'd so often thought of as insignificant, loathsome creatures. I am trying at this moment to imagine what appeal you hold." She narrowed her eyes and turned up her lip as he had done. "If any. Aye, your kiss is tempting to an untried girl such as myself, but aside from that—and cannot any man accomplish the same?—what have you to promote yourself? Honor? Compassion? Kindness? None of these things, not that I've seen." Her mood was so agitated by this realization and what looked to be a mountain of mockery in his dark eyes that she walked out of the water, daring him not to feast his gaze upon all of her, whatever the soaked and clinging shift might show him.

Behind her, Violet whispered with a combination of awe and smugness, "So it's like that, is it now?"

Alice ignored her and then Nicholas as well, giving her attention to her footsteps as the rocky parts of the lake bed were closer to the shore.

When her feet touched the grassy ground, she shook out the hem of her shift and sat with her back to Nicholas, tipping her face up to the sun. She was dismayed to discover that her words were truth: he had nothing to recommend him, not any virtue that should draw and hold her attention, as she'd just so bitterly realized. He wasn't worthy of either her disdain or what distress she'd known from his contemptuous appraisal of her.

"Get dressed now and come on back," he said sharply behind her, likely put out that she'd sat down as if he did not await her.

"I will when I am dry, and not before then," she said over her shoulder, staring out into the lake and at Violet, who didn't have too many expressions but just now showed widening eyes for Alice's daring.

Quiet sounds of movement behind her advised that he might be leaving. Alice kept her gaze fixed on Violet and the tremor of her chin to a minimum until the girl began to come to shore.

"He's gone," Violet said as she sat next to Alice.

Only now did Alice quake with all the emotions she'd held at bay during her confrontation with Nicholas. A harsh breath seethed out through her nose as she clamped her lips to keep from crying outright.

"That will no' see any boons come yer way," Violet predicted, "no' speaking to him like that. But aye, ye're no' too far from the mark. And I dinna ken ye before this day, but ye've sprung leap and bounds in my estimation."

An anxious and trembling laugh erupted from Alice, but her heart was sore.

She'd truly thought him a decent person, only bedeviled by circumstance, angry at everything around him but not exactly at her. Until he'd torn her to shreds with that ruthless and merciless gaze.

# Chapter Seventeen

It took several hours and a bruising ride atop his splendid stallion for Nicholas to recover. Even then, regaining both his wits and his equilibrium came only in bits and pieces for everything that the morning had thrust so unpleasantly upon him. Edgar's part in Nicholas' sour mood faded quickest, certainly in light of all that Alice had left him to stew and simmer with.

He struggled to recall exactly her words—her uncharitable set down, as it were—each attempt hindered by the memory of her, one of many from this day alone, one more mesmerizing as the next, though none could compare with his first glimpse of her at the loch. From that alone, he might need several days to recover.

All the anger at finding her gone and then so far from the keep had been overwhelmed by the sight of her when he'd come so quietly upon the loch, as she'd been gliding so artlessly and enchantingly upon the water. Aye, he'd noticed Violet as well, diving and swimming, seen and then not, but Alice...well, Alice had been mesmerizing, a sea nymph cast adrift, surely made to tempt any warm-blooded male to his demise.

But his reaction to the mere sight of her had angered him further, that he was weakened by only that.

Not least of all, not by the furthest stretch of the imagination, by what she had shown him, first unknowingly while she only floated about, her round and firm breasts highlighted daringly by the wet chemise; but next with that beguiling blush of hers when she'd realized what had garnered so much—all, for a time—of his attention when she'd righted herself; and finally with so much defiance as she'd walked out of the water, revealing the full scope of her glory and leaving him agitated and nearly breathless at the vision of her, her trim waist and lithe legs, the flare of her hips where the wet chemise had caught and sat, her nipples peaked to pebble hardness.

Aye, but that defiant strut from the water! Surely, by then she must have known that he was not immune to all that was displayed. And then she'd behaved so brazenly, thumbing her nose at him, as if she would have him believe she were unaffected by his inability to remove his hungry gaze. As if she were a queen, and merely thought to gratify a peasant with some nominal keepsake that would cost her nothing but ensure his faithfulness. Never in a year of days would he have imagined that she'd so audaciously march herself up upon the grass so scantily clad and exposed in front of him. It hadn't been done to entice him or tease him with the sight of something he could never have; she wasn't made like that, wasn't worldly enough to have recognized that kind of power and vindictiveness in herself just yet. It was simply her way of telling him that he meant nothing to her, that what he saw or thought bothered her little, that he wasn't worthy of her concern over something so trifling as her half-garbed state.

And all that exceptional bravado and for...what? Because he'd taken her to task for not adhering to what she herself had promised early, that she would stay within the confines of the keep and yard? Or for that grossly misjudged statement of hers, supposing he'd not wanted to be parted from her? Or had she sensed his fury, which he'd not been able to hide, but which was only self-directed, for yearning so intensely for something that could never be his?

*Could never be his*—not before this day and certainly not now. To do so, to know her, to touch that porcelain skin or stroke his lips or fingers over those flawless, pale breasts would only serve to reinforce her opinion of him, that he was without honor.

Reining in sharply, the curt action timed perfectly with his snort of disbelieving disdain, Nicholas blew out a harsh breath and gnashed his teeth.

*I think you mistake weakness*, she had said to him.

The words themselves had been exasperating, that she would dare to presume to know him or his mind. And then more infuriating, for the memory those words recalled, that of his own sire spouting a similar nonsense on the one and only occasion that Nicholas had called him out on his complete and utter devotion to his stepmother, when that woman was gone, and Robert MacRory could not seem to find his center of gravity anymore.

"Enough," Nicholas had railed at him with little tolerance. "Enough with the never-ending grief. She is gone but ye are no'. There is work to be done, a bluidy war to fight. Ye dinna need her to live yer life."

To this day, half a decade later, Nicholas could well recall the look his father had given him. A smile had come, not a soft and easy one, and not one meant to sneer. He'd been, Nicholas believed at the time and since, stunned by what he likely perceived as Nicholas' callousness, stunned that his son's thoughts leaned in such a way. The smile had evolved though, to some bittersweet thing exchanged often between the sage, old parent and the young, all-knowing child.

*This, you will learn*, the smile had foretold.

Without shame, his father had said to him, "I would do it again, and for so much less, would live all these years again to know only those few with her or even a fraction of that time."

Possibly, the old man had followed that up with a philosopher's guess, *One day you will understand.*

Bah. Nae, he would not.

Nicholas spent the entire day away from the keep, and then purposefully kept his distance from the loch, just in case. One small aspect of the otherwise disagreeable day did provide him with a measure of calm. Sadly, he did not consider it until much later in the afternoon. Part of his initial fury at discovering Alice gone had come when he believed that she might have fled. It did not occur to him until well after their meeting at the water's edge that she hadn't, that she was or had seemed at the time until his presence had been detected, at peace, if not with her circumstance then at least with Violet's company and their leisurely pursuit.

THANKFULLY, SHE DID not see Nicholas again for the remainder of the day. She'd visited briefly with Joanna when she and Violet eventually returned to the keep, possibly much later than Nicholas had hoped or expected. The fact that he had not waited on her and personally ushered her back to her prison imbued her with a sense of calm.

"Och, and he was fearsome, lass," Joanna related in her breathless way, her hand patting at her chest as if her heart raced. "Could no' find hide nor hair of ye, no' anywhere about. Raised such a ruckus, he did, had me fearing as well and I'll beg ye—and ye too," she said, pointing a finger at the unsuspecting Violet, "to be so kind as to save all that gadding about till when I'm safely dead. Could ye do that for me?"

"Yes, Joanna," Alice had obliged. "I apologize for having worried you."

"'Tis no' me that ye need to worry about, but yer own dear mam, and that poor woman tested beyond sanity already, is she no'?"

Alice dared a fleeting glance at Violet, who stood beside them, and caught her eyes moving back and forth between Alice and Joanna, her mouth open.

"Mayhap I should make myself scarce," Alice suggested, "and take a tray in the...or rather, abovestairs?" There wasn't any part of her that wanted to convene inside the hall with any other person for the last meal, certainly not if it meant she would be forced to suffer Nicholas' presence. 'Twas already weighing heavily upon her that she would spend the night with him in his bedchamber.

Joanna nodded with appreciation. "Aye, and that'll be one of your better ideas, lass. Like the meadow hare, ye should be, quiet and well-behaved, and leave no mess in yer wake."

Alice nodded and then grinned at the still-gaping Violet before she turned and ascended the stairs. Behind her, she heard Joanna say to Violet, "Ye had nothing to do with any of that, I should hope. Ye look like a good lass, but I dinna mind setting ye straight if ye need it."

Violet's murmured response was lost as Alice turned around the corner.

There was little with which to amuse herself until a platter arrived, courtesy of some unknown and very young kitchen girl, and at that, Alice only picked, not particularly hungry. So then she seemed only to wait until darkness came, so that she might sleep.

With the darkness came a roiling wind, which howled through the tapestry covering the window. A quick peek out in the gloom showed a darkening sky filled with black clouds, which were shoved swiftly across the night sky by the strong gusts, tumbling and turning and spilling fat droplets of rain, though this came without any great volume. Happily, both she and her shift were long-dry by now, but with the wind and rain came a chilling draft and seeping cold and Alice knelt before the cold hearth to replenish the peat and kindling and light a fire.

While she was about this chore, the door opened and Nicholas entered. She spared him only a brief and mute stare and when she found his gaze to be as unfathomable as ever, she allowed her gaze to be mesmerized by the beginning flames.

"I will see to that," he offered, his tone devoid of its customary bite.

His boots appeared in the boundary of her gaze.

Shaking her head, she advised, "It's fine. All set, I think." And she remained where she was, part of her fearful that if she claimed her corner space, she might once more have to bear witness to him stripping his body of his clothes. She wasn't sure this day could withstand any more upsets, certainly not ones of that sort. Thus, she lifted her hands out toward the flickering flames, pretending she only desired warmth at this moment.

Closing her eyes, she listened for his movements to speak of his actions: the trunk lid being opened, his belt and sword being removed and set near the bed, his boots as they were dropped to the ground.

"Alice," he said when several long seconds had passed with no sound discerned behind her.

Turning her head only fractionally on her shoulder, so that she saw only the door, but appeared to acknowledge him, she waited.

"I am compelled to—can ye no' turn and face me?"

No, she wanted that least of all. "I'm sorry. I am so suddenly chilled. The fire is soothing." It should be, the warmth of it, but nothing was soothing about being alone with him inside his bedchamber, and he probably garbed now as indecently as she had been earlier.

"I will wait," he said.

She growled her displeasure inwardly and heaved a weary sigh, before rising to her feet to face him, keeping near the hearth.

He sat on the bed, his head bent over with his elbows on his knees, his gaze on the floor between his legs.

He spoke without changing position. "I will apologize for my behavior...all of it today. I ken this is unbearable enough without my adding to it by being..."

She had to bite her tongue at his hesitation, so eager to fill in the space he'd left there. Intolerable? Unforgivably rude? A bloody beast? Yet, the very fact that he deigned to favor her with any show of contrition suggested the disharmony—it was so much more than that, in reality—sat unwell with him also, and thus Alice kept her mouth shut and her thoughts to herself.

Lifting his dark but possibly weary gaze to her, though he maintained his bent posture, he finished, "I apologize for my overbearing manner. Truly, I do understand that ye are innocent of any crime, that this conflict and impasse is between yer sire and me. I...I am sorry ye are caught up in the middle of it."

"But not sorry enough to see me home or send me home?"

He shook his head, piercing her with his complex gaze, filled now it seemed with genuine remorse.

She would not yield completely to him though, did not trust his stated remorse had not more to do with the tension and unease he knew rather than how wrong it was to treat her as if she had been the one who'd betrayed a promise. He wished only harmony, not some nagging captive who might be ready to blister him verbally at any moment. She wouldn't mind harmony. She'd been too long without it, she knew. He'd extended this olive branch. It would cost her little to accept it, and with graciousness. She nodded tightly and allowed a very small, "Thank you," to pass her lips.

It really was a shame though, she thought, that so much handsomeness was wasted on this man, who didn't deserve to be so beautiful when he'd proven how ugly he could be.

She turned and claimed the space in the corner closest to the fire, letting her back slide down the wall and drawing her knees up to her chest as she had last night.

"Dinna do that...Alice, take the bed," he offered next, coming to his feet. "I canna have ye—"

The quick shaking of her head forestalled the rest of what he might have said.

"I prefer this. Leave it be."

Laying her chin on her folded arms and staring again into the orange flames, she barely gave any notice to Nicholas moving the chest in front of the door again and then finding the comfort of his bed as he had the night before.

Instead, she'd just been overcome with her own remorse, for how this had played out. She would have been so much happier, she was certain, if he'd only left her at home with her parents. Before they'd arrived at the de Graham house, she'd wondered, albeit briefly, if she would ever see him again, if she would lament his leavetaking. She would have, she'd decided only days ago. He might have been the one by whom all subsequent interested males were judged.

So now, she wanted to erase all of today and yesterday, wanted to go back to that time when she'd thought him honorable and good, when his kiss had been cherished, having stirred her as she feared no one else's ever would. She wanted to return to that time when she'd only wondered how unbearable would be their parting.

Better that, a final parting from something yet in its infancy, the unrealized potential of him, of any possible *them*, rather than this, knowing the truth about him, so that she'd lost him all the same but more harshly now.

How mournful.

She struggled for quite some time, not at all comfortable but too stubborn to admit as much, and unable to sleep. He might be struggling as well, as Alice was aware of the sounds of his tossing and turning. She thought at one point that he was literally punching his pillow, either to pound it into a more suitable shape or to relieve what frustration might yet gnaw at him.

And then she was running, through a monstrous wind and in the rain, around that bend in the road in the little village outside of Lilliesleaf. Lightning sparked in the distance and thunder roared overhead while her sodden mantle tangled around her legs and its hood flapped about her shoulders. Violet and Ellen's uncle, Edgar Ailred, was chasing her, his face ashen and his black eyes akin to that of a rat, beady and lifeless. He held no weapon, but Alice perceived a feral threat about him. She kept tripping and stumbling, striking out her arms to stop her fall, and never seemed to get around the bend. Several times her hands met with the hard earth, and she felt the skin torn from her flesh. He was catching up to her and she fell once more, screaming, and glanced over her shoulder just in time to see his feet leave the ground as he leapt at her. He landed hard on her, rocking her entire body and then took her by the arms, shaking her roughly.

"Alice!" He raged at her.

She fought wildly against him, her hands connecting with his chest and face to ward him off.

"Alice! *Jesu*, lass. 'Tis but a dream."

The nightmare ended then, replaced by a dream, for that was Nicholas' voice and she was in Nicholas' strong arms. Alice went limp and clung to him, her fingers digging into the flesh of his shoulders, pulling him closer, yearning to be cocooned and safe. She laid her cheek against his hard, naked chest and wept, though she didn't know why tears came now, when the threat had been removed.

"Come now," he said, as gentle as she'd never heard him.

She felt his hand at the back of her head, stroking her hair, and she became aware of the quiet surrounding her. Opening her eyes, panting with the lingering haze of fright, she tried to make sense of what had happened.

She was not in that little village, but in the bedchamber at Braewood. The fog of confusion lifted instantly as she understood she'd suffered a night terror as she had not for many, many weeks. When she'd first been held at the de Lisle house, it had been rather a weekly occurrence that Joanna had been forced to wake her from something similar, something equally as terrifying, even as so often the villains of her dreams were undefined or as random as tonight's, with the unwitting and dandified Ailred assuming that role.

Awakening fully, Alice pushed lightly against Nicholas, realizing that they were crouched in the corner together, Nicholas on his knees and she in his arms, he once more without a tunic and she having clung to all that warm, strong flesh without hesitation. All that remained of her nightmare was the wind and rain, which howled wickedly outside, the rain slashing hard against the keep and the tapestry covering the window.

"Better?" He asked against her hair.

Under her hand and her cheek, his heart thumped at a sharp pace.

Swallowing what remained of her fear, she nodded against him and only then was made anxious by their position and her own embarrassment. "I am...I am so sorry to have—"

"Cease," he clipped. "Ye dinna apologize for things ye canna control."

He pulled back and looked down into the eyes she turned up to him. He moved his hand from the back of her head to the side, and with his thumb wiped away at the wetness of her tears from her cheek.

This tenderness was both unexpected and jolting, because he should exhibit such gentleness, because his eyes should be filled with such concern. Unnerved, she laid her hand over his and curled her fingers around his, drawing his hand down and away.

"I'm...I'm fine now."

His gaze followed their hands, lowering between them as she withdrew.

"*Jesu*, Alice, but ye've torn yer hand."

She followed his gaze and saw that indeed she had, likely on the rough stone wall in this corner while she'd believed she'd been fighting for her life. Disengaging completely from her, which oddly left her cold and inexplicably bereft, Nicholas got to his feet and helped her to stand as well.

"Sit there," he said, advancing her toward the bed.

She did, her actions still sleep-shrouded a wee bit, and watched as he went to the trunk barring the door and rifled through that, his back to her. He withdrew something and his arms lifted and flexed, and a rending of fabric was heard before he closed the lid and returned to her. He sat next to her and took her hand again, wrapping it efficiently in a strip of linen, bending over the end of it to bite a tear mark and making two ends, one of which he reversed and knotted at her palm. He ran his fingers over the knot and then her fingers and looked at her, offering a rare and slight smile.

Alice tried to return it, though could give no opinion on her success. "Better," she told him in a small voice. "Thank you." And she rose, intent on retreating to her corner, not sure what to make of or do with this solicitous, entirely too-tender Nicholas, this man she did not know.

"Nae," he said. "Ye'll no' sleep there now. I will no' have it."

"But I—"

"Aye, and there is no *but*. And I will no' argue with ye about it in the dead of night." He approached her and turned her around, a flash of lightning highlighting his hand as he pointed from around her shoulder toward the bed.

She surprised herself by not arguing further. Save that the night was damp and cold and the terror too fresh yet, so that she returned to where she'd sat upon the bed seconds ago, startling a bit at a booming clap of thunder.

Nicholas walked around to the other side and did not hesitate but stretched out on his back, his arm under his head. After a moment, Alice laid down, keeping as far to the edge as possible. Like him, she rested on her back and stared at the timber of the ceiling, which flashed bright white regularly for all the lightning streaking about in the night.

The silence between them unnerved her until she imagined some prosaic conversation and said softly, "I hate being afraid."

"None of us have control over the night terrors, lass, or what dread they introduce." He scratched lazily, mayhap mindlessly, at his chest. "I'll be right here, Alice. I'll wake ye again should they return."

Aye, he was a balm to fright, but then he was also the cause of so much distress.

And her heart twisted and tightened now for how that saddened her.

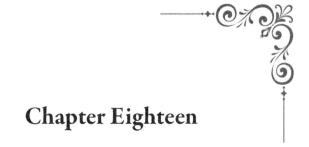

# Chapter Eighteen

Even after her nightmare had faded into the shadows of memory, so much still went bump in the night. The storm raged ferociously outside, forcing Alice to pursue the security and warmth of the pelts and woolens on the bed. She cocooned herself under these and listened to the fury beyond the stone and window.

She slept poorly and when she woke, she was facing Nicholas, who slept yet, on his stomach with his arms under the pillow beneath his head. His lion's mane of hair was tousled, the left side pressed flat against his head as if he'd slept for some time in that other direction. Small straight lines spread out from the corners of his eyes, the stamp similar to what she might see upon the ground in the wake of a crow's light steps; sadly, she knew they had not been formed by smiles but by his scowls. A wee and pensive smile turned her lips upward at his expression, or rather the lack thereof. In slumber, he was not quite so menacing, but then still striking for how handsome he was, but boyish now for the absence of his usual harsh countenance.

She lifted her hand, extending her forefinger with the intent of tracing that spot where creases normally furrowed deep between his eyes but were now only slight indentations, but caught herself and withdrew, folding her hand at her chest.

A thudding of heavy feet sounded outside the chamber, growing closer, and Alice was not surprised by the ensuing knocking at the door.

Nicholas did not stir with any severe jolting, despite the firm rapping, but opened his eyes slowly, meeting Alice's gaze almost instantly and holding it while he called out, "Aye?"

Dungal's voice answered while Nicholas held her gaze. "Sure and we'll be busy all the day. Plenty of damage to the village, and we've got flooding in more than one of the ditches."

Nicholas' gaze shifted, not away from her, but showed a full wakefulness now with this disturbing news. "I will be down anon," Nicholas advised.

"Aye, and ye take yer time, Laird," Dungal called back, a hint of mirth in his tone. "Whenever is convenient to ye, as ye will." Footsteps sounded again, fading away as Dungal left.

Alice bit back a grin but feared she'd not hidden it well from her eyes. Nicholas did not smile, of course, and neither did he remove himself from the bed or his eyes from her. Not for the first time, Alice felt imprisoned by his gaze, wondering what went through his mind when he stared so blatantly at her, with such probing determination.

"What are you looking for?" She thought to ask, and then immediately regretted the question.

He said nothing, not directly, but pulled his hand from beneath the pillow and used it to brush a stray lock of hair from her cheek. Alice's heart fluttered at so casual but intimate a gesture, something that mayhap should be reserved for two people who were better-acquainted or more relaxed with each other.

Perhaps he just now realized that was incompatible with their roles as captor and captive—their close and peaceful proximity, that gesture that nearly overstepped bounds, what she might have been seeking in her query—so that he closed himself off, rolling over on to his back.

"I seek nothing," he said, throwing back the furs and blankets and sitting up, his back to her. "Naught but resolution to whatever destruction is to be found today." He stood after a short moment and once more slid the trunk across the room, lifting the lid when it was parked at the foot of the bed. With nary a glance at her, he donned a fresh tunic, covering all that beauty of his superbly sculpted chest.

Alice blinked and sat up as well, rubbing sleep from her eyes and then running her fingers through her hair to push it all away from her face and shoulders. She had nothing to change into but went to the small cupboard with the ewer and basin and splashed water on her face while Nicholas had taken the chair near the hearth to don and lace his boots.

When he stood and affixed his belt and sword to his waist and while Alice used the cloth to dry her face, he asked, "Should I expect that ye will be with Violet again today?"

Turning from the cupboard, the square towel arrested at her neck, Alice wondered, "Unless I or we might be of some help in the village?"

"I dinna ken that at the moment, but Violet is no' adverse to helping when more hands are needed," he said. "It's a good wager if there's help needed, she'll show up."

"Then yes. Either way, I will find Violet and...go where she goes."

He nodded, blindly securing his belt, eyeing her steadily. For a moment, he looked as if he would say more, but then with only a spare glance over the bed in which they'd slept, he inclined his head again and left the chamber.

It was another fifteen minutes before Alice had finished her morning ablutions and arrived in the hall, which was not half as filled as it had been yesterday morning, but which saw many crossing from one place to another, including several soldiers who rose almost all at once from one table and left the hall. One table away, a group of three women sat, and looked to be about the chore of mending oil cloth window coverings. Alice was disconcerted that she did not recognize anyone seated at any of the trestle tables and thus aimed for the door, chewing her cheek, wondering how she might find either Violet or the village.

As it had been yesterday, the main door was fully open, and her first glimpse of the day showed nary a sign of rain or clouds, the opening bright with sunlight. Having a sudden fear that someone might believe she was trying to escape, Alice approached the door with caution, pleased then to see Dungal walking through it.

"Ye lost, lass?" He asked, lifting his brows.

"Not exactly," she said. "But Nich—the laird said I might be of help in the village but I'm not sure where it is."

"Och, and we'll need all willing hands," answered the old-timer, scratching at his long beard. "Now wait right here while I tell Cook and Nelly we'll be needing a hearty meal to feed the masses, and then I'll take ye there myself."

Smiling her appreciation, she followed him with her gaze toward the passageway that led to the kitchens, her eye then stopping on that Ailred man, who sat at the high table with his daughter, undisturbed it seemed by whatever went on around them, or what had befallen the cottages in the village.

Dungal returned shortly and lifted his hand toward the door and Alice preceded him outside.

"Aye and we're walking, lass," he informed her, "since most the horses, including the destriers, are put to work as draught animals today."

"Is there very much damage, Dungal?" She asked as they cleared the gate. In an aside glance, she noticed what she had previously, but not with any great attention, that his stride was even and steady, but that it involved so much of his body than only his arms and legs. He put his shoulders and hips into each step, and even his head bobbed more than most as he lumbered along.

"Aye and were they no' fierce last night, those bickering lovers, the wind and the rain?"

Alice laughed at this, agreeing, "Yes, they were. At times either one of them lifted the tapestry fully away from the window."

"And there ye have it, so now we've lost the kirk's spire and enough thatch to make half a dozen new roofs if we're of a mind to chase it down," he said, "and ye ken there was only one measurable tree about the village and did it no' get struck down and wasn't it tossed atop Finn's roof while he slept—like a babe, his old bride says. She had to rouse him though the closest limb lay in the bed with them."

"Good grief, how awful," Alice commented.

"Aye and yer a fine lass, Alice de Graham," Dungal said next, "no' holding against us that which had to be done."

Alice found this humorous, though she did not know why. "Is that you, Dungal, speaking of my kidnapping as if you MacRorys get about the same with some frequency, casual as you please?"

He snickered good-naturedly at this as they walked along the lane. "Och, and there's nothing casual about stealing a person, but must needs and all that—aye, and I ken that dinna excuse it, but there ye have it. If I dinna feel bad for the despair we surely caused yer sweet mam, I'd be little troubled by the rest of it since ye ken more than most yer in good hands, that all is well."

She might have stopped and called him out on this. All was most certainly not well, and as he'd just pointed out, kidnapping had many victims. But she understood that he was naught but a soldier following orders and she would not take issue with him or his blind adherence to his laird's directives.

All around, upon the meadow and up yonder, in the pasture where dozens and dozens of fluffy sheep grazed, the ground was littered with broken limbs and a few overturned trees and so many green leaves, torn from their branches well before they might have let go on their own.

The lane they followed dipped low into a glen and then rose upon the far hill, the road here more grass than dirt. Walking up the rise in the road showed the highest parts of the village first, the tops of the village kirk in the distance—devoid of its spire as Dungal had warned her—and the thatched roofs of the crofts before the walls and winding lane were revealed as they crested the knoll.

The village was unlike the one at home, where houses were only scattered about the road to the de Graham house, with sometimes as much as a quarter mile between, and then it was so vastly different from where she'd been kept in England, in that small town with so many two-story clapboard buildings. Brae-wood's village was a clustered community, the crofts set close-ly, some with not more than a dozen feet between them, and all with the short end of the long houses facing the lane. Alice thought there might be more than twenty homes and she saw in the distance, beyond the kirk, larger barns and what looked like a mill.

The lane and yards were crowded with both busy and idle people; some of the frontages were crammed with furniture, possibly as the cottars emptied their crofts to clean storm clutter from within. The roofs were crowded as well, almost every one of them supporting two or more men, soldiers Alice might presume, who'd climbed up to repair the damage from the battering.

She saw Nicholas first thing, near the closest hut, where nearly half the thatch had been ripped or washed away by the storm. He was on his haunches before an old woman, who sat upon a small stool, as bent and crooked as he was straight and strong, her white hair so thin one could make out the entire shape and size of her head and scalp.

As they approached, Alice overheard what he was saying to the fretting woman.

"Curstag, ye wily fox, ye ken I'd no' leave ye without a roof over yer head. Ye dinna need to bribe me," he said. He unfolded himself from his crouched position then, though was yet bent at the waist to be eye level with the old woman. "But if ye are going to start passing out bribes, aye, I'll take some of yer berry tarts. And dinna be telling Cook that hers'll never stack up to yers."

In response to this, the woman cackled like a lass many years younger, showing more gums than teeth as she took Nicholas' hand in both of hers. "I ken ye'd take good care of us, lad, and never have ye done otherwise. Ye come any time, I've told ye 'fore, whenever ye want the sweets done right."

"I'll keep that in mind, Curstag," he said and turned, slowly withdrawing his hand from the old woman's grasp.

He noted Dungal and Alice's arrival then and met them in the center of the lane.

Dungal said, "I've said to Cook and Nellie to bring up a cold meal so we dinna lose hours tramping back and forth and idling around the hall. And now I'll get on with the lads at the southeast ditch. Like as no', they're standing about, pikes and axes and shovels in hand, waiting for one with a brain to show himself." He indicated with his thumb Alice's presence. "And this one wants to work, though I ken she'll prove more distracting than useful." With a glance at Alice, he grinned and said, "Sure and no offense, lass, but they dinna make 'em so bonny at this elevation."

Alice shook her head at his foolishness and then spied Joanna exiting a croft with a banged up frontage.

Thus, when Dungal departed, Alice did so as well. "I, um, I see Joanna there. I'll see what help she needs," she said to Nicholas, already moving away from him.

No surprise, she learned, that Joanna had taken charge of some situations.

"Nae," she was saying to a middle-aged man, whose face was scrunched up while he listened to her, "we're no' going to sweep around what sits inside, living on naught but hope that we catch it all. Everything comes out, into the yard, all the furniture and belongings. We'll get it done proper first time, and ye'll be thanking me later when the air inside is as fresh as this out here."

She did not wait for the man to acknowledge this or contest this but turned to greet Alice.

Behind her, the man wondered of a teenaged lad standing next to him, "Who is that woman?"

Joanna's greeting was comprised of waving Alice forward to issue more instructions. "Aye and ye'll do fine with that lot over there," she said, pointing to a croft three away. "Too many un-walking ones and no' enough workers."

Alice smirked and headed in that direction, thinking she was not, after all, so unlike Dungal, as she'd just unconsciously followed orders given to her.

She introduced herself to the woman in front of the croft Joanna had indicated, whose efforts to clean her own home were hampered by an infant and a bairn not much older, and another no more than four or five. The woman was Fiona, she said, staring around Alice's shoulder down the lane, where Joanna was still directing.

"Aye and I was hoping I'd get the help of that one," Fiona said blandly, but with a longing gaze. "Seems she might only order the limbs and leaves to march outside and command the sodden earth within to dry."

Alice shrugged. "Sorry, you're stuck with me."

The woman looked her up and down, seeming to have no care that her scrutiny was nearly rude. "Aye, and I guess ye'll have to do."

Only an hour into her labors inside the village, Alice decided there wasn't a female here who was not, to some degree or another, smitten with her laird. Whether young or old, they smiled and blushed, while some stammered and gawked. The youngest lasses followed his progress around the village with darting eyes and high-pitched giggles, ignoring the young soldiers who were trying to make time with them.

She spied Violet eventually but found no sign of Ellen. The lass was hard at work at one of the farthest crofts, with what looked to be bed linens flung over a flowering bush, which she was beating ferociously with a stick to cast off the dust. On occasion, Violet brandished the stick as a sword and feinted toward the coverlet as if confronting a foe.

At one point, Alice stopped and gawped when she saw Baldred ride one of the large warhorses down the lane, slowing when he spied Joanna emerging from one of the crofts. Alice wouldn't have believed it if she hadn't seen it with her own eyes, but the man appeared to wink at Joanna, and in return, Joanna blushed bright red and shyly dipped her face to hide her responding smile.

"What has ye catching flies like that, lass?"

Alice jumped, startled to find that Nicholas had walked up behind her.

Still amazed at what she might have witnessed, she said with a hint of wonder, "I think I just saw Baldred wink at Joanna."

"Canna be," he replied evenly and without hesitation, casting his gaze down the street to where his captain still walked the horse along.

"Then how do you explain that blush on her cheeks?"

Nicholas squinted and peered more closely at Joanna. "*Jesu*, and is she giggling?"

"I believe so."

He shook his head and questioned, "What's the world coming to, Alice?"

Which struck her as vastly amusing as he sounded so put out, and before she could help it a laugh erupted from her.

The laugh shocked her as much as him, and she clapped her hand over her mouth while he stared at her with a slack expression which quickly evolved into a frown and then just as swiftly eased again, his eyes roaming over her mirth-filled ones and her cheeks and the hand covering her mouth. He lifted his own hand and rubbed it over his mouth and jaw and Alice had the impression he did so to conceal a bit of gaping.

And his gaze stayed powerfully upon her for many long seconds, until Alice's mirth faded away and she dropped her hand. Her heartbeat at first froze at his keen scrutiny but then began to pound. She looked at herself through his eyes, supposing he might question her ability to laugh at all at this time.

But no. Instead, he said quietly, "Ye should laugh more, lass." No sooner were the words spoken than he raised his hand to forestall what had been her ready reply. "Aye, and I ken, ye will say ye've no' much to laugh about of late and that is to be laid at my door." This, he mentioned with a confident scorn, which coincided with the return of his scowl.

Alice shook her head, pleased to enlighten him, "I *should* have thought of that as my initial response. But no, I was going to say, *I will if you will*."

And now his lips did part but only briefly before he closed and clenched his jaw and continued to eat her alive with his heated gaze and she knew—she was absolutely positive—that if they were alone, not surrounded by dozens and dozens of people, that he would kiss her.

Someone called out something above them, one of those lads on the roof, but Alice heard only noise and not words. But Nicholas glanced up and then attacked her, yanking roughly at her arm, pulling her nearly off her feet as he drew her so hard forward that she crashed against him. He covered her head with his hands and shielded her body with his as something heavy glanced off his arm and crashed to the ground.

Stunned, Alice squeezed her eyes shut and huddled against his broad chest, her hands flat against him.

In the next second, he was thrusting her away and examining her again, this time with a ferocious frown even as his hand was so gentle brushing her disheveled hair away from her face, for the second time today.

"Are ye all right? Did it hit ye?"

Though confused a bit, she did know that nothing had harmed her. She shook her head and Nicholas once more turned his attention above them, where stood a wide-eyed youth, his mouth hanging open.

"Bluidy hell, David," Nicholas cursed.

"I'm s-sorry, Laird," the lad stuttered. "I dinna see—"

"Aye," growled Nicholas through his clenched teeth, one arm still around Alice, "and that is why ye look first."

Alice turned her head to see what missile had been thrust from the roof, only to find a bundle of old thatch, bound with thick jute, which like so many others all through the day had simply been pitched off the roof.

Nicholas said no more to the poor lad but pulled Alice out from directly beneath the roof and closer to the two rutted lines of dirt in the grass that were the road.

She saw hers was not the only chest that heaved, but she thought the cause of this might have more to do with awareness and proximity and was less about missiles being launched from rooftops.

"I should..." she began but didn't know what she should be doing. Still, she flung a thumb over her shoulder as if something did await her attention.

"Aye. I'll uh...I've got to..." Hands on his hips, he turned and glanced behind him, where nothing particular seemed to beckon him.

"Yes," she said nonsensically and walked stiffly into the closest croft, from which she'd walked out not five minutes ago, having deemed its cleaning complete.

She smiled at the woman kneeling over her small kitchen fire and then at her husband, whose head poked through a gaping hole in the roof, from his position overhead.

The couple stared back with some question in their gazes, having bid Alice parting only minutes ago, having thanked her profusely for her help.

"This looks nice," Alice said, breathless and befuddled, not looking around at all to have been sure of that verdict.

When her breathing returned to normal and she heard Nicholas calling out to someone further away, Alice ducked outside again, her hand to her chest as so many twirling thoughts raced through her.

She sent her gaze down the lane, to where he stood with Baldred, since dismounted, pointing up at the small church, his strong arm lifted and moving left and right to indicate something along the roof line. After a moment and while she watched, he barked out a laugh and clapped his captain heartily on the shoulder, filling Alice with greater confusion, though the chaos in her head battled mightily to be known above her reaction to the sound of his hearty laughter.

Nicholas' laughter suited him perfectly, deep and rich, as large and as beautiful as was he. Alice was not unaffected by the noise or the sight. Indeed, she was warmed by the sound and smitten by the look of him now, so boyish and light.

Quite frankly though, she did not know this man with the heart-stopping laughter any more than she recognized the gentle, caring one of last night, who'd soothed her tenderly after her night terror. Or the one who had teased the hag, Curstag. Or the man whose waking gaze had been so soft upon her this morning. If she had met this version of Nicholas MacRory straight away at the de Lisle house, likely she would have come willingly to either of her own abductions.

Working to calm her heart as it seemed to want to race again, Alice addressed the chaos inside her.

Only half aware of her own movements, she lifted her hands and laid her fingers and palms over her cheeks, in reaction to her own shock for what she discovered of herself. She could not ignore the growing suspicion that suggested despite everything, despite even how unjustified it seemed, that she might be in love with him. She wasn't sure, but mayhap that explained the tightness in her chest, the warm feeling that enveloped her as surely and kindly as his arms had last night and only moments ago, her complete and exasperating inability to stoke the anger she should feel toward him. Perhaps such an outrageous notion then rationalized her desire to be the one to make him smile or a greater yearning to have his smile turned upon her.

She was aware that with this stunning revelation came a wee anguish for how unfortunate and unwelcome was such a thing. He was her father's enemy, her own captor—he deserved loathing and enmity and not...love, by all that was holy. Not even this intense...*like*, she amended, whittling it down to that lesser emotion, rejecting the idea that it could be anything greater or grander.

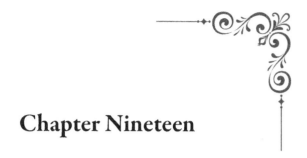

# Chapter Nineteen

As the day wore on, the work was accomplished one job at a time, made easier by so many willing hands. A neighborly consultation and exchange of ideas formed the latter part of the day, men and women gathered round in the small church yard while a flock of snowy geese waddled slowly down the village road. Men discussed the repair of the steeple, which would have to wait until the carpenter, Tom Pence, returned from Glasgow, where he'd gone for the funeral of his father. Women stood in a cluster, recounting what success their days had known prior to the storm—the number of skeins of yarn one had spun only yesterday, the yards of linens woven by another, while a third chimed in about *the crankiness of the dye-pot.*

They comported themselves well, from the pipe-smoking burgher who'd sat all day just outside his croft, about the industry of creating bundles of thatch, to the soldiers who labored atop the roofs and returned to solid ground at the end of the day with far more knowledge than they might have wished about those thatched roofs. After scrubbing and sweeping all morning, the women had gathered in the early afternoon to manage a communal laundry day, and all those linens and fabrics and clothes that had been dirtied by mud and wreckage falling from their leaking roofs had been washed. Even the youngsters helped, clearing smaller debris, loading it in to the cart at the end of the lane which would be carted away when it was full.

In the early evening, people gathered on stools or what seats they could find or arrange around a well-supplied board and an abundant supper of pork pies, smoked herring, and garden vegetables—cabbage and beans roasted with spices in bacon grease, all eaten upon wooden trenchers with pewter spoons or their own eating knives. The table had been laid in the yard of the kirk, with the cleric, Father Ioan, blessing the fare and the people gathered.

Nicholas had never discounted the sense of community that Braewood managed so well. Much like an army, a collective society worked best when they worked together. 'Twas a fine and hard-working group of people. Not to say that there weren't petty squabbles or even those of greater magnitude, but there was rarely scandal, for each one's business was every person's business, such was the life of a village of close-gathered homes.

If it hadn't been there previously, it was possible that his father and stepmother had fostered this general goodwill inside the village. They were forever hosting festivals and gatherings; the great hall had been opened to the peasants as never before; his stepmother, Maven, considered the health and well-being of each person as her own responsibility and could regularly be found within the confines of the village during the daytime, tending to people and matters.

Nicholas was drawn to the table by the elder men of the village and joined the supper there, though with a curious reluctance, half of his attention held by Alice. She took her meal with Violet and Ellen and three more unwed women of their age, seated on the soft grass under the lone fruit tree in the church yard, naught but a score of feet from the door of the kirk. Possibly they expected that Joanna would join them, but of course she did not. Instead, the tireless woman spent all of the meal time circling the table, refilling trenchers and cups, admonishing bairns to sit and eat, and generally playing warden to this simple feast.

When the peasants and soldiers were all mellowed with ale and sated bellies, and the sky sparkled with hundreds of shimmering stars in the gloaming, fires were lit at either ends of the long tables, kept in metal barrels, made and stoked by lads too old for wooden sword-play as another group was about but then too young to be received in the company of warriors. Nicholas sent his gaze once more to Alice under the apple tree. Three lasses, not ten-years-old any one of them, approached and goaded Violet and another lass into chasing fire-flies. Violet was always good fun, if quietly so, and Alice was unknown to them, which might explain why she was not invited to play. Or mayhap because she'd been deep in discussion with the sisters, Mary and Margaret, daughters of the farmer Findlay, was she excluded. But then the sisters were summoned out from under the canopy of the tree, henpecked by Findlay's wife who was not their mother, to help with the clean-up at the table, and Alice was left alone. With little forethought, other than that he might have been waiting for just this opening, Nicholas excused himself and went to where she was, sneering silently at himself, naught but a moth seeking the flame.

She was about to rise, he saw, when she noticed him striding toward her. He was pleased when she relaxed and lowered herself onto the grass as she had been, staring up at him as his shadow fell over her.

Without waiting an invitation or delivering any greeting, he sat beside her and drew up one knee and laid his arm over it. They both faced the long board where yet sat thirty or more people.

"It was a good—" he began.

"I've never—" she said at the same time.

They halted at the same time as well, Alice grinning nervously and ducking her head.

"Ye've never what?" He wanted to know.

Her blue eyes, sparkling as they reflected the fire, found his. "Oh. Um, I've never been part of so much industry and cheerful collaboration as I have on this day. It's all quite...wonderful."

No, he supposed the very layout of that scattered and small village near the de Graham home did not lend itself to any community spirit.

"Hard day's work," Nicholas commented.

"And they make a feast out of it," she said. "I like that."

"Aye, and Eachann Fraser just ran for his cithara, so it will no' end any time soon. The ale will flow and they'll start with the dancing and we'll be listening to their carousing long into the night."

"But well-deserved, is it not?"

"It is."

"*Their* carousing?" She questioned, tilting an impish grin at him, "Will you not be joining them?"

He scoffed playfully at this. "The laird does no' carouse, lass." It came to him suddenly that she was remarkable and he so unworthy. Remarkable for showing him anything of merit; he did not deserve any grin from her, impish or otherwise. He'd not earned it, had in fact done so much to preclude such a boon, which should be reserved for those more worthy. No sooner had this occurred to him that he upbraided himself for such sentimentality. He was only passing time with her right now. He desired no such dividend from her. *Then why did you seek her out?* asked a voice in his head. He cleared his throat. "The laird should...." He paused, picking up the sound of an approaching vehicle.

Several soldiers, those not lost in their cups so early, turned their ears as well and the overall din lowered until the elegant cart and mare of Edgar Ailred appeared over the ridge, coming from the direction of the keep.

"Curious, that he should sniff out the meal but not the work," Nicholas grumbled quietly and then sipped of his ale, his gaze narrowed over the top of the flask, upon the cart with Edgar and the insipid Marjorie inside.

"Possibly, he did not wish to risk the delicacy of his garments," Alice offered, a wee irreverent.

She regretted such impudence immediately, Nicholas might have guessed, if he read the wince that followed correctly.

Nicholas let her know that her assumption was not far off the mark by adding, "Nor the softness of his hands."

To his chagrin, Edgar had spied Nicholas under the apple tree with Alice, and he pulled the horse to a stop directly before them. Before he addressed them, Edgar put the village and the people under a thoughtful examination. When his moving gaze found Nicholas, he said only, "Ah, but I see these low-roofed houses shut their doors against pride and luxury."

*What an arse.* Nicholas said nothing, not of a mind to engage the wretch.

"But how wide their doors stand open to charity and relief," Alice surprised him by saying.

Surprised Edgar as well. While Marjorie tore her gaze from Nicholas to stare shrewdly at Alice, Edgar subjected her to a more thoughtful and thorough study. "Ah, the captive," said Edgar Ailred, "are you not?"

Alice raised her chin. "I am."

Edgar tittered a laugh that was almost grotesque for its insincerity and said, "One wonders under what treaty you might be held, partaking so generously of your captor's grace."

Because he so often did not deign to engage in any of Edgar's trivial gambits, and more importantly, because he was very certain that Alice could hold her own against the toad, Nicholas refrained from responding to the transparently manipulative affront.

"We have an understanding," Alice said.

Edgar let his gaze roam almost lasciviously over Alice while he said provocatively, "Aye, I would imagine you do."

Nicholas flexed the hand that draped over his knee and needed only a split second to decide that should not stand.

Before he might have risen, as had been his intent, he felt Alice's hand on his arm.

She smiled at him and pointed to another part of the church yard, where Violet and those children were chasing fireflies. "Look at them," she said, laughing briefly as if momentarily distracted by their fun.

And that was all it was, a distraction, to keep Nicholas from nipping at the bait Edgar had dangled before him. She turned her tight smile and bright gaze upon him, her look telling him it wasn't important, that she wasn't disturbed enough to wish his intervention.

"I thought to take you to task, lad, for such dishonor as you've brought to the MacRory name," Edgar said next, drawing their attention once more, "but then I hear with the lass comes an army, if—her sire, is it?—deems her worthy of the trade?"

"Ye presume too much, Ailred," Nicholas said lazily, caring little for Edgar's thoughts on the matter, but more greatly for his knowing of these details. "Nothing regarding her, or indeed Braewood in general, should be of any concern to ye."

Edgar pretended to be tremendously displeased. "Forsooth, lad. But it is only the—"

"Nothing at all," Nicholas reiterated, slowly and firmly. "And good night to ye now. We dinna want to keep ye out so late in so inhospitable a place."

With a pursing of his lips, knowing he could not advance his own agenda to lay low another, Edgar snapped at the reins and the small carriage burst into motion, taking those unwelcome visitors away.

"I am surprised you allow him entry to Braewood at all," Alice noted when the cart had moved far enough away, and her opinion would not be overheard.

Nicholas sighed, little affected by the simpleton's attempts to rile him. "'Tis Ellen and Violet's uncle and cousin, all the family they have—such as they are. I cannot bar the door to them." He frowned and asked of her, "Ye made it fairly clear that ye dinna wish to be kept in my bedchamber, lass, for what talk might come of it, so why then did ye prevent me from calling him out for inciting ye with his offensiveness?"

She sent a grin his way. "I more than most understand that you cannot be prevented from doing anything. But that exchange only made me think of what my mother is fond of saying about engaging with small-minded people—consider the speaker and judge them worthy or not of any rebuttal, indeed of any thought at all."

"Well thought," he agreed, satisfied with her response, and meaning to put Edgar Ailred from his mind this moment.

As ever, certainly when he was so close to her, he struggled to keep his gaze off her.

Just now, she adjusted her position, moving off her knees to sit with her legs crossed. She plucked a blade of grass from her side and twirled the thing in her lap. And sent the most beguiling and sly glances his way from under her long lashes, aware of his regard, but not willing to face it head-on perhaps.

"May I ask you something?"

He did not answer, would not until she looked at him. She did, eventually, when he said nothing.

"You should answer that one," she advised while one corner of her gorgeous mouth curved upward. "That was the easy one."

Though suitably charmed by her easy manner, Nicholas did not allow it to show. "Ask away."

She swallowed first, which should have alerted him to the significance or the weightiness of her coming query.

"Why do you smile so little, Nicholas?" The blade of grass stopped spinning in her lap. Her head tipped to one side. Briefly, she made a face that suggested she was sorry that he might not find joy in anything. "There seems so much to be delighted in, to be thankful for, right here in your home and with these people.

What happened to you that you don't find joy? Or do you...do you refuse joy?"

After his initial shock at her daring, the oft-used protective wall came down. He had no intention of sharing with her—her of all people—all the things he'd been and done and endured, all those things that made happiness not only impossible but unwelcome. And yet she regarded him with such hopefulness, as if she might know a solution if only she were made aware of the problem.

He shrugged, pretending little distress for so intrusive a question. "Why would ye suspect that something had to happen to have made me this way? Ye ken some people are simply born unhappy and stay that way all their lives."

Her response to this was to show him a look of irritation, for she knew damn well that he was hedging. But her lifted brows did not draw out anything else from him so that she supposed, "None of my business, I understand. I was only curious and I...I think you would be good at being happy, but it seems you fight against it."

He clenched his jaw at this. "You are ridiculous, of course, pretending to ken me."

For the space of a second, her next expression showed a hint of pity and Nicholas' hand fisted.

But then she only wondered, "Am I?"

Riled by her inquisitiveness, he heard himself give up more than he ever had at any time, to anyone. "A man lives his life having convinced himself that his deeds were justified, necessary mayhap, that he was—" he halted, deciding against finishing that thought, *that he'd been doing good.* He could no longer acknowledge or accept how ignorant he'd been at one time to have persuaded himself that he'd been doing good. That was only half the lie, though; truth was, he'd thought it wouldn't bother him in the long run, what he'd done. Stiltedly, he continued, "And then one day he meets...true good, and he realizes that wasn't what he was about all those years. No' so much to smile about."

Alice was unimpressed. Here, he'd pulled something genuine from the deep well of his tortured consciousness and she all but rolled her eyes.

"That's called regret," she told him pertly. "And it's not fatal, you know."

He did not care for the way she dismissed it out of hand. "Aye but it should be, in some cases."

"And that right there is self-directed woe, which is rarely if ever useful."

She stared at him, wanting to know more, possibly expecting it, but Nicholas was sure that exposing anything else of himself would require many long rounds of torture for him to give it up.

"You either have some experience in this regard to speak with such authority upon the matter," he guessed, not without a hint of ire, "or more likely, the folly of youth—idealism—has a good strong hold on ye."

"I...obviously, I haven't experience in so much of anything save being kidnapped of late, but...well, I imagine regret is like so many other wasteful things: it will not change the past but then it doesn't need to consume the future."

Nicholas scowled, wondering if this were a direct commentary on the aforementioned kidnapping of her. Or was there something else behind the original question and her misplaced concern for his happiness? If he thought she was getting on about the latter, he might also assume that she was, in her very apparent naiveté, trying to tell him that joy was available to everyone, even those who thought they ought not to have it. He wasn't sure that he believed this—actually he was pretty sure he did not.

But she did.

Why? Why did she care?

Eachann indeed had produced his cithara and Gillean Brockie must have fetched his wooden flute and while Nicholas continued to contemplate Alice and what she was about, the sound of the raucous melody they played filled the air. The night grew older and the boards where supper had been set were dismantled and returned to storage and no one was surprised when ol' Tearlach was the first to dance, spinning clumsily around the nearest barrel fire, well into his cups and expected to break something, mayhap parts of himself before the night was done.

Others soon joined in the cavorting, even as those with smaller children found their way back to their crofts. Soon the lane where all had gathered was crowded only by half.

After a while, Violet crashed onto the grass beside Nicholas and Alice.

"Och and will someone remind me at some later date no' to have bairns," she begged, panting. Despite her request, the smile she wore was serene.

Soon Ellen came, giggling with Violet about one of Nicholas' soldiers, Ráild, another one with two left feet in Ellen's estimation. And then they were joined by those other similarly aged and untethered lasses, and Nicholas excused himself, desiring to refill his ale and then not wanting to keep company with a passel of tittering women.

He joined Dungal and Malise and Henry and several other men on the opposite side of the fire and feigned interest in all the drunken nonsense they spouted, pretending that he wasn't still thinking about Alice. Even when Malise began to talk sensibly to him, about more training with lances, Nicholas had one hell of a time concentrating.

It wasn't but a half hour later that his sisters and Alice and those other three lasses removed themselves from beneath the apple tree entirely and walked along the lane. He thought they might be meaning to join the frolicking to the music but then the six of them skirted around the drunken dancers. Alice and Violet, he saw, were arm in arm, as they came close to where he stood.

Before he might have inquired of their intention, Ellen sang out, "We're off to the loch to erase the stench of our labors."

Nicholas scowled, recalling with confidence and not only a wee exasperation the scent of Alice, which was akin to bluidy innocence and all things off-limits and unattainable, but which in reality was likely still that primrose fragrance he'd grown to like.

Effie Unes, inside that group, who was not known for her reticence, added merrily as she waved an arm over her head dramatically, "And ye men stay away lest yer eyes be filled with visions of naked—"

"Effie!" Ellen chastised loudly and through her scandalized giggle.

Nicholas stepped forward and lightly caught Alice's hand as she passed. Instantly, her smiled vanished and her breath held.

"Lass, ye stay close to the others," he advised her. "Dinna go into the deep." To Violet, who'd stopped when Alice had been forced to, he said, "One hour or I'll come for ye."

Both nodded, neither looking pleased for the orders he gave them.

"Yes, brother dear," Violet said with so much sass. "Come on," she urged Alice, "before he changes his mind. We've only seconds to make a getaway before that happens."

When they moved on, Nicholas realized he still held Alice's hand. She did not tug to have it returned to her, but turned back to him, as if with some question about why he was still holding it.

He let her go, watched her hand slide away from his, watched her walk away. The crease in his brow deepened and he was surprised that the next thought inside his head came to him in his father's voice.

*I would do it again, and for so much less, would live all these years again to know only those few with her or even a fraction of that time.*

His lip curled and his stomach twisted as he watched her walk away.

Son of a...

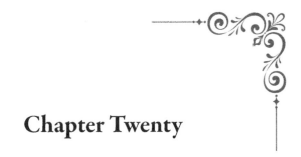

# Chapter Twenty

The bath was not as enjoyable as Alice had imagined, not as peaceful as her late-morning swim with Violet had been only a day ago. In the dead of night, when the water was only one massive pool of unknown black, she was suddenly concerned with bumping into fish or other lake dwellers and then was loath to put her bare feet on either the stony or smoother parts of the lake bed. And too, because Alice had been compelled to remove her shift as the others had done—"...and even if there were any creeping about, what could they see on this moonless night?" Effie had posed as part of her prompting—Alice had felt decidedly uncomfortable with her open-air nudity.

Still, she enjoyed the company of these girls, and was pleased to refresh herself as Ellen had not been far off the mark and Alice was sure she smelled no better than any animal in its pen. Alice, Violet, and Ellen parted ways with the other three ladies directly from the loch, as the night's coolness was felt so much more thoroughly since they were wet, and they wanted to make straight for the keep. Ellen had promised Alice a shift of her own since Alice had no others and they stopped at her chamber upon their return to Braewood. There, Ellen opened both a cupboard and a trunk, each stuffed and nearly overflowing with garments.

"And help yourself to a léine as well," she offered generously. "As you can see, I have too many."

"Indeed," Alice responded, overwhelmed by the sheer size of Ellen's wardrobe.

Ellen shrugged and mayhap blushed a little. "I enjoy creating the pieces," she said. "Actually, I find it quite soothing and have been known to make three or four in as little as a sennight...if I am troubled."

Alice paused, her hand arrested where it had pulled out just the skirt of a hanging blue gown. "What troubles you, Ellen?" She wondered.

"Oh, gosh, what does no'?" Was returned carelessly. And then she waved away Alice's concern and withdrew the very gown Alice had touched from the cupboard, holding it up against Alice's shoulders. "Should do fine," she said briskly and went to the trunk to retrieve a shift.

"I...might rather change here, if that's all right," Alice said.

"Och, but of course," Ellen said, understanding, and rushed to close the door.

Alice quickly doffed her unclean clothes and donned the borrowed pieces. Ellen approached with a long linen cloth and began to squeeze the water from Alice's hair.

"What troubles you, Ellen?" Alice asked again, concerned for what little she'd just revealed.

Her hands paused in the act of wringing wetness from the length of Alice's hair before she made a noise that might have been a harrumph or more likely a snort of derisive laughter.

"How silly of me to express even a hint of discontent," Ellen said, "when you've been treated so unfairly. Let's see what becomes of you, and how long your stay might be." There was a note of wistfulness, as if she wished for something or knew something that Alice did not. "Perhaps one day we'll exchange stories of what confounds us, shall we not?"

A knock came at the door, interrupting their tête-à-tête and when Ellen called for entrance, Nicholas showed himself as the thick, arched timber was pushed open. His dark golden gaze swept over them, where they were perched so closely upon Ellen's bed.

He'd had his own bath, it seemed. He held his belt and sword in his hand and his tunic hung loosely about him, outside the waistband of his breeches, clinging with some glorification to his damp chest. His hair was wet but not dripping, the locks curling with great charm about his face.

"I would rather be sleeping than chasing ye down." While the statement was almost offensive, suggesting she was naught but a fox or any other fleet-footed prey that he would run to ground, his tone suggested only weariness after the long day and not anything else that Alice could discern.

"Can she please stay with me?" Ellen pleaded, her hands clasped in entreaty.

"No, she can no' stay with ye," Nicholas answered curtly.

"Ye are so contrary, Nicky," Ellen whined to him. "Ye let her cavort in the loch, first with Violet and then tonight with nary a guard in sight, and ye dinna mind making use of her all the day to labor under your banner and for your people, and if she wanted to escape, I ken she would have at least made some attempt by now, but ye'll no' allow her any peace of mind but force her to endure the scorn that is already being mumbled about and all because—"

"That is enough," he snapped at Ellen, his hand tightening upon the door's latch. He moved his once-again angry glare to Alice. "Come."

Ellen growled her displeasure and smacked her palms on the feather mattress, to little effect, as Alice rose from the bed.

"Thank you," Alice said to her, "for your kindness and for trusting me."

Ellen showed her a bittersweet smile, which might have said, *For all the good it will do either you or I.*

She followed Nicholas from the chamber, made weak by the truth Ellen had just unwittingly exposed to her.

*If she wanted to escape.*

If.

Didn't she? It wasn't as if she thought Nicholas would have followed through on his threat to lock Joanna in the dungeon. Honestly, she couldn't even say with any certainty that he might have marched his army to the de Graham home to exact revenge if she had thought and then executed and then actually managed to flee and return home. He wouldn't put her in danger by storming her own home. Would he?

Good Lord, had she at least considered escape at all?

Nicholas held the door of his own chamber and when she passed by him, he closed it softly and moved around Alice as she'd stopped just inside, her shoulders slumped, staring at his bed. While she stood indecisive, everything inside her screamed at her for her failings, that she'd not made any attempt at all to pursue what should have been a great desire for freedom. She knew great shame that she'd not considered once that escaping would abet her own father's cause, that he would be safe from reprisal or persecution if Nicholas no longer had control of her.

Ah, but the control was not by means of restraint or vicious coercion, was instead garnered by the spell he'd cast over her, by what was in her heart, whatever she felt when he stared at her with those mesmerizing golden eyes, when her stomach fluttered with excitement whenever he was near...all the times she yearned for one more kiss.

*I am pathetic*, she decided, to be so easily weakened and turned traitor to her own sire, and for what? For a smile? A kiss? From this hard and angry man who would give her up without blinking an eye, with no regret, buoyed by the reward she brought him?

Distracted by her own glumness, Alice turned to seek her bed in the corner.

"Alice," Nicholas said behind her, "let's no' argue about this. Ye're no' sleeping on the floor."

"I cannot simply—"

"Aye, ye can," he snapped at her impatiently. "Same as ye did last night."

Her dander risen, she punched her hands onto her hips and confronted him, "There was a time that you were kind to me and I—"

"And ye've since learned that I am not."

"I've learned that you have anger and...something else in you, and that you might fight against it, but that you can't help but...like me."

He said nothing and neither of them moved, standing on opposite sides of the bed.

Alice swallowed and boldly confessed, "I suffer the very same affliction. I don't want to like you—I have every reason to hate you—but I...I seem to be powerless to...stifle it."

His nostrils flared. His jaw flexed. And then he said, his voice yet curt, "Aye, so we like each other. Will ye get in the bed now?"

Irked that he dismissed so callously this revelation, Alice abruptly doffed the borrowed léine and yanked back the covers and climbed into the bed, all her motions rigid and angry. She laid on her back and tucked the blankets and fur under her arms and stared at the ceiling. Nicholas doffed his tunic and came to bed in a mellower manner, as if nothing raged between them, good or bad.

Alice took a deep breath and wished for sleep to claim her immediately, but it did not. So then she was left to be tormented and agitated by what came next, wondering if he would kiss her again—wondering further what that said about her, because she very much wanted him to. It vexed her greatly that she would desire such a thing when he'd played the uncaring blackguard so well over the last few days. *Good grief, but what is wrong with me?*

"What will happen if my father does not send his army?"

"He will—"

"But what if he doesn't?"

"I've no plans to hurt ye, Alice," he said tersely, "ye ken that."

*But you will*, came unbidden as her response inside her head.

"I can hear your mind spinning," he said quietly next to her, dispersing the taut stillness that had lasted for more than a minute.

"Should it not be?" She sighed, tortured by what she wanted right now, and how awful and selfish a person that made her. "This is dangerous," she whispered, more an admonition to herself than any commentary to him.

"What is...? This is no' more dangerous than...."

He let that go as she turned her head on the pillow and met his amber gaze with her watery eyes for a long and silent moment. The seething pulse of desire that leapt to life inside her mocked her for this treachery now, this longing for him.

"I'll no'...touch ye," he clipped.

Alice's lips trembled. And all the bravery that she wished to possess but mostly believed she did not own gathered in her breast. "Too often, that is what I fear most."

Possibly, she would never again witness so much shock in him as was etched across his proud visage just now.

"*Jesu*, lass," he cursed darkly, rising up on his elbow to face her. "That will no' encourage restraint."

The husky harshness of his voice startled her. She nodded jerkily and removed her eyes from him, pulling the blankets higher up on her chest.

Nicholas didn't move, though she felt his gaze bore into her so that certainly he made note of the lone tear that spilled from her eye. Many more seconds passed before he spoke again.

"I'm no' good, Alice. Ye ken that."

She shook her head sadly and kept her gaze locked overhead, on those dark planks of the ceiling. *But you are, if you would let yourself be.*

"Ye have no idea of what I've...ye dinna ken me at all."

She said nothing. *I know what you are to me. I know who you are with me.*

"Bluidy hell, Alice," he growled and suddenly loomed over her, pressing her back into the mattress as his mouth covered hers.

Joy clutched at her chest and her exultation burst from her lips into his kiss.

His lips moved and probed, at first with some taut restraint that was at the same time breathtakingly demanding. Alice responded instantly, lifting against him, straining toward his searching mouth as his hands delved into her hair and he deepened the kiss.

Her response was as it had been on the occasion of their first kiss, instantaneous and enthusiastic. His elbows and arms flanked her head on the pillow, while the kiss improved as Nicholas seemed to let go of his restraint, his tongue plunging inside, stroking against hers with a hunger to match her own. She felt branded by his kiss, marked as his, and happily so. That part of her that had so little experience in these intimate matters was nervous, but even it was yearning for this, for more of his touch.

"*Jesu*, but how I want ye, Alice." The quiet need of his statement dissolved what little trepidation remained.

Alice put her hands on him and splayed her fingers out against the hard contours of his chest, which she'd dreamed of touching while underneath, his heart thrummed in time to her own. As a reply to her touch, he ravished her mouth and Alice had some notion deep inside that she was behaving wantonly to respond so eagerly, to behave as if she couldn't get enough of him. But then she decided she didn't care and found it so very easy to thrust aside any such self-reproach.

Nicholas shifted his body against her, and she was made aware of all the parts that touched and not only their mouths and tongues. He covered only half of her, his chest pressing against one side, but he'd thrown one leg over her thighs, his limb heavy and hard but not uncomfortable. He moved that now, sliding it along her leg as his kiss moved from her lips to her neck, his lips bringing hidden nerves to life wherever they touched.

"Nicholas," she breathed, but did not recognize her own voice, how husky and needful it sounded. She was dizzy with anticipation. She had never before considered what manner of person she might be within just this circumstance, hadn't ever wondered if she would be passionate or resigned or afraid, but she knew just now what she was: eager and ardent with need and want.

His warm fingers grazed the skin above the bodice of her shift. He pulled gently at the drawstring, unlacing the thing with excruciating slowness, his face in shadow as he'd lifted himself from her to witness the progress of his fingers. When the cotton laces opened under the whisper soft instruction of his fingers, he pushed the cotton away, revealing first one breast and then the other, his calloused palms gliding sensuously over her soft flesh. The only sounds in the room were the bare wind that sifted through the window and their heavy breathing. The dark fire of his gaze upon her bared breasts ignited all her senses.

"Ye have to ken, Alice, that every frown and every harsh word, what anger I own and ye perceived," he said, sounding a wee tortured, even as his face was devoid of all of the habitual fierceness as he gazed with so much adoration at her naked breasts, "was meant to avoid just this. But I've always ken, somewhere inside, that this was inevitable, that my want was far stronger than my will to control it, or rather to deny it. Aye, so much of me did no' want to control it, the urge to touch ye, to..." he paused, shaking his head before he met her gaze. "I've no' lied to ye, Alice. My heart is dark, my soul tarnished. But I promise ye, I'm no' that man right now, no' with ye like this."

His voice, thick with longing, was as arousing as was his kiss and the fingers that traced soft patterns around her breasts. She loved how strong he was, how solid was his body and how piercing was his gaze. She adored how fierce he sounded speaking of his longing and his inability to manage it. It enflamed her own desire.

Though his gaze was hot and hungry upon her, Alice felt no shyness. But before she might have reached for him to return his lips to hers, he bent and his mouth completed the path his hands had begun, chasing the fabric further away, pressing against the skin revealed, onto the roundness of her breast and over the hardness of her nipple.

Alice watched, unable to look away, saw the top of his head and the outline of his nose and mouth, intrigued and breathless at the sight of the connection of their bodies, where his lips now met her breasts. She trembled at the caress of his smooth lips, at the soft flick of his tongue over her pebbled nipple. Sensation of touch soon overrode her curiosity and she let her head fall back on the pillow, closing her eyes to revel in his glorious assault. She gasped when he pulled one taut bud between his teeth. She was awash in an unbearable heat, made more severe by the stroking of his tongue against the imprisoned peak. He repeated the delicate offensive upon her other breast and nipple and Alice was suddenly mindful of parts of her body that she regularly overlooked, those brought vigorously to life as he lit so many nerve endings on fire.

She could not prevent the cry of panic that escaped her kiss-swollen lips when he left her, but her disappointment was quickly forgotten as she watched him rise from the bed and begin to remove his clothes. He was already bare-chested, and Alice was pleased to gape audaciously at the corded muscles of his arms as his hands began to work on the ties of his breeches. He only loosened them and pushed them aside to next undo the other laces of his braies. His bold gaze met hers, likely kept on her even as her breath caught, and her gaze returned to his hands as he pushed both garments down over his hips and thighs and kicked them aside. He was magnificently aroused, his brazen erection straining upward from the short dark hair of his groin. Alice trembled at the sight but could not discount the shiver of excitement that coursed through her.

He paused only seconds after making himself so gorgeously naked and when he moved toward her, Alice's eyes lifted from the pulsing evidence of his desire to his smoldering gaze, and she was overwhelmed by the answering yearning and reaction of her own body, by the tingling expectation between her legs.

Nicholas returned to bed but did not lay his body against hers this time. Rather, he sat on the side of the bed and once more his eyes roamed with so much devotion over her exposed breasts. He lifted his hand and applied it gently to the top of one rounded globe, drawing it down over the nipple, which had receded for lack of touch but now responded sharply, rising for him. His hand did not stop where the fabric of her shift began, still holding just under her breasts. He skimmed his fingers over the cotton, over her flat belly, eliciting a roughly indrawn breath from Alice. When his fingers moved on, crawling down over the rise of her mound, her breath was stolen completely.

Alice eyed him as his gaze followed the movement of his hand once more. She watched his lips part as his hand swept over her hip, defining its shape by pressing the cotton against her and smoothing it down. He leaned forward, his strong arm flexing as he reached all the way down to her shins, where the hem of her undergarment ended. When he glided his hand upward now, it was beneath the cotton, warm and titillating upon her flesh.

Captive to his sweet torture, Alice did not move. As much as the touch of his hands aroused her, she was more aroused by the look on his face. She might almost believe she was some rare and precious thing for how he worshipped her with his eyes. She knew a moment's discomfort when his traveling hand had brought the shift upward, above the triangle at the juncture of her thighs, but the moment was short-lived, extinguished by his rapt gaze, by the quiet heaving of his chest.

"I have to taste ye," he said raggedly, impaling her with his amber gaze. "Ye have to allow me."

Keen to know more kisses from him, Alice nodded numbly. He climbed smoothly onto the bed and parted her legs with his knee before he knelt between them. She felt the hot rush of breath on her belly seconds before his lips landed there. When he moved next, it was not upward toward her lips but downward, toward her legs. As he did, his hands glided along the sides of her hips, pushing her chemise further upward.

He stroked one hand provocatively up her inner thigh, gently nudging her legs open wider. Alice's heart and breath spasmed erratically, not sure what he was about, until he dipped his head between her legs, and she nearly jumped out of her skin and off the bed itself.

There was only the faintest touch of his tongue along the silky triangle of hair before her squirming lifted his head.

"Hold, love," he commanded tenderly, a plea it seemed.

"Nicholas...." This was...this could not be proper, did not seem either respectable or...certainly there was nothing modest about it.

"I want to pleasure ye."

Her limbs and resistance turned liquid beneath him, for how very agreeable that sounded. Modesty be damned then.

He bent once more and boldly applied his mouth to her most secret and sensitive place, one about which she herself had little knowledge—indeed, for which she had little use before this moment now. Instantly, Alice became wide-eyed and rigid from the quick swell of tickling pleasure.

Nicholas slid his hands beneath her thighs and her buttocks. They did not stop moving until they surfaced at the tops of her thighs at the bend of her hips. There, his fingers held her prisoner, kept her enslaved to this forbidden kiss. He lapped his tongue with tantalizing softness over the flesh beneath the ebony hair there. The fire inside her, the want to know this with him, whatever this might be, overrode all sensible caution. Her breath caught but the drumming of her pulse only grew louder in her ears as he plied his kiss expertly. His hands moved, reaching under her thighs to spread her legs further apart and then he used his thumbs to part her folds and his tongue found the hidden nub within, stroking sensually back and forth.

Alice trembled at his ravishment. Her body ached while her senses reeled. She stretched her arms, her fingers clutching at the bed coverings, as if doing so would keep her tethered to reality while his tongue played and pierced her with fire. A moan oozed from between her lips, which did not make him cease his sweet torture, but seemed only to enhance his roguish onslaught. His hands moved again, this time settling under her buttocks, lifting her hips. And then, to her everlasting astonishment, and as a fan to the burgeoning flames, Nicholas pulled her against his mouth as he thrust his tongue inside her. Alice cried out now, not with any of the aforementioned modesty, but with need, en-thralled by his touch, by this deliberate act of raw possession. She fisted her hands tighter around the fabric of the bed linens at her sides and instinctively shifted her hips against his mouth, meet-ing each surge of his tongue.

"Nicholas..." was all she could manage as sound, both a ques-tion and an exclamation, that one sweet word given in a voice that came from somewhere very far away. "Help me," she begged, though for what she did not know. Death was near, it must be— her body damp with perspiration, her senses staggered, her limbs numb, while something teased her, something more.

Help her he did, over the edge, his hands and mouth mer-ciless in their play, until the sun burst inside her and she cried out and tried to thrust herself away from such delirious torment, shuddering with waves and waves of hot, molten release.

Dazed and shattered, she lay unmoving, her eyes closed while she absorbed all the rapture.

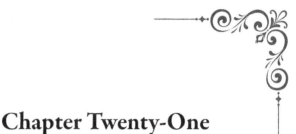

# Chapter Twenty-One

When she stopped writhing, and only lay upon the mattress, arms flung wide, either unwilling or unable to move, Nicholas grinned with a lover's delight and gently pulled the bunched chemise down, over her hips and legs, discarding the thing without care. She was now completely naked, and he let his gaze travel leisurely over her glistening skin, over each tempting curve and every sleek line.

But he could wait no more to claim her. He was rock hard for her, near to bursting with a desperate ache for her. He moved over her, above her, settling into the embrace of her lean thighs. He did not drop all his weight onto her but held himself aloft. She turned her face on the pillow and opened her eyes, her smile serene as she instinctively reached for him.

"I may never recover," she said.

"But we're no' done, lass. There is so much more I want to ken with ye, to show ye." And with that, he shifted his knees and his arms and urged the scorching tip of his shaft to touch the very essence of her, where she'd throbbed under his tongue only moments ago. A flood of primitive lust ripped through him for how wet and open she was to him, for being here, at this moment, and in this place, so close to having his heart's desire. He sank slowly into her, just a bit, allowing her to adjust to this new invasion. "This will make ye mine, Alice. Ye need to ken that."

She nodded, her lips parting at the wonder of his rigid length entering her, of her walls welcoming him, drawing him inside. He didn't care that her acceptance came under this coercion, amid the awe and the returned spark of arousal. When he met her virginal barrier, he withdrew and slowly entered her again. "Wrap your legs around me, love," he murmured hoarsely, nearly undone by the exquisite torture.

Laying her hands on his arms, she lifted her legs and clenched her thighs around his hips and Nicholas repeated his slow forward push and careful withdrawal with teeth-gritting restraint.

"I'm sorry, lass," he said to her, when he could stand it no more, when he was wild with need, only a split-second before he surged forward and broke the wall that wished to deny him entrance. Immediately, he was sheathed in tight, hot flesh, and closed his eyes, grimacing, understanding he could not move as he wished to, not as he longed to do.

Alice winced beneath him, going instantly still, her fingers digging into his flesh. He forced himself to stop, to wait, to give her time to become accustomed to this first before he asked her to accept his complete fullness. His brow beaded with sweat. He glided his lips over hers and stroked his tongue inside her mouth, allowing her to taste herself. Purposefully, he let the short hair of his chest graze over her nipples, returning them to peaked hardness, anything to distract her from the pain, to bring her back to pleasure.

But even these small things, which moved their joined bodies only slightly, drove him quite mad with a strong yearning to rock hard and relentlessly against and inside her, to find his own shuddering release.

"I want—I need—to move inside ye, Alice. Ye tell me when ye're ready."

"I think...I am. Nicholas, I didn't know...well, I didn't know I would *feel* so much."

Nae, she would have no idea. But he would show her.

To test her readiness, he moved once, retreating until the tip of his cock was poised at her entrance. When she released a breathy, "Oh," at that simple motion, Nicholas sighed raggedly his relief that it was safe to move now, and with excruciating slowness he shifted his hips forward again, this time embedding himself deeper.

"I dinna want to hurt ye," he said raggedly, which might have been some primeval attempt to beg her to stop moving so temptingly with him unless she wanted him to slam powerfully into her, as he was wanting to do now.

Alice was remarkable, though, rocking with him, her hands on his shoulders, her hips lifting to meet him.

"I want to feel that again," she said. "My body...all of me, it tingles and throbs and is raw, and...Nicholas, it feels so good."

*Jesu.* So then there was no slowing down or considering her fragility. And maybe he didn't need to. He surged into her, into her honeyed tightness, his rhythm measured until he could no longer help himself and his thrusts became hot and hard and his brow was dotted with perspiration and his brain filled with some vague certainty that there would be nothing else, in all his life, to compare to this pleasure now. And she moaned and cooed and rubbed her breasts against him, her own search for another climax leading him quickly to his. He stiffened when came the intense sensual pain that was also the pinnacle of pleasure and gentled his thrusts, prolonging the sweet agony while Alice clung to him and murmured his name in a beautifully husky voice.

He could not move, not for many long moments, and stayed on top of her, holding the bulk of his weight on his elbows while they were yet joined together, while the raging cadence of their breathing took forever to settle down.

He'd barely regained his wits before he knew he would want her again, tonight, tomorrow, all the rest of his life.

"Everything disappears, does it not?" She asked, her voice naught but a whisper filled with wonder.

Nicholas nodded against her forehead and slowly, carefully, he withdrew from her, falling onto his back beside her.

He struggled yet to level out his breathing, blowing slow breaths out from his mouth.

"Aye, everything disappears," he agreed. But that was true elsewhere, outside the bedchamber, outside this lovemaking. So often when she was near, he saw and heard and was attuned to nothing but her.

Nothing else mattered, it seemed.

IN THE EYES OF SCOTLAND and in some regions of northern England, he was the Brute of Braewood. If he wanted to, he could suppose that nothing had changed. He'd be lying if he said he hadn't considered it.

He might only avail himself to her sweet body while she was his, might revel in the wild abandon she'd shown to him. And when the army was conveyed to him, he would bid her farewell, perhaps even send her off with some of the truth, that no other would ever compare to her, that he would think upon her for years to come.

But then he'd been wakened by a soft and small hand, about a tentative foray of discovery, slim fingers skimming feather-light over his chest. On his back yet, Nicholas did not open his eyes immediately even as other senses were roused.

Alice was leaned against him, much as she had been all through the night, in the crook of his shoulder, safe in his arms. Possibly, her eyes were fixated on her intrepid fingers or mayhap she watched his face for any sign of wakefulness, but if she chanced to glance away, and downward, she would know that he did not sleep now, that her cautious venture provoked other parts to stir as well. When she flattened her hand and stroked her palm with agonizing leisureliness over his nipple, Nicholas covered her hand with his, pressing both of them onto his chest.

"Ye keep that up, lass, it will no' matter if ye're sore or not," he said lightly. "Ye'll end up on yer back all the same."

He opened his eyes, glancing down past his chin to find her looking up at him. In her blue-eyed gaze, he saw some conjecture, as if she might be wondering if she were indeed too tender.

She was not, she decided, as told by the way she bit her bottom lip but stared so steadily at him. So then it was hard to imagine he might suppose nothing had changed. He propped himself up on his elbow and slowly dragged the covers downward, until all of her except her feet were bared to his gaze. He took his time, his perusal slow and thorough, staring at the tumbled waves of her ebony hair strewn about her shoulder and near his planted arm. She'd rolled onto her back when he'd moved, and Nicholas was afforded a close and perfect view of her face. Her lips were slightly parted and commanded his attention for more than just a few seconds, with memories of her brilliant kisses of last night. There was a smattering of freckles across her nose and cheeks, pale and small, barely noticeable, and more that dotted the top of her shoulder. He ran his forefinger over the turn of her shoulder and down her arm, only a sigh of touch. Her hip flared into a gentle swell, beckoning his moving hand. His hand skipped from her arm to her side, and he stroked four fingers over the soft flesh, following the curve down to her thigh and then toward the front of her, into the short curly hair at the juncture of her thighs.

He woke this morning half hard already and his erection grew easily now, stimulated as were all his senses by her, naked and magnificent before him. Coupling with Alice was already met and known, found to be perfect, but Nicholas knew he hadn't yet satisfied his full desire for her. Not yet. It needed only a slight shifting to maneuver on top of her and settle into the cradle of her thighs.

"Mm," she purred sleepily, lifting her hands to splay them over his back. "Good morning," she said and flexed her hips against him.

"It's about to be," he promised her, a true grin coming for how pleasing was this circumstance.

"I think I dreamed exactly this last night, or something close to it," she said in a sweet morning voice.

He slid his shaft into her tight sheath, pausing only for a second, his jaw clenched, at the beauty of that action. "Let's see if we can make those dreams come true."

An hour later, when they finally left the bed, tossing back the bed linens, he was presented with the red stains of her surrender of last night, what she'd held dear for nearly a score of years, what she'd neither given nor had stolen over the last year within that captivity, what she'd offered willingly to him.

And only a short time ago she had opened herself again, without reservation, had given as much as she'd taken.

And so...yes, everything had changed, he realized.

But then, he wasn't sure he was keen to embrace the particular change that might be expected of him now.

They broke their fast in a quiet hall. Alice had been seized straight away by his sisters and kept company with them at one end of the table.

Nicholas was likewise accosted almost immediately by his bailiff, who reminded him of the court session scheduled for this afternoon and attempted to discuss other business with him. Nicholas favored him with half an ear, finding the remainder of his focus stayed firmly with Alice. Likewise, he ignored the conversation beside him, where Dungal and Baldred engaged in some hearty discussion while they ate.

He wasn't sure what it said about either him or her that for as often as he sent an eager gaze her way, she appeared not to be likewise afflicted with any desire to set her eye upon him. In fact, she appeared wholly transfixed by whatever his sisters were whispering and giggling about. Had she laid aside all memory of last night, all that was brilliant, as soon as she'd set foot outside the chamber? Was she not invigorated by any want to cast a fond and knowing glance his way? To share a secret smile with him?

No sooner had he considered this than he noticed her sideways glance, which did not quite reach him, not entirely, but which advised her of his proximity, mayhap was just enough for her to glean what held his attention. In the next second, a flush crept up from her neck and covered her cheeks.

Nicholas' mouth shifted ever so slightly, the smallest hint of a smile.

Ah, that was better. He would rather not be the only one of them bewitched yet by both the memory of last night and the titillating promise of more to come.

His attention was next diverted by the door to the hall opening, by the coming of Edgar—a surprising turn, this, for rarely was the man known to be out of bed 'fore late morning and here he was, dressed in the same everyday degree of pedantic devotion and seeming to have been about the day for some time already. He regularly carried a cane with him, as much an affectation as were the two darkly garbed men who shadowed his every move.

Nicholas had, years ago, decided his attending minions only made Ailred appear to be playacting at some larger role of importance; he'd not ever determined what purpose those two served, had often thought it all gratuitous pretension, had sometimes wondered if he might ever meet anyone who took any part of it seriously.

Edgar found Nicholas' probing gaze upon him and waved his hand daintily. "You might wonder what I am about, roused so early from the confines of a warm bed," he said as he claimed a chair at the high table. "'Twas naught but a jaunt to Drumard Glen, if you must know, to see if the market there might provide a more palatable wine than...well," he said, then flapped his hand more vigorously to dismiss the very question he himself had raised and the answer he'd given. "And fortuitous, the undertaking, I should say, and you might agree, lad. There was some hue and cry raised, the townspeople's jaws fluttering with tales of rogue English in the area—lost or forsaken, who can say? Not more than a score of them, they were sure, and little damage they'd inflicted, but bothersome all the same, you might agree."

Bothersome, indeed, though Nicholas was yet awaiting any words that would explain why he would find such news fortuitous.

"Deserters," Edgar posited with a shrug, before he took a long swig from his flask, presumably of the wine he'd found in Drumard. "Feckless men with more bravado than true ambition, meaning to steal life rather than earn it." He set down his flask and raised a finger, as if just recalling something. "Though they did harass a widow thereabouts, slaughtered her cows and stole her only good mare." Edgar pointed to his hired men, "Louis and Harailt gave chase a bit, but sadly to no avail, so that I imagine the infidels are familiar with the area, to so quickly make themselves scarce, leaving no trail."

Nicholas moved his gaze to those two men, who'd installed themselves at a trestle table and made free with the morning fare, and who took no notice of his attention. They were, Nicholas surmised, rather accustomed to Ailred speaking about them, in front of them, as if they were not of sound hearing, as if they were but mindless hounds ever silent at his side—devoted more certainly to their pay rather than their master's well-being, Nicholas had to imagine.

"And where was that ye last saw them, these infidels?" Dungal asked, attuned to the conversation as were any within hearing of Edgar.

Edgar shrugged. "I have no idea of directions or distances, no' in this area. But closer to Drumard, I should ken. Within a mile or two mayhap."

Nicholas contemplated Dungal's frown and Baldred's cheek-chewing at his left.

"Sheriff should be told," Baldred said.

Dungal scoffed at this. There were few sheriffs in this part of the country, and even fewer effective ones since the war had begun. "Resources and motivations being what they are these days—scarce and dubious, respectively," he said, "I dinna ken that would prove most useful."

"Only Ardros Abbey would be closer to Drumard," Nicholas said, thinking out loud. "But if they are no' made aware of this tale, then it seems most prudent that we, ourselves, investigate what is afoot, and rout those few English loiterers."

"Aye," said Baldred, rising now, "and the day's training will be had away from Braewood, I'll tell the lads."

"Three units," Nicholas advised as Baldred stepped off the dais and headed outside. He would leave nothing to chance and ride with a contingent of at least fifty armed men.

While Edgar had his face buried in a steaming bowl of porridge—delivered upon his arrival, after he'd snapped his fingers at one of the serving girls—Nicholas rose as well, half his day now scheduled away from Braewood. He had no worry for Braewood itself, being further north than any English should dare to roam, and since there would yet be another three score men-at-arms within the boundaries.

He approached his sisters and Alice at the end of the table, all of whom watched his coming, having heard all that he had.

Adopting a mask of coolness, lest his sisters find him regarding his captive with a warm desire, Nicholas addressed Ellen and Violet specifically. "'Tis likely naught," he said. "Surely by now, they've realized their mistake, foraging so far north. But we'll take a patrol out, across the demesne. And we'll be returned by last meal, either assured of their retreat or their demise."

As it would be unseemly if he gave any kind or individual word of farewell to Alice alone, he included her only with the admonition, "Stay with either Elle or Violet, all the day." And then he fought hard to keep his intense regard from lingering upon her entrancing face and this fresh and beguiling blush, the one raised by his nearness, he might assume.

He left then and knew by the heat that scorched his back that Alice watched him walk away. He couldn't say that he minded, rather liked the idea of her regard so rapt upon him as his so often was upon her. Likely, his day in the saddle would be uneventful—he didn't actually suppose they might stumble upon twenty foreign infidels within the thousands of acres between Braewood and Drumard—so that he supposed he might wisely invest the time imagining all that he hoped to discover with Alice inside his bedchamber later this night. Reflections of last night allowed him to easily call to mind naked limbs and bodies entwined, the soft glow of her skin, the rounded fullness of her breasts, how tightly she'd sheathed him, and most breathtaking, how she'd abandoned distress and certainly robust reservations to give herself so wonderfully to him.

Within a quarter hour, Nicholas set out with a troop of men toward the south, away from Braewood's boundary, toward the outlying spaces between them and Drumard as he planned to see for himself what might be noted about English bandits in the area. A handful of miles away from the gates of Braewood, as they approached the hills known locally as The Lady's Breasts for their twin peaks and soft swells. a flash of sun upon steel inside the trees of the hills advised that mayhap intruders had made a home on MacRory land. Cursing, Nicholas set his men to a swift pace and charged headlong toward the base of the hill and upward. He called out to split the party in two and angled his destrier toward the northeastern side while Baldred led half the party around and upward fifty yards away.

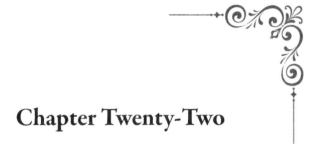

# Chapter Twenty-Two

S he watched him leave, as entranced as she had ever been, maybe more so now, by the feline grace of his walk, by the broad set of his shoulders, the proud tilt of his head. Possibly she would spend all this day in one constant blush, moments ago for detecting his powerful perusal, which she'd tried her best to ignore. And now, with his absence, for what memories assailed her—sweet memories of what they'd shared last night, ones that both shocked and elated her.

Violet and Ellen chatted around her, Ellen so like Joanna that so often no response was required. Alice was then left to consider the events of last night. As lovely as it had been, she wondered if she were strong enough, or had any capability to separate herself from that person she'd been inside his bedchamber last night, within Nicholas' arms. She wasn't sure that wasn't the more true person that she was, but it did not fit in with what her role *should* be. She ought to cast aside all thoughts, put the entire episode from her mind, unless she wished to risk torturing herself with guilt for how she had betrayed her father. She hadn't set out to do that, of course; she'd wanted only to know Nicholas, to know his touch, to feel his hands upon her, to be his, just for a little while. But in doing so—and with such eagerness—she had effectively betrayed her father all the same.

*Everything disappears*, she recalled saying to him. It had been more true last night than in all her memory. She'd thought of nothing but him, considered nothing but her desire and what she craved from and with him. And while she might spend all of today scolding herself, knowing such shame for her disloyalty to her father, she did not fool herself that everything was like to disappear all over again tonight or the next time she might know such intimacy with Nicholas, mayhap every night for as long as she remained at Braewood. She knew it was selfish, had advance warning right now of her inevitable failing and still, she had no desire to try and change it. This would likely be all she would ever have of him. She would take what she could get.

And she'd worry about silly things like heartbreak and repercussions and her own treachery when she was gone from him. But not at all while she was with him.

She was startled to attention as Ellen stood and left the table.

Violet caught her staring after her sister, while possibly Alice's expression wondered what she'd missed.

"Head in the clouds," Violet commented, her expression bland. And next, inclining her head toward her sister's departing figure, "She's off to the village with a basket full of bread and honey."

"Should we...?" Alice began.

Violet shook her head. Her hair was pulled into a ribboned tail which hung over her right shoulder. She fiddled idly with the long ends. "Nae, we should no," she said absently. "Or ye might, if ye wish. But I ken I had my fill of...people and crowds and noise to last me quite a while."

Alice grinned at this. "I understand."

"I'll be seeking the quiet again. Ye...well, if ye want," Violet said next, her brow furrowed a bit as she still fidgeted with the long strands of her flaxen hair, "ye're welcome to join me." And then, as if she did not wish to be considered particularly desirous of her company, she added swiftly, "I dinna care either way. But if ye want...."

Alice guessed that if she were going to be residing at Braewood for any length of time, Violet might be the person she would wish to spend the most amount of time—aside from Nicholas. She thought she might much prefer her serene and easy company to that of almost anyone else. And being out of doors in such hospitable weather, which she knew very well would not be theirs for long, was not anything to be discounted.

"I should like that," she said evenly.

Thus, thirty minutes later, Violet and Alice meandered along the shore of the loch, each with a basket in hand. Violet somehow managed to get away with rarely availing herself to household chores. She confessed that more often than not her basket contained bread and cheese, as she spent so much time outside the curtain wall and away from the meals.

"Or, sometimes," Violet said now as she idled along, barefoot, seemingly without a care in the world, "the basket might contain fishing nets—or parts thereof—and my short spear, which I honed myself, and which might be attached to any straight and useful tree limb found in the underbrush."

"You fish yourself?" Alice asked, swinging her arm deliberately and wildly in front of her as some black winged thing flew too close "And stab the fish with your spear?"

"When the nets do not hold my interest, aye," Violet answered over her shoulder, as she led the way.

"Why would the nets not hold your interest?"

"On occasion I like to actively participate, and not only sit back and watch and wait."

Alice thought that might be true of most of Violet's life, from what little she'd noticed so far.

"And what fills your basket today?" Alice asked the girl now.

Violet grinned, as she was rarely wont to do, which gave Alice pause. Violet stopped walking along the banks of the loch and turned to lift the long linen scrap that covered the contents of the wicker container.

Alice's initial gasp melted into a gratified smile. Inside the wicker, sitting upon another scrap of fabric, sat two tiny bunnies.

"I watched the hawk take their mother last week," Violet explained. "But I cannot continue to nurse them inside my chamber. They need to be...well, free and wild and learn their own way. Here's hoping the survival instinct is engrained in them and not only learned from their mother."

Delighted, Alice reached in and scooped up one of the furry kits. "Oh, you sweet thing," she cooed, holding it close and securely, stroking the downy coat between its ears.

Violet set down the basket and took out the sibling, holding it confidently with one hand while glancing around. "Fionn, in the stables, says ye should no' leave them so far from where ye found them, since they dinna ever move more than a few acres all their lives." She shrugged then, possibly suggesting she wasn't sure she subscribed to his theory. "But this is close to where their mam was taken, so aye, I ken it'll do."

They released the kits beneath the cascade of needled limbs of some unknown conifer, the branches and tips sweeping over the ground, the kits safely tucked beneath that canopy. Alice watched for a few moments but did not see either of them hop out from under the branches. When she turned, Violet had proceeded to the loch, was twenty feet away, already seated and removing her worn boots.

Alice did not demur, believing a plunge, quick or otherwise, might be just what her deliciously sore body needed. She sat and began to doff her own footwear just as Violet popped up to her feet and threw off her léine, walking without hesitation into the water, garbed in only her long chemise.

Alice stood, meaning to follow suit, beginning to pull the hem of her gown upward, when she was frozen by the sound of riders coming. She dropped the length of her skirt and cocked her head to listen, worried that a group of soldiers or peasants from the village might intrude upon the quiet.

Violet had dived into the water but now resurfaced, had caught the sound as well, her frown instant and for the same reason as Alice's hesitation.

Alice whirled when the noise grew closer and then was shocked to see Edgar Ailred come through the trees, upon horseback, and flanked closely by those two mysterious companions, likewise atop lean war horses.

Before Alice might have requested of Ailred that he remove himself from what she and Violet hoped would be their private swimming, Edgar Ailred lifted his affectation of a cane and pointed it directly at her.

"I must give you my appreciation, lass," he said, his gaze on Alice after it passed only fleetingly over Violet, neck deep in the water.

"Whatever for?" Alice wondered, bemused. She tried to focus only on Ailred and not let her gaze dart to those two men, whom she found quite menacing in this setting for the way they stared at her, as if she were naught but a fledgling bunny, vulnerable prey. Certainly she did not like the way they walked their horses forward a bit, as if they meant to circle around her.

"For making the task so much easier," Ailred said cryptically. "And here I thought I'd have to wrestle you away from under the noses of the house guards, now that the laird and surely a larger contingent are about chasing ghosts in the hills."

A prickle of unease disturbed Alice. Her polite smile was arrested as she shared a confused look with Violet across the distance, which contained no small amount of disquiet.

Edgar Ailred then followed Alice's gaze out into the water. Addressing his niece, his tone well-mannered, he called out, "Now, this here hasn't anything to do with you, dear Violet, and so it should not, as you've always been a nice, quiet lass." He turned to his mounted companions and said, in the same courteous tone, "It'll be the black-haired wench we'll be taking with us."

*Taking with them*? Alice's heart slammed into her ribs.

Stalling, hoping confusion evaporated or that some clarification was afforded her, she asked Ailred. "Did I hear that you rode down to Drumard this morn?"

He chuckled at the question, mayhap at her stalling tactic. Alice inched her bare feet backwards.

"Ride all the way to Drumard? On horseback? Nae, lass, I would have employed my carriage if that had been my plan. I merely rode outside the view of the castle guard, those on the wall specifically, and then tarried about the woods for a goodly time until I might return and relate that version of fiction about

English in the area. How else might I have gotten the laird and so much of his army away from Braewood? From you?"

"I don't understand...."

"No, of course you would not," he said as one of his henchmen slid from his horse and approached Alice. "I am sorry I cannot take the time just yet to explain," Ailred said, "But I really think we should get moving lest we are discovered."

Alice backed up a few more steps as the black-eyed man bore down on her. She wanted to run, but she was afraid to abandon Violet. And honestly, part of her rather thought this must be some jest, some prank intended to scare the hapless captive.

The man—Louis, he'd been called—grabbed her arm. Alice was unable to shake it off.

"I am not going anywhere with you," she said hotly.

"But of course you are," Ailred said as the man began to drag her toward his mount.

"Let her go!" Violet screamed from the water, beginning to walk out.

The other minion, Harailt, moved his steed to the water's edge and drew his sword, suggesting he would strike if Violet marched any further.

Violet raged, her face red, "He will ken! Nicholas will ken what you have done! I will tell him!"

"Oh, I do hope so, my girl," Ailred cooed ominously. "It would be nigh impossible to get what I want—what is my due—if he doesn't know who has done what, or where she is."

To Alice, who was trying to free herself from the brigand with the black eyes, Ailred advised, "Please do not make this tedious, my dear. Violet truly is an agreeable lass. I would so hate for her brother to find her with her throat slit."

She might have fought. She'd just thought that Violet could simply swim away from this terror. But in that brief moment when Ailred's words scared the bejesus out of her, Louis cracked her across the face, the blow ringing her ears and sending her stumbling back several paces, until she crashed into the side of his horse. While she tried to right herself, her head spinning while Violet shrieked an alarm, Louis slipped a loosely knotted rope over her hands and yanked the end tight, drawing her hands together swiftly as if she'd clapped them. She had just gotten both feet under her and lifted her hands to claw at the man's face when he spun her around and prodded her forward with a kick to her bottom, while yet holding the rope. She went flying toward Harailt and his steed and was lifted from behind and tossed unceremoniously onto the saddle before that silent man, plopped onto her stomach, the force of her rough landing forcing a whoosh of breath from her. Louis passed the rope beneath the horse's belly, and she felt the ends of it being knotted around her knees. She was wedged between the man's groin and the pommel and entirely too much of her was draped over the man in a grotesque fashion.

With escape seeming impossible now—she hated herself for her confusion and hesitation—fear rose to the fore.

My God. What was happening? Why was Edgar Ailred kidnapping her?

While Violet continued to scream, likely hoping to alert what soldiers remained at Braewood, which would prove either unlikely or simply too little too late, the three horses turned about and walked through the trees. They did not find the main road, either to the village or to Braewood, but crossed directly over it and walked their horses casually across the flat meadow, and up and over one of the many knolls which might be seen from the curtain wall. Once beyond that and down into the low valley again, they picked up speed, Edgar likely hoping to put as much distance between him and Braewood before Nicholas returned and was alerted of this travesty.

The ride, face down with her limbs tied and her stomach bouncing along unevenly, was an unimaginable horror all by itself. Her cheek and eye, where she'd been struck, felt as if she'd been kicked by a furious steed, the pain reverberating along one side of her face with every racing footfall of the steed. Her hip scraped and crashed against the man's knee with every up and down motion, as she had no way to control her ungainly bouncing. She was certain what little food and drink she'd put into her stomach this morning was about to come out. At one point she began to slide forward, her upper body being pitched along and down the side of the horse, until the man, Harailt, grabbed a fistful of her léine at her lower back and held her in place.

She could avoid neither the wrenching discomfort nor the crazy fear that perhaps Nicholas would not care, perhaps he might be well-pleased to be rid of her through no effort of his own. Perhaps he'd had some word that the de Graham army would not ever be his to command. He might only brush his hands back and forth against each other, the whole untidy affair at an end.

She was ashamed to admit that particular fear bullied her for more than a mile.

No, he will come for me. He feels...*something* for me. Something more than only what was expressed last night with his kiss and his touch. That mantra repeated in her head—*he will come for me*—until she believed it wholeheartedly. She was unworldly and unwise and possibly influenced by what she felt for him, but she just couldn't believe she might have misjudged him so much that he would leave her to this fate, whatever Edgar Ailred had planned for her.

They continued moving, their pace never less than swift, taking Alice further and further away from Braewood and Nicholas. She had no sense of where they were or where they might be going. She knew only that they moved north, but she had no true idea about direction or destination or miles left behind them. The motivations behind this scheme were impossible to imagine, as she'd only just come to Braewood and had exchanged so few words with Ailred. It was strictly between Ailred and Nicholas and she was, yet again, naught but a man's pawn.

Soon she could not control the ire that prickled her for this circumstance. It overrode every other ache and pain and concern. She'd had enough of being used and abused, as if she had no other worth but as that of a hostage. She wished she were stronger, or braver, to be able to terminate for herself this vexing pattern of her life. She was naught but a victim in the last year, and to several selfish parties—Nicholas included—and would be, all her days. Unless or until she did something about it herself.

They were forced to slow their pace as they entered a forest of trees. Thus far, Alice had mostly kept her eyes closed as it seemed to alleviate, if only minimally, the jarring and bumping of the ride. When her eyes were open, she'd watched the passing ground, having concentrated at some points on the earth and grass and mud being chewed up beneath the horse's hooves. Inside the trees, the ride did not improve measurably, for the uneven ground and sometimes sharp twists and turns. It was then less a steady cadence of bouncing and more jolting, and Alice's stomach roiled and she let it, doing nothing to fight the nausea. She felt the bile rising and was pleased then to lift and turn her face, as much as she was able, and spew her breakfast onto Harailt's leg and boot.

The man cursed and snarled, trying to lift his leg away from the path of her retching. He reined in abruptly, his hand removed from where it had held her at her back, and Alice was jolted forward and then down, with nothing to stop her steady descent.

"Bollocks," shouted the man.

But at least the horse was brought to a halt. Harailt dismounted, grumbling and spewing forth a litany of curses. The entire party stopped then, Edgar Ailred seeming to find the reason humorous.

"Oh, my," he said in his high voice. "Harailt, ye've got a mess there—but don't leave the wretched creature dangling over the side as such! Louis, attend the lass," he ordered when Harailt ignored him and walked away, beyond Alice's constrained view that she had no idea what he was about.

Louis appeared in front of her and took a dagger to the ropes he'd tied. He grabbed Alice's arm before she might have only toppled onto her head, and dragged her forward until her legs cleared the horse's back and dropped to the ground. Every inch of her was numb and bruised and sore and she could not help but fall to her knees. She lifted her arm and wiped the sleeve of her léine across her mouth. The ropes, cut and thus loosened, draped uselessly around her wrists. With her head bent, she gathered the drooping jute and pulled it close, to give the impression that her hands were still bound tightly.

Harailt was in her periphery, to her right, on his arse near the small brook, removing his black leather boot, which he was no doubt intent on washing. Louis stood directly in front of her, either waiting for instructions from Edgar, or for Alice to stand of her own accord. His hand had fallen away from her when she'd collapsed to her knees.

Edgar's voice came from behind her, behind Harailt's horse, by which she sat. "Be quick, Harailt. We need to put more distance between us and them."

Harailt shot back an insolent retort, more concerned with the state of his shoe than Edgar's wishes.

"If they give chase," Louis commented, "they'll be at least an hour behind us."

Still mounted, Edgar walked his steed around to loom above her.

Alice lifted her furious gaze to him. "He will come for me," she promised him with mad glee. "And he will split your gullet east to west when he finds you."

"Aye, he will try. Certainly he has done as much before. The Brute of Braewood was not only a designation imagined to frighten the English. He has earned that moniker and all by the tip of his blade, none of it honorably. But then ye ken that already, do you not?"

"He has more honor in only one limb than you have in all of your...yourself. He is nothing like you. He uses his sword for freedom and for country and—"

Edgar laughed uproariously, cutting her off. "I ken we're no longer speaking of the same person, lass."

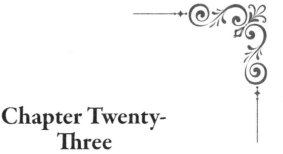

# Chapter Twenty-Three

Alice stared fiercely at the toad of a man. How dare he—whilst in the midst of his own abduction of her!—call into question Nicholas' honor.

But Ailred's next words silenced any further defense she might have given to Nicholas.

"Likely, amid all the calf's eyes ye and he were making at each other, he neglected to inform ye of his true self. The Brute of Braewood Keep was born not of the righteous war against the English, not his part in it—certainly not from his time spent as a captive of the English—och, ye were not told of that? Aye, a most ignoble circumstance to be sure, and one that no doubt formed the basis of the life he lived immediately after, that as a hired sword. He was a paid mercenary, lass. Generously paid, to be sure, as he was merciless in his profession and could demand any sum. God's bluid, but it appears ye were not made privy to this aspect of his life either. Ye poor, deceived thing," he said and laid his chubby hand against the brooch at his chest. He winced as if personally affected by her plight. "And now, ye see how foolish ye've been, romanticizing him, and aye, defending him as staunchly as ye have. 'Tis naught but misplaced devotion, is it not? He is a killer of men and women and—if the stories be true—of children as well, though I am sure, my dear girl, that some were deserving of it." He went on, gleefully it seemed, his eyes wide. "I heard tell of a most peculiar tale some years back, which said that the Brute of Braewood Keep had once aided and abetted the cause of four men, uncles to an heiress, who wanted her...well, gotten out of the way upon the death of her father. They called upon the man you claim is chock-full of honor, putting him under contract to remove what stood in the way of their own greed. And so he did, invading the home and making off with the lass—she was but a child, had seen no more than ten summers, mayhap—and he went directly to the forest nearby and slayed the child, burying her in a hole in the ground in the middle of nowhere. Collected his fee and off he went, without a backward glance, as I hear it told. Where, dear girl, is the honor in that?"

Alice was speechless, disbelieving—or wanting to be. But she had no words now to holler at Ailred in defense of Nicholas, not when Nicholas' own words sounded in her head, seemingly given credibility to what this insufferable man had just put forth.

*I'm no' good, Alice. Ye ken that.*

*Ye have no idea of what I've...ye dinna ken me at all.*

While she wrestled with all the trauma that rightfully was associated with this agonizing news, and more specifically with the possibility that Nicholas had once taken the life of a child—perhaps more than one—merely to collect coin, Edgar continued speaking.

"Ah but ye can't blame him, likely his time in that English prison made him that way. But still, such a rascal, is he not, lass? To have lived that life, to have all that blood on his hands, and then to rail against me for any effort of my own to end war and division in my little corner of the world. But then ye already ken what a shameful and self-serving brute he is, do ye not?"

Her shoulders fell, her gaze unseeing even as she continued to look at Ailred. Bereft, she wondered if she'd simply overlooked the truth, all for want of a kiss. The shame she'd convinced herself she would and could put aside while she was yet with Nicholas, while there was a chance that she might again find herself in his arms and in his bed, returned with blinding force until her chest burned and throbbed more powerfully than did any other part of her bruised body.

But no, she would not believe it. Lies, all of it, given only to distract her, to make her distraught, mayhap compliant.

But then, *A man lives his life having convinced himself that his deeds were justified, necessary mayhap...*

*No, no, no.* That was not the issue at hand, she decided. Her own precarious situation was.

To steer both herself and Edgar away from this unsettling portrait painted of Nicholas, she railed further against Edgar and his own dishonor. "And what of you? This, now, is a laudable kidnapping?" She sneered at him, "You only meant to save me from the clutches of the beast?"

Edgar shook his head, though was wholly unmoved by her scorn, his smug grin intact.

"Nae, lass. I dinna pretend so much. At least I am honest about my intentions. I seek what your hero Nicholas did—an army for my cause."

Alice gasped. *What?*

"Tis true," he said, enjoying her confusion, pleased to enlighten her. "I require either an army or the coin to procure one. Alas, I may have overstated the desperation in our little burgh to the north, when in fact 'tis my own desperation that fuels my concern. Oh, pray, don't get me wrong—the conflict is real. It is...well, it's just that I truly have no care for politics as such. But then, I am not absurd, not at all. I need the MacHeths and MacWilliams to hold power so that I may hold power. Presently, alas, I have little to offer. But with an army, I rise in the ranks of all those obnoxious goblins spinning their wheels to establish themselves as worthy and valuable. With great—"

"So, it's all about greed," she surmised bitterly.

"Never let anyone tell you it is ever about anything else."

Possibly, she was wasting her time trying to understand his motivations.

She jeered at Louis and Harailt, who'd returned from where he'd knelt by the slowly trickling water. "And you are willing to die for this odious man? Because die you will, when Nicholas MacRory comes for me."

Neither seemed overly concerned, nor said a word.

*Trust only yourself*, she decided then and there. For more than a year, and discounting both her mother and Joanna, she was the only person whom she might trust. To any other she was naught but a means to an end.

She dropped her head and looked sideways, but only to avoid facing the conceited and intimidating stares of these three men. It was then that she noticed a flash of light glinting off an object at the gravelly bank of the narrow stream. Squinting her eyes, Alice saw that it was a knife, sitting almost exactly where Harailt had a moment ago. A quick glance at the man showed he still possessed a longer dagger, sheathed in his belt. That one there might have been removed from his boot when he'd taken it off to clean it.

"I need a moment," she said, rising to her feet, not without difficulty. She was sapped of strength, sore and frightened, and her faith in Nicholas had been challenged mightily. "Let me at least rinse my mouth and soothe my stomach with fresh water lest there is more to be brought up."

While Harailt nodded stiffly his fondness of this plan, Edgar thinned his lips and advised, "Be quick. We must make haste."

Alice trudged the twenty feet to the water's edge, going to her knees once more, this time directly on top of the dagger that had been forgotten. She did rinse her mouth, and she even splashed a bit of water on her face but used only one hand while she let the rope joining her hands go slack as she reached the other hand beneath her legs, finding the wooden handled blade and tucking it discreetly up into her sleeve.

She didn't move then, stayed bent over the water, trying to imagine a plan. She thought her best chance might be now to affect an escape, before she was put up onto the horse again. To do so, to gain her own freedom, she would have to actually use the knife against someone, she guessed, would have to pierce skin and flesh, cause real damage, enough to incapacitate one or more of them. She couldn't outrun them, and it was unlikely she could manage to push Harailt off the horse, even if she was brave enough to use her tiny weapon against him and cause an injury. Mayhap her best chance was now, if she could run, and possibly put enough space between each of them that she had only one to contend with at a time.

"We need to move, lass, and now," Ailred called out. "Fetch her," he commanded of one of his hired goons.

Now or never.

Alice leapt to her feet and sped quickly along the uneven ground along the stream.

There was a curse behind her and then equally swift footsteps giving chase. This was followed by Ailred shouting another blasphemy and then roaring, "Get yer horse, man! Run her down!"

She would be caught, she knew, praying she had the courage to fight for her freedom, to possibly take a life.

As she ran, she tossed off the rope and withdrew the short dagger from her sleeve, her knuckles white as she clutched the warm handle. Then she picked up her skirts and ran hard through the brush and saplings near the stream.

NICHOLAS LEANED FURIOUSLY over the big black, his teeth bared and his heart thrumming in time to the swift and loud clomping of the horse's hooves. His gut churned with rage and worry, and he kicked his heels, urging the destrier to fly even faster.

Any previous self-criticism and derision, of which there had been plenty over the years, paled in comparison to what he felt now, that he'd been so easily duped. He should have known, should have suspected immediately when Edgar had said he'd ridden into Drumard so early.

But he did not know, had thought nothing amiss until they'd followed the flashing reflection of the sun upon metal up that hill, and had found naught but a non-descript sword thrust into the bark of a tree. Whether intentional or only inexplicably neglected some time ago, Nicholas had been overwhelmed with a sense that something was not right. Instinct troubled him. Edgar was up to something, he'd known right then. Up and about so

early when the man never showed himself before late morning. Riding to Drumard without a viable reason, not one that
Nicholas had heard. Small considerations, in the whole, but by
the cross, how they shouted and cried at him with hindsight.

Something was not right. He could feel it.

He'd ordered the men with him back to the keep. "We're
chasing fiction," was all he'd said and so was not at all surprised
by the uproar that greeted him upon his swift return to the keep.
Violet, in tears, spouting some unfathomable tale about Edgar
and his minions abducting Alice; Ellen made speechless by her
shock; Joanna wailing her fright, in her usual manner, wondering what she might say to Alice's *dear, sweet mam* if she'd lost her
child.

Edgar.

Abducting Alice.

It made no sense, not any at all until they'd been hard on his
trail for three quarters of an hour.

Edgar, abducting Alice, mayhap for the very same reason
that Nicholas had, as Longshanks had before him, all of them
seeking an army.

*Jesu*, but if she were harmed in any way—

"There!" Malise shouted over the thundering of hooves,
pointing to a continuance of the trail, made relatively easy to follow since the morning dew had not evaporated fully under the
dull gray sky.

"He'll be aiming for the northeast road then," Dungal surmised.

Aye, the only other option would have been quicker as the
northeast route skirted through the forest, but likely Edgar
would have supposed that Nicholas would have assumed he'd

gone in the other direction, or mayhap it was only hope that the MacRorys would not have so steadfastly followed their trail. It didn't matter but that Nicholas knew greater hope of catching up with them, since Violet was sure that Edgar had not more than a half an hour's head start. Nicholas did not dwell on what might have been if he'd not heeded that tingling of apprehension when they'd found that abandoned sword upon the hill.

They did not ease up on the brutal pace set, not even when the trees of the forest closed around them. The destrier might have had an awareness of Nicholas' fear and thought to cause him no more grief, and so his gait was sure and swift through the oaks and elms and pines.

They were naught but a half a mile inside the dark forest, the army spread out wide to cover more ground, when a call came from the extreme left flank. Nicholas dug his heels into the stirrups and pulled back on the reins, turning the destrier in that direction.

He found several soldiers prancing their horses around a wounded man, one of Edgar's minions, Louis, he thought it was. He was bloodless of face and holding his hand over the inside of his thigh, his fingers and breeches soaked in his own blood.

"Where is she?" Nicholas demanded, rearing the horse above him, the front feet coming perilously close to crashing upon him when they landed.

"Running," the man said, shaking his head, rolling onto his side. He met Nicholas' dark gaze. "Running scared." He lifted his bloodied hand and pointed north. The gash at his thigh reacted to the loss of pressure and red blood swelled and oozed from the slice.

"Leave him," Nicholas called and spurred the destrier into a gallop once more, having no care of concern for the man or his condition, or even how he'd come about that wound, which would likely be the death of him. He wouldn't—couldn't—let his mind address any other thing but Alice's safety. He must find her.

Another shout rose over the sound of a deafening noise made by fifty riders in the woods, but this cry was not one of his soldiers alerting him of someone found, but was Alice herself, raging and hollering. Nicholas crested a rise in the terrain and came upon a startling scene, which revealed Alice standing above a fallen Edgar Ailred, her hands clasped tightly about a stout tree limb, nearly three feet in length. She was shouting at the man and beating him about the shoulders and back with her club, while Edgar covered his head and cried like a wee bairn, his chubby legs drawn up to his chest.

"How dare you!" Alice thundered. "Think you have any right to my person!" She smacked him again with the branch.

Nicholas slid from the saddle before the horse had completely come to a halt and raced toward her. She continued to wail at Ailred, her words and charges bringing Nicholas to an abrupt halt, his feet skidding to a stop in the forest debris. As of yet, he was unseen by Alice.

"I am not a body to be used and abused!" She raged on and whacked him again. "I am so eternally sick and tired of playing the part of the pawn." Thwack. "I'll be damned before I do so ever again." Thump. "You can take your greedy plans"—smack—"and your bloody minions to hell with you."

She did not lift her arms or her weapon again. Instead, she struck the stick into the ground and leaned upon it, the fight expelled, her foe vanquished, quivering and whimpering.

"You are evil and selfish," she said, breathless now, weary. "And you don't deserve even this as attention." Then she lifted the club once more but only to toss it scathingly upon her victim.

Nicholas was...astonished. Beyond that.

"Alice," he called out to her, breathless himself at the raw hatred revealed in her voice and words and actions.

She turned her head, only marginally, before she straightened her shoulders and turned fully to face Nicholas and the fifty mounted men behind him.

His breath caught now in his throat at the sight of her. Her hair stood on end, clumped and tangled and peppered with leaves and one thin stick; her léine was torn and dirtied. Her face was bright red, swollen near her left eye, while a trail of tears washed a clean track down her cheeks.

Her chest heaved up and down and the gaze she sent to him showed not relief but still so much of the fury she'd just employed with Edgar Ailred. But then, that was not surprising, given that all the words she'd spat at the fallen figure might well have been spewed at Nicholas, for his sins were the same.

Despite this, he needed to touch her, to hold her. His heart split in two for what she had become, this bitter and broken person, for what part he'd played in it.

"Seize him," he instructed, regarding Ailred, as he strode purposefully toward Alice.

He put his hands on her arms and looked her over again, assuring himself she was, despite appearances, not suffering greater injury.

For the space of a second, she sagged with some known relief, and Nicholas pulled her tight into his arms. He breathed raggedly, ejecting his own torture, his throat tight with some unnamed emotion. He kissed her forehead and her filthy hair.

She allowed this but briefly before she shoved him away. "Do not touch me," she snarled in a voice he'd never heard before from her. "You are just as guilty and as awful as that one."

From two feet apart they stared bitterly at one another, she with her justified anger and he with the collapse of hope.

"Where's the other one?" Baldred asked, coming to stand beside them.

Without blinking or taking her gaze from Nicholas, she answered, "He fled when he heard your approach."

Neither startled nor paid any attention to Baldred then barking out orders, that the man was to be run down.

"How did ye...? We found Louis further back there, a mortal wound inflicted." He moved his gaze to her bloodied right hand.

"I don't know. He leapt at me from the horse while I ran. We...tussled and I...I just...." Her eyes swelled again with tears. She lifted the bloody hand to her inspection.

"Come," Nicholas said, holding out his hand to her. "I will take you ho—back to the keep."

Averting her gaze, Alice shook her head. "No," she said. "Take me home. If you have any feeling for me at all, take me home. I don't want to be this person, this angry person. I-I don't want to...know you. I want to go home."

"Alice..."

Her chin quivered as she leveled him with a bitter gaze, then brushed past him, stalking to where he'd left his horse. As before, she mounted herself. In truth, he was surprised that she waited for him, did not kick the patient steed into motion to be away from him.

Nicholas exhaled sharply as he reached her. Without a word, he gained the seat behind her and spared only a fleeting glance to see that his men had the scene under control—he did not suppose for one minute that the second ruffian would get very far before he was overtaken—before he started the short trip toward the keep.

They spoke not a word, not for many miles, not until they crested the last rise before Braewood, when only the flat meadow and rutted road and a quarter mile separated them from the keep.

At the crest of the hill, Nicholas reined in again, and watched, with both wonder and a fresh wave of anger as another army marched slowly toward the curtain wall and gate. He knew no fear. This was a walking army, not a hurriedly moving militia meaning to lay siege to his home. At the fore, banners waved in the hands of the flag bearers, the gold and red of the de Graham crest and colors clearly visible.

Her father had come to deliver his army.

Had come to take his daughter home.

Alice gasped a moment later, as she, too, identified the troops and the large man at the helm. She might suppose that the four-wheeled, enclosed conveyance carried her mother. The whole bloody family, come to wrest her away from his evil clutches.

When he didn't spur the horse to move down the hill, Alice turned her face toward him.

"Here is your army, sir, exactly as you wanted."

Nicholas cursed under his breath and angrily shoved off the horse, landing on two feet, holding the reins in one hand, Alice's skirt in the other.

Her face was pale now, gone the fight, and stricken with anguish, of which he might be mostly to blame.

He opened his mouth but did not know what to say, how to say it. He only knew that he was out of time but that he could not let her go.

"I want to go home," she said before he could piece together a credible plea.

In the most vulnerable way possible, such as he'd never shown in all his life, not to anyone, he said with only a hint of hope, "Home can be here, Alice. With me."

She frowned down at him. "What on earth are you suggesting?"

"That ye marry me."

"Why on earth would you want to marry me? The...the army is here. You've won."

"No' for that. Yer da can take them home. I dinna care about the army."

"Then why...why?"

"I have to," he said, still coming to terms with it himself, all the powerful and poignant emotions that were tied to Alice. "I canna all my life wonder and worry, is she safe? Is she well? Is she happy?"

He'd stunned her. She raised a shaking hand to her lips.

He went still, clinging to her, afraid to look away, afraid she might not recognize his anguish, which might possibly engulf him if she left him.

"And you think you can make me so? Any of those things?"

"All of those things."

"But you are not a good man, Nicholas," she whispered tonelessly.

With his hands yet on the reins and her thigh, he averted his gaze, staring down blindly at his own feet. "Nae. I am no'."

"I don't really know anything about you," she said softly. "You've hidden so much from me...about your past."

Ah, so Edgar had been chatty. It didn't matter. It would have come out eventually. Might have, he corrected, since Edgar's stunt of today and her father's arrival in all probability precluded the necessity of divulging any sorry truths to her now.

Sighing with a mental exhaustion he hadn't known was possible, he lifted his gaze to her. "It does no' matter now." He would have mounted again, returned her to her father, but that she forestalled him with her next words.

"It does matter. I have a right to know why you hid so much." She chewed her lip, looking suddenly more vulnerable than indignant. "From me," she added pointedly.

"I did no' hide anything," he told her quietly. "Until last night, we both fought against any deeper connection, did we no'? It was no' as if I'd introduce into any of our snappish and stilted conversation, *oh, by the way, did ye ken I was once abused and imprisoned and brought close to death at the hands of the English? Did ye ken I hired out my sword to assuage all the impossible anger I ken from all those months?* Aye, hired out my sword. I killed people. And it matters no' whether they needed it or no'. I see that now." His own frustration with his past made him bitter again. "But then I warned ye about that. I told ye I was no good."

"You didn't tell me that you murdered an innocent child, at the whim of her greedy uncles—"

"Of whom do you...? Ah, I recall."

"God's blood," she cried. "How many children have you slain, Nicholas, that you cannot recall that one poor lass?" Fresh tears fell from her anguished eyes.

"Never a one. I have...I have never killed a child, nor a woman. That particular tale is old and was no' ever...corrected." Though it pained him to admit it, he said, "My sword was worth more after...when it was believed I was without mercy, was merely heartless. She is...that was Hewlyn, daughter to the Gruffydd, a noble in Wales. Aye, I promised her uncles I would dispose of her. I took her instead to a convent out on Skye, where she has been well-hidden, safe from their schemes. When she comes of age, she will return from the dead to claim what is hers. She could no' do that as a child, will need a champion to wrest the castle from their avaricious hands when the times comes."

"But you...there have been others."

"Aye, that tale—and my uncommon...benevolence—is a rare tale. Mostly, I did what I was hired to do. Usually it involved putting down rebellions or petty skirmishes between clans. But...but no' always."

"What then? Of those others?"

"'Twas vengeance," he admitted, still unable to meet her gaze. "I returned to England, returned to the house in which I'd been imprisoned. I...left no one alive but the servants."

He stared now only at his hand on her leg. And closed his eyes when she traced her finger along the scar upon his cheek, from his mouth to his ear.

"Is that where you came by this?" She asked, her voice breaking.

Nicholas nodded, unwilling to read anything into the wrenching pain he heard in her voice, certainly not if it were only pity.

While he stood with his eyes closed, she laid her palm against his face and Nicholas turned his cheek into her hand.

"There is goodness in you, Nicholas. I know that. I could not...I don't believe I could love someone who was not."

His throat aching, he finally opened his eyes and confronted her. An incalculable hope flooded him when he saw her cautious smile.

"But I do love you, Nicholas," she said.

And the hope became joy and he laid his head on her leg and wept.

Embarrassed at his overwrought emotions, he shook them off and offered her a smile filled with peace, which he felt deep in his heart. "Then ye can no' leave me, lass. I am more... human, my most honest self when I am with ye. I need ye, Alice, but no' only to save my black soul. I dinna ken how to love, Alice. Or, I thought I dinna. But ye...lass, ye bewitched and mesmerized me, right from the start."

She laughed and cried at the same time. "That most certainly was not my plan."

This wrought a chuckle and he felt as light and unencumbered as he had not in years. He set his hands on her waist at the same time she reached for his shoulders. Slowly he claimed her from the saddle, letting her slide down his body until her lips were level with his. Alice twined her arms around his neck while Nicholas pressed his forehead to her.

"Ye will say hello and then goodbye to yer parents," he said, partly a question.

"Do you truly wish to wed me?"

"Aye, I do."

She winced a wee bit. "Then, likely we will be hosting them for some time. I miss my mother, Nicholas. And I cannot be wed without her at my side."

"I understand, love. It will be awkward, though, with the tarnished history between yer father and I."

"Awkward, aye, and on both sides," she acknowledged, "but not impossible."

"No' impossible."

Finally, he joined his lips tenderly to hers. "Say it again, Alice."

She smiled against his mouth as her arms tightened around him. "I love you, Nicholas."

"I will work every day to earn it, Alice. I give ye my vow."

# Epilogue

*Braewood Keep*
*Summer, 1331*

"SHE'S NO' GOING TO like this," predicted William grimly.

Robert looked down where he held his father under his shoulder on one side. His brother, Benjamin, had taken up the position on the opposite side, their father's arms slung around their necks. Having born him from the training field, they marched him through the Smallwood, as Alice MacRory had called it for years, the ground covered in brown and spent pine needles, the earth dipping and rising. Their father winced but did not cry out as his foot dragged over a gnarled root.

But his soreness of foot was of little consideration when his other wound presented so ghastly a sight.

Nae, she was most certainly not going to be happy to find her husband sliced across his chest, blood oozing all down the front of his tunic, the skin flayed beneath. Their da was not dead weight, but the going was slow, in deference to both the greater wound on his chest and then the minor injury, his sprained ankle, gotten when he'd tried to side-step the coming blow.

"Someone's head is going to roll," Patrick guessed, using one of Joanna's expressions. "It will no' be yers, Father, since ye are already near death's door."

"We can say it was Dungal," William suggested hopefully, walking ahead of them, half-skipping, sometimes turned and walking backwards, wincing every now and again when his troubled gaze landed on the damage he himself had inflicted upon the training field. "She'll no' take Dungal's head off."

"There's a lot of blood," Benjamin observed, a wince to his expression as well. "We should have ridden him back."

Robert, truly more concerned for his mother's reaction that any actual peril his father might be in—he'd witnessed firsthand far graver battle injuries—tried to lighten the very bleak mood of his three younger brothers. "But ye ken, at his age—the pitiful wound notwithstanding—it'd have taken him two days to get from the field to the keep upon the big red."

"I say we leave him at the door and make ourselves scarce," Patrick suggested, swatting a long and stripped twig along the ground as he walked on ahead.

"Bluidy hell, are ye more concerned for yer mother's sure grumbling or my own possibly mortal wound?" Grumbled their father, who just now for the first time let out a grunt of pain when his sore and lifted ankle was inadvertently kicked by Ben's swiftly moving feet.

The four MacRory sons exchanged glances. They answered unanimously.

"Aye, mam."

"For sure."

"Definitely. She's going to be pissed."

"I can safely say I had nothing to do with it," Robert said with satisfaction, pleased with this turn.

"Ye did, Rob," protested William, almost desperately, knowing right now only his arse was on the line. "Ye were standing right there, might have shoved the old man out of the way."

"*Jesu*, I was no' that close to him. And it's no' my fault age has dulled his reflexes."

"I can still hear you," their da said.

"Are ye sure 'tis no' threat to yer continued breathing, though?"

"It's a flesh wound, Will," Nicholas MacRory assured his youngest son, "more blood than damage I'm sure."

A huge grin spread across Patrick's face. "Aye then, but can we pretend it's worse? Close yer eyes, Da, pretend ye've been—"

"What the hell is wrong with ye?" His father barked at him, suddenly the robust and powerful laird once more. "Why would ye do that to yer mother?"

Patrick was the prankster, the least serious one, the third born son. While he was good of heart, some of what he considered funny absolutely was not. Either their mam or Joanna was forever reminding him of such.

Will dashed on ahead as they neared the gate. "Bluidy hell—hush!" He called out, when one of the soldiers up there, upon spying his bloodied laird being dragged toward the gate, lifted the horn to sound an alarm. "'Tis naught but a training mishap."

Baldred showed himself atop the gatehouse, leaning down between the embrasures.

"Best hide, all four of ye, when yer mother sees what ye've done." Otherwise he didn't sound too concerned for the condition of his laird.

By this time, Robert—as tall as his father though not yet owning the same breadth since he'd only just turned ten and eight—had broken a sweat for his efforts, and was sure that Ben might have as well, for having carried him the quarter mile from the training field back toward the keep.

Daisy, who might have been upon the wall with her father—she was never far away from Baldred—came tearing down the abutted stone steps, hopping off the last two to land just beside Robert and the laird and Benjamin as they shuffled by.

"Did ye kill him, then?" She asked, her blonde hair bouncing loose all around her shoulders. "Mam's been saying for years that one of ye would."

As ever, there was a bright light of mischief in her bonny blue eyes. As ever, Robert pretended that he didn't notice.

Patrick and William, in the middle of the yard, were brought up short, the first to stop, when the door to the keep opened and their mother stepped out into the bailey.

Her hand flew immediately to her chest and her face went ashen at the sight of her husband. Her feet froze so that the distance was not shortened between them until Robert and Benjamin brought her husband to her.

"Just a scratch, love," Da advised quickly, when no one else seemed eager to alleviate her sudden fright.

"Sweet St. Andrew," she breathed, moving her hand up to her neck. Her expression changed, swiftly and severely, as she looked from one son to the next. Planting her hands on her hips, she asked curtly. "Which one of you did this to your father?"

"It was Dungal," two of them said at the same time.

Robert rolled his eyes. His mother pursed her lips, not believing this for one moment.

"It was no' the lads, love, but—as they say—my advanced years and slower reaction time—"

"Aw, Mam, ye should have seen it," Patrick said, with entirely too much enthusiasm. "His face was all like, *God's ankles! What's this coming at me?* And then ye could see when he ken he could no' avoid it and his eyes widened—"

Their mam held up her hand to Patrick, putting it only inches in front of his face as he towered over her. "I suggest you take that charming retelling away from me."

Daisy giggled somewhere behind Robert.

Patrick went silent but his grin remained. William elbowed him viciously for antagonizing her when the whole thing was already fraught with so much tension.

Their mother waved the cloth in her hand and ushered them all in side. "Straight up to our chamber. I'll be right behind you," she advised. "I need the medicinal from the solar." She called over her shoulder, "Daisy, run to the kitchen. Tell them to put on a clean kettle of water to boil."

The four sons of Nicholas and Alice MacRory climbed the stairs and crowded into their parents' bedchamber, Robert and Benjamin depositing their father onto the bed.

"Dinna touch it," the laird barked when Patrick meant to lift his sore foot from the floor to the bed.

Joanna was the next person to enter the chamber, her daughter Daisy on her heels.

She squeaked a cry and ran toward the bed. "Och, and what are we going to tell yer dear, sweet bride? Oh, she'll perish of fright and dread and—saints alive! But what will she do without ye? And here, ye two getting on in years, the lads all grown, probably thought ye'd spend yer autumn years holding hands along a quiet loch in the—"

"Joanna!" Nicholas cut her off gruffly, before she would have painted a more grim picture.

"Mam!" Daisy scolded at the same time. She could, when she wanted to, be quite reasonable.

"Aye? What now?" Joanna turned her worry onto her daughter.

"'Tis but a scratch, they've said," Daisy told, looking to Robert for confirmation.

He nodded and swallowed.

His brothers would not let it go at that. They lived—absolutely lived and breathed—solely to stir Joanna's overwrought passions.

Benjamin started it, feigning a sniffle. "Och, but Joanna, ye recall Peter Fickle—remember him, in the village? Thought 'twas naught but a scratch, until came the fever, am I right?"

Joanna wailed a pitiful noise and clapped her palm against her forehead and held it there. "For mercy's sake," she breathed. "Yer poor mam. Now ye lads be strong for her."

"Aye," said Patrick, "light the candles, Joanna. 'Tis all we can do but pray."

"Aye, and that's no' a lie. But we'll see her through it—"

"Same as ye have, every other calamity that's befallen her over all these years," William finished for her, words she might have spoken a hundred times in their lives.

"Sure and so I will," she agreed. "I dinna ken what she'd do without me."

Daisy did not try to rein in her mother's misconceptions at this time but was busy trying to control her own smirk.

Robert glanced at his father, who'd opted to close his eyes, possibly trying to dismiss all of them from his mind.

His mother arrived then, her eyes only for the laird, having no care about Joanna's disconsolate weeping or the smirks worn by two of her sons. She went directly to the bed and to her knees and whispered something to her husband.

Robert leaned a fraction of a foot to his left to have a clearer view of both parents' faces.

His father's eyes were still closed, but a slow and easy smile turned up his mouth.

His mother kissed that smile, which was then shown to have enlarged as she whispered something else before rising to her feet and beginning to cut away at the laird's tunic.

Robert felt his cheeks color, same as they did any time he'd been subjected to his parents' almost embarrassing habit of being so openly affectionate. But his gaze strayed to Daisy, who was watching him, her cheeks also stained pink, her lips turned up in a speculative smile.

So aye, the affection between his parents might not be wholly understood or appreciated but when he gazed into Daisy's bright green eyes, Robert was quite certain he wanted to know more about such things.

"ARE THEY GONE THEN?"

"Every last one," Alice said, cleaning up the rags and implements from the bedside table. She turned, meaning to deposit them in the basin and remove all of it from their chamber. A hand caught on her skirts, halting her forward progress.

"Ye were—still are—the best thing that ever happened to me," Nicholas said solemnly.

He laid, bare-chested, upon the bed. She'd shooed out the crowd earlier, after she'd cleaned the grazing wound and applied the salve, and wrapped the linen securely around his broad chest, telling all the gawkers that he needed only rest now.

"Och," she said, grinning, "and I bet you say that to all the wenches who tend your wounds."

"Only the bonny ones."

"The things you do to have me rip your tunic from your body," she teased him. "You are quite obsessed with me, I fear."

"I dinna mind admitting I am, have been for some time."

Smiling still, Alice dropped all the things she'd just picked up back onto the table and lifted her brow coyly at her husband. She was neither young nor beautiful, but Nicholas always made her feel as if she were. In truth, she felt young again when he grinned at her as he was now.

"I do not want to cause you pain," she cautioned, "or undo my handy work."

Nicholas took her hand and pulled her down until she was draped across him. He lifted his face and crashed his lips on hers, as he'd done a thousand times by now. Alice still shivered with delight. He slid his hand around her neck and held her close and ravaged her with his scorching kiss.

Alice pulled back, employing a seductive grin she'd learned about fifteen years ago, which never failed to fill his gaze with the delight of anticipation. She sat up and straddled his powerful thighs.

"We'll take no chances," she said referring to the rather deep scratches on his chest.

She moved her hands down his hard body, toward the laces at his breeches, but was stopped by Nicholas taking hold of her wrists.

"I love ye, Alice. I canna remember a time when I did no."

Her smile now was serene. "And I you, my love."

"Do ye ken I'm a good man?"

Tilting her head at the significance of the question, wondering what had effected such deliberation, she nodded and easily spoke the truth. "You are a very good man, Nicholas. The best of men."

Leaning forward again, she pressed her lips to his. And she might have turned away all his worries with her loving but that the door to their chamber, which she had not yet latched, burst open.

"Aw, *Jesu*," croaked Benjamin. "Mam! What the—"

"Disgusting," decided Patrick.

Alice grinned at her husband, thankful they hadn't gotten any further and took herself off him, sitting at his side on the bed, facing her boys. Nicholas set his strong hand on her lower back.

"What's disgusting?" Wondered Robert, coming in behind his brothers. "Oh, shite, did ye catch them—?"

"That's enough," Nicholas commanded, which silenced his sons instantly.

William entered next, bearing a small bowl and spoon. "I dinna ken if ye'd come to the hall, Da. I brought ye Cook's pudding."

"Aye, he's got an arse to kiss yet," Patrick teased, "for skewering Da."

Nicholas sat up now, not without a small wince for his discomfort and took the bowl from William, who indeed appeared to yet feel terrible for what he'd done.

"There's no harm, lad," Nicholas said. "I can no' fault ye for being bold with the blade. That is what ye're trained to do."

William accepted this, his handsome face showing some relief. How awful must have been the last few hours, worried for the damage he'd caused his father. Alice was sorry that she'd been busy tending Nicholas and could not have been a greater support to her baby.

Their sons obviously were not too *disgusted* by what they'd walked in upon, since they'd taken up seats around their chamber, Patrick at the foot of the bed, Robert and Benjamin in the chairs near the hearth, while William sat just now on the floor near the side of the bed.

They must have missed their father's presence at supper and hence had come to claim some of his time.

As much as she loved her privacy with Nicholas, she adored when they were all together like this, when the lads sought them out, when they stayed and chatted with them, whether being silly or serious, whether the conversations were lighthearted or not.

She knew she was a good mother. She loved her boys fiercely and wanted only their happiness. She knew all the emotions that surely any mother did: all the worries and anxieties, joys and so many proud moments. And she knew her boys loved her tremendously. She'd known and cherished all those sweet moments when they were small, when she'd been the center of their universe, when they came to her for everything, large and small.

They'd outgrown her, of course, as boys must surely do. And she didn't hold a candle nowadays to the awe and respect and devotion they gave to their father. She was not jealous; she had enough love. She was thrilled, so pleased that this man was what they aspired to be. She saw it every day, in the way her sons walked and talked, how they dealt with people and problems, and in the manner in which they held themselves accountable for their own mistakes and misjudgments. For how they laughed and spoke and expressed themselves. For how like their father they were.

She would tell Nicholas later, when they were alone, would say to Nicholas that this was how she knew he was a good man. He need only to look at his fine sons.

*The End*

(scroll down for a sneak peek at *And Be My Love*,
the first book in my
**Far From Home: A Scottish Time Travel Romance** series)

Thank you for reading *Heart of Ice*.
Gaining exposure as an independent author
relies mostly on word-of-mouth,
so if you have the time and inclination,
please consider leaving a short review wherever you can.
Thanks!

---

*Other Books by Rebecca Ruger*

### Highlander: The Legends
*The Beast of Lismore Abbey*
*The Lion of Blacklaw Tower*
*The Scoundrel of Beauly Glen*
*The Wolf of Carnoch Cross*
*The Blackguard of Windless Woods*
*The Devil of Helburn by the Sea*
*The Knave of Elmwood Keep*
*The Dragon of Lochlan Hall*
*The Maverick of Leslie House*
*The Brute of Mearley Hold*
*The Rebel of Lochaber Forest*
*The Avenger of Castle Wick*

### Heart of a Highlander Series
*Heart of Shadows*
*Heart of Stone*

*Heart of Fire*
*Heart of Iron*
*Heart of Winter*
*Heart of Ice*

**Far From Home: A Scottish Time-Travel Romance**
*And Be My Love*
*Eternal Summer*
*Crazy In Love*
*Beyond Dreams*
*Only The Brave*
*When & Where*
*Get the Free Novella (Nicol and Eloise's story) by signing up to my Newsletter*
*A Year of Days*
And! coming 2024
*Beloved Enemy*
*Winter Longing*
*Hearts on Fire*
*Here in Your Arms*

**The Highlander Heroes Series**
*The Touch of Her Hand*
*The Memory of Her Kiss*
*The Shadow of Her Smile*
*The Depths of Her Soul*
*The Truth of Her Heart*
*The Love of Her Life*

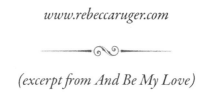

*www.rebeccaruger.com*

*(excerpt from And Be My Love)*

TWO DAYS LATER, KAYLA set out to join the search efforts for Eloise Cahill.

Previously, a five mile radius had been investigated by law enforcement and a local search and rescue organization, in every direction, they claimed. Today, more than one hundred people met in the wide gravel drive of the Camisky Lodge, a nineteenth century Victorian lodge in Torlundy, Fort William, set amidst the spectacular Inverness-shire landscape on the shores of the River Lochy. The lodge itself sat on five wild acres, all of which would be included in today's search. After signing in and showing ID, Kayla was put into a volunteer group that would hike straight away from the lodge, heading northeast along the River Lochy. They would be led by a trained search-and-rescue volunteer, Roger Darby, and would report directly to him while on the hunt. Some well-meaning volunteers became impatient with Mr. Darby's rather long-winded instructions to the group, but he reined them in with his reminders that they were now exposing themselves to danger.

"We will encounter some rough terrain," he said, "and it is essential that no one—not one of you—take off on your own, looking to become a hero, but more likely to become our next SAR mission."

He didn't give his credentials with his instructions, but he wore a lanyard and ID, which alone might suggest some measure of authority. Kayla listened intently, though he repeated himself often—two groups led by other SAR coordinators had already departed in their search maneuvers. Mr. Darby was British, she decided, and wondered if he had been called in just for this, or if he lived locally.

Eventually, her party of twenty began their trek away from the drive of the lodge, stretched out to cover more ground, but per Mr. Darby's instructions, never more than arms' length away from the next person. They would walk north close to the river and return, all at once, further south, only barely overlapping the ground already covered.

While they were upon the level, open space of fields or meadows or along the banks of the river, they were expected to walk closely, eyes on the ground, stepping forward uniformly, so that nothing would be missed. But inside the woods, with so much underbrush and so many trees, it was more difficult to keep up this formation. Kayla felt a little like an idiot, that she hadn't considered her outfit better, hadn't exactly taken into consideration dressing for the terrain or how much colder it would be as they began to climb. Hiking boots and a windbreaker might have served her well, better than the jeans and sneakers and sweater she wore. And something other than her thermos-ed latte might have also been a good idea as well. It had long since gone cold, and after the first two hours, she was thirsty for water now, not a sugary faux coffee.

In other words, she was fairly miserable. The falling mist of a rain didn't help and then she felt poorly that she was aggrieved by the weather and her own ill-preparations, when poor Eloise Cahill had been missing now for three weeks.

Ruta, a girl from Poland, with whom Kayla had several classes as they were both in the same program, sidled close to Kayla about half way up the side of the mountain.

She seemed to be suffering the same misery as Kayla, ill-prepared, cold and wet. At least Kayla was wearing her sneakers. Poor Ruta had only a pair of cute—but impractical—dock shoes on her feet.

"I did not know we would climb mountains today," Ruta said, with a self-effacing grin and a roll of her eyes, her English heavily accented.

"Nor did I, "Kayla commiserated. "And apparently, I'm pretty selfish, that I have to keep reminding myself that Eloise Cahill has more reason to complain about anything than I do."

"If she *can* still complain," Ruta said, with a shrug and grimace.

Kayla's eyes widened at the bleak suggestion that Eloise might have met with a more dire fate than simply being lost.

Defensively, Ruta went on, "It's been three weeks. If she is out here, she's lost to the elements. Otherwise, she was taken—stolen—and then she is probably dead as well. Or...wishing she was."

*Oh, my God*. Negative much? Lengthening her upward stride, Kayla hoped to put distance between her and Miss Doom and Gloom.

"I didn't sign up to search, hoping I'd find a body," Kayla stated, speaking to the side of the mountain, her tone biting even as she didn't care if Ruta could hear her or not. "I'm here to find Eloise."

Occasionally about the side of the mountain, there were little shelves of level ground where she could stand on solid, hard-packed earth and catch her breath. When she reached one that was more than just a shelf, was a long plane of level ground before the mountain rose again, maybe hundreds of yards away, Kayla paused and took another sip of her cold latte. When she lifted her arm to reattach the thermos again to her backpack, a flash of color caught her eye. Her gaze narrowing, she moved toward the object, which looked to be only a scrap of fabric. Plucking it from the ground, Kayla inspected the torn piece of bright yellow cotton. Once bright yellow, she amended. It was now grimy and faded, looking very old, as if it had been up here longer than only three weeks. She had no idea if it was connected at all to Eloise, but would not discount any possibility, and tucked it into an outer pocket of her backpack, intent on turning it in at the search's base camp when she went back down. She was about to turn back when another flash of yellow caught her eye. It was the same yellow, further ahead in the trees. This one floated on a breeze, which made no sense since Kayla had not been aware of the wind once they'd moved up the mountainside and inside the trees. Curious, she followed the drifting piece of fabric, imagining it was not coincidence that there was more than one piece of what looked to be the same fabric. A prickle of unease lifted the hairs at her nape as the scrap of material continued to float just outside of her reach.

The sensation was strong enough that Kayla stopped abruptly and glanced around.

"Ruta?" She called out, not with any great volume, some frisson of fear shaking her voice. All morning, along the initial path and then up the hillside, she could see and count six to ten people at any given time in close proximity to her. Right now, she saw no one. She called again, louder now, a hint of panic tainting her tone. "Ruta!"

Blinking, trying to sort things in her brain, Kayla spun around, taking in all the woods around her.

She hollered again for Ruta, and then for other people in her small group. "Taylor! Scott!" Her heart thumped wildly in her chest, and she ran in one direction and then another. Nothing was familiar. No one was here.

"Mr. Darby!" She shouted.

She could not find the side of the mountain, only seemed to be lost, adrift in a forest of trees. The ground was laden with pine needles and moss while the trees stretched high into the sky with thick boughs, and canopies heavy with leaves.

Squinting through the forest, which included so much underbrush, Kayla spied what looked like a path about fifty feet away. Approaching the flattened line of brush and grass, she supposed it might be some kind of deer path. She'd seen plenty of these back home in New York. She followed the narrow trail, occasionally calling out names to the empty woods. After about fifteen minutes, the trail wound around a small pond, the ground having hundreds of indentations which Kayla seriously suspected—hoped—were deer tracks. She had some fear that the path might only lead her deeper into the woods but as she felt she had no choice, she followed this for several minutes. It veered eventually away from the end of the pond, and through a thicker, taller growth of trees. Here it was darker and chillier than whence she'd come, and she was now more than earlier regretting her lack of warmer clothing.

Still, if she weren't so earnestly frightened, Kayla might have appreciated the beauty of her surroundings; a chipmunk scurried through the underbrush and raced around the stem of a fat oak tree; overhead, what probably were several squirrels appeared to be leaping from branch to branch, causing quite a ruckus in the otherwise quiet of this wood; what little sunlight squinted through the canopy of trees made streaks of light all around the forest.

Sunlight?

Kayla tipped her head back, holding her hand in one of those shafts of light, touching the motes that frolicked within. But sunlight? It had been gray, the air heavy with a misty rain. It had been like that all morning, had seemed one of those all-day gray skies.

Where—when!—had the sun come out? Why were there no clouds in the sky now?

She wasn't one to sprint from calm to panicked like zero to sixty, but she was increasingly unnerved by how lost she was, how different everything was from only five minutes ago, and where everyone else had gone. Staunchly, she resisted entertaining any wicked ideas, wondering if this is what happened to Eloise Cahill? Had she just been out hiking, and the entire terrain and atmosphere shifted and morphed into something unrecognizable?

Kayla tripped over something and went flying, striking out her hands at the last second to stop herself from landing face-first. Her backpack, which had hung from only one shoulder, fell to the ground beside her. Kayla spun around, putting her butt on the ground and her hand to her chest, glaring with some accusation at a slight swell in the ground. All around her the earth here was flat, except for that spot, which was lifted as much as half a foot, being almost eight feet long, she guessed.

Kayla considered the size and shape of the mound, aware of the lingering eerie sensation that made her more than a little cautious.

She reached out her hand toward that spot of earth but then jerked it back and scooted a bit backward.

Her eyes never left that heap and she pulled back her lips in a wince, deciding that the shape of it clearly looked like someone had filled a shallow grave and covered it with leaves and dirt.

Her brain went into overdrive then, thinking of things like forensics, wondering if she should touch anything at all; should she take pictures before she disturbed the area? Had her sudden fright at becoming lost and separated made her fanciful? Was she only imagining that the mound was shaped like a body? Did she really want to dig to find out if Eloise was under there?

Clamping her lips to keep them from trembling, Kayla crawled forward on her hands and knees and gently brushed away a few leaves.

She stopped when an unknown voice told her to find him. *He's right there.*

She swiveled her head left and right, looking behind her. There was no one here with her.

She hadn't expected to find anyone, having an unnerving suspicion that the voice had only been in her head.

*I'm going crazy.*

And yet, inexplicably, she was drawn to the bump in the earth, having a sense that she should not ignore it.

Swallowing her fright, Kayla began to sweep her hands over the raised earth with some steadiness, moving away all the forest debris. She crawled around the mounded earth as she worked, something inside her urging her to dig deeper, beneath the loose stuff, into the earth.

She couldn't say what propelled her or guided her, but she became more and more anxious that she must unearth whatever was here, and then became more and more fearful that she was about to uncover poor Eloise.

When all the leaves and lichen and loose earth were pushed aside, the swell in the ground clearly resembled a raised tomb. Inside her head, that same indistinct voice implored that she keep digging and so she did. She dug into the ground, pulling away dirt and twigs and buried leaves, and then softer mud underneath. It was not an easy task, but she kept at it, terrified by some notion that if Eloise was under here, she needed to get to her; Eloise probably couldn't breathe under all that earth.

When her fingers connected with something that was undoubtedly not mud or dirt but then clearly not rock or stone, she paused, but only for a split second while her mouth formed a wide *o*, before she began digging more feverishly.

"Help! Someone!" she howled wildly, but with little hope when she'd exposed what was clearly skin. "Oh, my God." Kayla kept at it, swiping and scratching at the dirt, uncovering a bare shoulder and part of a neck. Tears rolled down her cheeks as she moved more dirt away from where she now guessed Eloise's face was. The jaw and cheek were revealed, and Kayla wrenched the scarf from around her own neck and used that to more gently remove all the grime from the face.

The skin was dirtied but not discolored. This body had not been here for three weeks.

And the more she cleaned the face of all that had covered it, the more sure she was that this body did not belong to Eloise. Her relief was only wobbly. Too many questions consumed her now. Who was this? And how was this body not decayed? Not even a little bit. The earth she'd moved was not freshly turned before she touched it.

Carefully, she exposed a square chin and jaw, stubbled but not heavily. The mouth was shown next, lips as pink as any living person, full and still, moving only when she wiped the scarf across them before settling back into a pleasing shape. Kayla's frown grew but her tears lessened, confused by how real, how alive this person appeared. A man, clearly, but who? Other questions jumbled and spun in her mind while she worked to expose all of him. His nose was narrow, and she used her fingernails to scratch away at the dirt crusting inside his nostrils, though she wasn't sure why she should. Next, she unearthed his eyes, closed, dark lashes fanned against his hollow cheeks.

Stunned and beyond bewildered, Kayla sat back on her heels and considered what she found.

A man, dead and buried, under six inches of earth, in the middle of the forest.

A body actually, she amended, but one that had not long been buried here.

She turned her head again, this way and that, trying to make sense of... at this point, anything.

And when her attention was drawn again to the man's body, she was struck by something that had escaped her notice at first. Another frown furrowed her brow. Kayla lifted a shaky hand and gingerly touched the man's shoulder, the lone corner of his body excavated.

And she gasped when she felt how warm was that flesh. He should not be warm.

"Please someone come and help me," she whimpered and went onto her knees again, digging out the man's chest, just enough that she could lay her ear against him. She could discern nothing, no sounds, no vibrations. She sat up and tapped at his cheek. "Sir?" She took his face in her hand, thumb to the right of his nose, fingers to the left, and shook him. "Are you dead?" Grimacing, she pried apart his lips, now able to determine that all of him was warm, like any living person. And his skin was smooth and... lifelike. Inside his mouth, there was no dirt, no debris. Kayla put her ear there now and closed her eyes, willing her brain to silence so that she might hear or feel any sign of life. When she straightened, she laid two fingers against the side of his neck to check for a pulse. After five seconds, she could discern nothing, not even a thready beat of life.

She started CPR, more as a *just in case* thing, not with any hope that she could actually revive him. Recalling her training from her lifeguard days, she cleared more dirt away from around his head so that she could tilt his neck and raise his chin. She placed her hands on his chest, one on top of the other in the space she'd already cleared of dirt and pushed hard and fast. She did this thirty times and then pinched his nose and covered his mouth with hers, delivering two rescue breaths. Nothing. She went back to compressions, using a steady rhythm in her thrusts, up on her knees to use her body weight to accumulate force. And then she administered two more rescue breaths. Still no response.

"Come. On. Man," she urged, the plea given in time to the first three of the next set of compressions on his bare chest. Her next two breaths, over his warm lips, were answered with a gasp. "Oh, Jesus." She pulled back and froze, waiting for more. The mouth beneath her moved, the bottom lip trembling. "Yes, that's it. Breathe." She laid her palm against his warm cheek. "Breathe." The man's lips pursed, inhaling and exhaling. And Kayla cried again, this time with relief. When his long black lashes began to move, Kayla used her scarf again, wiping away more loose dirt from his face.

"You're alive," she cooed. But then she didn't wait for his eyes to open, but began digging out the rest of him, beginning with his other shoulder. "I can't believe it." She kept digging, glancing between her task and his face, waiting for those eyes to open. "Oh, shit. I'm so sorry," she said, when she inadvertently scratched his arm. Her own eyes widened as she exposed more of the man's body. Holy crap. The guy was built. But then she saw no marks on him, no bruises or bullet holes or stab wounds, or whatever had knocked him out but had not killed him.

Pulling her gaze from the sculpted chest, matted with black hair, Kayla returned her regard to his face, entranced to find a pair of black eyes watching her.

"Oh," she squeaked, and her hands went still.

He blinked several times, struggling to focus, it seemed. She held off with the dozens of questions that assailed her, wanting to be asked. She settled back onto her heels once more and waited. His arms and hands began to move, stirring the loosened dirt around him. Roused to action again, Kayla assisted, scraping away more earth from around him.

He lifted one hand, and then his whole arm, up and out of what was supposed to be his grave, and held it above his face, curling and extending his fingers. The other hand appeared so that only the bottom half of him was buried.

"How did...what happened to you?"

"The witches." His voice was scratchy, weak even.

"Oh." *Oh, boy.* Maybe he had been conked on the head, maybe the mark was in the back, still buried.

She glanced around the forest again but despite all hope, there was no one else around. When she turned back to him, he was struggling to sit up. Kayla sprang into action again, standing and taking his hand, pulling him to an upright position, though he remained seated, his lower half still wedged in the earth. Without a word, he pulled his hand away from hers.

The man rolled his shoulders and shifted his waist left and then right, as if warming up at the gym. He lifted a thick, muscled arm and applied his hand to the back of his neck, seeming to rub out kinks or cramps, his fingers lost inside his longish, black hair. Kayla slowly walked around so that she could see the back of him, to find the injury that had knocked him out. His head and wide back were coated in enough mud yet that she could discern no injury or blood.

"Who sent ye, lass?"

Confused once more, and then more so by the anger in his tone, Kayla took a cautious step backward, away from him. He was forced to turn his head to have her in view, which he did, and leveled her with a dark scowl. "Who sent ye?" Harsher now, impatient.

"No one sent me," she returned defensively, rushing out the words to appease him.

Growling something unintelligible, he set his hands on either side of him, on the ground that was not disturbed, save for what excavated dirt had been thrown onto it. He bent his elbows and his muscles rolled and flexed as he lifted his lower body out of the grave. Though his motions were stiff and slow, he managed to lift himself first from the hole, sitting himself on the ground while his feet remained within. In the next moment, a bit unsteady still, he pulled himself to his feet.

And turned an impatient glare upon Kayla.

"Who are ye? And why did ye no' kill me?"

Gaped-jawed, Kayla stared at him. Even if she did understand what he was asking for, or insinuating, she couldn't have answered. The guy was wickedly gorgeous, with broad shoulders to hold up that thick neck, and arms that suggested a brutal weight-training regimen. He was tall, and though there was no spare flesh on him, like not an ounce of it, he wasn't lean, was too powerfully built, too...huge to be considered lean. His hair was as dark as midnight, a perfect match to his angry, obsidian eyes. But honestly, as fabulous as his body was, Kayla found her gaze again and again drawn to his face. Ferocious fury aside, he must have originally been sculpted in granite, so chiseled were his jaw and cheeks. On a lesser man, one with a narrow face, it would have appeared gaunt, she decided, but on him...well everything looked good on him.

Moments ago, she'd had a brief concern about his bare chest, when only that was available to her gaze; she'd wondered if he was naked under the remaining dirt. Thankfully, he was not. But what clothes—and accessories—he did wear did nothing to lessen her anxiety. He was dressed in some sort of baggy pants, the color of a young deer; they looked to be made of wool. They were tucked into leather boots, to which she could give no evaluation because so much mud clung to them still. Of greatest concern, and what held her focus just now, was the scabbard that dangled from the leather belt around his waist, which seemed to serve not as a means to hold up those pants, which perched deliciously low on his lean hips, but only to keep the weapon attached to him. The scabbard was leather as well, but the hilt of the sword it kept was metal, dull and carved, the detail lost as well to the crusted dirt.

"Do ye have a name, woman?" he barked then, his voice recovered enough to be imposing.

"I do," she answered mechanically, foolishly.

He talked slow, but his accent was not easy to understand, even as he was heard clearly, his deep voice slicing through her fear, low and almost soothing for the commanding presence of his tone. Almost soothing, but not quite, as this situation still hovered somewhere between fantastic and alarming.

He might have barked again for a proper reply, that she give her name, except that he was now staring at her as if she were the one uncovered from a hole in the ground, bare-chested, and wearing a sword around her hip. His dark gaze raked her from head to toe in such a fashion as to make Kayla glance down at her jeans and sweater and sneakers. She plucked self-consciously at the oversized sweater, which, like her jeans, was covered in almost as much grime as all of him was.

When he'd looked his fill—and his scowl only intensified—he brought his gaze to hers. Kayla swallowed and looked at him. His expression morphed from confusion to suspicion.

"Who are ye?"

"Kayla. Kayla Forbes." And then words just started tumbling out of her, as often happened when she was nervous—and she'd never been this nervous. "I was helping with the search party—looking for Eloise Cahill?—and I don't know what happened, but I seem to have gotten separated from the rest of the party. I was lost and I stumbled over"—she pointed to the freshly dug hole—"over that. I don't know what... I mean, I didn't see...you, so I'm not sure what made me start digging. Oh, my God, what happened to you?"

He didn't appear as a man who might ever be caught slack-jawed—he gave off solid and heavy alpha vibes: always in control, surprised by nothing, able to manage any situation—but he was now.

But then he seemed to dismiss her babbling, setting his big hands onto those trim hips to consider the hole in the earth, from where he'd come.

Kayla supposed she'd do a lot of frowning as well, if she were in his shoes, but this guy so far had only that one expression. He turned it onto her again.

"What is the day?"

"Um, May the twenty-third."

"Nae."

"Um, yay," she maintained. "It is. Should we get you to a hospital?"

"I received a missive on the third day after Whitsunday, in the fifth year after the English invasion."

"Missive?" *Whitsunday? Invasion?*

"To come to Gairlochy."

"Gairlochy?"

He glanced around, ignoring her parroting. "But this is no' that place."

"Wait," Kayla said. "Are you saying you were summoned here? And...like, ambushed?"

He responded to this with another frown, this one quizzical. "Were you surprised by an attack?" she clarified.

"Aye, from the witches."

*Okay, buddy. We definitely need to get you to a hospital.*

He must have sensed her disbelief, that he rather growled at her, "'Twas three of them. A mortal can no' hope to best only one, but three, a man has no chance."

Skeptically, Kayla asked, "And um, what did the witches do to you?" One day, she thought, I'll meet a hot guy who *doesn't* have serious issues.

Now he gave her a look that suggested her question was ignorant. "They cast the sleep spell onto me. But it could no' have been today," he said, pointing to the grave from which he'd escaped. "It must have been some time ago, to have been overtaken by the earth."

More to be polite, and pretend an interest in his babbling, Kayla asked, "When did they put you to sleep?"

"On this day."

She couldn't have said what prompted her to ask for further details, but that something was off about him, something was just not... right. "Um, what year?"

"I've said, we are in the fifth year since those mongrel English began the war with us."

She laughed nervously, trying to decide which English invasion he might be referring to. To her recollection, the English made a regular habit of it, in every century between the 13$^{th}$ and the 17$^{th}$—but not since the latter. "Okay, but we're anywhere from four to eight hundred years away from that."

"What say you?" He narrowed his eyes at her.

"It's two-thousand and twenty-one." She cleared her throat while he stared at her as if she'd spouted nonsense. "In the year of our Lord," she added, hoping that lent credibility to the truth as she knew it.

(End of Sample)

———— ๑๑๑ ————

Happy Reading!

Made in the USA
Las Vegas, NV
23 December 2024

15195112R00193